CIVVIES

LYNDA LA PLANTE

Civvies

BCA

LONDON NEW YORK SYDNEY TORONTO

This edition published 1992
by BCA
by arrangement with Sinclair-Stevenson Ltd

CN 9878

Printed and bound in Great Britain by
Mackays of Chatham PLC, Chatham, Kent

I would like to thank the BBC for producing CIVVIES as well as the director, Karl Francis, the producer, Ruth Caleb, the co-producer, Ruth Kenley Letts, and the script editor, Sheryl Crown. My thanks must also go to the great crew, the make-up and costume department, the stunt arrangers and casting. Indeed, there was a dedication from everyone involved in the making of CIVVIES that I have never seen before in any other production. My deep gratitude also goes out to the superb team of actors and actresses whose professionalism and talent I cannot praise too highly. I thank you all sincerely and wish each and every one of you a successful future. You have held in your hands a piece of work that I had a deep and personal belief should be made and to have it enriched by your talent and produced with such loving care has touched my heart.

Thank you.

Lynda La Plante

I would like to acknowledge the talent of the writer Trevor Hoyle without whom this book could not have been published.

I dedicate this book to Bob's four daughters

THE BOMBING

1

An alarm bell clanged through the haze in Dillon's head, faint yet nagging as toothache, the instant he laid eyes on the place, stuck out there in the middle of nowhere. Trouble was, by then his brain was half-pickled by the four pints of bitter and three Grolsch sloshing around his gut, making his head spin slightly and giving him that keyed-up flutter in his chest – Saturday night had started right and could only get better.

Yes!

And Jimmy Hammond, squashed against him in the front passenger seat of the jeep, can of lager in his hand, was yelling in his ear, 'Got the best beer for miles around – and there's a disco, Frank!'

There were ten of them in the jeep. The four in the front were seasoned veterans and old mates, while crammed in the back were six fresh-faced 'Toms', as the privates in the Parachute Regiment were called. After passing through the living hell of 'P' Company selection (twenty-seven had made the grade out of ninety-eight hopefuls), followed by months of intensive training, this was only their second week in Northern Ireland and their first chance to get tanked up.

Dillon had promised 'his lads' a barnstorming binge, and Sergeant Dillon always delivered.

The jeep swung into the parking area – little more than a patch of cindery earth bordered by concrete posts slapped with whitewash – and tried to find a spot amongst the thirty or more cars already there. Dillon got his first gander at Hennessey's Bar, and was none too impressed. Not much more than a two-storey barn tricked out with

3

fairy lights, he reckoned, the shanty-like toilets housed in lean-to shacks at the side. And nothing for miles around except a few trees and the impenetrable darkness of fields, hedgerows and tilled farmland.

Harry 'Big Gut' Travers switched off the engine, and everybody piled out to avoid his thunderous fart. They groaned in unison and threw a few choice curses as they extricated themselves from Harry's fumes. The six young lads jumped around, faces all aglow, trying to get the circulation going. The noise from the entrance, double doors flung wide, was horrendous – a thumping disco fighting it out with a live Irish folk band.

'Popular, isn't it?' Dillon looked around, tucking his shirt into his jeans, pulling his windcheater straight. All wore their scruffs, jeans, T-shirts, battered Puma trainers, outside the base. 'Sure it's got clearance?' That bloody persistent alarm bell.

Jimmy drained his lager, crumpled the can as if it was a paper cup and tossed it over his shoulder. He grinned and thumped Dillon's arm. 'Trust me, I've been coming here for months.' Leading the way, he waved them forward, tall, broad shoulders on a muscular frame, red hair cropped short. 'Right lads, get a move on!' he yelled. 'First round's on me!'

Crunching over the cinders and broken glass, Harry on one side, Steve Harris on the other, Dillon caught sight of Malone talking to another guy just outside the entrance. Tony Malone, plainclothes military police, six-foot-four, built like a brick shithouse with a personality to match. Dillon wasn't given to hating people, he didn't care to waste the emotional investment, but Malone made a career of being stagnant pond life and proud of it.

'Oi! Malone,' Dillon called out as they approached. 'This place given the all-clear, has it?'

Malone turned, eyes narrowing under the black bar of his eyebrows, Brylcreemed hair gleaming slickly in the fairy lights. He didn't like being addressed as if he were a

4

common craphat, even by a staff sergeant in the Paras. He spat the words out, hardly moving his lips.

'You and your mob drinking, Dillon, no place is – '

No love lost between them, Dillon went straight to him, staring up past Malone's hairy nostrils, though he kept his voice low and neutral. 'I asked you a question, mate.'

Malone stared back, eyes like slits, as if seriously considering whether to have a go, right there and then. He'd taken on bigger guys and beaten them to a pulp, but there was something about Dillon, a kind of chilling stillness and brooding intensity about the man, that warned him off. And Dillon's face bore the marks of someone who'd been through the wars and lived to tell the tale. The NAAFI brawl in Belize that had slit his cheek wide open and left him with a thin cruel scar. Nearly losing an eye 'down south' on Mount Longdon, the sniper's bullet grazing his right eyebrow and leaving a pale puckered abrasion. The kind of face that could take punishment and come back for second helpings.

'Come on, Frank – ' Jimmy pulled Dillon away from the simmering confrontation. 'We're wasting valuable drinking time . . .'

As the six young lads pushed past him, Malone vented his spite over their heads, twitching his size-seventeen neck. 'I checked it out personal, so screw you and . . .'

The rest of it was lost as noise, heat and smoke hit them like a solid wall. At the far end of the long, narrow room, beams and nicotined stucco plaster overhead, the live group was twanging away, and through an archway disco lights were strobing over a packed dance-floor. He'd been dead right, Dillon saw, following Jimmy's broad back. This was about as basic as you could get, a bar running almost its entire length, tables against the walls, bare floorboards, and a crowd into the serious business of getting pissed as farts in record-breaking time. They were all young, mostly soldiers, with a fair sprinkling of local girls sitting on laps, some openly necking. Dillon felt the tiny coiled spring of tension at the base of his spine unwind.

Odd how after three tours in the Province he was more wary now than he'd been on his first. What was it – creeping paranoia or just plain old senility? Jesus wept, past it at thirty-one.

Jimmy – Mr Fixit as usual – was doing the organising. He'd spotted a table round the corner from the main door vestibule with only a couple of young blokes sitting there, just finishing their pints, locals judging by the length of their hair and five o'clock shadows, and Jimmy was in before they'd put their glasses down. Harry Travers and Steve Harris were grabbing spare chairs and passing them over the heads of nearby crowded tables. Dillon and Jimmy started clearing the table of empties, pint glasses and bottles of Guinness, telling the six Toms to get sat down, first shout on them.

'Thanks, mate.' Harry plonked two more chairs down as the Irishmen got up to leave. Their table was filled with empty glasses and bottles. 'You had a good night's session by the look of it.'

One of them nodded, gave the thumbs-up, and stood aside as the young lads eagerly crowded in.

Jimmy raised his arms. 'Right – pints all round. What you having, Harry? Scotch? Steve, want to give me a hand?' Counting on his fingers, backing towards the bar. 'Guinness for you, Frank, yeh?'

'Harry, give us the kitty.' Steve reached across, palming notes and coins. His long-lashed, green eyes in his clean-cut handsome face were already a bit fuzzy. One or two of the young girls had given him the swift once-over as soon as he walked in, and Steve, glassy-eyed or not, had taken their rank and number. Might get his end away later on, with one, both, or several. Can't keep a good prick down.

But first things first. Drink, crisps, drink, peanuts, drink, and more drink.

They were still a few chairs short, Steve saw, and gestured to Billy Newman, the youngest of the Toms, just turned nineteen, to get it sorted. 'There's two up at the end, Billy – grab 'em. Hey mate,' Steve called to a squaddie nibbling the ear of the blonde girl on his knee, 'that seat being used?'

Over by the door, on their way out, one of the two young Irishmen glanced back. His gaze drifted casually down beneath the table. For a mere fraction of a second it lingered there, on the brown carrier-bag against the wall, wedged behind and partly hidden by the old-fashioned iron-ribbed radiator.

His gaze flicked over the six young men sitting there, expression frozen, eyes hooded. Then taking all the time in the world, he pulled the collar of his leather jacket up round his ears and strolled out after his companion.

Taffy Davies hailed Dillon from the bar. A large beefy man, with a broad, friendly mug and a nose that had taken a bashing in the Battalion boxing squad, Taffy and Dillon had been close mates ever since they'd signed on and gone through basic training together – thirteen, fourteen years ago – both young shavers practically straight out of school. Since then they'd done a roll-call of tours all over the world: Jordan, Bahrain, Cyprus, British Guiana, Belize. Not forgetting their time in the Falklands, when they'd been under continuous artillery and mortar fire for almost two days and nights. Wherever there was a shitty job to be done, send in the Paras. The Regiment's motto, *Utrinque Paratus*, said it all – 'Ready for Anything.'

'Hey, Frank, wanna drink?' Taffy raised his pint mug.

'We're on a round,' Dillon yelled back. 'Come and join us.' And turning to Harry, 'Got a coin for the juke-box?'

Dillon pushed through the ruck of bodies, passing Jimmy and Steve at the bar, frantically signalling to get served. Harry went over to give them a hand. Taffy drained his glass and waved it aloft. 'I'll have a pint, Jimmy!'

'I'll be a second.' Dillon pointed to the crudely-painted sign reading GENTS' TOILETS tacked above a scarred green door at the far end. 'Gonna take a leak.' On the way he stopped at the juke-box and did a quick recce

7

through the Fifties section, then with a grin inserted the coin and punched up his all-time favourite. Christ, if he had a quid for every time he and Susie had bopped to 'Great Balls of Fire' . . . go for it, Killer!

Heading for the Gents', he had to laugh at the antics of the Toms, pounding the table and yelling at Jimmy and the others to get a move on: six young faces, slightly flushed with heat and the few they'd had on the way, bursting with health and high spirits. And Billy Newman acting the comic, sprawled back in his chair, grasping his throat, tongue lolling out, as if he'd just crawled across the desert. Smashing lads, Dillon thought, the best, and felt a glow of real pride. My lads. Better than those fat knackers you saw on the streets back home, hair dyed green and purple, safety-pins through their nostrils, with pasty, drab faces like dead fish on a slab.

Feeling good, more relaxed now, he pushed through the door into a narrow, dank-smelling concrete-floored passage with mildew eating the walls, having to squeeze past crates of empty bottles stacked nearly to the corrugated iron roof. The Gents' toilets consisted of two cubicles, one already occupied, and as Dillon stood back to let someone pass, he glimpsed Malone entering the other. A girl, seventeen or thereabouts, lank mousy hair tied back in a pony-tail, was standing outside one of the Ladies' cubicles opposite, tapping ungently on the door with bitten fingernails painted a day-glo yellow.

'Come on, Kathleen, you bin ages!' The lilt of her accent made even her whine sound attractive to Dillon's ears. She tapped again, gnawing her lip. 'Kathleen, are you coming out of there?'

Amused, Dillon leaned against the wall, stroking his dark moustache. He watched as Kathleen emerged – a transformed Kathleen apparently – having strained and struggled into a skimpy, tight-fitting knitted top that showed every nook and cranny. She smoothed it down over her puppy-fat tummy, blue-lidded eyes under frizzy blonde, home-kit permed hair, an attempt at being

8

Madonna falling flat. She mouthed through glossy red lips, 'Me mother'd kill me if she caught me wearing this . . . do you like it? It's crocheted – '

Catching sight of Dillon, she tossed her haughty head in the air, and the pair of them went off, squealing and giggling.

Hell, he was bursting. Dillon banged on the cubicle door.

'Come on, Malone!'

BAM-BAM-BAM-BAM!

You shake my nerves and you rattle my brain -

(Loud enough, even here, to drown out the sound of the live band.)

BAM-BAM-BAM-BAM!

Too much in love drives a man insane -

Dillon banged again, harder.

Jimmy backed away from the bar, loaded tray held high, Harry nipping in to grab the one being filled by the perspiring barman. Taffy, having filched his pint, was already on his way to the table, licking a moustache of foam from his upper lip. Given the glad eye, Steve was leaning over a pale girl with glossy black hair draping her shoulders, putting in a useful bit of spadework for later on. She Taurus, he Pisces – sweet combination! – was the bill of goods he was selling. And she was buying, gazing into those sexy green eyes of his.

I laughed at love cos I thought it was funny –

BAM-BAM-BAM-BAM!

You came along and moved me honey –

BAM-BAM-BAM-BAM!

I've changed my mind

This world is fine –

Goodness Gracious! Great Balls of . . .

Weaving through the crowd, twelve feet or so from the table, Taffy saw with his own eyes what a £6.50 Woolworths' alarm clock, some copper wiring and thirty pounds of Semtex could do.

It was the stuff of a twisted, tortured nightmare dreamt by a madman. In an instant the table and the six flushed, laughing young faces vanished, obliterated in a rocket blast of intense white heat and a curling, orange-streaked fireball that blew a hole through the ceiling. In a dragged-out eternity of suspended time Taffy actually saw it happen, before the upsurge of the blast sucked the big Welshman in – sucked him towards the heart of the inferno, towards the gaping hole left behind as the front wall was ripped out and spewed into the carpark.

Then the roof caved in, a massive oak beam smashing across Taffy's shoulders and pinning him to the floor.

The shockwave lifted Jimmy, the loaded tray of brimming pints disappearing over his head, and flung him into a writhing knot of hot bodies, tangled arms and legs, splintered tables and chairs, shards of broken glass. Harry, his back to the explosion, head-butted the bar and in a dazed, instantaneous reflex rolled under a table as another huge beam came crashing down, missing him by inches. Further away from the epicentre of the blast, near the archway to the disco, a giant hand swatted Steve between the shoulder-blades. Sent him skidding along the floor into a mass of bodies, feeling them pressed close to his face, the mingled smell of perfume, aftershave, sweat, beer and Babycham stinging his nostrils like fetid, suffocating incense.

And then a strange unearthly silence. After the boom and searing flash and shockwave had died away, it settled over the wreckage of broken bodies and falling debris, illuminated by a single stuttering fluorescent tube hanging crazily from its bracket. It lasted a couple of heartbeats, this dreadful silence in the flickering semi-darkness. Long enough for the horror of what had happened to sink in, for the brutal fact of it to penetrate the numbed brain of the injured and the dying. Not as bad though, nowhere near, as the screams and moans and cries for help that now went up, a shrill, piercing, endless cacophony of human anguish.

A tongue of yellow flame licked. It lapped up the walls, touched the curtains, turning to orange, and raced upwards in a sheet of bright crimson.

As if this was the signal, the real panic started.

2

'Come on, Malone, get back in there!'

In a white fury, Dillon wrestled with the big man who had burst from the cubicle, all around them was mayhem, and Malone, even after swearing the pub was clear, seemed frantic to save his own skin, pushing Dillon backwards, as he tried to do a runner out the side entrance to the carpark. Dillon screamed at Malone to follow him back into the pub, but Malone was herding the crush of people jamming into the narrow passage, all of them struggling hysterically to get out. His bellowing voice yelling, 'Move . . . move keep it moving. This is my bloody job, Frank,' and he pushed and half carried out the screaming teenagers, as Dillon gave up on him, and now fought against the tide, pushing bodies aside in a frantic effort to get back inside. His lads were in there – maimed, mutilated, perhaps even dead. His head still rang with the tremendous boom of the explosion, which had sounded in Dillon's ears like a door slamming in the bowels of hell. And then, even worse, the terrible screams and moans and cries for help.

Squirming through, Dillon saw blanched faces crisscrossed with bloody streaks from flying glass, eyes wild with terror and blank from shock, desperate to get clear before the upper floor collapsed and buried them under tons of masonry. The girl with blonde frizzy hair stumbled into him, hands covering her face, blood pouring through her fingers and soaking the crochet top. 'Help me . . . somebody please help me, help me . . .' Behind her, a teenage boy with half his scalp ripped away, eyebrows and eyelashes burnt off, staggering blindly forwards, hands outstretched. 'Can't see, oh God I can't see . . .'

Dillon struggled on against the wall of human panic,

12

the babble of voices all around, mingled with weeping and choking screams as the horror of it all sank in. 'My wife, where's my wife' . . . 'Brian, where are you' . . . 'Me sister's in there somewhere' . . . 'I lost me handbag' . . . 'Get out, gotta get out' . . . 'Johnny help me, please, please' . . . 'Where's me shoes' . . . 'Meg, Meg, MEG!' . . .

There came a soft *whooosh*, a sudden brightening of flames from the darkened interior of the bar, and a coil of smoke like an evil black tongue writhed through the gap where the door had been blown off its hinges.

'FIRE! . . . FIRE! . . . FIRE! . . .'

Above the pandemonium Dillon heard the braying wail of sirens – fire engines, ambulances, police – racing along country lanes, converging on the pub from all directions. But there wasn't time to wait for them. Minutes, seconds, were vital. *He had to get in there now!* Dillon had almost given up, raging and despairing that he'd never make it, but suddenly, magically, a space appeared and he dived for it, head down through the smoke, crouching low, eyes tight and stinging as he scanned the carnage of what five minutes earlier had been a roomful of happy young people enjoying themselves, having a great Saturday night to the sprightly rhythms of the folk group and the pounding of Jerry Lee's piano.

Now, to Dillon's right, the smashed juke-box lay on its side, a dim glow blinking feebly from its innards. In the lurid light of flames he saw Harry, legs braced apart, holding aloft a table to shelter those underneath from the debris showering down from the jagged, gaping hole in the ceiling. Directly above, one of the severed oak beams, a good half ton of it, made an ominous groaning sound and started to slant down. A chunk of concrete hit the table-top and Harry's legs buckled. Somehow he held on, gritting his teeth and yelling for help. Dillon scrambled towards him. But Jimmy, red hair now totally white with plaster, eyes raw-rimmed, was nearer and got there first. The muscles on his tattooed arms bulged as he gripped the table's edge, back-to-back with Harry, the two men

13

straining to shield the injured beneath as they tried to drag themselves clear.

A couple of them managed to, the third couldn't, lying face down with his legs trapped. 'Get him clear!' Jimmy shouted, coughing and spitting out dust. 'Somebody – !'

Hands reached for the man, gripped his collar, and he screamed in agony as they pulled him free.

Jimmy glanced down. 'Is he clear?' His face tautened under its mask of plaster. He could see legs. A girl's blood-streaked legs through torn and shredded tights – Christ Almighty! He looked round for help, saw Dillon through the smoke, but Dillon was twenty feet away with a mountain of tangled wreckage to climb first. More concrete and brick thudded down on the table. Any second now the whole bloody roof was going to cave in. Harry again took the entire weight on his back, sweat dripping off his chin, and snarled at Jimmy, 'Go on, move her – I can't hold on much longer. Move her!'

Alive or dead, or just concussed, Jimmy didn't know, getting an arm around the girl's waist and lifting her, limp as a rag doll, from the debris of splintered tables and chairs.

'Jimmy . . . Jimmy!' Harry's legs were giving way, his body doubled over under the terrible strain. 'For chrissakes, I can't hold it, I can't . . .'

The table shuddered as another load fell, split in two, and as Harry went down, scrabbling on hands and knees to get out from under, Jimmy executed a swift side-roll straight out of the para landing technique manual, the girl clasped in his powerful arms.

It was a miracle, Steve thought. A total freak that the kid, young Billy Newman, had survived and was still alive, if barely, after sitting right on top of the bomb that had killed his five companions outright. Somehow Billy had been thrown horizontally instead of vertically by the force of the blast, and when Steve had found him and hoisted him onto his back, the boy had been groaning and muttering something about his jacket, he was wearing a new jacket, 'Is me jacket torn? Is me jacket damaged?' His eyes were unfocused, childlike, and he seemed unaware of his injuries. A terrible gash down the left side of his face, the pale cheekbone exposed through the ragged open wound; his left arm hanging uselessly like a tube of jelly; both legs charred to a black crisp, giving off the sweet sickly stench of barbecued human flesh. Cowardly murdering swine . . . choking hatred burned in Steve's throat like stale vomit. Round up all the IRA scum, stand 'em against a wall, have done. What the fuck did the politicians know, the bleeding-heart, so-called 'human rights' groups? What about Billy Newman's human rights?

'Steve . . . Steve!' Dillon was at his side, sliding his arm across Billy's back, taking half the weight. 'That front wall's going to give any second, get out this way . . .' Dillon swung round, bellowed through the smoke: 'EVERYBODY MAKE FOR THE BACK . . . STAY CLEAR OF THE FRONT ENTRANCE!'

Above their heads an ominous creaking and splintering as another oak beam tore itself loose and canted down, teetering in mid-air.

'Taffy!' Dillon yelled. ' – Taffy!'

Scrambling through the debris, the big Welshman got his broad back underneath the beam as it came down, bringing with it a snowstorm of plaster and shredded laths. Hands clamped to his knees, Taffy heaved upwards, giving Dillon and Steve the space to duck underneath with the injured boy. As they dragged him towards the bar at the back of the room, Dillon knew for certain – once that beam went, the entire front wall would go, taking half the ceiling with it. Only one escape route. One chance any of them would come out of this alive.

'Make for the stairs . . . GET UP TO THE NEXT FLOOR!'

The unwritten rule, the unspoken code, in any kind of situation, in any kind of emergency, you never abandoned a comrade, no matter what. Steve had darted back, tossing

15

furniture aside like a madman, to go to Taffy's aid. Harry was there too, the combined strength of the three of them hurling the beam away so that it swung in a wide arc, hanging in space, and then came hurtling down, smashing through the floor with a crash that shook the building to its foundations.

Hoisting Billy in a shoulder-lift, Dillon gripped the banister rail and hauled himself up the narrow staircase. He heard the rumble and felt the shudder as the ceiling caved in, filling the air with a whirling duststorm. Behind Dillon, Jimmy halted halfway up the stairs and looked anxiously down. 'Harry?' he called hoarsely. 'Taff . . . ?'

The complete frontage of Hennessey's had collapsed. One moment the upper storey was lit by flames, the next obscured by a pall of black smoke, clouds of red sparks billowing through the rafters of what was left of the roof. Behind the fire engines, their hoses snaking over the cindery, puddled ground, police cars and a cordon of uniformed men kept the groups of survivors at a safe distance. The Army had arrived, three Bedford four-tonners, MPs in jeeps, officers in quilted flak-jackets deploying their men to seal off the perimeter. Through the hissing of hosepipes and the roaring crackle of the inferno, a child's voice could be heard, screaming 'MUMMY!' and screaming again 'MUMMY!' and again 'MUMMY!'

'Oh God Almighty . . .' The landlord's wife, face blackened, hair singed, a blanket around her shoulders, tried to break through, screaming hysterically, 'My kids . . . My kids are still in there!' Held back, she stared up with wild, petrified eyes, white runnels on her cheeks where tears had eaten through the grime.

The door splintered and swung wide, hanging off its hinges from Dillon's force-kick. Smoke was sifting through the cracks in the floorboards. Dillon charged inside, Billy Newman draped across his shoulders, and turned to the wall, shielding both their faces as Taffy and Steve came through the doorway like an express train. Without break-

16

ing their stride they hurled a long section of what had been the bar-top through the window, taking out four panes and part of the frame. Grabbing the end, they held firm, the bar-top forming a slippery, slanting bridge between window-ledge and toilet roof ten feet below. Dillon checked it out, a cold inner core of his brain insulated from the noise, chaos and confusion, the total professional coolly estimating angles, the breaking strain of the corrugated roof, the risk of over-balancing under Billy's weight. Thank Christ he had his Pumas on, Dillon thought, stepping up onto the window-sill, inching out one foot to make sure of his grip.

'Frank, wait – ' Steve leaning out, gripping his elbow. 'You'll never make it!'

Through the smoke and flying sparks, Dillon glimpsed a fireman on a hydraulic platform rising towards him, but prevented from coming too close because of the spread of flames. Dillon gritted his teeth. If he could just get Billy those extra few feet nearer the fireman's reaching arms . . . he edged further along the treacherous surface, feeling Steve right behind, the two of them balanced precariously on the wooden bar-top, now starting to bend under their combined weight.

'Hold onto me, Steve,' Dillon ground out. 'When they get Billy I'll lose my balance. Keep me steady!'

'I got you, mate.' The collar of Dillon's windcheater bunched in one fist, Steve's other arm was clamped like a vice to the inner wall. 'Another couple of feet . . . easy now . . . easy . . .'

With a final heave Dillon got the boy across the gap, saw him clasped safe and secure in the fireman's arms, and felt the wood split beneath his feet. His leg went through, he dropped, arms paddling thin air, and then hung, legs dangling as Steve hauled him up by the collar.

'Couple of Hail Marys, Frank.' Steve's handsome mug was split in a broad grin, the pair of them in a heap on the floor. 'Then I reckon we should get the hell out of here!' Dillon stared at him, raising his fist, then gave him the grin back, punching him on the arm.

Taffy was at the door, thumb jerking frantically over his shoulder at the smoke-filled passage streaked with orange. 'Frank, there's kids up here!'

Dillon leapt up, cursing. At the window he shouted down to the knot of firemen spraying the side of the building. 'Drench us! Come on – get those hoses on us, we're going back in!'

Standing in line, bracing each other, the three men took the full force of the jet, which sent them staggering backwards. Dillon wrapped his sodden windcheater around his head and dropped to his hands and knees, preparing to scuttle back in, when Harry, crouched low, appeared through the smoke, a little girl cradled in his arms.

The firemen, aiming their hoses to either side, formed a sheltering spray for the platform as it rose level with the window-ledge. The gap slowly closed, the platform inching nearer. Holding the little girl close to his chest, Harry stepped across.

Dillon stood next to an Army fire tender, drenched to the skin, gazing with sick eyes at the flames leaping towards the sky. The front of the pub was practically burnt out, the fire still raging at the back, rapidly devouring the upper storey and roof.

The little girl Harry had rescued was nearby, wrapped in a blanket, being comforted by her mother. Her two boys, barely a couple of years separating them, were huddled in their father's arms as he knelt between them. God knows how Taffy had done it, Dillon thought . . . the bloke was asbestos, somehow finding them in there and smashing his way out through a rear window, bringing them out alive with hardly a scorch mark apiece. That brand of courage didn't grow on trees.

Dillon closed his eyes, jaw muscles clenched tight making the scar on his left cheek stand out through the smeared dirt. His lads. None of them over twenty, with all their young lives ahead of them. If he lived to be a hundred, two hundred, he'd never forget this, never forgive. Jimmy's voice brought him back to his senses.

'They're bringing them out now.' Jimmy was pointing to where the firemen had hosed the front entrance to a charred frame of smouldering timbers. Bodies were being stretchered out.

'I'm game.' Harry, his hands bandaged, was staring at Dillon with bloodshot eyes, one old pro reading the thoughts of another. 'Come on, let's go for another try . . .'

'You crazy?' Jimmy tried to grab Dillon's arm as he started forward. Dillon shook him off. 'Frank, the whole place is gutted. Frank!'

'My lads . . .' Dillon choked on the words. '. . . are still in there.' A spasm creased his face. 'My lads.'

'Frank, for God's sake, don't be crazy!'

'I'm with you, Frank,' Harry said. 'Let's go for it!'

'FRANK!' Fists clenched at his sides, Jimmy watched them get another drenching under the fire hoses and head towards the building, a fireman and two MPs trying to cut them off.

'Oh shit!' Shaking his head wearily, Jimmy started to run. 'Wait for me . . .'

The young doctor, fair hair ruffled by the breeze to reveal his premature bald spot, moved along the line of stretchers, stooping every now and then for a closer look, moving on, signalling to the attendants those to be taken to hospital and the others who were beyond the power of medicine.

Doors slammed and ambulances sped away.

The firemen were reeling in their hoses, working mechanically, faces blackened, weariness etched into every pore. A single hose still played on the pile of smoking rubble, the damp hissing of the embers the only sound, clouds of steam and mingled soot drifting away into the darkness.

Jimmy came through the huddle of Army trucks and found Dillon having cream and gauze applied to his hands by a civilian nurse, who despite looking about sixteen

19

seemed to know her job. Jimmy hesitated, watching the nurse lightly wrap and tie a bandage around the raw wound. The frozen stillness of Dillon's face, the absolute fixed, unblinking intensity of his eyes, scared Jimmy. The man looked possessed.

'You okay?' Jimmy asked at last.

Dillon gave a tight nod, the harsh lines of his face carved out of stone. 'Did any of them make it?'

Steve came up, overhearing Dillon's question, his mouth set grimly. 'No, they didn't stand a chance.'

'What about Billy?'

Steve shook his head, almost in tears. He gestured vaguely. 'They want you over by the trucks. Taffy's refusing to go to hospital – '

'Harry?' Dillon asked.

'With the medics. He's okay.' Steve tried again. 'They want you to – '

Dillon ignored him and walked over the wet cindery ground to the dark-grey body bags ranged side by side in a neat, military row. Some already had plastic tags, name and rank in black felt-tip, the ones in bits or too badly burned for recognition didn't. Dillon sank slowly to his heels, head bowed. He reached out, as if in silent meditation, his fingertips resting gently and briefly on one of the anonymous shapes. He stood up, about to turn away when he realised they were grouped round him, the four of them, his comrades and best mates, the men he'd crawled through shit and bullets with, two of them, Harry and Taffy, for getting on twenty years.

Without anger or emotion of any kind, as if all feeling had been drained out of him, Dillon spoke to them in a drab monotone.

'Those two guys, the ones at our table when we came in. They must have planted it.' Dillon looked at each of them in turn – Jimmy Hammond, Harry Travers, Steve Harris, Taffy Davies – searching each face with a cold, implacable scrutiny. 'I want them, no matter how long it takes. We find them, agreed?'

20

The C.O. had arrived, climbing out of his staff car. Jimmy touched Dillon's arm. 'C.O.'s here, Frank,' but Dillon brushed his hand away and went on in a throaty rasp, 'We make this *personal*. Agreed? We're gonna get those two bastards, agreed?' Fixing each man straight in the eye. 'Yes? YES?'

They were with him, he knew it, and only when he knew it and was satisfied did he turn to acknowledge the C.O.'s presence, standing a little distance away.

'Dillon, there's a truck waiting for you and your lads, get yourself cleaned up and then . . . well,' he cleared his throat, 'soon as you're fit I'll need – you know, the usual procedure.' Looking down at the row of body bags, his voice sank to a whisper. 'I'm sorry. Tragic . . . it's bloody tragic . . .'

Dillon nodded once, staring at the ground, made a pretence at saluting, and turned away. Taffy drew him forward, hugging him, almost like a father comforting his son. 'Like you said,' Taffy muttered under his breath. 'We make this personal.'

One by one they all touched Dillon's shoulder, each man making his private, unspoken vow.

The truck was chugging blue diesel fumes, the tailboard down, and Dillon was about to climb aboard when he stopped and went rigid. Across the carpark, standing between two MPs, Malone was staring about him with a look of dazed bewilderment. Dillon pushed the others aside, growling in his throat to get at the yellow bastard, beat the holy shit out of him. Jimmy and Steve hauled him back. 'Cool it, Frank – let's just get the hell out of here.'

Dillon was ashen, trembling. 'Okay, okay . . .' He subsided, wiping his mouth. 'But one day I'll have him for this!'

Two scores to settle. The IRA and Malone. One day for certain, both of them. He'd never rest till it was done. Never.

Dillon stood, holding onto the swaying truck as it bumped over potholes to the road, seeing them lift the

21

body bags, so very carefully and gently, and slide them into the military ambulance. And even when the truck turned and the sight was hidden from view, Dillon continued to stare out. *Never.*

FRANK DILLON

Thin curtains of chill wintry drizzle swept over the gleaming drill square, neat gravel paths and sodden grass verges
of Browning Barracks, Aldershot. Known as The Depot,
this unlovely collection of flat-roofed, slab-sided buildings,
resembling nothing more than an inner-city council estate,
housed the three regular battalions of the Parachute Regiment and units of Airborne Forces. Through the rain-
streaked window of the Sergeants' Mess, lingering over his
second cup of lukewarm coffee, Frank Dillon watched two
truckloads of raw recruits just pulling in, 'Joe Crows'
fresh from Civvy Street. Some of them would jack it in
tomorrow, Dillon knew, others not last till the end of the
week. As for the rest, they would go on to experience the
joys of twelve weeks of mental and physical torture before
they faced the ultimate test of 'P' Company – five days of
sheer undiluted hell on earth.

Steeplechase, Log Race, Endurance March over twenty-
eight kilometres of rough country, bergen rucksack loaded
with 22kg of bricks and gravel, Speed March, Assault
Course, including the dreaded Shuffle Bars – scaffolding
poles fifty feet off the ground and no hand-holds –
Stretcher Race with a twelve-man team hauling 75kg of
steel bars and sandbags over twelve kilometres of Welsh
peaks and gullies.

The ones that came through it would know – with the
bright shining certainty of hardened survivors – that they'd
earned the right to proudly wear the Red Beret with its
winged badge of lion and crown above a floating parachute.

Their first day in, Dillon thought, watching the Joe

Crows disembark, with it all before them. After eighteen years, four months and sixteen days, he was going out. Back to Civvies. Back to a world he hardly remembered. Another lifetime, a different Frank Dillon altogether, so it seemed to him, all those years ago – a gangling lad with a shock of floppy black hair, an attitude problem, and a sheaf of pathetic school reports, plus two scrapes with the law that had nearly landed him in Borstal. The Paras had sorted that out, hair, attitude, even the required discipline of book-study, the lot. They had shaped and trained and hammered him into the mould of a professional fighting man, a member of one the finest and fittest elite corps in the world, Commandos and SAS included. At thirty-six he was still remarkably fit. Still possessed the skills necessary to strip down and assemble blindfold the SA80 family of weapons, stalk an enemy through brush and bog, hurl himself into space through the door of a Hercules C–130 at eight hundred feet. That was Frank Dillon's story in a nutshell, serving Queen and Country. Question was, what the fuck was he going to do now?·

Dillon pushed his cup away and checked his watch against the wall clock. 7.20 a.m. Better snap to it if he was going to catch the London train.

A Radio One DJ was babbling something about Red Nose Day as he went through the double-doors and ran along the covered walkway to the NCO's billet, feeling the sting of cold rain whipping through. His suitcase was packed, lying on top of the four grey blankets, plumbline straight and squared off at the foot of the bed; just a couple of things for his leather grip on the four-drawer chest, and that was that. The small room with its single window and plain cream walls had the austere look of a hermit's cell, but it had been home.

Dillon tossed in his shaving bag, opened the top drawer and took out a metal case tooled in dark leather. He didn't intend to open it but he did. Sergeant Dillon gazed at the three medals embedded in green velvet, the UN, the NI, the SA, not really seeing them. Now they too belonged to another life. He snapped the case shut, dropped it in the grip, zippered it.

In the square wall mirror he gave himself a final regimental inspection. A stranger in dark blue blazer with breast-pocket badge, maroon tie embroidered with the Para motif, grey trousers pressed to a knife-edge, stared back at him. But for the moustache and the scar, a thin straight line below his left eye on which stubble never grew, he mightn't have recognised himself. As long as Susie and the kids did, Dillon thought without humour. *Daddy's coming home – for good!* Good or ill, that remained to be seen.

One last call, to settle his NAAFI account and collect his rail warrant. Dillon handed over forty quid, received his change and a receipt from the Duty Sergeant, who then gave him a pink slip.

'Rail pass, and that's it.' Duty Sergeant Sinclair watched Dillon fold the paper and slip it into his wallet. There was a brief, awkward silence. Then Sinclair, instead of saluting, took Dillon's hand in a firm, rough grip. 'Good luck in Civvy Street, Frank.'

The Dakota from World War II, parked on the quadrant of grass outside the Regimental Museum, flanked by an equally ancient artillery piece and heavy-duty machine-gun, looked in better nick now than in its operational days. Kept spick and span not just for show, but for a purpose.

Under a grey, restless sky, a few bright patches breaking through, Dillon walked by the aircraft, raincoat buttoned up to the neck. His eyes moved from the bulbous nose and along the clean sweep of the fuselage, slick-wet and shining from the downpour. Those new recruits he'd seen arriving earlier would be standing in front of the old war-horse in a few days, lined up with their instructors for the course photograph. Some of them, a highly selected few, would make it from the despised DPM forage caps – craphats – to Red Berets, from Joe Crows to proud new Toms. They'd take over where he left off.

Dillon walked on, not looking back.

27

The minute Susie Dillon heard the phone ring, she knew. So did Helen, Susie's mother, eyes narrowed, mouth pulled down at the corners in that told-you-so expression. She tugged her cardigan straight and folded her arms, glaring at the table, moved specially into the centre of the small living-room for the occasion, laden with plates of sandwiches, cakes, biscuits, bowls of peanuts, even a bottle of sparkling Spanish wine. All that time and trouble and effort wasted, would her daughter never learn? But it was the two boys she felt most sorry for, Kenny and little Phil. Hair brushed, faces shining, self-conscious in their brand-new Marks & Sparks shirts and shorts, they sat happily together on the sofa, dive-bombing the hearth-rug and vari-flame gasfire with a model Spitfire.

Susie went through to the tiny cluttered hallway, glancing at her watch to avoid her mother's eye. She stepped round the children's bikes and picked up the phone. Helen heard her say, 'Hello?' and then call to the boys. 'Quick, it's your Dad!' They were off the sofa and gone in a trice, giddy with excitement.

And then, as might be expected, Susie's puzzled, rather plaintive tone. 'But . . . where are you, Frank?'

Helen shook her head at the ceiling, sighed, and picked up a sandwich and gouged off a corner. Don't let it go to waste — she chewed, grimacing — even if it was fish paste.

Pissed as arseholes. Or very nearly — but sufficiently in control to keep the slur out of his voice, Dillon hoped. He concentrated through the din of voices and 'Peggy Sue' thumping from the juke-box. 'I gotta go, Sue . . . no, tell 'em I'll see 'em later. I'm fine, really — ' He smothered a belch. 'Sorry about this . . . Bye.'

After the second attempt Dillon got the receiver back in its cradle. He blinked and contemplated the five pints of Courage bitter lined up on the bar by his elbow. He'd had . . . how many? Eight, nine, ten? Couldn't remember, as if it made any bleeding difference. He took a deep gulping swallow, head thrown back, and plonked the glass

28

down, wiping his mouth with the back of his hand. Four to go.

It was somewhere around late afternoon, he could tell that by the rays of sunlight slanting in low through the red and green panes of the Haverlock's front bow-window, spotlighting the thick blue smog of cigarette smoke over the pool table. First call had to be the ex-Paras' watering-hole. Because, Dillon thought with sudden blinding clarity, he was one of them now. Ex-Para. He knew what it meant but the words wouldn't sink in.

'Eighteen?' Harry Travers was saying to a young guy further along the bar, waving his pint glass and slopping beer everywhere. '*Eighteen?* You're looking at a man,' belch and a sway, '. . . at a man who sank twenty-five . . .'

'Cheers, Harry,' Dillon said, raising the next one and taking the head off it. But Harry, his face a torrid hue, sucking beer from his gingery moustache, was jabbing the air with a blunt finger, fixing the young guy with watery blue eyes. 'Get this . . . security company wants three drivers, one armoured car and a motorbike. I said, "For a grand, mate, I'll get the Royal Tattoo and Joan Collins." ' His mouth twisted. 'Wanker.'

Dillon surveyed the packed bar. One or two young blokes, probably still regulars by the lean, trim look of them, but mostly older hands, a couple of years out and already getting slack around the middle, beer guts hanging over their belts. Not for him, Dillon made a drunken pact with himself. He'd work out, keep a tight grip. Or else he'd end up like Wally over there, balding, fagging it, looking ten years older than his forty-five, shirt-buttons straining to hold back a phantom pregnancy nearing full term.

At least Jimmy seemed to have adjusted well to civvy life, Dillon thought. There he was, the wheeler-dealer, plenty of scams cooking and more on the back-burner, handing out folding stuff.

'And you get double,' Jimmy was saying to a young, tanned bloke who looked as if he was just back from a

stint in Belize, 'if you can get me a dozen MBC suits. An'
I can take as many DMBs, jungles, as you can lay your
hands on. I got transport, no problem.'

Jimmy glanced over, winked at Dillon, flashed his confident grin. Looking very sharp in an expensively tailored,
shot-silk blue suit and crisp white shirt, a fine gold chain
fastened with studs to the collar points and looped across
his matching necktie of gold and red diamonds on a blue
ground. He'd let his red hair grow longer and wore it
slicked back with grease; seeing Michael Douglas in *Wall
Street* had left a lasting impression.

'Two of us on the door,' Wally draped his arm round
Dillon's shoulders, droning on with another of his intermi-
nable stories, 'thirty-five a night, an' I'm not jokin', mate
– I've had more fuckin' fights than I had the whole time
I was in Belfast.' He gestured to the blonde landlady,
working like a Trojan behind the bar. 'Two more here,
Sybil, three over there . . .'

Dillon made a token protest, knowing he should be
making tracks, but Wally was in full spate.

'You can keep hittin the Irish an' they bounce . . . I'll
tell you, Frank, there are more of those bastards over here
than they got over there!'

Feet apart, legs braced, Dillon tried to keep the floor in
place. Gazing straight ahead at the optics, he stated, 'I
gotta go home . . .' the fixed dead stare of a man recognising an ultimate truth.

Somebody came through the smoke and whispered in
Harry's ear. He beckoned Jimmy over and they closed
around Dillon, Harry bending close, giving the word,
Dillon half-catching something about 'Kilburn' and 'bunch
of paddies' and the name of a club.

Wally's face lit up. Letting out a yell, he hooked Dillon's
neck in the crook of his elbow, announcing, 'Let's send
this man out into civvies fighting! Yesssss! Come on!'

Getting wind that something was up but not knowing
what, Dillon said vaguely, 'Where we going?' as he was
carried in a scrum to the door.

30

At the cigarette machine, a tall, ashen-faced man with hair hanging in his eyes, pissed as a fart, did a staggering turn and collided with Dillon. About to brush past, Dillon stopped dead in his tracks. He gripped the man by the shoulders, stared into the lost, bleary eyes.

'Steve -? Steve Harris?'

In place of the handsome Jack-the-Lad, six-feet-two in his stocking-feet and with, as he never ceased to tell anyone within ear-shot, a dick that was perfectly in proportion with his Adonis body, was this pathetic, shambling wreck. Unshaven, bloated and boozed out, Steve 'the Puller' Harris, renowned for his sexual exploits, not allowed near anyone's wife, or sister, and on one occasion, Smother Smith's mother! . . . Steve, one of Dillon's best lads, was almost unrecognisable.

'Leave him, Frank, just leave him, he's a waster,' Jimmy said contemptuously, and as if to add insult to his remark, he stuffed into the drunken Steve's torn top pocket a tenner. 'Right, we mustered? Let's go . . .'

Dillon held Steve's face in his cupped hands. 'Steve! It's me, Frank, Frank Dillon, what's happened to you, sunshine, eh?'

The lost eyes, sunk deep in unknown depths, roamed about and finally registered a tiny spark. The slobbering mouth opened, but instead of words, a choking, throttled growl issued out, grotesque and mechanical and meaningless as an alien's.

Dillon's heart filled his chest. He put his arms round the lad and pulled him to him, mumbling, 'Steve, oh Steve, Steve . . .'

News at Ten was just starting when Susie's mother decided she'd had more than enough, thank you very much, and put her coat on to leave. The table had been cleared, except for one plate, one cup and saucer, and the bottle of Spanish sparkling, now half-empty. The boys were long gone to bed, asking where Daddy was even while Susie was tucking them in. Now she drained her wineglass, trying not to ignore her mother at the hall door, at the same time fighting to stay calm, not lose her temper. But Helen wouldn't let it go.

'Some homecoming. Bloody hero doesn't even turn up.' She tucked her woolly plaid scarf under her chin. 'I'm sorry for the boys . . .'

'He'll need time to adjust, Mum.' She hated the plaintive tone in her voice, but it just came out that way.

'He's not going to find it easy to walk into a job with no qualifications.'

'He's doing this for me and the kids, and if he wants to let off steam for a few days, then that's his business.'

'Eighteen years, and all he's got to show for it is three thousand quid.' Helen's blue rinse quivered. 'That mate of his got near a hundred thousand . . .'

Susie snapped off the TV and faced her. 'That was for his leg. He lost his leg. You ask his wife which she'd prefer – better still, ask him. Goodnight, Mum.'

4

Jimmy Hammond swung the re-conditioned jeep into Kilburn High Road, shouting into the slipstream and not giving a damn who heard, least of all Steve, 'He's a waster, Frank!'

Harry leaned back from the passenger seat, poking Steve's knee as he addressed Dillon. 'Just make sure he stays put. He's a bloody liability.'

Steve sat between Dillon and Wally, apparently insensible to what was being said, or even the universe at large. After about quarter of a mile the jeep turned off the main road and jinked down several badly-lit backstreets, darkened shops and shuttered industrial premises sealed tight for the night.

As they drew up beneath a streetlight, Jimmy said tensely, 'How many did he say there were, Harry?'

'Five. Said we'd recognise one of the bastards . . . here's Johnny now.'

A figure muffled in a scarf and donkey jacket emerged from an alleyway, collar up around his ears, and skipped along the damp pavement on rubber soles. 'Frank – how you doing, man?'

Johnny Blair, another old mate from the Regiment, shook Dillon's hand. Then he noticed Steve. 'What you brought him for?'

Wally clambered out, a bit unsteady on his pins. His feet were bad anyway, ever since he'd lost three toes to frostbite on Wireless Ridge in the Falklands. 'It's Frank's first night in civvies!' he chortled.

Johnny laughed, rubbing his hands together. 'Right, there was five at last count, up in the snooker hall. Could be more. . . .'

Jimmy was pulling on a pair of leather gloves, heavily

reinforced along the knuckles. Under the gloves he wore three chunky gold rings.

'What's going down?' Dillon asked, sobering up fast.

'Bit of paddy bashin', Frank,' Harry grinned. He jerked his thumb, glancing towards the green light that glowed above the entrance to a club, half a block along on the opposite side. Then spun completely round saying, voice way back in his throat, 'Holy Shit! Look who just walked out – it's Keenan. Any money Tony McKinney's with him!'

Keenan, apparently, wasn't slow on the uptake either. Seeing the group under the streetlight, he flicked his dog-end into the gutter and hurried back inside.

'How do you want to do it?' Wally said, fumbling in his pocket. 'You want a cosh?' he asked Dillon.

'Wait.' Jimmy laid a hand on Wally's arm, looking into Dillon's eyes. They were a team once more, a professional fighting unit, and Sergeant Dillon was back in charge. 'Over to you, Frank.'

Dillon straightened up, sucking in a breath. The haze of alcohol evaporated from his brain, in its place cold, crystal-clear reality. 'How many exits? We do it in or outside? We'll need a man either end of the alley . . . an' we need to know how many there are.' He hooked his arm around Wally's shoulder. 'Let's flush 'em out . . .'

Three minutes later they were set, men posted, exits covered, Wally as the decoy stepping through the doorway, the light above making a green bird's egg of his bald head. He looked up the narrow staircase to where Keenan was standing, shapes rippling on the frosted glass panel behind his back.

'Wanna game?' inquired Wally casually.

'It's members only.' Keenan's eyes were flat, hard. 'And you're on our turf, so back off!'

'Wrong, you Irish git,' said Wally softly, mounting the stairs. 'This is our territory . . .'

'Stay put . . . You bin warned.'

'Then come on down!'

The provocation had the desired effect, as Dillon knew

34

it would. Wally grabbed Keenan's foot as he kicked out, the next second the pair of them rolling down the stairs and into the street – the signal for all hell to break loose as the staircase was suddenly filled with Irishmen wielding billiard cues, one with a baseball bat, some with bottles.

Flattened against the outside wall, Dillon, Jimmy and Harry Travers bided their time. The important thing was to work as a team, backing each other up, using the techniques of karate and kick boxing against an undisciplined mob used to street brawling. Dillon chopped the first man down with a blow to the windpipe, employing the straight edge of his hand like a knife-blade. He sidestepped to avoid a swinging bottle, swept the attacker's legs out from under him, and let Jimmy finish him off with two stiffened fingers in the eye-sockets. Harry got a crack across the back of the head with a billiard cue, grabbed the man by the lapels and broke his nose with a single head-butt. But the Irishmen were a tough bunch – biting, kicking, flailing about with their weapons – while the Paras worked with clinical, methodical patience, covering each other's backs.

Left behind in the jeep, Steve saw a bunch of men charging along the alley, having piled out of the rear exit and doubling round to cut off the retreat. Steve yelled a warning but nothing came out, just a harsh guttural croak. He stood up, smacked his hand against the car horn and kept it there. This alerted Dillon all right, it also drew attention to Steve, a lone target, and three of the men broke away and ran across the street, hauling Steve down onto the road and taking it in turns to kick the living shit out of him. Dillon saw it happen, but he had one or two little problems of his own. He dealt with one, knee to the groin followed by a rabbit punch, the other a bent-elbow thrust into the larynx. And then he was up and running, aggression pumping through him, his tunnel vision directed at going to Steve's aid. In the distance, police sirens wailed. Without breaking his stride, Dillon yelled back to the others: 'Cops! Move out – it's the cops. *Pack up . . . Pack up!*'

Steve was on the ground, both hands protecting his throat, curled up in his suede jacket as the boots thudded in. Dillon kneed one of them in the small of the back, got a fist in the nose that rang through his head, and took another out with a leg sweep. He wiped blood from his chin, hearing the sirens blare as two, maybe three police cars came screaming off Kilburn High Road, less than five hundred yards away.

The jeep whinnied, then roared into life. Jimmy gunned the engine, Harry and Wally legging it across the street and leaping in, Johnny Blair close behind clutching the side of his head. Down on one knee, Dillon took Steve's wrist and hoisted him across his shoulder, tossing him into the back as Jimmy crashed into first gear and shot off. Dillon ran, arms reaching out to him, and was hauled on board. The jeep did a screeching two-wheel U-turn, missed a parked van by millimetres, and raced off, leaving behind a dozen slumped, groaning bodies as the police cars wailed up, blue lights strobing the dark street.

Smothering a yawn, Susie Dillon side-stepped the kid's bikes and opened the front door of the flat, wrapping the dressing-gown around herself more firmly when she realised that Frank had someone with him. For a moment she just stood there blinking, brushing a hand through her tousled russet hair, smoothing her fringe down while she took in Dillon's bloody nose and the yellowish bruise on his right cheek.

If anything, the young man he was holding up looked even worse, his face like chopped liver, as if he'd been given a right going over.

'Hello, love!' Dillon greeted her, tossing his suitcase into the hallway and shrugging off his leather grip, looped over his shoulder. 'This is Steve Harris, he was one of my Toms. Steve . . . ?'

But all that came from Steve was a croaking rasp as his head lolled forward. Dillon manoeuvred his way into the hallway. 'He can't talk – had his throat shot out by a sniper in Belfast. . .'

'Where do you want to put him?' Susie asked, shifting the bikes out of the way.

'Shut the door . . . fix up the spare room eh?' Susie closed the door and stood watching him helping the boy upstairs. First day out of the Army and he looked like he was back from the bloody wars.

'You gonna chuck up, Steve?' she heard Dillon say. Susie sighed and propped up the bike her husband had still managed to knock over.

'He was awarded how much?' Susie gaped at Dillon and repeated in a hoarse whisper, '*How much?*'

Dillon shot her a fierce look across the bed they were making up in the spare room, warning her to keep her voice down, though going by the retching and spluttering as Steve threw up in the bathroom next door, there wasn't much need.

'Over a hundred grand, and he's not got a cent left – nothing. He's had to tap me for a few quid.'

Susie unfolded a sheet and shook it out. 'What did he do with it?'

'Stupid bastards hand over a cheque to a twenty-six-year-old, already having head trouble. He was a right handful when he first joined up – he took some beatin'.'

'A cheque?' Susie said incredulously, tucking the sheet in at one side while Dillon did the other. 'They gave him a cheque? I don't believe it . . .'

Dillon scowled. 'Captain told him in hospital he'd never jump again. He went from A1 fit to P6 – P7's deceased. They tried to say he was forty per cent fit, the CO had to appeal. Eventually got put down seventy-five per cent disabled, so he'd been through it before they sent him the cheque. By then he was – ' he indicated the pillows ' – pass 'em over, a head case.'

Susie tossed over the pillow slips, studied Dillon as he

37

stuffed the pillows inside. She said quietly, 'How long is he staying, Frank?'

'It'll just be until I can get him back on his feet – ' He glanced up as Steve appeared behind Susie in the doorway, and said in a cheerful voice, 'Hi, Steve! You want a cup of tea?'

Susie edged past Steve, giving him a quick smile. 'I am just going to get a blanket,' she enunciated loudly.

'He's not deaf, Susie.' Dillon beamed at Steve, beckoning him in. 'Come on, get yer head down!'

'I'll put the kettle on.' Susie lingered a moment on the small landing with its square of MFI cord carpet, looking in as Dillon helped Steve off with his suede jacket, torn at the shoulder seam, a muddy smear down the back. The boy seemed permanently hunched, hair hanging over his face, and she knew now why he wore that paisley-patterned scarf, tied gypsy-style, round his neck.

She hissed at them, 'And keep the noise down, the boys are asleep. They wanted to wait up, but – ' Susie couldn't keep up the frost, she sighed, resigned over the years for the unexpected, 'Welcome home, Frank!'

Steve up-ended the bottle of Tuborg into his glass, filling it to the brim, with the studied deliberation of the experienced piss-artist intent on not spilling a drop. They had been sinking the booze all afternoon, after Dillon had dragged Steve to meet the head of the 'Swallow' club, a club organised to assist men from all sections of the military with vocal chord damage. The membership entrée was simple, if you had had your throat cut, or blown out, you were in. The major who ran the club showed Dillon his scars, and with eerie clarity explained that he spoke on a burp of wind, having no vocal chords. They had a speech therapist and a number of men who would gladly assist Steve. It would be a long slow process, but, joining them in the nearest bar, and gulping a frothing pint, he suggested that this was the best way for the 'beginners' to learn, as the beer was good and gassy. The major had thoroughly enjoyed demonstrating his prowess, but Steve had remained stubbornly silent, simply downing one pint after another. They had virtually had to pour the burping major into a taxi, before deciding to return home and continue the 'lessons'. Dillon was beginning to think the entire episode had been a waste of time, even more so as Steve was very obviously an alcoholic, sinking more and more pints in rapid succession, but remaining in stony silence.

'For chrissakes Steve, you got to just try it.'

Dillon having joined Steve in the boozing was getting as pissed as he was. 'Go on, just try . . . burp and say a word.'

Steve raised his glass to his lips, sank a good half of it, and emitted a raucous belch that somewhere had 'Fuck off' in it. Steve had been offered speech therapy sessions, but the attractive woman had been at such pains to make him comfortable, she had made him feel more and more inadequate. A woman he could have pulled spoke to him as if he was ten years old, kept on saying that as soon as he had a break through he would feel better, as if he was sick, or mentally retarded. He was not sick, he was not mentally sub-normal, he was just dumb, and his frustration turned into aggression until he was asked not to return unless he was sober. He had attempted one more session, and was sober, but hearing his efforts replayed on tape, hearing himself speaking like a distorted Donald Duck finished him off completely, he decided that he would prefer to remain silent.

Dillon kept on and on, even trying it himself, until Steve burped out a few words, almost as if to show Dillon that he could do it, but chose not to. Dillon thought Steve sounded like a Dalek with laryngitis, but he heard an entire sentence. 'Piss-Goff an' gleeeve glme gl gla . . . lone!'

Dillon applauded Steve's effort, doing his best to focus, elbows in a puddle of lager on the formica kitchen table littered with their training session.

Steve gulped down another mouthful and, riding on the

back of a huge belch came ... quite clearly, 'Baaa ... ssst ... aaard.'

'Yeah, great, that was great,' Dillon nodded, with an effort forcing his eyelids wide, as if they were lead shutters. '. . . bastard, right? Am I right?' Dillon grinned crookedly. 'You bastard.'

Steve doubled over in a wheezing laugh that turned into a paroxysm of gurgling and bubbling. He went a shade of blue and had to thump himself in the chest to clear the air-lock in the plastic tube that served as his wind pipe. Only Steve knew the terror of the tube getting blocked. Even though he had been told over and over by the doctors and the specialists just how dangerous it was to get drunk, to be out of control and that a vomit attack could suffocate him, he ignored the warnings. He could no longer laugh, but gave guttural snorts, the sound to his own ears hideous. Steve hated his disability, was incapable of caring for himself because he felt he was a social misfit, his only way of dealing with it to become even more of one than he already was. Dillon was not the first to try and help him, but somewhere in the Steve's confused, drink-befuddled mind he had a premonition that, maybe, Frank Dillon was the last hope he had of straightening out. He couldn't as yet thank him, he didn't know how to . . .

Susie walked in to find them laughing like drains, noting the rows of empty bottles with a decided coolness. 'Frank, I want to make the supper! The kids are hungry – '

Dillon waved her to silence. 'Show her how you talk . . .'

Susie waited patiently, her hand on Dillon's shoulder, as Steve drank straight from the bottle, held his breath, and belched, 'Suu – sss – ieee'

Dillon, three sheets into the wind, didn't catch it, though Susie did, and couldn't help smiling. 'My name – did you say my name?'

Steve gave her a boyish gleeful grin, tickled to death. Susie's smile faded at the edges as she saw Dillon pick up a crate of lager and make off with it. 'Where you taking that?' she demanded suspiciously.

But all she got was a muffled profanity as he collided with something in the living-room, followed by a yell, 'Steve – upstairs. Mind the bikes!'

Susie stood on the blue-and-white squared linoleum, surveying the wreckage of her kitchen, listening to their unsteady progress through the hallway and up the stairs. A bell tinkled, a clash of tangled spokes, one of the bikes was over. Susie closed her eyes and counted to fifteen.

5

Steam rose from Dillon's face. His hair was wringing wet. A towel around his neck and tucked into his tracksuit, black Puma trainers on his feet, he reached the third-floor landing and turned, jogging on the spot, and bellowed down at Steve: 'Come on, come on, keep your knees up! – *come on!* One-two, one-two, on your toes – '

Two flights down in the block of red-brick council flats that formed a square surrounding a paved central court, Steve Harris laboured up the concrete steps, a bergen containing four house bricks wrapped in newspaper strapped to his back. Ten-past-eleven in the morning and he was on his sixth climb, chest heaving, his tracksuit top practically drenched. Still, in better bloody shape than he was a week ago, Dillon thought with satisfaction. Couldn't beat the tough Para training regime to work the flab off, tauten muscle tone, get the old heart-and-lung machine functioning.

And in the process drag Steve up from being the useless fat knacker with no future he'd turned into after two years in civvies.

Susie came out of the flat, buttoning up a fawn topcoat that had seen better days, a shopping-bag in the crook of her arm. 'I'm going to the shops,' she announced to Dillon, still jogging, elbows back and forth like pistons. 'You want anything?'

'Where are the kids?' Dillon asked, but he was more interested in Steve, who'd stopped, panting for breath, on the floor below. 'Oi! Move it, Steve, don't slack off. Keep moving.'

'They're at school.' Susie's voice had a sharp, irritable edge that had nothing to do with kids and school, everything to do with the subject she'd tried to raise at breakfast.

'Are you going to sign on, Frank? You said you'd go today . . .'

Steve finally made the last few steps, stood with hands on hips, head thrown back, gasping for air, totally wiped out.

'Go on – down again.' When Steve didn't immediately respond, Dillon stuck his arm straight out and pointed. *'Go on!'*

Off he went, staggering a little under the heavy pack. Susie tapped her foot. 'Frank? Did you hear what I said?'

'Yeah, yeah, I'll go this afternoon . . .' Dillon brushed past her on the stairs, jumping three steps at a time, calling out, 'Right, back up, Steve, come on, push yourself.' He skipped down and started pushing Steve up from behind. Susie had to flatten herself against the wall as they came by. 'Don't leave it too late, Frank . . . you should have gone yesterday.'

'I said I'd go, all right?' Dillon snapped back at her. From the landing above he called down, 'Oranges. Get some oranges for juice, not that bottled stuff!'

'Oh, right – ' Susie said, marching down, heels ringing on the concrete steps. ' – I'll just go and pick 'em for you! You want them, get them yourself.'

Wiping his face with the towel, Dillon silently cursed himself and hung his head over the brick parapet, but she was lost to sight. That was all he knew, rapping out orders to squaddies and Toms – *Do this, soldier, do that* – expecting to be obeyed on the instant, and it was hard to break the habit, even with his own wife. He'd better start learning. This was Civvy Street, where anarchy ruled. Nobody took orders from anybody.

Dillon, about to turn away and suggest to Steve a shower and a well-deserved beer, happened to notice a car parked by the estate entrance. Nothing too unusual about that – except the locals in this part of the East End who could afford to run a jalopy just scraped by with a clapped-out Skoda or a Lada with a failed MOT. Not a sleek black J-Reg Jaguar Sovereign 3.2. The Jag's push-button window slid down, a face appeared flashing a cocky grin, red hair plastered straight back, and Dillon ducked away, but a fraction too late.

'Hey, Frank!' Jimmy Hammond hailed him. *'Frank!'*

'How ya doin'?' Jimmy greeted him, climbing out, all smiles, giving Dillon a bear-hug and a punch for good measure. 'You okay? Everythin' okay?'

'Yeah!' Dillon's glance slid sideways to the passenger in the back seat. 'Just been workin' out.'

Jimmy followed his look. 'You know Mr Newman, don't you?'

Dillon gave a brief nod, went over as the rear window glided down; a slender elongated hand encased in blue-black leather took his in a soft, limp handshake. 'Hello Frank, you remember me, don't you?'

Dillon remembered the voice too, flat and expression-less, nearly as soft as the handshake, so you had to listen hard. Some people had to take orders after all, Dillon reminded himself, and this was the voice that gave them. He said politely, 'How ya doing?'

'Jimmy said you were looking for work . . .'

Dillon cast a sidelong glance at Jimmy, cool and sharp in his tailored blue suit leaning against the Jaguar's glossy bonnet, arms nonchalantly folded, wearing his fat grin. Always the fixer, trying to run other people's lives for them. Newman uncoiled from the car, a tall emaciated figure that with his dark business suit and leather gloves put Dillon in mind of a long dry-skinned lizard. And yes, there was even something reptilian in the sunken flaking cheeks and deadpan grey stare, the tongue flicking out along the thin wide mouth.

Newman strolled a few yards, a cheroot trailing smoke in his wake, and indicated with a small incline of the head that he wanted a private word. Dillon followed, waiting as Newman sent a plume of smoke thoughtfully into the air.

'I've never forgotten the way you came round . . . it, well, it meant a lot to me.'

'I was just sorry it had to be him.' Dillon shuffled, staring down at the soiled black Pumas. 'He was a really good soldier . . .'

'My boy thought the world of you, always mentioned you in his letters home . . .' Newman's flat delivery skirted the edge of something near real emotion. 'We never hit it off that well, I reckoned he joined up to get away from me.' Newman's pale grey eyes sought Dillon's. 'I've sort of made it my business to give a helping hand to his pals when they get into civvies.'

'Billy was a good lad,' was all Dillon could think to say.

'Meant a lot, you coming round the way you did, to Maureen. She's dead now. I think Billy's going took the heart out of her . . . we only had the one, just the one son.' Newman studied the glowing tip of the cheroot. Outwardly, the neatly-parted grey hair and grey moustache gave him the distinguished yet dated look of a thirties matinee idol, but Dillon wasn't deceived. He didn't, never could, trust those cold flat eyes, a predator waiting to pounce.

Dillon shifted uneasily as Newman placed a hand on his shoulder.

'I reckon I owe you a favour. I can offer you a lot of work, and with Jimmy on my payroll, be like old times . . .' The sunken cheeks creased in a smile. 'He's a card, isn't he? Eh? Jimmy . . . I think you'd make a good team.'

'Thanks, Mr Newman, but – ' Dillon shrugged, staring at the ground. 'I've got a few things in the pipeline . . .'

'Have you?'

'Yes.' Dillon cleared his throat. 'I want – well, eventually – to open up a security firm. Me and a few of the lads.'

'Good.' Newman seemed genuinely pleased. 'That's a good idea. Well, if I can be of any assistance, you know Jimmy can always put you in touch. I'd like to see you set up with a few readies in your hand. I know it's tough coming out, and, well, I'll be straight with you, Frank – '

Dillon stepped back, held up his hand. 'That's just it, Mr Newman. I want to go straight. Whatever Jimmy does is his business.' He turned quickly away, jogging off. 'But I appreciate your offer . . .'

Newman stared after him, the friendly warmth instantly extinguished by a glacial stillness, as if Dillon had struck him. With a flick of the wrist he tossed the cheroot away and made an abrupt gesture to Jimmy, who slid off the Jaguar's bonnet and went after the running figure, now leaping up the concrete stairway, two at a time.

'Frank . . . wait! Wait a minute!'

Dillon halted on the first-floor landing and looked down as Jimmy reached the bottom of the stairs, swept-back hair bouncing, features strained in a matey grin.

'No, Jimmy, you wait.' Legs braced apart, outstretched arms pressed against the brick walls either side, Dillon looked in no mood for the old pal's act. 'I don't want any involvement with that crook. I don't want him brought round my place, near my place. And if you'd got any sense, you'd walk – '

Jimmy broke in. 'He's trying to do you a favour!'

'Whatever I did for Billy, I'd do for any of my lads. I joined up because of men like Newman. His own son tried to get away from him. He's rotten. Billy knew it, I knew it.' Dillon's voice sank, but the intensity didn't. 'I know it, Jimmy, because his type was all I had going for me when I was a kid. Now I want more, Jimmy, and I want it legit.'

A slight flush mottled Jimmy's cheeks. He gave one last guarded look at Dillon, as if he'd been caught out in a lie, then turned sharply away, muttering tersely, 'I hope you find it, Frank!'

Dillon watched him go. Angry, bitter, but most of all sad.

Jumped-up pompous twits with their bloody bits of papers and petty rules! Newman's visit had put him in a foul temper and his trip to the DSS office later that afternoon didn't improve it one iota. Christ, he could have sat on that plastic chair staring at the muddy green wall till the cows came home for all the good it did him, till his teeth dropped out. What did they care? Three, four years ago Dillon had run across an old mate with sixteen years' service under his belt who'd recently got his discharge. This bloke, ex-sergeant, had asked the C.O. for a reference, set him up in Civvy Street, and the C.O. had written in his file: 'Suitable for petrol pump attendant.' After all the bullshit about serving Queen and Country and upholding the honour of the Regiment and drumming it into you that you were the cream of the Army's élite fighting men, that's how the system treated you. All of a sudden you were a social leper. Brain-dead. About as much use as a wet fart in a wind-tunnel. Thanks ever so much for all you've done, old chap, now kindly fuck off.

Well, the DSS could go fuck itself, in spades, as far as he was concerned, Dillon thought savagely, slamming the front door shut behind him and stopping in the nick of time from cracking his shin on the bikes in the hallway. He went through, wrenching his tie loose, feeling sweaty and ridiculous in his best suit that Susie had pressed for him that morning. She looked up, eyebrows raised, hopefully or expectantly, he was past caring.

'I been in that dump all afternoon, waiting like a prat, for my number to be called out – '

'And? Well, what did they say?'

'*Number twenty-three to cubicle four . . .*' Dillon mimicked a prissy officious voice. '*Number twenty-four to cubicle five.* I was number fifty-three. Went to the friggin' job centre section, came back and I'd missed me number!' He took a pale-green ticket from his breast pocket, tore it in half and scattered the bits on the coffee table.

'So you didn't sign on, did you?'

Dillon was on his way back through the hallway, jacket half-off. 'I'll get Steve, go for a run.'

'Fine, you go and see Steve.' Susie was up quick, after him. 'And while you're up there could you tell him to

throw out his empty bottles and his dirty bandages . . .
Did you tell them about your experience in the Army?
Frank?'

Leaving his jacket draped over the banister post, Dillon
started up. 'Anythin' I've done was in the Army, and that
don't mean nothin'. Bloody IRA think more of us!' He
suddenly turned, hot angry eyes burning down into hers.
'Every Para's worth seven grand to them. Six, if you're
dead.'

Steve leaned over the banister, mouth working, croaking
at Dillon. 'YoU'D bE – *burp* -BetTEr ofF cOMin' OuT –
burp – Of thE nIcK!'

'Too right, mate.'

'What did he say?' Susie frowned.

'He said I would be better off comin' out of the nick!'
Dillon threw a punch. 'Move, Steve – *let's be havin'*
yaaaa!'

Steve gurgled something and Dillon responded with
force, 'Right, mate, half-way houses, career officers,
counsellors, subsistences, therapists, psychiatrists,
physiotherapists . . .'

The phone rang on the hall table, Dillon's voice floating
from above ('An' if that's Jimmy, I'm not in.') as Susie
snatched it up.

'Hello?' Susie listened, eyes growing bigger, then in a
rush, 'Oh, yes, yes, he is, just hang on a second . . .' Head
craning up the stairs, yelling excitedly, '*Frank*, it's that
friend of Mum's – he owns a building site . . . quick!'

Dillon cleared the banister rail and did a free-fall drop,
arms parallel with his sides, to land at Susie's feet, springing lightly up and grabbing the phone. He coughed and
said, 'Frank Dillon . . .' listening and nodding as Susie
stuck both thumbs up. '. . . there's two of us, yeah.' He
grinned then, nodding harder as if somebody had tightened
his spring. '. . . Fantastic!'

Beaming a great big smile, Susie punched holes in the
air, fists raised high. Yippee!

6

The tinny blare of a transistor playing Radio One echoed round the building-site, some berk with a mid-atlantic accent and no sense of humour trying to crack jokes at seven-fifteen on a dismal grey Monday morning. The young bloke alongside Dillon in the cradle, twenty feet up, supposed to be – literally – 'showing him the ropes', considered himself something of a joker too, and a patronising bastard into the bargain. Making clever cracks ever since Dillon and Steve had walked on the site at seven o'clock, bang on time.

'You okay?' he asked Dillon with a smirk as the cradle swayed and bumped against the side of the half-erected five-storey apartment block. Scaffolding poles rose above them, forming a skeletal framework nearly a hundred feet into the drizzly air.

Dillon watched as the ganger manipulated the ropes on his side of the cradle.

'Right, first you make a figure of eight like this . . . you know how to make a figure of eight?'

'Sure,' Dillon said. What did this prat take him for, a kid straight from school? Not much more than a kid himself.

'Right, you in the parachute regiment then, were you?' The ganger grinned, as if this was something funny in itself. The other building workers down below seemed to think so too, an appreciative audience with the ganger as comic, Dillon the stooge.

Keeping up a running commentary, he demonstrated, releasing the rope with his right hand, holding firm with the left. 'You let it run through nice and easy, from your left to your right, keep it slow for safety . . .'

Then gave a sly wink to the builders below, leaning on

their shovels watching. 'You'll be used to this kind of thing, then' – suddenly letting go so that the cradle jolted and tilted to one side. If he was expecting a reaction from Dillon, he was disappointed. Not a flicker.

'Okay, you wanna have a go an' lower the other side?'

Dillon hauled himself up the sloping cradle, released the figure of eight, gripping the ropes tightly – then just as quickly let out double the drop, tilting the cradle even more steeply the other way.

The ganger slid cursing down the cradle, grabbing the rail to save himself. His flailing foot dislodged a half-full bag of cement which tipped over, sending a thick shower of cement dust swirling down directly on top of Steve, who fell to his knees, hands clutching his throat, a pitiful helpless figure like a caked snowman.

'Steve?' Dillon yelled down anxiously. 'You okay Steve?'

The ganger gave Dillon a venomous look and shouted down, 'Turn the hose on the stupid bugger!'

The other workmen whistled and cat-called as one of their mates let Steve have it full blast, knocking him flat so that he slithered around in the mire of wet cement, half-blinded, trying to protect his vulnerable throat as he gasped for breath.

'You *bastard!*' Dillon made a swipe at the ganger and shouted, 'Steve, get up here!' On his feet now, Steve was like a hunted man, backing away, shaking his head, unable to handle the fear and humiliation.

Dillon leaned right out, hanging on the ropes. 'On your feet, Harris – move it!'

This time it was an order, and Sergeant Dillon was giving it. The same voice that had whiplashed men up Mount Longdon, pushed them on through the pain-barrier of sub-zero temperatures and hostile terrain and the constant threat of sniper fire, and kept on pushing them to the limit of human endurance and beyond.

'I want you up on them shuffle bars, on those bars, you prat. I said move . . . *you deaf? You deaf as well as dumb, Harris, are you?*'

The ganger and the workmen gaped as Dillon used the ropes to swing himself from the cradle, and with amazing agility began to climb the fretwork of scaffolding until he was balanced, sixty feet off the ground, on two parallel bars above the well of the building. Every fledgling Para had to go through the ordeal of the high shuffle bars, a test of nerve, skill and overcoming the fear of heights to find out if he had the bottle to jump on command from a balloon or aircraft. Dillon had taken a thousand Joe Crows through it, showing by example that you could shuffle along on the soles of your boots, arms spread wide, touching your toes at the halfway point.

'Come on, you bastards, any takers?' Adrenalin pumping, enjoying the mental challenge, Dillon taunted the men far below. 'Any takers, come on! Show 'em, Steve, get up here . . .'

In stunned silence the workmen watched as Steve obeyed the order, clambering up through the well of the building to join Dillon, the pair of them facing each other, legs apart, balancing like trapeze artists, and both of them grinning like loons!

'Ready, Harris . . . Wait for it! Go – Go – Go – Go Goooooooohh!'

Steve was back in his element. Just like old times, him and the Sarge risking their fool necks. But a calculated risk all the same – calling for mental and physical co-ordination, daring, guts – because that's what you'd been trained to do and you took pride in doing it well. And that's what had been lacking, Steve knew full well: pride. He'd sunk lower in his own estimation than a snake's belly. He exulted in the chance to re-live it all, feeling suddenly re-energised with the joy of applying the old skills he'd almost forgotten he possessed, the exhilaration of flirting with danger . . .

It's me, Sarge, it's Harris . . . when the fireman grabs him, hang on to me . . . I'm right behind you!

Flames spurt from the side of the building as the ladder edges up, smoke billowing all around. Dillon inches out,

51

Billy Newman draped across his back. The fireman reaches out across the gap, Dillon sliding one cautious foot after the other, knowing that when he transfers the weight he's going to overbalance. But Steve's there, Dillon's collar bunched in his fist, his other arm braced inside the shattered window-frame.

Watch yer balance when you get lift-off . . .

Voice calm and reassuring in the confusion of sirens, flames, screams, the stench of burning flesh.

Dillon nods to show he gets the message. Shouts to the fireman: Lift, on the count of three – One – two – three!

The wood buckles and splits under Dillon's feet, he teeters, hands clawing thin air, and falls, Steve hanging on for grim death, teeth gritted as he hauls the dangling Dillon back onto the ledge.

Steve grins, white teeth in a smoke-blackened face, green eyes twinkling as if he's damn-well enjoying this. Couple of Hail Marys, Frank, then I reckon we should get the hell outta here!

Bleeding understatement of the year. Mad bastard. And Steve keeps on grinning, even when Dillon gives him a whack for his pains.

What had happened on that terrible night had broken something inside Dillon; Susie sensed it but had never pressed him, knowing that sooner or later, in his own good time, Dillon would want to talk about it, unburden himself. Now was the time. Propped up on the pillows, she listened to the quiet, unemotional voice of her husband, the lamplight gilding his head and shoulders, making dark swirling patterns of the tattoos on his forearms and the paler skin of his biceps as he sat hunched on the side of the bed.

'It was all for nothin', as it turned out . . . the kid was dead. It was Barry Newman's son, that friend of Jimmy's.'

'So you feel you owe Steve – '

'No!' Dillon's tone was sharp. 'I owe nobody nothin'.

We were all doing a job of work, no more, no less.' He stared into the darkness. 'It was a job.'

Susie was silent for a moment, then: 'What about the job you had today?'

'Didn't work out.' Dillon raised his head as a muffled thud came from Steve's room next door. He closed his eyes and sighed. 'Susie, I can't just dump him. I can't do that . . .'

She didn't need to be told. He was her husband, the father of her children, her lover, and she could feel his pain. She stroked his arm, leaning forward to nuzzle his cheek. Dillon gathered her in his arms and they slowly subsided onto the bed, their gentle lingering kiss becoming urgent, more intense. Dillon brought his hand up to cup her breast, Susie moving her body against his, needing to feel the hardness of his chest, the heat and passion of him.

Something thudded against the other side of the wall, a few feet away from where they lay, followed by the crash and tinkling of broken glass.

'Oh *shit!*' Dillon extricated himself and rolled off the bed. What in hell was the prat up to? He got to the door, holding up his hand as Susie raised herself. 'No, you stay put. I'll sort him!'

Too late anyway – the racket had woken the kids, little Phil bawling – and Susie went to see to them while Dillon pushed open Steve's door to find him sprawled half on the bed, half on the floor. The phone in the hallway started to ring as Dillon went in, checking his anger when he saw the bright red face shiny with sweat, the soundless gaping mouth, Steve's hand pulling feebly at his throat.

'What? What is it?'

Dillon was scared. An ominous gurgling rattle was coming from Steve, his face now beetroot red. He kept pointing at the bedside table. 'What is it?' Dillon asked again, lifting him upright. 'The filter blocked? *Steve?*'

Amongst the clutter of personal belongings Dillon found a small plastic bag, and snatching it up he scanned the printed instructions. 'Okay, Steve, gonna be all right.'

Dillon was very calm, his voice low and soothing. 'Now, tip your head back, just try to relax . . .'

Dillon's head rested almost against Steve's chin as he sucked out the blockage, spat it out, and re-inserted the tube. He then checked over Steve's so-called medical box, re-read all the instructions and, working patiently and methodically with the thin piece of fresh tubing, prepared clean gauze and adhesive tabs.

'Gonna fit a clean tube, okay? . . . Now get ready, get a good bellyful of air, and I'll fix it in place, you ready? . . . One – two – three – right, you're all set, I'm gonna do it now.'

Steve sucked in a lungful of air and flopped back on the pillow, growing quiet, his hair stuck to his forehead as he held his breath while Dillon worked inexpertly with the tube. His hands were steady, his face strained in concentration, eyes flicking to the instruction leaflet. Steve watched him and saw no sign of distaste, no gawping at the gaping hole in his throat, but that steady, hawk-eyed look as he carefully inserted the clean tube and placed the square of gauze across Steve's throat. He nodded proudly to Steve, as Steve breathed easier, giving a small wink to Dillon to show he was okay.

'You're gonna have to get this medical box shipshape, it's a mess.' Dillon sat on the edge of the bed, sorting through Steve's tin box. Steve reached out and gripped Dillon's hand, needing the physical contact to quell the fear that was still lurking in his eyes like a dark shadow.

Dillon pulled up a chair and leaned forward, elbows on his knees, speaking quietly in an easy, conversational tone that had the desired effect on Steve, relaxing him. 'We're gonna have to set up some kind of routine, so this doesn't happen again. Always check equipment, first rule – you know that, Steve. How many jumps you done, for chrissakes? Always check the equipment!'

'Thanks – mate.' Steve found a smile. 'Give us – a couple of – Hail Marys – will ya?'

Dillon grinned back. He glanced round as Susie inched

the door open and put her head in. 'It was that Jimmy again, said he'll pick you up.'

Turning back, Dillon caught the disapproving look in Steve's eyes, more reproaching than accusing, but it still pissed Dillon off.

'Lay off me,' he warned. 'Everybody's on me!'

Susie glared at Dillon's back. 'I was just passing on his message!' she snapped and banged the door shut.

Steve looked at Dillon, and Dillon returned it, square in the eyes.

'If it's bent, I walk away,' he said.

7

Jimmy went in first, then ushered Dillon into Newman's rabbit-hutch of an office above a clothing shop in Leather Lane, just off Hatton Garden. In contrast to the dingy surroundings, Newman was his usual immaculate self, a royal-blue tie and matching handkerchief adding an acceptable touch of flamboyant flair to his neatly groomed appearance and dark business suit. He didn't offer to shake hands, and for an empty moment Dillon just stood there in front of Newman's desk, self-conscious in his rumpled tracksuit and battered Puma trainers, pushing a hand through his still-damp hair. 'Hello, Barry.'

Newman watched him through half-closed eyes, and it was left to Jimmy to break the permafrost, telling Newman with a grin, 'Grabbed him off the track.'

As Newman could see, and probably smell, for himself, stroking his grey moustache with a manicured fingernail. He gestured to the swarthy man, five o'clock shadow and receding hairline, leaning against the filing cabinet, who came instantly to life. 'Get him a decent suit, on the firm.'

Dillon hesitated. He glanced at Jimmy, who gave him a quick wink, and only then reluctantly followed the swarthy man out.

Newman waited until the door closed behind them.

'How much does he know?'

'Nothin' but he needs cash,' Jimmy said.

'Okay. Let's get down to business.' From a drawer Newman took a black velvet bag and placed it on the desk. 'You carry them to this address,' unfolding a slip of paper. 'Come back to me with the cash.'

The cheap off-the-peg suit chafed him, but Dillon didn't dare scratch where it itched, anyway not in a public place.

Newman's largesse had run to the suit, check shirt and polyester tie, but not to shoes, so he still wore his Pumas, which he was glad about. Doing a job for Barry Newman gave him the edgy feeling that at any moment he might have to leg it.

Like right now, on the northbound platform of the Piccadilly line at Holborn, waiting for Jimmy to make up his frigging mind which train to catch. They'd let two go — for no apparent reason that Dillon could see — and it was making him nervous.

'So far so good.' Jimmy did a recce of the scattering of people on the platform. He tilted his head, mouth almost touching Dillon's ear. 'How does it feel to have half-a-million against your inside leg?'

'If you really want to know,' Dillon ground out, a mist of perspiration on his forehead, 'I'd prefer the firing squad. I mean, why all the skivin' around if this is legit?'

'Insurance — to cover the insurance of these babies costs an arm and a leg!'

A rumble, a cascade of sparks, and a warm wind blew in their faces.

'We on this one, or trying for the next?' Dillon asked tensely, feeling like a walk-on in *Godfather III*.

At King's Cross they came up the escalator to the main-line station and walked briskly across the marble-slabbed concourse to a side exit leading to the warren of back streets fanning out eastwards to the Caledonian Road. Dillon didn't know the area all that well, but Jimmy seemed to, and eventually, as they came into yet another indistinguishable street, he nodded and said, 'This is it.'

A door with a tarnished brass nameplate and creaking hinges led them into a wooden passage that smelled of dust and mildew, and up a narrow staircase that doubled back on itself. Jimmy rapped lightly and after the sound of locks and bolts, a door opened a cautious three inches, held by a heavy chain. A pair of pouchy eyes appeared in the gap.

'This is Frank, Morris —' Jimmy motioned Dillon

forward, to be scrutinised – he's a friend of mine, okay? Just the two of us.'

They sidled in, following Morris's shambling bulk into a tiny workshop that was sweltering to death from a Calor gas stove, the single grimy window screwed up tight. A youth with lank greasy hair parted in the middle sat on a high stool picking his nose, pin-prick eyes impassive as Dillon unfastened his belt and lowered his trousers, releasing the leather carrying pouch strapped to his waist and dropping it on the workbench. Morris switched on a powerful desk spotlight, swung a magnifying lens on a bracket into position. With long slender fingers he extracted the velvet bag from the pouch and tipped it out. Dillon felt his mouth go dry as the stones tumbled out, mesmerised, dazzled, the diamonds like a heap of white-hot embers flashing sparks on the blue velvet pad in the stifling, airless room. He ran a finger inside his collar. Couldn't take his eyes off Morris, who set to work, closely examining each stone through the lens, then weighing it, making a notation in a ledger, setting it aside and taking up the next.

'We on the move?' Dillon whispered to Jimmy as Morris, task done, funnelled the stones into the velvet bag, pulling the drawstring tight.

'Yep. I'll wear them now, just in case.' Jimmy dropped his pants.

Fine by me, Dillon thought. The more he saw of this set-up, the less he liked it. Taking risks for Barry Newman, he must be out of his tiny skull, with brains to match.

Back on the street, walking quickly, Dillon glanced behind. The young lad from the workshop was following them, keeping up the same brisk pace. 'What's with the kid?'

'So we don't switch stones,' Jimmy explained. 'An' he knows which apartment, I'm not sure.' He called back, 'Eh, kid. Is it much further?'

'Two minutes now.' The youth jerked his head, indicating a large block of flats, stained concrete and tiny balconies fronted by corroding ironwork, an architectural gem with a grandstand view of the gasworks. 'Better follow me in,' the youth said, and scuttled on ahead, the wind whipping up his hair like bits of dead grass.

'Money for jam this, I told you,' Jimmy chortled as they went in through a pair of glass-panelled doors, one of them boarded up with plywood. 'But keep your eyes peeled. Anyone gonna clobber us, this place is perfect. What a dump!'

The thought stayed with Dillon as they followed the youth along a dim corridor and turned a corner, arriving in a cul-de-sac at what appeared to be the porter's flat, judging by the spyhole in the centre of the door. Standing in plain view, the youth knocked, and then stood aside to let Dillon and Jimmy enter as bars slid back and chains rattled. A big, bearded man in a fawn polo-neck with a beer gut he'd been nurturing for some time did a rapid, expert frisking job. From Jimmy he took a portable phone, a neat little folding item in black and silver, and placed it on a side table. He went on down the passage, tapped on a door, pushed it wide, waving Dillon through.

As Jimmy went by, the man barred his way, and very lightly brushed the small of his back. Raising both hands, Jimmy smiled and gave a little shrug. 'Just for protection.'

Unimpressed, the man nodded, reached under Jimmy's jacket and removed the Browning 140-DA semi-automatic, dropping it in his pocket.

Dillon was fidgeting by the door when Jimmy came in. The small room smelled of stale whisky and even staler sweat, and the wheezing thick-set man in the shabby suit, brown Hush Puppies and black shades, standing at the open safe in the corner, neatly rounded off Dillon's stock memory of a British B movie circa 1953. He felt lost, out of his depth, and besides, Dillon thought moodily, this was Jimmy's picnic. Let him get on with it.

A silent ritual took place. Jimmy fetched up the velvet bag, held onto it until the man in shades had transferred several thick bundles of notes from safe to table, fifties and twenties. The man spread the diamonds on a velvet cloth, wheezing whisky fumes as he bent over to examine them. Jimmy flicked through the bundles, a quick rough tally, but enough to satisfy him. Confident, done it before. No sweat. He straightened up, opening the front of his jacket and unbuttoning his shirt. 'You got the belts for us?'

Two black money-belts were produced. Jimmy stashed the notes away in the zippered pockets, handed one of the belts to Dillon, who wrapped it round his waist, securing it with velcro fasteners. When they'd finished, Jimmy said to the man in shades, 'Kid stays put until we're out of here, okay?'

The man nodded, pointed to a chair. The kid sat, picking his nose.

Dillon waited until they were clear, had put a corner between them and the concrete block. 'You think I'm blind?' Jimmy gave him a guarded, puzzled look. 'You're carrying, aren't you?' Dillon blazed, the tension erupting out of him, making his neck muscles bulge. He pushed Jimmy roughly. 'Aren't you!'

'I got a licence, Frank – it's okay!'

Fists clenched, Dillon walked off. He stopped and turned, nostrils twitching. 'Where do we go now? Come on, what's next?'

Jimmy took out the portable phone, pressed numbers as they walked back in the direction of King's Cross. Jesus Christ Almighty, Dillon was thinking, I must have fucking scrambled eggs for brains. Walking down some poxy back-street with fifty grand, a hundred grand – he didn't know how much and he didn't care – strapped to him, talk about a soft target . . .

'Everythin' watertight this end,' Jimmy was murmuring low into the phone. 'We're on our way back to base – ' He listened, brow furrowing. 'What?'

Forward, sideways, back, Dillon was doing slow sweeps, wishing he had eyes in the back of his head. There was a bloke, forty, fifty yards behind, red anorak, pasty-faced, who might be out for a stroll, or going to the shop for fags, but Dillon had his doubts.

'Well what you want us to do with it?' Jimmy's voice rose half an octave and he brought it down. 'Strapped round our waists, where you think?' He glanced meaningfully at Dillon. 'Wants us to hang onto it!'

'You're bloody joking – you tell him we're coming in. I've had enough.' Dillon grabbed the phone. 'We're not wanderin' around friggin' London with . . . hello? . . . hello?'

Dillon thrust the phone back, eyes swivelling over Jimmy's shoulder. 'I think we've got a tail on us. Guy in a red anorak, see if he's still with us . . .'

Jimmy sneaked a look, a quick nod at Dillon. They kept on walking, picking up speed but trying not to show they'd rumbled him. The street they were in branched into another, running parallel with the lines that went into King's Cross. As they neared it, Dillon said, 'He's still behind us, an' he's still on his tod. What you think? Next corner? Make a run for it!'

'Okay. Soon as we hit the bend, next left, do a runner, split up. See you at King's Cross taxi-rank . . .'

The instant they turned the corner it was heads down, diving into a sprint, running like crazy; they'd covered all of thirty yards before either of them realised. Dillon skidded to a stop, staring at the high brick wall topped with broken glass, blocking off the street.

'*Shit!* You don't even know where we are! You prat! It's a dead end . . . *it's a dead end*!'

They whipped round, but it was too late. Red Anorak had turned the corner and was coming towards them.

Jimmy said, 'We're gonna have to take him – '

Before Dillon could say anything he was charging back, running like the clappers. Red Anorak stopped, started to turn and run, but Jimmy was fit and fast, on top of him like a ton of bricks, bringing him down with a flying tackle. The man's head bounced on the pavement, and

61

before he'd rolled into the gutter Jimmy was up and at him, putting the boot in.

'For chrissakes, take it easy,' Dillon panted, coming up as Jimmy delivered another kick, seeing blood pouring from the man's gashed head.

'You see anyone else?' Jimmy's eyes were rolling in his sweating face. 'Go on, get to the corner, see if he's got anyone else with him – hurry. *Move it*!'

Dillon ran off. Jimmy ferreted inside the anorak, found a wallet and flipped it open. 'Oh shit!'

Encapsulated in a 4 × 3 inch plastic slip cover, a colour print of the man's ruddy face and ginger moustache. Above it, his name, rank and number: D.C.I. RIGGS.

'Come on,' Dillon hissed, racing back. 'What you waiting for?'

Shielding it with his body, Jimmy snapped the wallet shut and slipped it into his pocket.

8

Dillon nearly lost all his shirt-buttons getting the money-belt off. 'Here, take it – I never want to see that bastard Newman again!' He thrust it into Jimmy's lap, sitting alongside him in the back of the taxi parked on the hard shoulder of the Shepherd's Bush flyover. Two close calls in one afternoon, and he was sick of it. First Red Anorak, then evading the cops literally by seconds, ducking into a cab at King's Cross as squad cars came zooming in from all directions.

Dillon wiped his damp palms on his trouser knees. 'I lost half-a-stone sweatin' what would have happened if we got rapped over the head an' lost it.'

He jerked round, staring out into the gathering darkness as a police car, lights flashing, siren wailing, appeared over the flyover behind them and shot past towards the main roundabout. They watched it vanish towards White City. Dillon flopped back, limp as a wrung-out dish-rag.

'Come on, it's okay. So we had a bit of aggro,' Jimmy admitted, pulling the money-belt free and folding it with the other. His old cocky bravado was back, as if being chased by the police was all in a day's work, which probably wasn't far from the truth, Dillon was starting to realise.

The cab driver was looking over his shoulder and Jimmy rattled his knuckles on the sliding window. 'Oi! Keep your face to the front. What you think we are, couple of woofters? We're waitin' for a pick-up.'

A mite pissed off himself, the driver slid the panel open, beaked nose and bristly chin outlined in the green dashboard lights.

'I don't give a shit what you do, but parkin' here is

illegal. Pay the fare – you wanna wait, that's your business! I can get fired for parkin' here.'

Dillon nodded curtly at the money-belts Jimmy was holding. 'Pay him, Jimmy. Sure as hell got enough dough!'

Jimmy peered out, banging the window with his fist. 'Where the hell is he?'

'How long does he expect us to wait?' asked Dillon, getting jittery all over again. 'You think we aren't drawing attention to us now, parked here?' He grabbed the door handle. 'Next thing a bloody cop car'll stop . . . I'm out of here!'

'*Wait!*' Jimmy pulled Dillon back, face pale and twitching. The last time Dillon had seen him so hyped up was standing in the open doorway of a Hercules C–130, line rigged up, cheeks rippling like a rubber mask in the slipstream, ready to jump. 'That guy I whacked,' Jimmy said. 'He was a police officer.'

Dillon slowly blinked at him, unable to take it in. Assaulting a copper and he'd been accessory to it. They were talking prison here.

The cabbie's patience finally worn though, he stuck his head in, telling them straight, 'You think I'm stupid? I've given you the warnin', now I'm gonna call the law!'

Without a second's hesitation Jimmy viciously slammed the panel shut against the cabbie's face, and in a fury started stuffing fivers in the gasping mouth. 'Here's your soddin' money . . . I know your cab number,' he was shouting, 'I know your name!'

The driver dragged his face free, groping for the security lock button. Jimmy reached through, grabbed him by the scruff of the neck, and yanked his head back hard against the glass panel. 'Try anythin',' Jimmy snarled, 'and I swear before God you're fuckin' dead.' Again he yanked the driver's head back – *clunk* – against the panel, and once more to make sure the idea had sunk in.

Scooping up the money-belts Jimmy slammed the door shut and shouted after Dillon, walking head forward along the hard shoulder with the look of a man who's had it up to here.

'Frank, where you going?' Jimmy broke into a trot. He looked up to see the Jaguar coasting down to the roundabout, signalling to make a left. '*Frank! He's here!*'

Dillon swung an angry face towards him, aiming along his pointing finger. 'I've had enough for one night, Jimmy, an' don't try an' tell me this is all legit! It reeks, it stinks. It's got nothin' to do with insurance an' you know it! I just got into civvies, an' I don't intend going to jail for you – or that bastard Newman!' He marched on, yelling over his shoulder, 'I got a wife, I got kids . . . *I don't need it*!'

'Frank, listen to me – '

'I'll make it, Jimmy,' Dillon shouted, marching on, his voice becoming fainter, echoing under the sodium-yellow streetlights. 'You do whatever you want, just stay clear of me!'

Jimmy tried to shout, but nothing came out, his throat choked tight. The last thing he wanted was to alienate Frank Dillon, his best mate in all the world. Frank knew Jimmy, possibly better than anyone else. There *was* no one else. He saw Dillon moving away over the frozen tundra, pale Antarctic sunlight slanting down, his figure silhouetted against the blue wash of sky. That day they'd tabbed fourteen miles with thirty-eight kilograms of kit – L1A1 weapon, thirty-round magazine, fighting order, bergen stuffed with ammo and emergency rations – sneaking up the enemy's backside after a march the Argies thought humanly impossible. Dillon had set the example, and Dillon wasn't a man you let down, not if you wanted his respect. Worth more than rubies, and he was throwing it away for two money-belts of soiled notes. 'Frank . . . Frank, I'm sorry,' Jimmy whispered.

'Sorry about the wait, but the filth were crawling round my place, Newman said, placing the money-belts inside his pigskin briefcase and snapping it shut. He inclined his head towards Jimmy, sitting subdued in a corner of the back seat. 'Frank all right, is he?'

'Yeah. Just needed some fresh air.' Staring without seeing anything, blur of lights, smeared faces.

Newman held out two thick bundles secured with rubber bands.

'This is your cut, and you both get a bonus. Three grand!' Newman permitted himself a faint smug smile. 'Glad Frank worked out, but then I knew he'd come round. Everyone's got a price.'

'You can't buy Frank Dillon,' Jimmy said quietly, his chest so full he hardly had the breath. Then softer yet: 'I'm the type you can buy, Mr Newman . . .'

The Jaguar sped on, Jimmy stared bleakly out.

He was in luck. Dillon was mooching across the paved courtyard, hands in his pockets, just as the taxi turned the corner. Jimmy hopped out, told the driver to wait, and intercepted Dillon at the bottom of the stairs. 'Here's your cut!' The grin was back, but not quite sure of itself. 'An' we got a bonus!' Jimmy handed over the thick wad, keeping his back to the cab driver.

'How much?'

'Three grand – not bad for one night's work, eh?'

Dillon's surly expression faded as he gazed wonderingly at the money in his hand. 'What – each? You kiddin' me?'

'Naaahh!' Jimmy slapped Dillon on the arm. 'Look, I gotta go, Frank, be in touch soon, yeah?'

Dillon looked him in the eyes. 'You sure, Jimmy . . . no strings?'

'No strings, Frank.' Jimmy ducked his head, turned away. 'Night.'

'G'night you thievin' bastard!' said Dillon, cuffing him. 'I'm sorry I sounded off on you . . . don't get in too deep, Jimmy.'

Jimmy looked back. 'Steve Harris still dossin' down at your place?' he asked quietly.

'He's got no place else to go.'

'He'll bleed you dry, Frank.' Bitterness there, even a tinge of envy maybe. 'His kind always do.'

'He doesn't lie to me, Jimmy.' Dillon's voice had icicles on it. 'I trust old Steve, an' I'll get him back on his feet.' He went up the stairs, footsteps ringing out on the concrete.

Jimmy nodded to himself, listening as the footsteps faded, knowing Dillon meant every word. He said to the empty stairwell, 'What about me, Frank? What about me?'

Susie was mending the kids' shirts when Dillon walked in, snipping frayed cuffs, binding them with strips of cotton she'd bought down the market. There was soccer on the telly, but the sound was off, vividly coloured doll-like figures darting about on smooth emerald-green baize, chasing four shadows at once. She said, 'Where've you been?'

'Ran into a pal of Jimmy's, did a bit of collectin'.'

Dillon looked at the screen, at the carpet, at the ceiling fixture, and turned to go.

'Buy you the suit, did he?' Susie carried on sewing.

'What?' Dillon fingered the lapel as if seeing the suit for the first time. 'Oh . . . yeah.' He turned again.

'What's the matter, Frank?'

Dillon slowly faced her, tugging at his moustache, eyes on the screen. He said quietly, 'It's not going to work.'

'What isn't?' The words like twin pistol shots.

'Civvies.' Dillon cleared his throat. 'I'm signing on for mercenary duty . . .'

'You can't do that to me – the kids.' She'd started to flush up, eyes bright and stony. 'The whole point of you leaving the Army was so you could be with us.'

'But if I can't get a job . . .'

'You telling me with eighteen years' experience training men they can't help you?' Susie said, incredulity straining her voice.

'Who's they? Eh? Go on, tell me!' As if she had touched a raw nerve in him, the bottled-up resentment and bitterness spilling out. 'I was in the Army, now I'm out of it.

That's it. And if you want the truth – I didn't leave for you or the kids.'

'What?' Susie mouthed, stunned.

'We used to pride ourselves we were the toughest, the best fighting men, but they want to change it all, change our image. It was my life, my lads ... but I got as far as I could go, as far as they'd let someone like me go.' Dillon stood there in the cheap, wrinkled suit and battered Puma trainers, fists clenching and unclenching at his sides, the thin line of the scar a whiter shade of pale on his cheek.

'Yes-men, that's what they want. Yes-men. They don't want soldiers, they want blokes with good education.' He gazed off somewhere, suddenly very still, far away. 'The Falklands was the best time in my life. Everything I'd been trained for came together. It was the same for all of us – everything I was made sense.'

'And it doesn't now?' Susie asked quietly, getting up. Emotions that frightened her were chasing themselves across his face. She reached out to hold him, comfort him, and Dillon backed away, the cords in his neck standing out.

'Frank, please, I'm trying to understand – don't get angry. Talk to me, help me ... the Falklands was a long time ago, I know you wanted to go to the Gulf – '

Dillon pushed past her, slamming open the sideboard cupboard to get a bottle of Famous Grouse and a glass, poured out a large measure. 'For your information, there's still a war going on in Ireland,' he said, scathing, as if talking to a cretin, his face ugly and twisted. He took a huge gulp and yelled, '*Steve ... Steve! Get down here!*'

Susie walked out – very nearly. At the door she turned back, gave it another try. He was her husband, she loved him, he deserved that much at least. 'I knew it wouldn't be easy, Frank, but ...' she hesitated, 'the bills have to be paid, and I've been thinking – with the kids at school now – I could get work.'

Dillon's knuckles showed white on the hand holding the glass, the scotch jumping and splashing his fingers. He barked hoarsely, 'I can provide for my wife and kids!' Black rage seeping out of his pores, making his eyes hot.

'I don't want to be provided for with a dead man's pension,' Susie told him calmly.

Dillon swung round, his face so tortured and strange she feared for her safety. As if, without a single qualm, he could have smashed the bottle and gouged her eyes out with the jagged edges.

'Steve! . . . STEVE!'

Steve burst in. He only needed one look at Dillon. He gripped Susie and bundled her roughly out of the room and before she could open her mouth slammed the door in her face. Susie furiously gripped the handle, ready to storm back in, freezing as she heard the splintering crash of the bottle and glass being flung to the floor. Another crash, more glass breaking, and then came a high-pitched whinnying laugh that chilled the blood in her veins. She stood, unmoving, staring at the door, listening.

'I'm going crazy, I'm going crazy . . . For chrissakes I'm dying . . . Don't let them bury me here . . . ' That awful weird, whinnying laugh again. 'All night he screamed "Help me, I'm dying, I'm wet, my chest is bleeding" . . .'

'No – he said his – heart – was bleeding.'

Tears streamed down Susie's face. Turning, she slowly began to mount the stairs, then paused on the third step at the sound of her husband's sobbing. Wiping her eyes with the heel of her hand, Susie went back down and opened the door. Shards of glass littered the carpet. Over in the corner the toppled lamp standard lay broken, it's flowered shade bent and torn, and in the dim glow of the vari-flame gas-fire she saw Dillon and Steve crouched together on the sofa, arms around each other's shoulders.

Suddenly aware of her, Dillon seemed to cringe away, hiding his wet face.

Very softly, Susie murmured, 'Turn the fire off when you come to bed, Frank . . . Goodnight Steve.'

Steve looked at Susie, and gave her a kind of tentative half smile. Then a small wink. It was then, in that moment, that she knew — for the first time realised the truth. That it wasn't Steve who needed Frank. She'd got it totally, completely wrong. It was Frank who needed Steve. Needed this boy with the shattered throat to help him heal his own wounds. Frank's were different from Steve's, his were inside, raw and open, he needed Steve to heal them, and Susie would simply have to wait, he hadn't really come back to Civvies, yet.

Susie silently closed the door and went to bed. She lay curled up, waiting for him, hearing laughter from below, hearing the muffled sounds making it impossible for her to sleep. She tossed and turned, and hours later heard the thud-thud of them both coming up the stairs, heard through the thin wall Frank making sure Steve's filter was cleared, the strange, garbled interaction that she still found difficult to understand, yet Frank was able to carry on long conversations with Steve, as if he were so in tune with his gasping burped sentences there appeared nothing unusual, and the truth was, she had witnessed with her own eyes Steve's transformation. His confidence was growing stronger every day, whereas Frank seemed more and more unsure of himself.

At last Susie heard the click-click of lights being turned out, of toilet flushing and still she waited, waited for her husband to come to bed. Eventually, she got up and crept from her bedroom. Standing on the landing she caught sight of Dillon in their kids' bedroom, standing staring at the old Habitat felt board with all his photographs pinned up. She hesitated, and then inched open the bedroom door.

'It's very late Frank', she whispered.

He nodded his head, and then turned slowly towards her, he seemed so vulnerable, so at a loss. She reached out and took his hand, and he allowed himself to be drawn from his sons' bedroom into his own. She helped him undress and then folded away his clothes as he slipped into their bed, wearing just his jockey shorts. He lay back on the pillows, and she got in beside him and snuggled close, not too close, she was content with just being near him, feeling his body heat. Everything inside her wanted him to reach out, hook his arm around her and draw her even closer, but he remained distant, staring up at the ceiling.

'Steve is gonna be okay,' he whispered.

'Yes, yes I think he is . . .' Susie didn't say what was in her mind or ask all the questions she wanted to ask, she knew intuitively that he meant that he was going to be all right. She could wait, she had got used to it over the years, and she loved her husband deeply. It was Susie's understanding that had kept their marriage steady, when many of their friends' had fallen apart, and, as if he knew it, Dillon drew her to him, easing his arm around her, pressing his hand in the small of her back until she was cradled beside him. He was maybe unaware of the impact this simple gesture meant to Susie, he had always done it and she had never been able to describe to anyone what it meant to her. She could never, or would never, make the first approach to him, it was not in her nature, but when he reached out and drew her close to him, it was, to Susie, like a great warrior claiming his woman. She liked that, liked his domination of her, and trusted him totally, not only to take care of her, but of their sons.

'I am so proud of you,' she whispered.

He looked down at her, the scar etched in his face, white and translucent in the darkness, and then he smiled . . . and he was no great warrior, no sergeant, he was the man she had fallen in love with, and when he gave her that sweet gentle smile, seen so rarely, but a smile that altered his entire face, she felt for the first time he had come home.

Rifles held aloft, grinning through blackened faces. A pair of boots, steaming gently, inscription: 'Wally's Boots!' An Argie with half his face missing, the other eye hanging on his cheek. Steve clowning around, draped in a Union Jack. A gang of them in the NAAFI canteen at Port Stanley, toasting the camera with fifteen Budweisers. The enemy dead, stacked three deep. Dillon, Harry Travers and Jimmy

71

Hammond on their haunches, raw-eyed, bone-weary, a soiled dressing above Dillon's right eye. Four or five of them grouped round a subaltern (an anonymous hand sticking up behind giving the vee-sign). Three shivering Argie prisoners, smiling scared at the camera, waving. Drunken Taffy pissing in the snow, writing his name.

Steve tapped this last one, shoulders shaking, the jerky wheezing breath that passed for his laugh puttering out of his gaping mouth. He wiped his eyes. Dillon, grinning, turned a page, and this set Steve off again. He'd had it, helpless, wiped out. He pointed at the photograph in Dillon's album, tears dripping off his chin.

Dillon straightened up, stuck his nose in the air, and did a perfect officer's accent, braying, 'What —? What did you say, Harris?'

Dillon put his hands to his ears, miming headphones, and did Steve's part. 'Tank. It's a tank, sir! *Tank*.'

Officer: '*Where's the bloody tank, man?*' Neck straining forward, peering through binoculars. '*Tent you blitherin' idiot*! TENT. That's a ruddy tent on the beach, not a tank!'

Dillon broke off, chest heaving, and the laughter swept through him sweetly, and once he'd started he couldn't stop. He fell back into the sofa, legs splayed and quivering, head flung back, shouting out his laughter.

Steve, growing quieter now, sat and watched him, eyes shining with tears of utter devotion and love.

TAFFY DAVIES

9

It was a dream. Taffy wasn't fooled, he knew that full well, because it was always the same dream. But he was still trapped in it, and there was no escape. Always the same crushing pressure on his chest. Smell of burning flesh, possibly his own. Screams of agony mimicking the distant wail of sirens. The taste of blood, like salty glue, in his mouth (he recognised the taste). Thick black smoke swirling up past a flickering fluorescent tube dangling from its bracket. And the dream had a musical soundtrack too, thud-thud-thudding in his head, keeping time with the pulse throbbing in his temples.

BAM-BAM-BAM-BAM!
I've changed my mind
This world is fine –
Goodness Gracious! Great Balls of . . .

The song always ended right there, Jerry Lee cut off in his prime, old Frank's all-time favourite rock classic. Funny how it still went on in his head, the lyric completing itself, even when all he could actually hear were screams and moans and choking and sobbing.

Taffy pushed, straining to shift the massive beam pinning him to the floor. What didn't make it any easier, the frigging thing was alight, pretty blue and yellow flames dancing along it, scorching his eyeballs and searing the skin off his palms.

He was aware of a body close by – a girl's – the beam across her legs, a dark ugly stain seeping through the bright green of her skirt. Taffy gritted his teeth and heaved with all his might. It was moving, definitely. He'd got the bastard! Another shove and they'd be free. The girl screamed as the weight lifted off her. Taffy wanted to tell her it was okay, he'd soon have her out, but he didn't have an ounce of breath to spare . . . holding the bastard at arm's stretch now, gathering himself for one final push, the muscles in his shoulders nearly tearing themselves loose as he tried to fling it aside.

Something cracked, splintered up above. Taffy stared and through the smoke he saw the rest of the ceiling, sheets of flame racing across it – Holy Shit! – start to give way. Taffy shut his eyes and began to pray. He covered his ears as the crackling roar suddenly welled up, angry and deafening, and the ceiling fell in.

Instinctively, Taffy twisted away, bringing his knees up defensively, and rolled off the bed, ending up in a foetal crouch on the strip of thin carpet under the window. He opened his eyes, blinking warm sweat away, and gazed with trembling relief at the bubbled pink paintwork of the skirting-board, six inches from his nose: his arms, his shoulders, his entire back, aching from the strain of wrestling with that eternal bloody burning beam.

Daylight poured in. What time was it? Morning, afternoon, he hadn't a clue. Only eight pints of Murphy's stout last night, no reason to sleep past ten. He unwound and pushed himself up, feeling through the floorboards a steady throbbing vibration, coming from the bass beat of the stereo next door. Night and day it went on. Day and bloody night. In warm weather it blasted through the open windows, Queen, Phil Collins, Dire fucking Straits, and the lad's so-called music was even worse – a jangled thrashing of tuneless noise like a dozen panel-beaters on piece-time, polluting a quarter-mile radius of the council estate with its mindless racket.

And as if all that wasn't more than flesh and blood could stand, the seventeen-year-old son – dyed black dreadlocks, rings through his nose, ripped jeans, knee-high lace-up boots – was also a drummer in a punk band. Three, four times a week he had his mates round in the back bedroom, smashing hell out of their instruments and loosening the foundations. To Taffy, the singer sounded like he was having his back teeth pulled.

He looked up from buttoning his shirt at Mary's voice, down in the hallway, and listened, frowning. Not arguing exactly, more like pleading. Then an answering man's voice, laying down the law in a flat, nasal drone. One of the kids started crying, and this set off the toddler. What the hell was going on?

Taffy strode out onto the landing, brushing strands of greying hair from his forehead. Two men in brown coats were coming out of the front room, humping the big 16-inch television set between them, while another bloke in a suit and dingy white shirt with curling collar points was waving a sheaf of documents in Mary's face. Taffy caught something about 'Poll Tax' and 'default' and 'reclaim' and he didn't need to hear any more.

Bastard bailiffs!

In stockinged feet Taffy vaulted down the stairs in three leaps, grabbed a bunch of shiny lapel in his meaty fist, fumbling with the front door Yale lock. 'I'll give you bastards two minutes to get out of this house!' Yelling in the man's face, flecking him with saliva.

'Taffy, don't – ' Mary clawed at his arm, her chin quivering, brown eyes large and moist, swallowing back the tears. She dragged him off. 'It'll do no good . . . just get back up the stairs. We can't stop them.'

The big Welshman stood there, panting with rage, wiry grey chest hair exposed through his half-buttoned shirt front. He jerked his thumb towards the kitchen. 'They take the fridge, what'll you do with the food?' he demanded.

Mary shook her head helplessly, biting her lip. The men in brown were edging towards the front door, hands locked under the TV set.

'Put – that- down!' Taffy pointed to the kitchen doorway where his two eldest were clinging to the door jamb, bawling their heads off, the toddler shrieking in the background. 'We've got an eighteen-month-old kid in there . . .'

Trying to make him listen for once, to get some sense

77

into that bone-solid head of his, Mary gave it to him straight: 'It's either this or they'll evict us – just *stop it!*'

Taffy immediately stepped back, raising his hands. Fine, okay with me, go right ahead. As the men got to the front door Taffy bent down and yanked the carpet, bellowing out his defiance, taking their legs away and sending all three of them colliding into each other, the TV set doing a wobbly as they very nearly dropped it. 'I'm helping them, woman,' Taffy explained reasonably, coming forward with a strange smile on his face. 'I'm not gonna hurt anyone.' Mary cringed, hating the blank expression that gave away nothing. It was as if his face was a mask – only his eyes were alive, and very very dangerous.

The two men in brown got the door open and got out, having gently deposited the TV set at the bottom of the stairs. Taffy helped the man in the suit on his way with a shove in the back and a boot up the jacksi, and slammed the door on the whole mangy pack of them.

'You don't say a word unless you have to. I'll do the talking, just nod your head, right?'

Steve nodded and said, 'Right.' Or that's what Dillon thought he said. Sometimes he could understand Steve plain as day, other times it was a mangled croak, like a bullfrog with an attack of hiccups.

The radio had said cloudy with the possibility of showers, but there was blue sky and a faint breeze, not cold, almost a touch of spring in the air. They came down the concrete stairway from Dillon's flat, brisk and purposeful, wearing identical grey suits (bought off adjacent pegs), slim black ties, and rubber-soled black shoes. Freshly shaved, hair trimmed and groomed, the pair of them moved with a lightness of step and casual agility that only came with a regime of hard punishing exercise, coupled with the discipline to maintain the body as an efficient fighting machine, because in their profession if you weren't superbly fit, you were dead. Most civilians were slobs; ten minutes on Heartbreak Hill at The Depot in Aldershot would give them cardiac arrest.

'Frank . . . *Frank*!'

Dillon looked up to see Susie's tousled head poking over the third-floor parapet. 'What?'

'Somebody called Taffy – said it's very important.'

'What?'

'On the telephone!'

'Tell him to call tonight,' Dillon shouted, striding off with Steve across the paved courtyard, not bothering to look back.

As they came round the corner into the street, Dillon nodded towards a royal-blue Mercedes idling at the kerb, a young black guy at the wheel. Done out in a chauffeur's garb of neat dark jacket, crisp white shirt and black tie, he exuded the same hard, clean energy as the other two, giving Dillon a broad cheery grin.

'He was only on transport,' Dillon told Steve in a muttered aside as they came up, 'but he's a good lad.'

They climbed in the back, Dillon doing the introductions. 'Cliff Morgan, Steve Harris . . .' Cliff stuck his hand out, but Steve seemed too busy settling himself on the contoured, brushed upholstery, taking in the walnut trim, the plush fixtures and fittings.

'Appreciate this, Cliff,' said Dillon, slapping his shoulder. 'We owe you one!'

Cliff gave a quick nod, shifted into Drive, and off they shot.

Avoiding the gridlock of Oxford Street, Cliff cut across Tottenham Court Road and jinked up the backstreets to Portland Street, the Merc surging smoothly into Regent's Park Crescent, the classical, elegant façade of white and pale cream stonework bathed in gentle sunshine. To Dillon, this part of town had the alien reek of wealth and power; he felt like a non-swimmer whose feet couldn't quite touch bottom, and a knot of apprehension tightened in his stomach, making it hard to catch his breath. Embassies and trade missions – diplomats and bureaucrats – the nameless, faceless power-brokers of the globe inhabiting a rarefied stratosphere he knew nothing of and could barely imagine. Of course, blokes like him and Steve weren't meant to – that was the whole point. That was how these high-flying wankers kept their closed shop nice and cosy and exclusive.

Blokes like him and Steve were just expected to sort it all out when they'd made a balls of it. Shovel up the shit after it had hit the fan. It seemed to Dillon he'd been doing that all his life.

From the glove compartment Cliff took a glossy laminated folder, fancily embossed with the name Samson Security Company, and handed it to Dillon. Cliff seemed a bit on edge himself, Dillon thought, even though it was their picnic.

'Here – just do exactly as I've told you,' Cliff said, eyes steady and serious. 'You got all the legit stuff here, but any letters you got from HQ, show 'em.' Dillon patted his jacket to show he'd remembered to bring them. 'They particularly asked for guys with terrorist training – your Army records should clinch it.'

'Oh yeah?' drawled Steve sarcastically. 'Yours ga-get you – this – did it . . .'

'Shut it!' Dillon snapped from the side of his mouth.

'What did he say?' asked Cliff.

Dillon opened the door. 'Nothing, and look, thanks mate.'

'Don't foul up on me Frank, this is a good firm, a good job, I don't want to lose it.'

Dillon winked. He didn't intend to blow this one, with or without Steve's help. He shoved Steve out ahead of him and warned him to keep his mouth shut, but Steve brushed his hand aside.

'He ga – a ugh-pratt, only-Ever g-hone transport.'

Dillon straightened his tie, giving a warning look to Steve, who, for all his problems seemed incredibly relaxed. His hair was washed and combed, he had shaved and was wearing a clean shirt that Susie had pressed for him and one of his suits from when he had been in the money. He looked more like the old Steve, handsome, his green eyes clear, and standing a good three inches taller than Dillon. Steve was back. This was the first time Frank realised how far he had come in so short a time.

'G-after'gu – Mate', Steve smiled, giving a mock bow, but he did follow Dillon, nervously touching his throat, aware that the tie was irritating his skin. He hated wearing collars, they restricted him, made him fearful he would not be able to get to his tube fast enough if he had an emergency . . . but then he knew Dillon was there, that made him feel safe. As if in confirmation he tapped Dillon's shoulder, and winked . . . 'We'll G-it gub job, – no problem.'

Dillon shrugged Steve's hand away. Bloody Steve was his problem and he knew it, even doubted if getting him back on his feet was all that good a thing as he was now bound to help him even further. It was like the blind leading the blind.

The house was a fortress. After the battery of security cameras covering the portico entrance, the white-barred windows of double-paned, shatter-resistant glass, the steel-lined bombproof front door, Dillon was expecting at least an X-ray scan and body frisk. But the letter of accreditation did the trick, that and their neat, respectable appearance – amazing what you could get away with wearing a suit and tie, Dillon always thought. Stroll into Buckingham Palace, have tea with the Queen, maybe even get to sit on her bed.

They were conducted across the marble-floored hallway, large black and white squares like a giant chessboard, and along a carpeted corridor into an ante-room with dark red walls and a gleaming parquet floor, and told to sit and wait on ornate gilt chairs outside a pair of huge double doors with curved handles in the shape of scimitars. They looked to be made of solid gold, and it wouldn't have

81

surprised Dillon to learn that they were. A crystal chandelier tinkled faintly from some non-existent breeze.

Given the choice, Dillon would have opted for a ten-
mile tab in Advanced Wales with full pack rather than
endure this. He was glad he'd showered that morning and
put on fresh underclothes, he didn't want to sully the
opulent atmosphere.

'You okay?' Dillon asked in a whisper after Steve had
cleared his throat six times in as many seconds. Steve
nodded glumly, staring at the polished floor, wrapped in
his own thoughts. He had to wear his tie loose and shirt
collar undone, a strip of gauze and adhesive tape just
visible below his Adam's apple.

Dillon started as one of the double doors silently opened
and a slender dark-skinned man with oiled black hair
and gold-rimmed spectacles glided into view. He wore an
immaculate silk suit that changed colour as he moved,
hand-stitched shirt and grey silk tie, the dull gleam of gold
on his wrist, fingers and from the fob chain looped into
the pocket of his embroidered waistcoat.

Salah Al-Gharib crooked his finger. Dillon wet his lips
and obeyed, Steve trailing a couple of feet behind.

It was like being summoned into the sultan's palace.
The large room had white-panelled walls edged with gold,
a Persian carpet floating on the polished floor. Over by
the window overlooking a walled garden, a six-seater sofa
and three deep armchairs in white leather were grouped
around a low table of beaten copper and mosaic tiles.
Above the marble fireplace, a mirror with scrolled edges,
and in front of this a huge desk, made to seem even
bigger because all it contained were four telephones, each a
different colour, and a leather blotter without a mark or
blemish on it.

Behind it, reclining in a winged leather chair, Raoul Al-
Mohammed gazed into the remote distance with heavy-
lidded eyes, dark folds of skin beneath resting on swarthy
bloated cheeks. Never once did he look at Dillon and
Steve, nor acknowledge they were even breathing the same

air. In their grey suits they were no more substantial than vague grey blurs, so it didn't matter that they shuffled uneasily like two schoolboy miscreants summoned to the headmaster's study, awaiting the clap of doom.

Raoul Al-Mohammed twitched a finger, and Salah Al-Gharib, his principal secretary, ghosted forward and placed Dillon's folder in front of him. He flipped it open, laced his dark-haired fingers across his stomach, and with heavy, sombre eyes began to read.

Dillon sneaked a glance at Steve. But Steve was still in some faraway place, not of this world at all.

Ignoring a black cab's furiously tooting horn and its driver's mouthed obscenities, Cliff pulled out into the swirl of traffic and headed north round the Crescent towards Marylebone Road. In the back, Dillon was chortling and jumping about with almost childish glee, as if he was the birthday boy who'd just been given the present he'd always wanted; even Steve seemed a mite excited, cheeks flushed, some of the old devilry dancing in his eyes.

'He closed the folder, looked over my letters, never said a word. He just gave a nod to the other geezer and walked out of the room!'

Cliff looked at Dillon through the rearview mirror. 'He's a real bastard. Used the firm six times in the last two years.' His lip curled. 'Fired two or our guys because one of 'em was caught smoking. But take his crap and you could see two grand minimum in the hand on top of your fee . . .'

'How you gonna handle it,' Dillon was concerned to know, leaning over the front passenger seat, 'when they pay the company?'

'Taken care of.' Cliff flashed his confident smile. 'I'm having a fling with the secretary, she'll lift it before it gets to accounts.'

'SaiD he WanTs uS – rouNd tHe clOCk – onE dRiviNg – oNe –'

'What did he say?' Cliff interrupted, frowning.

Dillon interpreted, 'We're to be on call twenty-four hours, one driving, one baby-sitting. Two weeks definite, could be longer. Start Monday.'

Cliff gunned the car to beat the lights and spun right into Baker Street at the Planetarium, broad black hands caressing the wheel, steering with his fingertips. He laughed aloud, shaking his head. 'You lucky so-and-so's . . . you just got yourselves a class A earner!'

10

Bugger this for a game of soldiers, Dillon was thinking. He looked down at his new pair of shoes, up to the welts in mud, and then glared round at the heaped-up wrecks, rusty engines, crazed windscreens, leaking sumps, the assembled detritus of a thousand crashes stacked under the viaduct that carried the lines south-west from Waterloo. Leave it to me, Steve had said. Famous last fucking words. Might as well leave brain surgery to Stevie Wonder.

Dillon could see Steve through the window of the lean-to shack that passed as an office – at least see as much of him as the cracked, filthy panes and cardboard covering the gaps allowed. Patience worn to a brittle point, Dillon was about to storm in when Steve emerged with a mechanic in overalls sagging with grease and engine-oil. The mechanic, sixty if he was a day, was thumbing through a dog-eared ledger, pausing now and then to wipe his nose with the back of his hand.

Dillon unfolded his arms. 'Where's the car, Steve?'

The mechanic said, 'Hopefully picking up the bride – it's not due back until four.' He looked up from the ledger, eyes bloodshot in the corners. 'How many days did you want it for, Steve?'

Dillon's nostrils were white and pinched. He burst out angrily, 'What is this . . . ?'

'The only day it's needed is the Wednesday of the first week,' the mechanic went on, 'there's a big funeral from twelve till – '

'Forget it.' Dillon made a sweeping gesture with the flat of his hand and turned away, yanking his shoes from the mire. He took one look back at Steve. 'Stay away from me, okay?' And really meant it.

'Arms dealers, that's what they are – and the prat gets a weddin' Roller lined up!'

Dillon stood at the press-ups bench, his hands underneath but not touching the bar Jimmy was hefting, acting as safety back-up as the big lad did ten reps with forty kilos. Face contorted, lower lip between his teeth, Jimmy strained with the last one, got it full stretch, and Dillon eased it onto the dead-weight brackets.

'You know he's a liability . . .' Jimmy panted, taking in deep breaths. He relaxed, broad muscular chest beaded with sweat, the veins standing out over the bulge of his biceps. He not only looked good, he had all the gear to show it off: black cutaway singlet, dark-grey exercise shorts with purple stripes and high vents at the sides, Reeboks that must have set him back a hundred and forty pounds. 'Don't know why you waste your time with him.' Upside-down to Dillon, his forehead wrinkled as he looked into Dillon's eyes. 'You wanna see if I can line something up?'

'Not with that crook Newman. Why do you keep trying, Jimmy? I don't wanna know.' Dillon wasn't angry, just a bit pissed-off. He slid another two ten kilos onto the bar, snapped the locks shut. He sighed. 'If this had worked out, Cliff could have farmed out more work on the QT . . .'

Jimmy snorted derisively. 'I heard Sambo Morgan was still doin' transport – just switched his uniform. He's another prat!' He jerked his thumb, indicating the bar. 'I'll need a hand with these, just do three to five reps. I don't understand you, Frank. At The Depot you wouldn't give Cliff the time of day, now . . . *Uggghhhhhh* shit!' His arms tautened, muscles solid and bulging as he took the strain. 'Okay, I'm set.'

'Right now I need any break I can get,' Dillon said grimly.

'What do you come out with – *uhhhh!* – at the end of the day?'

'Fair whack – course, we got to hire the uniforms.'

Dillon's cupped hands followed the rising and sinking bar. He said, 'Don't strain, mind your back . . . easy now . . .'

The three character traits most highly valued – and actively encouraged – by the Parachute Regiment were aggression, aggression, and aggression. Not only directed at the enemy, but internalised too, to make a man overcome his natural inclinations of fear and self-preservation when standing at the door of a Herc, hooked up to the static line, Red on, Green on – go, go, go! You didn't just fall out of the aircraft (that way the slipstream would whirl you round and you'd end up with a faceful of rivets), you had to punch yourself into the air in order to get clear. Dillon had seen a seasoned Para freeze at that moment, and it took three despatchers to heave him out, bashing his arm to make him let go of the strop. Focused, controlled aggression, that's what was required.

And that's how Jimmy went at it now, grunting and scowling each time he pushed the bar to arm's length as if he bore the sixty kilos a personal grudge. Possessing a good physique, strong bone structure, and being in peak condition did the rest.

'We'll have to shell out a few readies to Cliff for puttin' us on it,' Dillon grunted, settling the bar on the brackets.

Jimmy sat up, towelling his neck and shoulders. 'But you need a motor, right?' he said. 'I'll see what I can do.'

'No kiddin'?' Dillon's face lit up.

Jimmy put his arm round Dillon's shoulders, gave him a fat smile. 'Let's have a shower first, eh?'

Mary Davies let herself in and dumped the two plastic carrier-bags of shopping next to the hallstand, kneading her fingers to get the circulation going again. She stared with undiluted hatred at the wall at the foot of the stairs.

Thump-thump-thump-thump-thump –

Behind the pounding bass, the sharper staccato rattle of a snare drum coming from next door's back bedroom. The punk drummer paused, a moment's blessed respite, and then started over again, practising the same machine-gun attack, paused, repeated it.

'Taffy?' Mary shouted up the stairs. '*Taff?!*'

When there was no answer she picked up her shopping and headed for the kitchen, calling, 'Meg, did your Daddy go out? Can you hear me? I'm surprised I can hear myself with that racket! *Megan . . .*'

Mary pushed open the door with her backside and stopped dead at the sight of the contents of her fridge stacked on the kitchen table: packets of frozen foods, processed cheese, carton of eggs, fruit juice, a full and a half-empty bottle of milk. And next to the washing machine, a gaping hole where the fridge had been. Mary slowly shook her head, faced screwed tight. The bailiffs had even taken the Wylex plug.

Thump-thump-thump-thump-thump –

Dillon side-stepped the bikes and went through into the living-room, dropping his carrier-bag just in time to catch Kenny who came hurtling out of the kitchen, scoop him up and swing him onto his shoulders. Little Phil tugged at Dillon's trousers, wanting his turn.

Dillon yelled towards the stairs, 'Steve, you in? *Steve?*'

Susie was halfway down, carrying the Hoover, dragging the flex after her. She mouthed at him, 'Bedroom,' and gave Dillon a dark look. 'He's drinking,' she said in a low voice, 'came in with it.'

Dillon swung the boy down and went past Susie on the stairs. He paused and looked back at her. 'We got the job.'

'You did? That's marvellous!' Smile breaking, eyes aglow, making her look about eighteen. 'Does that mean he'll be leaving?' Susie whispered, glancing up at the ceiling.

'Soon as we're paid,' said Dillon crisply, and carried on. 'Hey, Steve!'

The phone rang. Susie plugged the Hoover into the hall socket and got up off her knees to answer it.

British Telecom's modernisation programme hadn't reached this part of south Wales. It was a wonder the old-fashioned cast-iron telephone box was even in working order, considering that most of the windows were broken. There was a soggy bag of stale chips in the corner and the distinct whiff of urine, bi-lingual obscenities scrawled in felt-tip on every flat surface. Forehead pressed against the cold glass pane, Taffy Davies stared out at the rain sweeping down from a grey Cardiff sky, words tumbling out of him, just glad there was a familiar, friendly voice at the other end.

'The bastards play music all day, all night,' he mumbled into the phone, 'I can't sleep, the kids wake up, it's driving me nuts . . .' His voice quaked a little. 'I'm going crazy, Frank. I had to talk to someone – I don't know what to do, man!'

In the hallway, Dillon pressed his palm flat against his ear, struggling to hear the faint, crackling voice above the Hoover, the toilet flushing upstairs, and now the damn kids, playing shunting engines at Clapham Junction.

Dillon whirled round, red in the face.

'Pair of you, out! Get out!' He pointed. 'Susie, shut that off.'

Susie didn't appreciate being barked at as if this was a parade-ground, and nearly didn't, but one look at Dillon's face changed her mind. She stamped it off with her toe and crowded the boys into the kitchen out of harm's way.

'Okay, now listen, Taff . . .' Dillon spoke slowly and calmly. 'They can't play music all night, it's against the law.' Clicks and buzzes. 'You there . . . Taffy?' Dillon had to listen hard to the faint, croaking voice, on the line from purgatory. 'And what . . . they've taken your fridge? Who has?'

Taffy banged his head against the cracked pane, clawing with dirt-rimmed nails at his unshaven cheek. He didn't know he looked a slob, and wouldn't have cared if he had. It had gone beyond that, it was out of control, tears of rage and frustration stinging his eyes. It was pathetic and pitiful, but he just didn't care any more.

'The cops are bloody useless,' he mumbled hoarsely. 'If I go into that house, I'll kill somebody . . .' He yanked a sliver of glass from the broken pane and squeezed it in his bare hand.

Steve was on the sofa, groggy-eyed, listening to Dillon who was pacing up and down, smacking his fist into his palm.

'And the same bloke – given a medal for riskin' his neck and savin' God knows how many people – is goin' nuts because some bastard won't turn his stereo down. He can't find work. His kids are yellin', and his wife doesn't understand why he can't get a job . . . What does he expect me to do?' Dillon spread his hands helplessly. Turning, he saw Susie in the hallway, about to continue Hoovering, and pushed the door shut in her face.

All right, stay cool, Susie thought with tremendous forbearance, let it ride, and put her foot out to start the Hoover again. Then she flung the Hoover aside and kicked the living-room door open instead, standing there hands on hips, eyes blazing.

'I am sick to death of having doors shut in my face in my own home! Maybe the reason she can't understand is the same reason *I can't understand*. What do you think we are, Frank? Mind-readers? How am I to know what triggers off these moods if you won't tell me!'

'What moods?' Dillon snapped at her.

'Oh come on, Frank!' Susie's boiler was stoked up and blowing sparks. 'You breeze in on top of the world because you've got work – next minute, one phone call later, you behave as if I'm your worst enemy.'

Dillon said sullenly, 'Kids were just gettin' on my nerves . . .'

'It's half-term – instead of taking on responsibility for every soldier that leaves the Army, you should spend more time with your kids – '

'It's not every soldier,' Dillon interrupted. Wearily he turned his back on her, infuriating Susie even more. 'Why don't you play another record, you're getting to sound like your mother.'

Steve got to his feet and weaved towards the door. As he went by her he muttered, 'oNe lAMe – DuCk's enOUgh . . .'

Susie watched him go and rounded on Dillon. 'What did he say?' she demanded, spots of colour burning her cheeks.

Dillon grabbed her arm and dragged her towards him until his dark, dangerous eyes were two inches from hers.

'You want to have a go at me, do it when he's not around – '

Susie yanked her arm free. '*He bloody lives here!*'

'You want to talk?' Dillon murmured, raising his eyebrows. 'Well, I'm all ears.' He went past her, kicking the door shut, turned about, folded his arms. 'What do you want to know?'

'Oh stop this, Frank,' Susie pleaded. 'I can't take this!'

'What do you want to know, Susie? Want to know about the job?' Susie flinched as Dillon lunged forward. He made a grab for the carrier-bag propped against the end of the sofa and ripped it open, holding up a chauffeur's uniform of dark jacket and dark grey slacks with knife-edge creases. He bared his teeth in what was supposed to be a smile.

'Okay. Exchange one uniform for another, all right? You think this is what I want? You think I came out for this?'

When she had her breathing under control, Susie said quietly, 'It's a job. At least you can pay the rent.' She swallowed, her face nearly crumpling. 'You – you did take the rent money from the drawer, didn't you? Oh Frank, you're not playin' the horses, are you, you promised me . . .'

Dillon carelessly let the clothing fall in a heap over the back of the sofa. He said huskily, 'I'll pay the rent, Susie,

I'll pay it and anything else you want.' His eyes bored into hers. 'In answer to your question, no, I did not put a cent on a bleedin' horse . . . even if I did it's my business, not yours.'

He went to the door and threw it open, and Susie thought, if he yells for Steve just once more I'll scream. But he didn't, instead he almost fell over the Hoover.

Susie took a pace forward, trying one last appeal.

'You have so much time for everyone else . . . I need some too, Frank!' Dillon glared at her over his shoulder. 'Think about it, will you?'

Between tight lips, only just audible, Dillon muttered: 'Everyone wants a piece of me, and I need some space, okay? I need – '

What he needed was lost as Susie swept her hand out and slammed the door, this time in Dillon's face. A second later it crashed back on its hinges from Dillon's kick, and he stood in the doorway, the blood draining from his face, fists clenched.

'Don't ever do that again!' Dillon snarled, eyes glittering.

Susie held up her hands and backed away, her insides shrivelling at this proximity to a wild man with so much naked violence pouring out of him she could almost smell it. Or perhaps it was her own fear. Frank had never struck her but now she saw him fight for control, his hands rigid fists.

'I'm sorry.' Susie said quietly.

Dillon walked out, this time closing the door quietly and firmly, somehow it was worse than if he had slammed it. Susie buried her face in the cushion and burst into tears. She knew she couldn't take it much longer, she had tried, no one could say she hadn't tried, but she was beginning to wish he had never left the Paras.

11

With the tip of his finger, Dillon touched the bonnet of the Mercedes-Benz 300SE three-litre and watched the little round patch of condensation evaporate from the flawless silver surface. The caged wall lights of the underground garage gave the car a ghostly, almost supernatural aura. Thunderbirds are go! Dillon thought, and felt a little tremor of excitement and apprehension.

He was conscious of Jimmy watching them both from behind the wheel, no doubt revelling in their awe and trepidation – and of course envy too – because who else but Jim'll Fixit had the clout and the contacts to graciously bestow such a favour?

'What do you think?' Dillon said, a bloody sight more nervous than he cared to admit.

Steve gulped air and rifted, 'It's up to you – you'll be driving.'

'What d'you mean? You're driving, mate. I've never driven an automatic.'

'Okay but . . .' Steve shrugged indifferently. 'I've got no licence.'

Dillon's head came round in three distinct movements, his eyes burning holes through the air.

'Banned,' Steve burped. 'Three years, drunk driving . . .'

Dillon turned away, and hissed under his breath, 'Banned, you pillock!' Here they were with a job all lined up, he depending on Steve having never driven an automatic himself, and now Steve blurted or burped out he was bloody banned from driving. Dillon faced Steve, looked back to Jimmy, and in a low voice warned Steve to keep his mouth shut, not to let on to Jimmy, just drive the Merc out, he'd take over after a practice.

Jimmy beckoned to them. They leaned in, inhaling the

rich mingled odours of Cuban mahogany, deep-pile carpets and whole-hide leather in Antique Burgundy. 'Telephone . . .' Jimmy indicated the handset in its walnut box, 'you got everythin', even clean-air spray — and if you want a tip, use it. Nothin' worse than gettin' into a car reekin' of stale farts.' With a look of dire warning he tossed the keys to Steve. 'But so much as a scratch — an' I'll have your balls.' He tapped the steering-wheel. 'Thirty grand's worth of motor.'

'Okay, it's simple,' Steve told Dillon fifteen minutes later, having driven the car to a piece of waste ground. They'd swapped seats and Dillon was frowning at the unfamiliar controls while Steve played driving instructor.

'Just remember not to use your left foot . . . this is Reverse, this is Park, then 'D' for Drive . . . that's it.'

He folded his arms and settled back as Dillon pushed the stick into Reverse and pressed the accelerator. The fat wheels skittered stones and dirt as the silver Mercedes shot back at high speed towards a brick wall, Steve unfolding his arms quick to stop his head bashing against the wooden fascia. Dillon slammed down on the foot-size brake pedal and they skidded to a halt, rocking on hydraulic suspension, inches away from the wall.

Gasping and choking from the shock, Steve wiped his forehead, weak with relief that Dillon hadn't crumpled anything at first attempt. Then he was thrust back deep into the leather seat as the car suddenly hurtled forward, heading towards a pile of rubble. Steve covered his eyes. But Dillon reckoned he was getting the hang of it, even starting to enjoy himself.

Taffy made his preparations. He placed a blanket, crosswise, on Megan's single bed, and with neat, orderly movements stacked her toys and dolls in the centre of it, added the pictures off the walls to the pile, finally the toddler's fluffy animals, plastic bricks and colouring books. He gathered the four corners together and quickly and expertly knotted them, then carried the tight bundle out and dumped it on the landing.

Thump-thump-thump-thump-thump –

The drumbeat in his head pounded out its unrelenting rhythm. The phantom drummer was at it too, repeating the same riff over and over and over again. But Taffy stayed calm. It was all very clear and simple. No sweat. He knew what he had to do.

Megan crouched at the top of the stairs, biting her knuckles as she watched Daddy, singlet and shorts under the dressing-gown flapping at his calves, go back into her bedroom. He'd stripped down the bed and now he was dismantling the cot. He took it apart like a Bren gun, working with military precision and economy of effort, gathered the pieces and stacked them neatly against the banister rails.

Megan cowered away but Daddy completely ignored her, went back into the empty, bare room and closed the door. As a welcome change the phantom drummer was now practising triple rolls, but the *thump-thump-thump* continued as before, as always, as ever.

On Radio 5, Danny Baker was slagging off a new film with undisguised glee while Susie Dillon tidied away the breakfast things. She wiped her hands on the tea-towel and hurried through the living-room, using her fingers to comb back her hair, checking on the way that Kenny and Phil were still decent and presentable. She grabbed her coat from the hook and called up the stairs, 'Frank? Frank, I'm taking the kids to school – did you hear me?'

Susie took a step back, trying to hide the glimmer of a smile as Dillon and Steve came down the stairs, done up like dogs' dinners in their brand-new chauffeurs' uniforms, crisp white shirts and black ties, complete with peaked caps.

'You look great . . .' Susie said, proud and impressed. She waved her hand. 'Hey, kids!'

'Don't . . .' Dillon's neck was red with embarrassment.

He glanced at Steve, and then, finding a weak grin, raised his cap as the boys came charging through. 'How do!'

The telephone rang as Susie opened the front door and ushered the boys outside. She gave Dillon and Steve a big bright smile. 'Good luck! Know what time you'll be home?'

'Hello?' Dillon said into the phone, then covered the mouthpiece. 'We could be late.' Susie winked and shut the door, but opened it almost at once, flagging for Dillon's attention. 'It's Frank speaking, who is this?' Through a blizzard of static he caught the name 'Mary' before his attention was needed elsewhere.

'There's a gang of kids around the car,' Susie alerted him, jabbing her finger beyond the parapet.

Dillon sighed, glanced three ways at once, at Susie, at the phone, at Steve adjusting his cap in the hall mirror. Jesus, if it wasn't one thing it was ten others. 'Go and take a look, Steve . . . I'll call Jimmy, ask if we can leave it in the garage.' Dillon's lips tightened as Steve dawdled, now putting his tie straight. 'Steve – just go and check the car . . .'

Steve brushed past and went out banging the door behind him.

Dillon said, 'Hello . . . hello?' The beeps sounded. Impatiently Dillon checked his watch, waiting for Taffy's missus to feed in more money. Calling from south Wales and she was dropping in ten-pence pieces one at a time. Come *on*.

'Hello? Mary? Yeah, I'm still here, yeah . . .' Dillon listened to the distant voice, faint yet obviously distressed. 'Look, love, I don't know what I can suggest. I mean, I'm here, if he wants to call me again – '

beep-beep-beep-beep-beep-beep-beep

'Christ!'

'Frank!' Steve thumping the door with his fist. 'Come on, we'll be late!'

Dillon plonked the receiver into the cradle, set his cap straight, and went out at the trot.

Mary went cautiously up the stairs, the toddler, drowsily sucking her thumb, clasped in her arms. Megan lagged behind, peeping round her mother to the piles of stuff Taffy had placed on the landing. She pointed and whispered, 'See . . . he's moved everything out!'

Mary looked down at the bundle, Megan's and the toddler's clothing piled on top, the dismantled cot, the blankets and bedding beside it in military order. Handing the child to Megan, she shuffled forward to the door and listened. Not a sound from within, and blessed silence from next door as well, which probably meant they were all watching Noel Edmonds with their tea on their laps, thank God. Mary raised her hand to tap on the door, but didn't.

She called softly, 'Taffy? Do you want something to eat? Taff?'

Frowning and shaking her head, Mary went back down, silently shooing her daughter ahead of her. From the bend in the stairs she saw the light under the door go out. She hesitated, but carried on down.

In his dressing-gown Taffy lay on the bare mattress, arms straight at his sides, watching the light fade through the net curtains. The streetlamp came on, throwing a yellow trapezium on the flowered wallpaper and the pale areas where the pictures had hung, and, as if this was the signal triggering something in his brain, Taffy got up and began the final stage.

Opening his Airborne-issue bergen rucksack, he laid out his kit on the bed. DPM Para smock, olive green denim trousers, 'Hairy' KF woollen shirt, '58 pattern webbing order, cloth puttees, DMS rubber-soled boots, green lanyard for compass, maroon belt with regimental badge in bright metal on the circular buckle, maroon beret with matt-black cap badge. All present and correct, *sah!*

Taffy unscrewed the lid off the black boot polish and worked up a nice smooth paste with a globule of spit. Dipped the yellow cloth into it, set to with a will, bulling up the toe-caps. In the silent, darkened room Taffy polished industriously away, a frown of rapt concentration on his face.

'What time is it?'

Dillon, dressed only in jockey shorts and socks, carrying his uniform on a hanger, halted in mid-creep halfway across the bedroom floor. Susie's eyes watched him from above the covers as he hung the uniform on the wardrobe door. Dillon arched his back and crawled into bed with a groan. 'After two . . . I got terrible backache.'

'What time are you on in the morning?'

'Seven-thirty.' Dillon tried to relax, let the tension flow out of him. 'We've been sittin' in that car for twelve hours solid . . .'

'Well,' Susie retorted, 'at least you're sitting down.'

'Might have known I'd get no sympathy from you,' Dillon mumbled sleepily. He stretched and made a noise somewhere between a yawn and a groan, and snuggled down, totally whacked.

Crash!

From downstairs, but loud enough to wake the dead, Steve falling in through the front door, colliding with the bikes in the hall and thudding headlong to the floor.

Floating away on the soft pink billow of deep wonderful sleep, Dillon came bolt upright in the bed, eyes sticking out like organ stops. Another thud, clang of bike frames, and Dillon, realizing what it was, flopped back, the pillow over his head.

Steve, muttering drunkenly to himself, was now attempting the impossible, death-defying ascent of the stairs. Halfway up he missed his footing and tumbled to the bottom, landing with a *thud* that jarred the floorboards and made the wardrobe door swing open.

From the boys' room, a shrill plaintive 'Muuuu-mmmmmm!'

With a heavy sigh, Susie whopped the bedcovers aside and prepared to get up. Dillon whopped them back again.

'Leave it – just leave it!'

'But it sounds like he's fallen downstairs . . .'
'Good! Hope he's broken his ruddy neck!'

12

There was a red line around Dillon's forehead where his cap had been. He drummed his fingers on the steering-wheel, glancing every now and then at Steve, bent over in the passenger seat with a Little Chef road map spread across his knees, marking the motorways with a felt-tip. Bloody wonder they'd ever got here. And how long had it taken them – over two hours? Jesus wept.

Dillon kept a wary eye on the clients, just in case. Three bags full, sir, that was the drill. At the moment they were on the farside of the cobbled yard, talking to a tall thin man wearing baggy cord trousers and a polo-necked sweater under a tweed jacket, trainer or stable manager, Dillon guessed. He didn't know it for a fact, but the horses all looked like thoroughbreds, a row of glossy necks and proud heads arched over the stable doors, lively, intelligent brown eyes. He wondered how many of them Ali Baba owned.

Dillon wrinkled his nose. Was that horseshit or what?

He said, 'And for chrissakes, Steve, make sure we get the right route back to London. We go the same way we got here, we'll never get back.' He leaned nearer, sus-picions confirmed. 'An' I told you, use some deodorant, you stink!'

Steve sniffed his armpits. 'It's not me!' he protested, and nearly poked a hole through the map with his pen. 'Your fault – you said Newmarket was near Ascot!'

'Give. You always were bloody useless on directions.' Dillon snatched the map off him and glared at it with weary disgust. Thirty-grand silver Merc and they were using a Little Chef free road map to ferry their clients the length and breadth of the Home Counties . . .

'I told you, Steve, get a decent map . . . we need to check

how we're going for gas.' There was a low rasping sound as Steve released a fart. 'Very funny,' Dillon said. He glanced worriedly at the fuel gauge. 'We got any cash?'

'I'm skint.'

'We can't ask them.' Dillon looked across the cobbled yard to the two Arabs. The slim dapper one, Salah Al-Gharib, was beckoning, his gold ring winking in the sunlight. 'Hey, they want you.' Dillon nudged Steve. 'Go on. I'll check the route.'

Grumbling, Steve climbed out, and shambled over. Dillon swore, long and loud, discovering his squashed cap Steve had been sitting and farting on. He bashed it into shape, too busy straightening the bent peak to notice Steve was shaking his foot in the air, having trodden in a heap of fresh horse dung.

The black and chrome JVC stereo deck (nearly five hundred quid's worth) was the first item on the agenda. It smashed through the upstairs window and landed on the concrete path, disintegrating in a tangled heap of plastic and metal and solid-state circuitry.

Taffy stood at the broken window, spick and span in parade-drill order, maroon beret pulled low over the left eye in the approved Parachute Regiment manner, and let fly with a stream of tapes, CDs and records, showering down over the scrubby patch of lawn. A portable TV set followed, and a transistor radio followed that, hurled out with a methodical calm efficiency that was strangely at odds with the crazed, wide-eyed expression on Taffy's face.

The front door opened and the phantom drummer shot out, dreadlocks flying, a look of sheer terror in his eyes. He stumbled down the path, screaming abuse as a bass drum smashed an even bigger hole in the window and scored a direct hit on the garden gnome casting his rod in the flower bed. Out sailed the rest of the drum-kit, hi-hat cymbals setting up one hell of a racket as they skimmed and bounced into the road.

101

Mary came out of the kitchen next door and ran screaming round the side of the house, arriving to see Taffy
emerging through the front door. 'Oh God Almighty –
what have you done?'

Taffy strode down the garden path, kicking the mangled
remains of the stereo deck out of his way. 'Got some peace
and quiet,' Taffy said. 'That's what I've done.'

He turned sharp left through the gate, straightened his
shoulders, and setting his beret at the correct angle,
marched off.

'Where are you going? . . . *Taff?*'

'For a quick drink,' Taffy said, arms swinging.

Dillon was crouched forward in the passenger seat, brow
furrowed, speaking on the portable phone: 'I told her
this morning! I mean, what am I supposed to do, Susie?
Hello . . . ?'

He shook the handset. 'This ruddy thing keeps cutting
out . . . Hello?' He shook it again, and this seemed to do
the trick. He listened, nodding, and in a quick muttered
aside to Steve: 'It's Taffy's wife again, she's freakin' out
about something.' He said into the phone, 'Susie? Can you
hear me . . . ? Okay, give her this number, if she calls
again, or you get her number, but Susie – '

Snap, crackle, pop.

'Bloody hell! Hello . . . can you hear me?'

Steve nudged his elbow. 'Here they come.'

'I got to go,' said Dillon quickly. 'Don't call me unless
it's an emergency, 'cos I'm working!'

He cradled the handset and hopped out, tugging his
jacket straight and squaring up his cap.

'London, sir?' Dillon asked, opening the rear door.

Salah Al-Gharib gave a curt nod. 'White Elephant,' he
said, climbing in after the big man.

Dillon pulled a face at Steve through the window, who
returned Dillon's blank look with one of his own. Dog
track? Indian restaurant? Mosque?

All the way down the M11 Dillon anxiously watched

the red needle of the fuel gauge creeping to within a hair's breadth of Empty. Finally, scared to death they were going to run out, he ordered Steve to pull off at the service station just outside Epping. Luckily the clients were going through some papers, taking no notice; even so, Dillon blocked their view of the petrol pump meter as he carefully measured out £2.72 pence' worth to the drop, then surreptitiously palmed the handful of loose change from Steve. Now they were both skint.

It didn't take them long to find him. Taffy's glass of Murphy's stout was still half-full when the phantom drummer's redheaded older brother, a couple of his mates in tow, walked into the saloon bar. Three customers took one look and shifted rapidly out of the way, leaving Taffy alone on his bar-stool in the corner. Slowly, all the time in the world, Taffy turned his head to look at them. They were a mean-looking bunch but his expression didn't alter, kept its same level, sullen stare, unimpressed by this walking pond-life.

'Oi! You three – ' The landlord was across, pushing his rolled-up shirtsleeves further up his arms, pointing at the door. 'Out! Out now!'

Taffy's red head neighbour stopped in the middle of the floor, head lowered like a bull about to charge, eyes glittering. 'Gonna have you,' he murmured softly, just loud enough for Taffy to hear. 'You want to come outside?'

'Police – call the police,' the landlord told the blonde barmaid, who scuttled to the phone. He put both hands flat on the counter and leaned forward. 'Did you hear me? I'm calling the cops. Now – all of you – out. Get out!'

Redhead and his mates stood their ground, a tight little knot of hatred, and as the landlord raised the hatch, Taffy saw a stealthy movement and there was a knife in the redhead's hand.

'No trouble, lads . . . come on now . . .'

Taffy stood up. He lifted both hands, palms open, to indicate that he didn't want any trouble either. The redhead came for him. Taffy side-stepped, got an elbow lock on the knife-arm, twisted the redhead round to the bar with his arm up his back, wrist bent double. Taking the knife off him, Taffy dragged his head back by his red hair and slit his throat.

'Put your hat on,' said Steve. 'Get the doors open!'

While Dillon rammed his cap on and fixed his tie his eyes never left the wing-mirror, which he'd been anxiously studying for the past fifteen minutes. He gripped the door-handle and said, 'You clocked that red Sierra parked at the back of us? They've been around the block twice and come back. They seem very interested in us . . .'

Steve flicked the air-spray round the back of the car and switched on the engine. He waggled his thumb urgently, indicating that Dillon better attend to the clients, stepping out of the White Elephant after a dinner that probably cost as much as Susie spent on food in a month.

Dillon held the door open, and while they were settling in he glanced sideways under the peak of his cap, attempting to make out the occupants of the Sierra and how many. In the darkened interior he saw the glow of a cigarette, nothing more.

He nipped round and climbed in. 'Back to base is it, sir?' Dillon inquired, glued to the wing-mirror. Steve flashed the indicator and pulled out into Curzon Street, the Sierra's dimmed headlights springing on. It began moving off without indicating.

'Yes,' the secretary replied, polishing his gold-rimmed spectacles. 'Then that's it for today!' His boss, the big man, was dozing off, hands clasped comfortably on the swell of his paunch, recently replenished.

Steve drove up Park Lane, crossing into the right-hand stream to make the approach into Oxford Street. At this late hour, traffic was fairly light, at least by London standards, and Dillon could see the red Sierra merging into the same lane, two cars behind. He spoke quietly, hardly moving his lips, 'Keep your eye on 'em, they're right behind us.'

Steve nodded, the Mercedes surging smoothly forward, whisper-quiet under the power of its three-litre, 140 bhp engine. Dillon, after a minute's private debate with himself, inclined his head to the rear of the car. He kept his voice calm, no sign of agitation.

'Excuse me, sir . . . we've got someone following us. They were parked outside the Club, and they've been on our tail since we left. It's a red Sierra – take a look for yourself.'

Raoul Al-Mohammed immediately blinked open his heavy eyes and with his secretary turned to stare out of the tinted back window. They turned back, eyes locked together.

'Are you sure they are following?' the secretary asked quietly, leaning forward.

'wE cAN maKe SUre iF yOU liKe . . .'

'What did he say?'

'We can drive around a bit,' Dillon explained, 'see if they are really following . . . Okay?' He glanced behind and got a single, firm nod.

Steve was too expert and experienced a driver to tip off those behind that they'd been rumbled. Besides, this wasn't ideal territory to lose a tail. Better to get them into a warren of back streets they possibly weren't too familiar with – but he was. So in no great hurry he turned into Tottenham Court Road and proceeded at a stately pace towards Euston Road, eyes doing a constant slow swivel from the road to the rearview mirror. Actually, he was starting to enjoy himself. The Merc was a joy to drive, he'd never got his mitts on such a large powerful, beautiful motor before. Plus – and it was a big plus – he felt the old tingling thrill of pitting himself against an adversary. Didn't matter who: it was the enemy, the bad guys, the ones who had to be beaten at all costs. That's what he'd been trained to do, and Civvy Street had no use for his talents and specialist skills. No use for him, period.

Slowing for the traffic lights at the junction with Euston Road, Dillon turned round in his seat. It was make-your-mind-up time, so he called for a decision. 'He's still with us, what do you want us to do?' He raised his eyebrows. 'We head back into Regent's Park and we'll play follow-my-leader all the way back to the house . . .'

Salah Al-Gharib moistened his lips. 'What is the alternative?' he asked, and now his voice had the suggestion of a tremor in it.

Steve sucked in air, burped, 'I can lose 'em, Frank. No problem.'

'You sure?'

At Steve's nod, Dillon turned back and said tersely, 'He thinks he can lose them, sir.'

The lights changed, and being in the left-hand lane Steve had no choice but to turn left into Euston Road. There was a confab going on in the back, the secretary doing most of the talking, his boss interjecting the odd comment or question now and then. Both men seemed distinctly uneasy, rather fearful in fact, Raoul Al-Mohammed clutching his alligator-skin briefcase to his chest, resting it on his heaving stomach.

At last the secretary leaned forward. Behind the thin gold rims, the whites of his eyes gleamed against his dark complexion. 'If it is possible, lose them. Do what you have to do.'

Dillon touched Steve's arm. He took off his cap and said to the men in the back, 'You want to put your seat-belts on?'

They did so, Dillon pulling his tight. Steve operated central locking, securing all four doors, took a long searching look in the mirror, and put his foot down.

13

In the illuminated green dial the needle swept smoothly past fifty. Steve kept his foot down, the acceleration pressing them back in their seats . . . fifty-five — sixty — sixty-five in less than seven seconds, the needle hovering at seventy as they neared Regent's Park.

Through the wing-mirror Dillon had a clear view of the red Sierra, lagging behind but gradually picking up speed to match theirs; nothing in-between them now and very little traffic, so the two cars had virtually this entire stretch of road to themselves.

Dillon hadn't a clue what Steve intended doing. He hoped to God Steve had. But what Steve did, totally unexpectedly, as they raced towards the lights at the junction with Great Portland Street, was to flick on the left indicator. Crazy, Dillon thought, lost his marbles, Steve meant to turn into a one-way system, meeting the flow of traffic head-on! They were doing seventy, and Dillon braced himself for the turn, but what Steve did next was even crazier. Twenty yards from the lights he decelerated, and spinning the wheel hand-over-hand in a continuous, co-ordinated movement, he swung the Merc sharply to the right in a sliding 180-degree turn, tyres squealing and smoking, leaving burnt rubber on the tarmac as he completed a U-turn at the traffic lights and gunned back along Euston Road.

Rocking in his seat, Dillon glimpsed the flash of red in the mirror as the Sierra skidded into the turn, nearly losing its traction, then righted itself and came after them.

Whoever they were, these guys weren't amateurs, Dillon realised. And the Sierra had more soup under its bonnet than its un-extraordinary exterior might suggest. He ought to have known that playing nursemaid to a couple of Middle-Eastern arms-dealers wouldn't turn out to be a vicarage tea-party. What had that prat Cliff gotten them into, him and his favours?

Nudging seventy-five, Steve took the centre lane down into the underpass, the yellow lights inset in the concrete walls smearing like racing stripes along the aerodynamic silver body. The 300SE barrelled through the echoing tunnel and up again onto the main road, the glass and granite splendour of the mainline Euston terminal flashing by to their left. The traffic lights were changing to red, but Steve went through them anyway, and so did the Sierra, as a glance in Dillon's wing-mirror confirmed. After that hair-raising U-turn back there he was beyond offering Steve any advice. The lad might be crazy but he could handle the Merc all right, sitting back in his seat, head up, arms at full stretch, displaying the cool nerve and aplomb of a stunt driver, a faint grin on his face.

All four of them were flung against their seat-belts as Steve suddenly slammed on the brakes and veered left off the main road, taking to the labyrinth of dimly-lit streets backing onto King's Cross. To Dillon it was a dark maze of terraced houses and small blocks of flats, shops and pubs, the whole area shut down for the night. Every street a replica of the one before. Not to Steve, apparently, who seemed to know the district like the back of his hand, jinking left and right and judging gaps between cars parked either side as if he possessed a built-in slide rule.

But the red Sierra was a tough bastard to shake. It kept right with them, never more than fifty yards behind, headlights now on full-beam flaring in the mirrors.

Without warning, Steve hauled the car down a right-hand fork, the brick archway of a rail viaduct looming up ahead. He gave himself a quick nod, as if making up his mind, and half-turning his head but keeping his eyes front and centre, rapped out: 'Tell 'em I can double back on the Ford – there's dead-ends all along here.'

Dillon craned back. 'You want us to stop their car? We can double back, come out behind them . . .'

A quick gabble of Arabic, and the secretary gripped

108

Dillon's shoulder, his usual fluent English jerking out disjointedly.

'. . . we have no diplomatic immunity . . . they could be armed . . . we cannot risk . . .'

'Hang on, Steve.' Dillon reckoned it was about time to view the situation realistically. One thing, letting Steve have his fun like a big kid on the dodgems, quite another to find themselves in the middle of a shooting war that was none of their business. He said quietly, 'They seem to think these guys'll have guns. Maybe just lose them.'

Steve pointed to the fuel gauge. 'Petrol . . . no petrol.'

Dillon stared at the needle, hard against Empty, and closed his eyes. That was that then. Hobson's Bleeding Choice. He glanced behind. 'Get down – keep your heads down.' He shot a look at Steve. 'Can you handle it?' Steve grinned. Bastard was loving every minute. Best time he'd had in three years, since leaving the Paras.

Dillon had another disquieting thought, concerning thirty grand's worth of Mercedes-Benz 300SE. He turned to the rear, raising one eyebrow. 'What about damage to the car, sir?' The secretary was huddled in the corner, his fingers digging in the padded arm-rests.

'Sir?'

'Please . . . get us out of here . . .'

Steve adjusted his grip, hands crossed on the wheel, face lit up like a Christmas tree. 'Here we go . . . !'

The Merc slewed to the left, did a shimmy with its rear end, the bumper almost scraping the road, then went like the clappers as Steve jammed his foot to the floor. Two more screeching turns and they were back at the brick viaduct, which was exactly where Steve wanted to be – this time passing through the adjacent archway. A flick of the wheel, foot hard down on the brake-pedal. Hidden momentarily by the central arch, the Merc went into a spinning half-turn just as the Sierra shot out from under the bridge and passed them, the driver's head whipping round in dismay and disbelief.

Steve whooped.

Gotcha!

Grinning from ear to ear, he applied reverse lock and the Merc's tyres steamed as he performed another spinning half-turn, gave the 140 bhp engine its head and zoomed up behind, the Sierra's arse-end in his sights.

Closing fast, he gave the Sierra a gentle nudge, pulled away and gave it a harder one. There was the tortured sound of grinding metal and then a clang as the Sierra's bumper was wrenched half-off, the dangling end scything a trail of orange sparks down the centre of the road. Getting desperate, the driver took the only evasive action he could, picking at random one of the streets to his left to get the hell out of the way. Turned out it was a desperate mistake too, because as Steve was well aware, all those streets finished in a sheer brick wall that bordered the tracks out of King's Cross.

The Sierra's driver very quickly got the message. Reacted fast too – but by then all he could do was slam on the brakes and helplessly watch, frozen at the wheel, as the car went into a skid and slid sideways, left side on, smack into the wall.

Dillon expected Steve to slow down, but unbelievably the crazy bastard didn't. He kept right on going. He was doing what he'd been trained to do, following the anti-terrorist manual to the letter: when you have the enemy pinned down and cornered, take all effective steps for total disabling action. In this case it meant ramming the Merc's beautiful gleaming bonnet into the side of the Sierra, trapping the two men inside and preventing further hostile action.

Dillon covered his face. In the back seat the two Arabs were crouched double, petrified with fear, the big man uttering a kind of sing-song dirge. Steam hissed out, and there was a fizzing and crackling as the electrics shorted, the fascia display flickering like mad.

Dropping his hands, Dillon peered through the steam rising from the crumpled bonnet. The Sierra's driver was slumped over the wheel, his head at a nasty angle. Blood was streaming from the other man's nose, and he looked groggy, but then Dillon saw his hand move – saw him reaching inside his jacket – and he didn't wait to see any more, screaming at Steve, 'Back off! Back off!'

There was a horrible jangled cacophony of tearing metal as Steve reversed, leaving the Merc's radiator grille and the remnants of all four headlights in the roadway. Dillon was out even before the car had stopped, flat to the ground, snaking forward on elbows and insteps. Behind him, Steve scuttled head down below window-level and did a neat shoulder-roll to land up against the Sierra's front wheel.

Dillon pointed to the door handle, pointed at Steve, made a twisting motion. Steve nodded and reached stealthily for the handle. Dillon rocked himself onto the balls of his feet, hands curled, ready to make the dive the instant the door was opened. The man inside the car was yelling something, difficult to know what because his voice was high-pitched with panic. Cautiously, Dillon raised his head and took a peep. Steve did the same. They bobbed back down again and stared at each other with a sagging, sickly realisation.

Not a gun the man had been reaching for at all. But a badge. He was holding up a silver badge. The man was a police officer and they'd just rammed a Flying Squad car.

Squatting on his haunches, Taffy listened to the police siren getting nearer and nearer. Further off in the distance, the clanging of an ambulance bell. The two sounds converged, competing with one another, loud and clamouring, and then suddenly died away as both vehicles reached the pub three streets from where Taffy was crouching in a vegetable patch in someone's back garden. Reflected on the chimneys and slate roofs opposite, flashing blue and red lights, like the blue and red tracer fire spewing from the machine-gun emplacement the night they took Mount Longdon. Some of the blokes thought it made a pretty display, arcing out of the darkness, until they remembered

111

that between each blue and red streak there were five live rounds, any one of which could have your name on it.

That had been some firefight. Taffy's bowels had become liquid and he'd nearly cacked in his britches. Belly-down in a rocky crevice, cushioned by his bergen, he'd stuck the business end of his L1A1 SLR rifle over the top and pumped the trigger. Didn't matter a flying fuck what you were aiming at, the object was to overwhelm the enemy with sheer firepower. That John Wayne Hollywood crap about picking off individual targets, with your head out in plain view, was strictly for the punters. You kept your finger on the trigger until the magazine was empty, slapped in a fresh mag, did it all over again. There was always more ammo where that came from, there was only one of you.

And yet, for all the bowel-churning fear, it was bloody great. What you'd sweated through years of training for, and never dreamed, in all your wildest hopes and imaginings, to be actually engaged in a live firing attack against a real enemy who were trying to kill you. Suddenly everything made sense. You had a role, an identity, a purpose. You were doing the job you'd been made for, doing it with skill, guts, pride, and total uncompromising commitment, and you were going to show those Argie bastards what it was like to come up against a real soldier.

That's what Taffy had been then, a real soldier, still was, always would be.

A fine chill drizzle settled on his face. Time to get mustered. In FIBUA training – Fighting In Built-Up Areas – he'd had to crawl through sewer pipes as a means of infiltrating enemy lines, but bugger that for a lark. Taffy didn't fancy the Cardiff sewerage system, and besides, speed and distance were the top priorities.

Spitting on his palms, Taffy dug into the soft damp earth and plastered his face, smeared the backs of his hands. He could hear shouts now, running footsteps. He straightened up, and taking a couple of deep breaths, ran swiftly across the garden and leapt at the high brick wall,

112

scaling it with ease, and dropped down into the deep shadow of a cobbled alleyway, light as a cat.

A few minutes after 1.30 a.m. he was standing on the hard shoulder of the ring road that connected with the M4. Probably his uniform helped, because only the third truck he thumbed – a Bristol meat packer's refrigerated artic – slowed down and pulled over.

Taffy climbed on board.

14

From the holding cell Dillon, tieless, beltless, and with no laces in his shoes, was taken two floors up to the interview room. Little more than a cell itself; a bare table, one metal ashtray, two chairs, a sixty-watt bulb in a green plastic shade that threw a cone of light over the man already seated there, somewhere in his thirties with puffy, handsome features gone to seed and a flourishing head of hair streaked with grey that overlapped his collar. He was smoking a Marlboro, and he offered the packet as Dillon sat down opposite him, more out of icy politeness than as a gesture of friendship. And his voice too had an antiseptic ring to it.

'Mr Dillon. I am Alastair Sawyer-Smith.' He pushed a rather dog-eared card across the table. 'I am acting on behalf of Mr Salah Al-Gharib.'

'Thank Christ –' Dillon accepted a light, sucked in smoke. He had a headache and his eyes burned. It was long gone three and he felt strung-out. 'Look, this has all got out of hand . . . and I have to call my wife, she'll be worried stiff.'

But Sawyer-Smith wasn't listening, glancing instead to a man staring in through the glass panel in the door, studying Dillon hard. Dillon met his eyes and quickly turned his head away, recognising him as the detective who had followed him and Jimmy the day they delivered the diamonds. Whom Jimmy had clobbered and cracked his skull in the gutter.

'Oh shit,' Dillon muttered, closing his eyes.

'I hope you will co-operate fully, as this has been an exceedingly long night. Firstly –'

'It was all a misunderstanding,' Dillon was at pains to explain.

'My clients have been released,' continued Sawyer-Smith smoothly, 'without any formal charges being pressed. Furthermore – '

'What about me and Steve? We've been here all night – your clients got us into this!'

'No, you are mistaken,' Sawyer-Smith contradicted him gravely, his baggy-eyed stare perfectly level. 'The reason the police followed the Mercedes driven by your associate Mr Steven Harris was because the car is owned by a man currently under police investigation.'

Dillon slowly leaned forward into the light, the scar on his left cheek a thin cruel crevice. 'What . . . ?'

But the lawyer had it signed and sealed, all stitched up.

'Clearly you were working for my clients under false pretences, fraudulently using documents which they believed were from the Samson Security Company – a company that denies all knowledge of either hiring you or the driver of the vehicle, Mr Harris.' Having his man on the floor, Sawyer-Smith put the boot in. 'Mr Harris, who by-the-by has no licence, no insurance, and was given a suspended sentence in January of last year . . .'

'But . . .' Dillon's hands came up, clutching thin air. 'I wasn't driving . . .'

'No doubt the security company will take this matter up personally.' Sawyer-Smith got to his feet, picking up a somewhat shabby briefcase with a broken clasp. He looked down on Dillon. 'As far as my clients are concerned, they have agreed to forget the whole embarrassing episode.'

'But what about the damage to the Merc?' Dillon was half-out of his seat, blinking rapidly. 'It's not mine – who's gonna pay for that?'

For the first time Alastair Sawyer-Smith permitted himself a fleeting chilly smile. 'I would say that is the least of your problems, Mr Dillon,' and was gone, leaving Dillon with a dazed expression and two smoking stubs in the metal ashtray.

A shave, a bath, ten hours' kip, that's what Dillon wanted,

but it wasn't what he got. Immediately he entered the flat, Steve shambling behind, it was bedlam. He ignored the phone ringing in the hallway and was confronted with Susie's distraught face as she came charging through from the kitchen.

'Where in God's name have you been?' Susie jabbed at the phone. 'You'd better answer it, Frank, they've been calling all morning – half the night.'

Dillon turned haunted, red-rimmed eyes on Steve. 'Jimmy couldn't know about the Merc yet, could he?'

'Frank, answer it.' Susie gave him a shove. 'It'll be the police!'

'We just come from them, we got bail – ' Dillon tried to grab her as she brushed past. 'Don't answer it . . . *Susie!*'

Somebody hammered on the front door. Susie held her arms out. 'Don't answer, don't open the door,' she warned Dillon, but it was too late, Steve already had. He took one look and slammed it shut.

'It's Jimmy!'

'Open this door, you bastards!' The door shook under the onslaught of kicks and thumps. 'Open it or I'll smash it!'

Dillon said wearily, 'Let him in . . .'

Susie shook her head at Dillon, her eyes large and fear-filled, as the phone finally stopped ringing. 'Frank, you should have answered that.'

The tiny hallway was suddenly filled with bodies as Jimmy swelled the crowd. He swept Steve aside contemptuously and stopped in front of Dillon, his face livid with fury. 'I've just seen that heap of metal they towed . . . *towed* into the garage. Thirty grand's worth, completely wrecked!'

Dillon swayed out of reach as Jimmy threw a swinging right, knocked his arm away. It was Dillon's turn to see red. 'We've had the friggin' Flying Squad chase us all over London, and we got arms dealers in the back, thought they were gonna be kidnapped.' He pointed at Steve and himself. 'We thought it was an ambush!'

116

'Flying Squad? Pull the other one,' Jimmy snorted. He kicked out at Steve, who shied away. 'It was this . . . this *lunatic*.' He landed a stinging smack across Steve's head. 'You get pissed – was that it?'

Dillon got between them, held Jimmy off with the flat of his hand, quietly simmering.

'You think if I'd known it was Newman's car we'd have used it? You should have told us!'

'I told you he was in Spain. I was doin' you a favour – '

'Bullshit!' Dillon stuck his finger under Jimmy's nose, his eyes blazing. 'Now he owes us one. You tip him off – he's under investigation.'

'Frank!' Susie said. And then screamed it. '*Frank*!'

Dillon snapped, 'Get in the kitchen, get out,' not through with Jimmy by a long chalk. 'We're up for wrecking a patrol car, falsifying records, and that cop you whacked – he was there. He was clocking me. I could go down for this, but by Christ, I'll – '

He wasn't allowed to finish as Susie gripped his arm with both hands and literally dragged him through the doorway.

'Frank – if you don't come in here this minute I'll scream the place down!'

'You got a code book?' Jimmy was rooting on the hall table, scattering the two fat London directories.

'If you're calling Spain, make it collect!' Dillon yelled, vanishing as Susie pulled him into the living-room and slammed the door.

Footsteps marched along the landing and in barged Cliff, sweat covering his black brow, lips twisted in a snarl. 'Thanks lads!' he yelled, and seeing Steve, hurled his chauffeur's cap and jacket at him, hysterical with rage. 'Thanks a bundle, you bastards! You really done me in!'

Dodging round Jimmy, crouched over dialling the international operator, Cliff went for Steve, clipping him on the side of the jaw. Steve crashed against the door, just as it opened and Dillon came through it like a rat out of a trap. He parried a wild lunge from Cliff, who was lashing out in all directions, yelling, 'Eighteen months I've had that job!' taking another wild swing at Dillon for good measure.

There was a deadly calm about Dillon. An icy stillness etched into his face and menacing blue eyes. Almost in slow-motion he swivelled his body, taking the blow harmlessly on his shoulder, and hit Cliff with a short-arm jab to the solar plexus that doubled him over, clutching his stomach.

Dillon took the phone out of Jimmy's hand and Jimmy snatched it back, ready to take a sock at him. But the look on Dillon's face stopped him.

'Shut it – all of you!'

The unmistakable voice of Sergeant Frank Dillon stopped everybody.

'Put the phone down, Jimmy. Taffy Davies has gone AWOL. He's killed a bloke in Cardiff . . .'

The four ex-Paras looked at one another, all grudges, personal grievances and petty hatreds wiped off the slate.

Dillon said quietly, 'I think he's headin' for Aldershot.'

Taffy jumped from the slippery scaffolding pole and splashed knee-deep through the ice-flecked surface of the water-jump, clawing up the steep muddy bank on all-fours. Breath pluming the air, streaming with sweat, he gritted his teeth and slogged it up the meandering valley set with man-made obstacles and natural hazards. Designed to test heart, lungs and legs to the utmost, every recruit had to do two continuous circuits of the notorious Steeplechase in order to pass 'P' Company selection. But those behind him on the course were young men, not an old campaigner on the downward slope of forty.

Even so, they could run their goolies off and they'd never catch him! He's still beat 'em!

Punishing himself, chunnering to himself, giving himself orders, Taffy ran ahead of the field, maintaining a clear lead. He reached the crest of Heartbreak Hill, not even pausing to glance behind at the straggling figures in red

118

singlets, blue shorts and plimsolls before plunging down the narrow track through gorse and brambles.

Thump-thump-thump-thump-thump –

It was a joyous sound, healthy and pure, the steady pounding rhythm of his own heartbeat.

Dillon came out of the guardhouse and stopped to have a word with one of the MPs at the main gate. He nodded his thanks and walked past the two police patrol cars parked just inside the striped-pole barrier, returning to the others sitting in the Renegade jeep next to the perimeter fence. Jimmy was standing up in the back with field glasses, doing slow sweeps of Browning Barracks and the wooded hillside beyond. He glanced down as Dillon came up, and shook his head.

Dillon leaned against the jeep's wheel cowling, gazing round and tugging distractedly at his moustache. 'Law's been here for hours, nobody seems to know anything. Army's desperate to keep the Press out of it.'

'He could be anywhere, Frank,' Jimmy said gloomily.

Dillon nodded and sighed. He stepped up onto the running board, about to climb into the bucket seat when his eye fell on the old Dakota on its swathe of grass outside the Regimental Museum. Somebody was sitting under the shadow of the wing, hunched against one of the plane's fat rubber tyres which hid him from the main gate. Somebody in a DPM Denison smock and Red Beret.

Dillon stepped down. He said quietly, 'Keep the MPs busy. I'm going over the fence. I've found him . . . he's by the Dakota.'

Taffy squinted up into the sunshine, hearing the clatter of blades as a Lynx helicopter whirred across the blue sky and vanished beyond the flat rooftops of the barracks. Face caked with mud, hands filthy and scratched from the run, he felt bone-weary. Not just from lack of sleep, and the gruelling punishment of the Steeplechase, but weary deep inside. He closed his eyes and rested his head against the wheel, the shrill whine of the Lynx's engine and thudding blades fading away in the distance.

The sound reverberated inside Taffy's head, seemed to expand, become magnified into the thunderous roar of four mighty Hercules engines at full bore. Slipstream howled in the open doorway and swirled inside the C–130's cavernous interior, two rows of heavily-kitted men hanging onto the strops which attached the static lines to the cables running the length of the aircraft. Third man to go, Taffy's eyes were locked on the red light, waiting for the green. He experienced the familiar sensation of a nest of vipers writhing in his stomach. At the head of the line, first man to go, Dillon stood in the doorway, the wind rippling the flesh of his face in waves, eyes slitted against the blast.

'Tell off for equipment – check!' shouted the despatcher. 'Stand by for green, Number One – check! Number Two – check! Number Three – check!'

That was him. Shuffle forward. Left hand gripping the strop. Make sure the static line runs free. Other hand holding the container bag to his stomach. Ready for the despatcher's cuff on the shoulder, telling him to go. Taking a breath, preparing to scream out as you leap into space, 'One thousand . . . two thousand . . . three thousand . . . check canopy!'

Here we go, boys. Showtime. Shit or bust.

Tensing his entire body, Taffy got ready to jump, the roar of engines and howl of wind buffeting his eardrums.

'Taff . . . Taffy . . .'

Taffy opened his eyes to silence, sunshine, blue sky. A slight breeze rippling over the grass. 'You come for me, Frank?'

'Yeah, me and a few of the lads.' Standing next to the propellor blade, Dillon edged forward, eyes smiling but wary. 'Don't want the wankers in blue takin' you in.'

Taffy stared at the ground. 'I beat those new recruits,' he said with quiet pride. 'Not made of the same stuff today, are they? I went the whole course in me rubbers . . .'

He indicated his heavy, rubber-soled boots, thick with mud and dried leaves.

Dillon came a little closer. A muscle moved in his cheek. His throat was tight and dry, his eyes unnaturally bright, moist.

'I couldn't make it in civvies, Frank,' Taffy said slowly, and gave a sad half-smile. 'Price of beer, that was the first thing that knocked me sideways.' His hand was gripping something, but Dillon couldn't see what. He edged nearer as Taffy said, his face stiff and tense, 'I didn't let the Regiment down, Frank.'

'You never did, Taff.' Dillon saw it was his parade baton that Taffy was holding. He squatted on his haunches next to the big Welshman, elbows on his knees. 'Maybe it let you down,' he said.

'Bloody stupid . . . I don't know what came over me.' Taffy choked down a sob, wiped his wet eyes with the back of his hand. 'If I'd have waited, I'd have been okay.'

Dillon's fists involuntarily clenched as Taffy delved into his pocket, and Taffy looked at him with hurt, reproachful eyes.

'It's over, Frank,' he said softly. 'I've no fight left in me.' He held up a grubby, folded envelope. 'Want to show you this, maybe you'd be interested.' He pulled out a letter for Dillon to see. 'There's work going, if you want it, cash in hand. Up in Scotland, on the salmon farms. They want blokes like us. You know, pro's to . . . to try and catch the poachers. You'd have to live rough, and you'd need . . .' his throat worked. 'Ammo, tents, night-lights – '

A spasm raked through him, and his face suddenly crumpled. Dillon took the letter and put it in his pocket. He eased down on the grass, next to Taffy.

'I just snapped, Frank. God forgive me. Is the kid dead?' Dillon put his arms around Taffy and hugged him hard. 'Will you take care of Mary? See she's taken care of? Poor Mary, all the time I was in Ireland, she waited for the knock on the door.'

Dillon nodded. 'I'll see her.' The two men stood up, and

Dillon looked him in the eyes. 'You were the best back-up bloke I ever had, and that's what me and the lads are here for now.' He touched his shoulder. 'You know the score?' and then, 'Wait, just a minute,' adjusting Taffy's Red Beret the regulation two inches above the left eye. 'You all set?'

Straightening his shoulders, baton tucked under his arm, Taffy took a deep breath. 'All set!'

The cluster of uniformed police and three MPs at the gate turned as a body as Taffy marched towards them, arms swinging, back ramrod-straight. Chin up, his voice rang out in the best drill-square manner, 'Colour Sergeant Major David Davies reporting!'

Jimmy, Steve and Cliff were lined up by the perimeter fence when Dillon joined them, as if presenting themselves for military inspection. Then all four watched as the open jeep came through the main gate, Taffy seated in the back between two MPs. And all four ex-members of the Parachute Regiment saluted as it went by, Taffy half-turning to give them a brief, farewell smile before snapping round, shoulders squared, eyes front.

As the jeep went down the road they could hear him singing, his big Welsh voice roaring out:
'Ten green bottles
Hanging on the wall,
And if one green bottle
Should accidentally fall,
There'd be nine green bottles
Hanging on the wall . . .'

STEVE HARRIS

15

Dillon had not really paid any attention to the scrap of paper Taffy Davies had thrust into his hands, he didn't even recollect stuffing it into his pocket. The moment Taffy was arrested, seeing him from the back of the wagon as they took him away, turning, that one last time, as Dillon and the boys saluted him, was a moment Dillon would never forget. There was still that flash of pride on the Welshman's face, still that kind of 'take any bugger on, man!', his shoulders straight, his fists tensed, his chin out. But in his eyes hung the shadow of pain, the silent cry for help. There was no one who could give it to him, no one who could get him off a murder charge, or manslaughter with diminished responsibility tagged on the end of it. Taffy knew what he had done and would take his punishment. That was the shadow of pain, he knew, and asked for no pity, just forgiveness.

Susie found the note and stuffed it on the dressing table as she gathered the clothes for the weekly wash. Since Taffy's arrest Dillon had been sullen, uncommunicative, staying in bed until eleven or later. She was surprised when she heard him on the phone, not that she could hear what he was saying as the tumble-dryer sounded like an express train shuddering through the kitchen.

Susie could still hear the phone pinging even when the washing was out of the dryer, and stacked up in the basket for ironing. She was filling the steam iron with water when he breezed in, and dangled the scrap of paper.

'Got a job! Cash in the hand, wallop! Nice little earner, me and the lads'll be gone a couple of weeks.'

'Gone? Gone where?' Susie asked, as she plugged in the iron.

'Scotland, they got problems with poachers.'

He was out yelling up the stairs for Steve to get his gear packed. Susie came to the kitchen door and looked up as Dillon charged up the stairs. 'You're not poaching, are you?'

He leaned over, too far over, as he beamed, 'No sweetheart, we're catchin' 'em, they need army blokes – got to camp out!'

'How long will you be gone for?'

'For as long as it takes . . . OI! Come on you lazy bugger let's be havin' you!'

Susie thudded the iron over the folded sheet on the ironing-board, as footsteps banged and crashed around upstairs. She heard Dillon laughing. They were acting like kids, and she took out her fury on the ironing. He hadn't even asked if she minded, not even bothered to talk it over with her, no sooner home than he was off again.

The doorbell started ringing, and she heard Jimmy arrive, then Cliff, more yells and bangs, and then Dillon walked in with his arms full of dirty washing.

'Some of Steve's gear, can you run it through the washer? The lads have arrived, we'll be off any minute.'

The dirty linen and T-shirts and a couple of pairs of filthy jeans were dumped on the kitchen floor.

'Frank! . . . FRANK! Just shut the door a minute!'

He kicked the door closed, 'What?'

'How long will you be gone?'

'I dunno, but we'll bring you back some salmon.'

'I see, so how much they paying you?'

'Fair whack.'

'Will this mean Steve can find a place of his own? This isn't a ruddy hotel! And it would have been nice if you'd talked it over with me first!'

'Oh, sorry, didn't know I had to ask permission to get a job!'

'Oh, stop it, I just meant that you should have discussed

126

it with me, I don't know how long you'll be gone, you've only just got home!'

He reached out and slipped his arms around her waist. 'It's a job, we make enough dough we maybe can open our own business.'

'Pay that good is it?'

His arms tightened. 'It's good enough, now give us a kiss.'

She put the iron on its end and was about to turn in his arms when Jimmy barged in.

'Come on, we should get cracking, it's a hell of a drive – Hi, Susie – and Frank, can I have a word?'

'What?'

Jimmy inched the door shut. 'You're sure we should take Steve? He's a bloody liability you know!'

Dillon wafted his hand. 'He's coming! You just get the gear loaded, I'll be right out.'

Jimmy hesitated and then winked at Susie. 'Bring you a fresh salmon . . .'

Susie shook her head. 'You sure you lot are catching the poachers not joining them?'

Jimmy laughed, and then looked back to the hallway. 'Let's get on the road then!'

Dillon gave Susie a quick kiss, eager to be gone, and followed Jimmy out. Susie looked at the stack of dirty laundry and began to stuff it into the washing machine, as Steve edged in.

He said something, but she wasn't sure what it was, then he gave a soft pathetic smile. In his crumpled clothes, the scarf he always wore knotted round his throat, his knees showing through his ripped jeans, there was still the ghost of 'The puller' about Steve, the nickname he had because the women always fell for him. Maybe it was the sweet smile, but Susie went over and stood on tiptoe to kiss his cheek. 'You take care of Frank, okay?'

He nodded mutely, then delved into his pockets, and brought out two crumpled ten pound notes. His Donald

Duck voice burped out 'Get something for the kids, and some flowers for you.'

Susie watched them pile into Jimmy's jeep. They waved and yelled up to her from the courtyard as she leaned over the railings. Steve was sitting up in the back with Cliff who was already drinking a can of lager. They were like kids on some kind of school outing, singing at the tops of their voices, happy they were playing at soldiers again. But Susie knew they weren't really playing, Frank wasn't back in civvies, not yet . . . Maybe the time in Scotland would get it out of his system.

The Clyde Hotel was a solid, sturdy building of dark red sandstone that at one time might have been the residence of the local laird. Built on the crest of a small hill, it had magnificent views to the north of Loch Tummel and the Forest of Atholl, and further to the west of the Grampians, grey peaks lightly dusted with snow.

Cliff drove the old Renegade jeep up the curving driveway and halted on the gravel forecourt next to the main entrance. Too early for the hunting-shooting-fishing season, the hotel had a slumbering look about it, an impression reinforced by an ancient sit-up-and-beg bicycle with a straw pannier at the front, propped against the steps.

Climbing out, Dillon has a quick look at the tripometer which they'd set that morning on leaving London. 451. Bloody well felt like it too; his arse was as numb as a witch's frozen tit. Groaning and stretching, Jimmy and Steve jumped down from the back seat they'd had to share with the bags, personal effects and other assorted paraphernalia that Dillon reckoned they needed for the job. More gear than they'd had disembarking at Port San Carlos, Jimmy thought sourly. What were they going to do, invade Perthshire?

'What time do you call this?' Harry Travers clattered down the steps in DPM camouflage pants and army boots, big beefy grin on his chops. He'd put on a few pounds since last Dillon had seen him, but on top of a barrel-chested eighteen stone it hardly mattered, and he looked in fighting trim.

Harry stuck out his hand. 'How ya doin', Jimmy? Frank. This is Don Walker from One Para . . .'

A younger bloke, late twenties, with longish dark hair kept in place by a bandanna, nodded to them from the top of the steps. Harry's grin changed to a scowl as he noticed Steve Harris in the background.

'Hey, what's with Harris? You never said you were bringin' him.' Still grumbling, Harry led Dillon and Jimmy up the steps, Steve trailing after, head down. 'I got a bone to pick with him – he borrowed me mate's Honda Prelude and that was the last we saw of it. He's a prat!'

Left behind with a bag in each hand, Cliff contemplated the loaded jeep and shouted after them as they all disappeared inside, 'Oh thanks lads, thanks a bundle!'

Hamish MacFarland, the hotel's owner, was already well into double figures with the Glenlivet, by Dillon's estimation, as they came into the bar. He was balanced precariously on a bar-stool, glass in one hand, his other arm draped around a stag's head that for some mysterious reason was plonked on the counter next to the beer pumps. Harry did the introductions, and MacFarland invited them all to have a drink with him, 'a wee dram' before dinner. He had another wee dram himself to keep them company.

The mention of dinner got Dillon's gastric juices flowing: motorway coffee and sandwiches had sustained them on the trip, but he realised he was starving. But he forgot about his stomach for a minute when MacFarland's daughter came through to take their orders. And a hush fell amongst the others too, the banter dying away to silence.

Dark hair, shoulder length and naturally curled, a wide mouth that smiled easily, Sissy MacFarland had a creamy complexion that didn't need make-up, lightly sprinkled with freckles, and a figure that most women could only dream of having and every man couldn't help drooling over. She treated their admiring looks and silent whistles with good-natured amusement, not offended, not affected or preening either.

'Can I take orders for dinner?' she asked, looking around, licking the tip of her chewed pencil, using an old notepad to take their orders. She was flushed from cooking, her simple cotton dress had sweat marks under the arm pits and her apron ribbons were undone. She was a mother figure whose curves and heavy breasts encouraged a man to trust her and to want her to cradle him in her lovely strong arms. And when they felt her softness, the desire for those breasts to break free, to be cupped and kissed, made Sissy, sweet Sissy the object of every man's desire. 'Salmon, Jugged hare, roast venison?' She could have said, 'I am free, I am obtainable, I am here for each one of you, I am the woman you dream of!'

The menu received a spontaneous round of applause that set every man laughing, as if knowing each other's minds. 'I'll have that!' Jimmy laughed louder than the others, giving Sissy a wink. 'Eh! Is the rest of him on the menu Gov?' Jimmy pointed to the massive stag's head, still being embraced by MacFarland. 'If it is, I'll have the jugged hare!'

MacFarland didn't seem to get the joke, or the fact that the entire menu was obviously poached. He was getting into a drunken state over his prized stag.

'I brought him down with one shot,' he slurred, misty-eyed with nostalgia bordering on the maudlin. 'They got a big 'un up at the Estate, three grand on his head for anyone lucky enough to get him . . . BUT, he's not a patch on my boy. I had him mounted in Edinburgh, nineteen fifty-five . . .'

Sissy came round taking their orders, getting a lot of smiles and compliments, then she crossed to Steve sitting on the fringe of the group. Steve hadn't taken his eyes off her since the moment she had entered.

'What would you like?' Sissy asked pleasantly and all the lads gave a cheer, knowing full well what Steve would like.

130

Steve gulped air, trying to speak, but nothing came out. The lads were already encouraging Macfarland for another round of his special malt, only Dillon watched Steve. He saw Sissy repeat her question, saw the deep flush come over Steve's face. Sissy thought Steve was just drunk, she said, 'You want the jugged hare?' and he nodded. Sissy went out, back to the kitchens. Busy in her roles as cook, waitress and receptionist she never gave Steve a second thought, but Dillon had seen his helplessness, his deep humiliation at being unable to reply to a simple query. In the old days there could have been competition, Steve would have been in like Flynn. Then he had it down to a fine art, the shy look from his wide beautiful eyes accompanied by a slow, sexy smile, and the toss of his thick black hair, had the women within seconds. The female species couldn't resist him. Now, dirty lank hair hanging over his flushed crimson face, and drunk, befuddled eyes gave no indication of what he had once been capable of as 'The Puller'; all he could do now was stare helplessly into his whisky glass. It was empty. Dillon placed a fresh glass in front of Steve, rubbed his head, and returned to the lads at the bar. He turned back. Steve was looking at him and it was to Dillon that he gave one of his smiles, as he mouthed, 'Thanks Mate.'

Wearing her best outfit, fresh lipstick and Boots' pale peach eyeshadow, Susie Dillon stood at the waist-high counter of Marway MiniCabs, nervously clutching a Sainsbury's carrier-bag of groceries. She hadn't realised till now (Marway hadn't struck her as a foreign name, when she'd noticed the ad in the evening paper) that Mr Marway was Indian, or Sikh, or something – anyway he wore a turban, and had a small pointed beard. Not that it mattered. A job was a job.

Sitting at the control panel, looking a bit out of place in a well-cut dark suit and immaculate collar and tie, Marway spoke into the microphone on its silver stalk. He flicked a couple of switches, checked off the fares on a clipboard, and then gave his attention back to Susie and her somewhat strained smile.

'Day shift is from nine until three, night shift from four until three, and you'll be driven home.' Marway's voice was a dead fit with his appearance, anyway: tasteful, evenly modulated, an educated man, no question.

'I have two boys at school, so that would be fine,' Susie said, anxious to reassure him. 'My husband is working in Scotland . . . I'd need someone to show me how the – er – ' She made a little nervous gesture towards the control panel.

'Of course.'

Marway got up, smiling, lifted the flap in the counter and extended the palm of his hand, bidding her enter. 'What about right now?'

'You mean start straight away?' Susie said, taken aback.

'If it's convenient, and the pay is acceptable.'

Susie's eyes lit up. 'Oh yes! Yes!' She smiled delightedly, absolutely thrilled. 'I've got the job then? Oh, that's marvellous,' she said, taking his hand and shaking it. 'Thank you!'

It was that simple. Literally walking off the street and into a job. She could hardly believe it. Wait till she told Frank! But that thought didn't exactly fill her with unbounded joy, knowing his old-fashioned views on women going out to work when they had a couple of young kids to look after. Anyway, Susie thought defiantly, that's why she was doing this, for the kids, for the family. They needed money, so why not go out and earn it?

Simpler getting a job than actually doing it, Susie soon discovered. Marway wrote out a sheet of instructions, gave her an A-Z, and left her to get on with it. In-between taking calls and relaying instructions to the drivers, she managed to sneak in a call to her mother, asking her to pick up the boys from school. Bit of a white lie, that, telling Marway the job fitted round the school routine. Helen moaned at first, but then agreed, as Susie knew she would.

132

Less than an hour later, Helen rang back. Didn't want to panic unduly, but Kenny was complaining of a sore throat and his temperature was up. The panel started buzzing and flashing, calls piling up. In a rush, Susie told her to put him to bed, take up his favourite meal if he could face it, fish fingers and beans, chocolate-chip ice cream. She'd be home soon. 'Has Frank called?' she asked before ringing off, and instantly regretted the question even before Helen's reply came through the headphones, tart as vinegar. 'No, he's not called. But then you know him!'

Susie cut her off and went back to work.

'Marway MiniCabs . . . is it cash or account? . . . Be about half an hour, okay . . . Right, your name . . . ?'

Susie was getting the hang of it now, it hadn't taken too long, and as soon as she had got over her initial fear of fouling up the switchboard, she grew less and less flustered. She was actually beginning to enjoy working and the newfound confidence it gave her. If Frank hadn't called, it was nothing new, she'd spent half their married life waiting for him to call or write – at least in Scotland there was no fear of the call or the telegram to say he was dead.

16

Apart from the Tower of London, Dillon couldn't recall ever seeing a real castle, complete with turrets and ramparts, before he laid eyes on McGregor Castle, the centre-piece of the vast McGregor Estate. Riding up in the jeep with Jimmy and Cliff, the castle suddenly presented itself at the head of the glen, grey, jutting, uncompromising, outlined against a clear blue sky with faint wisps of cirrus high above. At the wheel, Jimmy gave a low whistle of awe and admiration, and from the back seat Cliff muttered grudgingly, 'Some have it all, don't they? Bet it freezes the bollocks off 'em in winter.'

The jeep juddered over a cattle grid, and the countryside became more cultivated, with sweeping lawns, groves of trees, and carefully tended flowerbeds. Harry Travers waved them down as they came up the drive and hopped on the running-board, directing them to take a side road leading to the stables and outhouses.

'You know who's in charge, do you, Frank?' Harry looked down, broad florid face and ginger moustache, wide-set piercing blue eyes fixed on Dillon. 'Old friend of yours. Malone.'

Malone. Dillon shot a venomous look at Harry, suspecting that the big man was winding him up. But Harry wasn't smiling.

'He's been in civvies for four years now.'

It was five since Dillon had seen him last. The night Hennessey's Bar went up, and the yellow bastard had run off, left the injured and dying behind, including his own comrades, in that hellish inferno.

Jimmy stopped the jeep outside the stable block. Don Walker, bandanna around his head, was in the paddock, feeding an apple to a beautiful chestnut mare. Don nuzzled the horse's soft nose, whispered to it and at the same time he clocked the lads' arrival, but he made no effort to cross over or even welcome them. He found it difficult to interact with anyone, even his own kind, his shyness and his inability to form personal relationships made him a loner. It was only with the animals that he felt at peace, felt the anger inside fade. Dillon was about to stroll over when a tall black-haired figure, dressed in an old Denison smock, emerged from one of the outhouses into the sunlight. Malone started towards the jeep, and then halted mid-stride, took a pace back as he saw Dillon. The two men locked eyes, the mutual hatred passing between them like a electrical charge.

'Well, well,' Malone said, getting a sneer into his voice, 'finding it tough in Civvy Street, are we, Frank?' Face stiff, black eyes sweeping coldly from Dillon to take in the others. 'Any aggro from any of you and you're on your way, understand?'

'Malone? Can I have a word?'

The estate manager, John Griffiths, appeared at the office door and beckoned him over. A tall, slender, fair-haired man with a beaked nose and receding chin, he had public school written all over him, and sounded it too, a drawling, negligent tone as if all the world was at his beck and call, which of course it was. Jodhpurs tucked into green wellington boots, thick polo-neck sweater, heavily darned, with leather patches on the sleeves, he was fashionably scruffy in the approved upper-class manner, and played the part to perfection.

'You think they'll be enough? Sure they can handle it?' asked Griffiths, nodding to the group clustered round the jeep.

'The dark-haired guy's an ex-sergeant, explosives expert,' Malone said, indicating Dillon. 'We were in the same Regiment. The other four are good, steady soldiers.'

'Yes, well, this isn't exactly a war, Malone,' Griffiths retorted, a trifle testily.

Malone grinned at him insolently, not bothering to hide

135

his distaste. He turned his head to look at Dillon, muttering under his breath, 'Wanna bet?'

Griffiths took Dillon and the others on a tour of the estate, pointing out the lie of the land, and where he felt they were most vulnerable to the poaching gangs. The scenery was breathtaking, but after seeing Malone Dillon wasn't in the mood to have his breath taken. Had he known the score, he wouldn't have accepted the job in the first place. He sat beside Griffiths in an open-topped Land Rover, the rest following on in the jeep, and tried to show polite interest, though his heart wasn't in it.

'Malone tells me you were in the same Regiment.'

'Yes, sir.' Dillon stared straight ahead. 'Then he quit, went over to the RMPs.'

'Explosives expert I believe,' Griffiths said, getting a nod and nothing more. 'How long have you been out of the Army?'

'Couple of months, sir. Eighteen years' service, sir.'

Griffiths pulled over suddenly and produced his field glasses, aiming them towards a rocky crag about five hundred yards away. 'There he is, see him?'

Dillon took the field glasses and found himself gazing at the proud, uplifted head of a magnificent stag with a huge spread of antlers. The animal surveyed the glens and lochs below, his world, his kingdom.

'He's the one with the price on his head, sir?' Dillon said, handing the glasses back.

Griffiths pursed his lips. 'Word certainly travels fast . . . some bloody taxidermist in Edinburgh,' he muttered darkly. 'He's very rare, and with antlers that size, a fair trophy. But he's worth a lot more than five thousand for stud.'

They drove on, Dillon glancing back. Five grand standing up there on the hill. He stroked his moustache, frowning thoughtfully.

Next stop on the itinerary was the main event, and it was clear from the boyish enthusiasm in Griffiths' voice that the salmon tanks were his pride and joy. Enclosed in a compound of chain-link fencing topped with razor-wire, the three huge steel tanks, lined with polythene sheeting, were teeming with full-grown salmon, silver bodies flashing and tumbling in their thousands. To Dillon and the others the sight was mesmerising, almost hypnotic. They stood on a wooden gangway while Griffiths gave them the low-down.

'These are the big 'uns, the ones the poachers go for. We lost the entire stock last year, more than fifty thousand pounds' worth.' Griffiths shook his head. 'Can't afford to lose out this year.'

'How did they do it?' Dillon was curious to know.

'Very simply – Hoover them up! They move fast, and with that machine it doesn't take long . . .'

Cliff's jaw dropped. 'Did he say *Hoover?*'

'You have any guard dogs?' Dillon asked, looking around.

'They were shot with a .22 rifle in '89. Bastards used Cymas that year; they also took the stock from the other tanks, so we were wiped out . . . fish and financially,' he added gloomily.

Dillon jumped down and Griffiths followed him over to the edge of the compound, the two of them looking out at the banks of heather stretching away to the stony ridge. Casting his military eye over it, Dillon was less than happy. 'You're wide open,' he said, rubbing his chin.

Griffiths spread his hands. 'To electrify the fences would be astronomical . . .'

Don Walker strolled up and offered an opinion. 'The one plus – if you can call it a plus – is that these men are professionals and dealing in bulk, so they need big trucks, not only to take the fish away, but to freeze it.'

'I think Malone's right,' Griffiths said. 'Best protection has to be manpower. That's why I got you chaps up here.'

Spoken like an officer, Dillon thought, which was what Griffiths was, in effect, certainly of the officer class.

The estate manager went off somewhere. Don had his

field glasses out, checking the terrain. The other lads were messing about, joking and laughing, and Don waved them over, obviously excited about something.

'There he is, see him?' Don handed the glasses to Jimmy, pointing, chuffed as a schoolboy. 'Just on that ridge!'

'Oh yesssss . . .' The word hissed through Jimmy's grinning mouth. 'A fair set of coat hangers.'

Dillon said, 'Where's the nearest Para base to here, Jimmy?'

Jimmy turned to Dillon with a sly wink.

'This taxidermist on the level, is he? We heard last night he's got three grand on his head.'

Don grabbed the glasses off him. 'You touch him and I'll mount *your* fucking' head,' he promised, and stumped off.

'Nature boy's a bit touchy about the hatstand, isn't he?' Jimmy shrugged, raising an eyebrow.

Dillon said, 'Let's get the security sorted first.' He gave Jimmy a deadpan stare. 'And it's not three, it's five grand.'

'Five?' Jimmy looked towards the ridge and quickly back at Dillon. '*Thousand? Five?*'

They both turned to contemplate the ridge for a moment, and then each other. A low growl of laughter came up from Jimmy's chest and he punched Dillon on the shoulder.

Steve Harris was having one of his filter problems. Leaning against the jeep, face puce, coughing and spluttering, thumping himself. Dillon went over as he was getting his breath back.

'All right, mate?' Steve nodded, sweat glistening on his brow. Dillon fished out a list and gave it to him. 'Okay, I want you to go into the village, get some stores.'

Dillon had intended to hand over the list to Griffiths, but seeing Steve in trouble he decided he would get him out of the way. 'Get yourself rested up, check your filter, okay mate? . . . Steve?'

Steve nodded. At that moment Jimmy walked past, he

gave Steve an icy stare. 'Ruddy liability, I told you not to bring him!'

Dillon glared at Jimmy, then patted Steve's shoulder. 'Pay no attention.'

Steve stuffed the list into his top pocket, and climbed back into the jeep. His breath rattled, a hoarse sound in his chest and he couldn't look at Dillon, knowing he was already making excuses for him. He hated it. He started the engine, released the handbrake.

'Take your time, get back when you're done . . .'

Steve nodded, the errand boy, the waster, the liability. He looked back at Dillon, but he was already walking away, so Steve headed into the village. The simple errand of getting the stores, the packs of beer, the food for the camp was an effort. He had to write everything down and pass the note to the shop owners, and, already feeling depressed, he became worse. He needed a drink, needed something, anything, to give him the confidence to face them.

Hearing the jeep crunching over the gravel, Sissy Mac-Farland nipped out from behind the reception desk and skipped through the doors and down the steps.

'Mr Harris, can I talk to you for a minute?'

Steve nodded, giving her a shy smile. He gulped down some air and brought up a burp: 'Yeah! Sure!'

Sissy looked startled. He was polite all right, and very good-looking too, but she hoped he wasn't drunk at this early hour.

Steve pointed to his throat, swathed in the loose silken scarf, and said in a slow croak so that she understood, 'I just had – my tonsils – out.'

'Oh! I'm sorry.' Sissy smiled, dimples in her cheeks. 'I was wondering when your friends would be back. I really need to talk to them . . .' She bit her lip, and went on anxiously, 'There's two local boys going to get themselves hurt – this Malone could even kill them. They're going for him tonight.'

139

Steve's mouth opened, worked soundlessly. The poor boy's throat must hurt terribly, she thought, because he then scribbled something down on the back of the list and handed it to her. Sissy read it and quickly shook her head, dark curls bounding against her pale neck – 'Och no! It's not Malone they're after . . . It's the stag.'

Steve felt better, he'd put a few pints down, and now he had something to do. It was important, he had to warn the lads about the poachers. He took a heavy swig from a bottle of scotch, and then turned the jeep round to head back to the camp.

Dillon tensed up, listening again for what had sounded like somebody or something disturbing the bracken a few yards away from the hide. Wearing his one-piece DPM combat suit with hood, lying full-length on a bed of straw, he peered through the six-inch gap, trying to discern a distinct shape in the darkness. Not a bloody sausage. Then a low whistle, and Dillon relaxed as Jimmy slithered in, teeth white against his blacked-up face. He crawled between Dillon and Harry, cradling what looked like a brand-new weapon. Dillon stared more closely. An L42 sniper rifle fitted with an IWS night sight.

'I dunno how you do it!' Dillon marvelled, envy in his voice.

'It's all down to contacts,' Jimmy bragged, chuckling.

'That prat Steve come back with the nosh?' Harry grumbled. 'I'm starvin'!'

Dillon reached for the headset as the radio emitted a couple of snaps and crackles. He twisted a dial, boosted the power with the slide control, listening intently for Cliff.

'You know what we should do?' Jimmy ruminated, lovingly running a lightly-oiled rag over the L42. 'Entice him down onto low ground . . . they like apples. We get him as near to the truck as possible – give ourselves a hernia if we try and lift his carcass, and – ' he squinted through the night sight, crooked his finger alongside the trigger. *'Pow!'*

140

'Word of advice, mate – keep stum about nobblin' that stag,' Harry advised him. 'Don's passionate about it!'

Dillon held up his hand for quiet, pressing the tiny button microphone nearer his mouth. 'Zero contact,' he confirmed.

Blur of static and Cliff's voice, clear as a bell.

'Alpha One to Zero. Two kids moving out of grid range south-east. Suspects armed. Looks like a crossbow. Over.'

'Zero to Alpha One. Maintain position and surveillance. Out.' Dillon flicked off, frowning. 'Going the wrong way for the salmon,' he said, and turned to Jimmy, eyes narrowed. 'Sounds like they're after the stag . . .'

'Shit! He's ours.' Jimmy wriggled backwards. 'Okay, I'm on my way.' He hesitated for a second, waiting for the nod from Dillon, and crawled out.

Harry folded his arms and stared morosely into the darkness. 'I wouldn't mind nickin' a salmon,' he said with feeling. 'I'm bloody starvin'.'

Pacing himself, Steve jogged for a quarter-of-a-mile, alternated it with a 'double' – double-quick-time march – over the same distance. To his right, behind the chain-link fence, the compound and the salmon tanks, to his left open countryside. Judging roughly where the hide was, he came off the lane and onto the grass verge, intending to cut across below the ridge. In the pitch-darkness he had some difficulty locating the trip-wire the lads had laid, eventually found it, and carefully stepped over. He set off at an easy run, not because he was knackered, but because the little hummocks of tough, wiry grass were treacherous as hell, and he didn't want to finish up with a sprained ankle or, worse, a broken leg.

Steve had remembered the trip-wire. He'd forgotten about the pressure pads, set at fifty-metre intervals, until he stepped on one, triggering the battery of sulphur flares which zoomed up into the dark sky, blinding white bursts of light that blanked out his vision, turning night into day.

Stumbling, almost falling, blinking furiously, all that

141

Steve could see was a mass of whirling red dots imprinted on his retina. High above, the fizzing flares drifted slowly downwards. Steve covered his face, mouth flapping open and shut, realising too late that he was caught out in the open, exposed to enemy fire. Where was the rest of his section? Why the hell hadn't he taken cover, the first rule when encountering SF, Sustained Fire? Tracer was coming at him. Masses of red streaking dots filling the sky. He heard the rattle of machine-gun fire, opened his mouth to scream, to howl, to cry for help, and nothing came. A mortar shell landed right in front of him, and in the gritty explosion a voice yelling, *Corporal Harris, take cover: Harris, get down! Harris, take cover, get back, Harris, this is an order!*

The voice echoed through Steve's head, but he could see Big Blackie Jeller crunched up, howling with pain, could see him, and no way could he turn back and run for cover. Big Blackie was his mate, and he hesitated just a fraction before he disobeyed the order and went back for him. As he gripped Blackie's hand, he felt the burning red-hot sensation rip through his neck, the blood filled his eyes, his mouth, everything was red, everything was over. Then came the darkness, weeks of darkness, of terror. He didn't remember being stretchered back, airlifted to the hospital, he remembered nothing but that moment of terrible scorching pain, and now it was back, squeezing the life out of him. Rooted to the spot, Steve shook all over, his arms in uncontrollable spasms, fingers twitching, and his mouth, gaping, filled with his own blood, unable to cry out.

Don found him, curled up like a child, hands over his head. For a second Don thought someone had been caught in one of the traps. He slithered and eased his way closer, and then he realised it was Steve. Steve huddled in wretched mute hysteria, his eyes wide, staring into oblivion. Don gently eased him to sit up, but Steve seemed afraid of him, and not until he had wrapped him in his arms repeating that it was all right, that he was safe, did

Don feel the rigid tension released. But Steve's hands were still like a vice, holding on to Don, and Don sat with him, rocking him, talking to him. Don, who was too shy to talk to anyone, understood, had no need for words, because he had been in that darkness, he had been in that mute land of fear.

Steve tried, once, twice, and then burped out, 'Poachers – two kids.' Don gave a pat to Steve. 'Good lad, I'll go tip off the lads . . . they're up in the hide, can you make it there?'

Steve nodded, watching Don move like the clappers, bent low, zig-zagging out of the way of the flares, heading back to the camp. Steve was alone again, listening to his own heartbeat slowly returning to normal, unlike the rest of him, that would never come back.

17

Kids, that's all they were, one of them barely fifteen, caught out there on open moorland which a moment ago had been inky black, now lit up to the horizon with the brightness of a film set.

Even while the shock of it was still registering, their young faces frozen with panic, Harry and Cliff broke from cover, running swiftly and silently down the slope, and were upon them from behind. It was nasty, quick, brutally efficient. Grabbed by their collars, kneed in the back of the legs, stamped into a prone position, faces pushed into the ground, arms twisted behind their backs. Handcuffs slapped on, sacks rammed over their heads, muffling their terrified screams.

Worse was to come, and it came in the shape of Malone, crashing through the bracken, red-faced, veins bulging in his neck. Pumped up like a mad bull, he charged forward and took a vicious, swinging kick at one of the hooded shapes, swung round and booted the other with all his sixteen-and-a-half stone behind it.

'Hey! That's enough, Malone. Back off!'

Dillon ran up as the two boys rolled and squirmed in agony, shrieking and slobbering in pain. 'Cliff, get the bag off the kid's head,' Dillon ordered. And stepped in front of Malone as he was about to land another brutal kick, shoving him in the chest.

Glowering at Dillon, Malone snarled. 'You don't like it? You got somethin' to say about it . . . ?' He extended his hand, fingers curled, gently beckoning. 'Come on then, come on, Dillon, let's have you!'

Dillon didn't move, didn't speak.

Slowly, deliberately, Malone unzipped his quilted jacket and tossed it down, flexing huge shoulders, hairy tattooed arms and hard biceps straining the sleeves of a black T-shirt. He beckoned again, smiling.

'Don't, Frank!' Cliff spoke quietly in Dillon's ear. 'He's a madman, he'll kill you . . . back off him.'

'Don't tell me,' Dillon said in a tone like cold steel, 'what to do.' Turning away, he cupped his hand under the blood-smeared frightened face of one of the boys. 'You okay, son?'

Dillon ruffled the boy's hair, then stooped to pick up Malone's jacket, was about to throw it to him when Malone flicked out a left jab, catching Dillon off-balance. Clutching the jacket in two bunched fists, Dillon took a threatening pace forward.

'Frank – don't,' Harry said, shaking his head.

Cliff stepped in, snatched the jacket from Dillon and handed it to Malone. For perhaps five seconds nobody moved. Everybody waiting to see if Dillon, seething with rage, was going to take Malone on. Nobody else wanted to, but was Dillon the man to do it? Did he have the bottle? The fifteen-year-old kid was whimpering, and as Dillon went to him, wiping blood from the boy's nose, Malone laughed. A loud, derisive laugh from the belly. And, shrugging into his quilted jacket, started to make soft little clucking chicken noises, black eyes glinting with triumphant bravado.

Turning his back on Malone, as if he hadn't heard, Dillon said stonily, 'We got a job to do, all right? Now, let's get on with it!'

But he had heard right enough, and everybody knew it.

Little Phil's hacking cough had awakened her, and as Susie hurried through in her bare feet, Kenny was at it too. She didn't turn on the light, didn't want to wake them. A chink in the curtains let in an orange glow from the corner streetlamp, giving a sepia tint to the glossy photographs pinned to the walls. Dillon and the lads, kitted up in jumping gear, boarding a Hercules, thumbs-up to the camera. A couple of the less gory shots from the Falklands.

145

Two photos of the platoon in smart No. 2 dress – parade uniforms, collars and ties – sunlight flaring off their cap badges, taken on the square at The Depot. A large blow-up in full colour of a sky filled with blossoming white and yellow parachutes – NATO manoeuvres in Germany. And postcards and mementoes from all over the world, every continent Dad had served in, plus bits and pieces of Para equipment: webbing, HALO goggles, tropical-issue water bottle, Parachute Regiment shoulder flash, the quick-release box off a PX1 harness, camouflage pattern forage cap, empty magazine clip. To the boys a hallowed shrine, material proof that Dad had been one of the famous 'Red Devils' – the meanest, toughest, fittest bunch going.

In the lower bunk, duvet kicked off, Phil was burning up, twisting and coughing in his sleep. Susie felt his forehead and the backs of her fingers came away sticky. Anxious now, she checked on Kenny in the top berth, pyjamas soaked with sweat, breath rasping. Both boys were really sick, no doubt about it.

The door was pushed open and Susie's mother peered in, hairnet over bulging curlers like an alien's headgear.

'It's mumps!' Susie whispered, distraught. 'Look at their throats . . .'

Don Walker found the tell-tale signs at first light, and shouted Dillon over to have a look. The two village kids had been taken into police custody, and now it was back to the more serious business – the business they were being paid for – protecting the salmon tanks. It was at the northern end of the compound, sixty yards or so from the fence, where the lane branched off into a rough moorland track. Thick hedgerows of thorn and thistles stretched away, clumps of juniper bushes dotted about.

Squatting on his haunches, Don pointed out the tracks to Dillon and Cliff. 'They've been here all right – look, tyre treads, five fag ends. There was two of 'em, and it wasn't the kids, they came in a van.' He prodded the soft

146

churned earth with his finger and looked meaningfully at Dillon. 'These are scrambler bike tracks.'

Dillon walked a little way up the lane, surveying the general area, and came back. 'Cliff, you and Don start cutting this hedge back, it's too good a hiding place . . .'

'What about Steve?' Cliff interrupted, dark face a bit haggard from lack of sleep. 'He's always pissed, Frank, we want him off our backs.' He jabbed his thumb into his chest. 'We're doin' all the work!'

Dillon nodded wearily. 'I'll talk to him.'

'*Hey! Frank!*'

'Kick the waster out – why should we split our dough!' Cliff grumbled.

Dillon made an impatient swipe to shut him up as Jimmy drove up in the jeep, slammed on the brakes and skidded to a stop. Christ, Dillon thought, somebody else with a grouse. Jimmy leapt out, eyes blazing.

'I just caught that bastard Malone red-handed! All that gear I got, the sod's been paid more'n five hundred quid. And two hundred for the radio!' Jimmy leaned nearer, fist up, voice getting throaty. 'I tell you, Frank – you don't take him, when the lads hear about this, you'll have to fight 'em off.'

Dillon closed his eyes, just for a second, to keep his sanity. Knowing Malone for the devious bastard he was, he sussed out what must have happened. Malone had been giving Griffiths some bullshit about how he'd organised the operation, got the radio and the latest sophisticated weapons, smooth-talked him that he was masterminding the whole show. The estate manager had swallowed the story, and forked out seven hundred to defray Malone's out-of-pocket expenses. Only Malone hadn't paid a red cent for the gear – Jimmy had, or Jimmy had made deals – didn't matter how they had come by the gear, the point was they had done it without Malone.

Somehow Jimmy had caught Malone bragging that he had pulled it all in, dogs, flares, radios, weapons, and the piece of shit was collecting a rake-off on the sly, as usual crapping on his mates from a great height. Dillon couldn't even pretend he was surprised: par for the course.

He said, 'You catch him at it up at the office then?'

'Yeah!' Jimmy was totally fired up. Reaching into the back of the jeep, he grabbed a pair of shears, snapped them under Dillon's nose. 'I'll cut his balls off!'

Half-an-hour later, when they returned to the compound, Malone hailed them. Dillon sniffed more trouble. A police car was parked outside the wooden office building, and over by the tanks Griffiths was talking with two uniformed officers and doing a lot of gesticulating.

'What's going down?' asked Dillon as Malone strode up, looking thunderous.

'That bloody wimp Griffiths, he's shittin' in his pants – ' Malone's black brows met in the middle as he glared towards the tanks. 'He wants all the weapons in his office . . . the kids reported us to the cops.'

Still boiling about the money, Jimmy snapped at him, 'That was down to you, Malone!'

'I'm doin' my job,' Malone rasped through his teeth, and Dillon half-expected him to stick one on Jimmy. 'You don't like the action, you know what – '

Jimmy cut his short. 'Gettin' well-paid for it, are you!' – his voice like a whipcrack, and Dillon had to act fast. He had the jeep in first, spun the wheel and shot off even before Malone could bunch a fist.

Griffiths was standing by the desk, talking on the phone, when Dillon walked in. Dillon hesitated, but Griffiths gestured him in, a casual twitch of the wrist, nodding and saying, 'Thanks . . . fine, and I'll see you first thing in the morning. 'Bye.'

He put the phone down and blew out a satisfied gust of air, smacking his palms lightly together. 'That's a relief! They've bought the entire stock . . .'

His pleased expression wilted into one of consternation, even alarm. Dillon had dumped a large canvas holdall on the desk and was taking out a small armoury of handguns,

148

rifles, night sights, ammo, CN canisters, commando knives in leather sheaths.

'Good God! Any of you hold licences for these?' He held up his hand. 'Second thoughts – don't answer.'

'You mind if I give you some advice?' asked Dillon, watching as Griffiths stacked the weapons in a cupboard with a heavy padlock. 'Get shot of Malone. You've got a good man in young Don, he knows the land and he's got military training for security. Give him Malone's job and hire a few of the locals on a permanent basis. Pay them enough so they won't have to poach. Lot of unemployment up here.'

Griffiths shut the cupboard and secured the padlock. Straightening up, he glanced guardedly at Dillon through his fair eyelashes. 'Not as easy as you think.' He hesitated, then went on in his educated drawl, 'Most keepers, you know, supplement their wages. So I give the butcher a few rabbits and he gives me a steak, eggs and so on . . .'

Dillon waited, knowing there was more to come as Griffiths went over to the window and looked out at the wooded hillside, pulling at the lobe of his ear.

'Sometimes during the pheasant shooting season a couple of the protected birds get clobbered. I mount them and sell them off in Edinburgh. Malone brought me a couple of falcons, said he'd found them after the shoot, and we split the profits. It's illegal, and I obviously knew to start with he wasn't simply finding them . . .' He gave a slight shrug, cleared his throat. 'Now? Well, I'm in a Catch–22 situation. If he goes to the landowner, that's me out of a job and a cottage, so I doubt I could get him to leave without a hell of a fight.'

Dillon nodded, getting the picture, and smoothed his fingertips along the line of his scar. 'There's one on the cards, sir,' he said almost inaudibly.

Griffiths looked over his shoulder, and he got the picture too, seeing the dark, threatening shadow in Dillon's eyes. Maybe there was a way they could each do the other some good.

149

He turned then, and said softly, 'You get Malone out of here and I'll see it to it you get a bonus on top of your wages, and Don will take over . . . Deal?'

They shook hands.

18

Dillon couldn't make head nor tail of it. First off, it wasn't Susie who had answered the phone, it was her mother; then Helen was going on about the boys, something about being feverish, poorly. Leaning against the reception desk, one hand pressed flat against his ear, he tried to make sense of what the cold, clipped voice was telling him – as it always was, of course, that same austere, snide tone, whenever she had occasion to speak to her son-in-law. Dillon tried again.

'Well, where is she? What? She's what?' Even more mystified now. Why was Helen rabbiting on about minicabs? Had Susie gone off somewhere in one? 'What did you say? *Mumps?* Hang on!' He fished in his pocket as the beeps sounded, pushed a fifty-pence piece into the metal slot.

'Hello? Look, I'm gonna gave to go . . . what? No, I dunno when I'll be back. Just tell Sue I called.' Dillon glanced up, aware of a presence, Sissy MacFarland standing in the entrance to the bar, one hand holding the edge of the doorway. She hung back a little, waiting for him to finish his call.

Dillon said, 'Well, maybe it's a good job, it's catching, isn't it? Look, just tell her I called, okay, and . . . hello?'

Hung up on him. Bloody typical. Dillon banged the receiver down and pushed his hand through his hair. He could never get a straight story out of that woman. All the time she had that icy, accusing tone to her voice, as if she was blaming him for something. As if he'd made a hash of things, couldn't provide for his own wife and kids.

'Could you give me a hand?' Sissy asked diffidently. She pointed behind her. 'Only I want to close the bar . . .'

Dillon followed her through. Head down on the table

151

amongst a collection of pint glasses and whisky tumblers, hair hanging over like rats' tails, Steve was gently snoring, the breath rustling and gurgling from his open mouth. One hand trailed on the floor. Dillon's lips tightened, and he shot a glance of apology at the girl, who returned a tiny shrug.

'Has he been drinking all morning?'

'I'm not sure . . . Dad was doing the bar, I've been in the kitchen.'

She didn't sound annoyed, more concerned than anything, Dillon thought, standing there with a small anxious frown. She looked as fresh as an advert, like a dairy maid, wearing an old print dress with coloured buttons down the front, and the hem half hanging down at the back. There was a small hole by the waist, maybe it had once held a belt, but it wouldn't have mattered, it was not the dress he was interested in.

'I tried to haul him up myself, but he's too heavy, if you knew how many times I've half carried the old man up to bed, but . . .' Sissy laughed. She was so free and easy and he noticed she wore no stockings, just small slip-on sandals, her legs still tanned from the summer.

Together they hauled Steve upright in his chair, both got an arm around him and hoisted him up. He was well out of it, eyes swivelling, legs like rubber and it took the two of them to get him to the stairs. He swayed, hands up to say he could make it, but then Dillon caught him as he was about to fall flat on his face.

Steve had an arm slung round Dillon and the other round Sissy as all three made it up the stairs, along the corridor to his room, and he was sagging between them as they heaved him onto the bed. It was then that Dillon noticed as he looked up and across to Sissy, that in the struggle one of her buttons had popped revealing a milky white, heavy breast. It gave him an erection at just the first look. He didn't even have to think. She wore no bra, and was still unaware of the fact she was on display, still trying to get Steve out of his jacket but as she turned him over she looked up, not into Dillon's eyes because, she realised, they were focused on her tits.

Sissy laughed, a marvellous throaty giggle, as she pulled her dress closer. 'I must have lost a button . . . sorry, can I leave it to you to get him undressed?'

Dillon nodded, thinking what he would give to rip that floral print right off her – he was almost as flushed as Steve. Sissy went out, leaving the door open as Dillon dragged off Steve's jacket, then eased off his shoes. His feet stank! Dillon pulled the duvet round him and as he bent forward, Steve's eyes opened. 'I thi-gulp-she fan-gulp cies . . . me!'

The beer fumes disgusted Dillon, and he let the duvet flap over Steve's head. He heard a drunken guffaw as he let himself out. Sissy was on her hands and knees, skirt up, searching around the corridor for her lost button and her arse was as much a turn on as her beautiful heavy breasts. Dillon moved towards her, trying to think of something, anything, to say but he was as dumb-struck as Steve.

'I found one! The other may be on the stairs!'

Sissy held up the button, and turned as if to walk down the stairs. Then she paused, 'Is he okay, maybe he needs some coffee?'

'He's okay.' His voice sounded hoarse, he wanted to hold her, draw her to him, but he couldn't, he just stood there, and then she cocked her head to one side and smiled.

'You hungry?'

Oh God! Was he hungry? He wanted to eat her, suck those big beautiful tits, wanted to hold her, he pushed at his pants, the pecker was talking for him. He knew if she came within arm's length he wouldn't be able to resist, he'd have to drag the rest of the little floral number off her, but it was just a fantasy . . .

'Ah! Well, isn't that lucky, I've found another button.' She held it out in the palm of her hand. He smiled and leaned against the wall.

Sissy slipped the two buttons into her pocket. She looked

at Frank Dillon with his head slightly bowed, his cheeks flushed. He had the most piercing eyes she had ever seen on anyone, but he wouldn't lift them, he seemed afraid or embarrassed to look at her.

'That room's empty . . .' Sissy looked at him and slowly he raised his head. He gave a low soft moan, and she crossed to him, lifting his right hand and slipping it inside her dress. The softness of her made him gasp.

Dillon still could not really believe he'd scored, but when she drew him towards room 22, opened the door, and walked in, turning back just for a second to look at him, he knew he had, as Sissy read in his ice-blue eyes what she had hoped, wanted from the first moment she had seen him.

A few minutes or several hours, he had no notion of how long he slept – or rather dozed – because whenever he drifted off a sour bubbling nausea rose up in his chest, and the bed, the ceiling, the universe went into a corkscrew spin that made him clutch the sides of the mattress, anxious to stay on the planet.

On one of these endlessly whirling voyages, ill with dizziness, Steve decided he could stand it no more. He gathered up a few shreds of willpower, groped his way off the bed and lurched to the door.

Bathroom. Which way? He could feel the prickle of cold sweat erupting on his forehead, each individual bubble breaking out, trying desperately to quell the gobbet of sickness rising in him and keep it down until he found a friendly lavatory bowl. Stumbling along the corridor, hand out to steady himself, he heard a low moan, quite unmistakable. The moan was heavy with sex, heavy with pleasure, heavy . . . someone being fucked, well and truly fucked. Steve went very still, listening, then moved closer to the door of room 22, just two rooms down from his, and pressed his ear to the wooden panel. The rhythmic creak of bedsprings, the woman gasping, the man grunting as he thrust into her. Swaying back on his heels, Steve

154

realised there was a fractional gap, the door not fully on the catch. He pressed his hand against the panel, inching it open, and craning forward, slid his head round the edge of the door.

In the dim light filtering through the drawn curtains he registered two naked forms, the pale blur of a face turning towards him –

'Sod off!'

The bedsprings twanged, hard thudding footfalls across the bedroom floor, and next thing Dillon's hoarse bark of anger, *'Go on – get out!'* as the door was slammed shut in his face.

In the bathroom Steve fell to his knees on the tiled floor, bent over, retching, speaking on the big white telephone in fluent Swahili.

Sissy waved to Dillon from the window, and gave him a warm, affectionate smile. He climbed into the jeep, switched on, and as he was reversing, tooted the horn and blew her a kiss. Sissy giggled, waved again, and watched him head down the drive, disappearing through the trees.

She spun round then, letting the curtain fall back, at the sound of a handle turning, her eyes widening as Steve came in and kicked the door shut with his heel. He leaned his head back against it, watery eyes in an ashen face, breath rasping harshly as if he'd run a mile. With a trembling finger he pointed to his throat.

'It's not my tonsils . . .'

Gathered the neckerchief in his hand and pulled it down.

'See . . . you want to see?'

Sissy shook her head, drawing the bedcover tighter, white rounded shoulders and the upper slopes of her breasts lightly dappled with freckles. 'I think you'd better leave . . .'

The tremor in Steve's fingers had taken over his entire body. She could see the pent-up emotions physically raking through him, and as he tried to speak, and failed, in his rage and frustration he thudded his side with his fist, trying to release the log-jam inside. But what frightened Sissy most of all was the glazed look of rabid desire in his eyes; not seeing her as a person, as a woman, merely an object of lust with which to satisfy his own cravings.

'Just leave, please . . .' Sissy could feel her cheeks quivering in a nervous half-smile she couldn't control, moving away from the white rectangle of the bed as he pushed himself off the door and shambled towards her.

'I want you . . .'

Grunted, garbled, the words were incomprehensible to her but their meaning and intention were plain. Sissy backed away, knuckles white where they gripped the bed-cover, real palpable fear making her eyes bright and bringing a fluttering, breathy laugh of nervous release.

Steve's mouth twisted, turned into a snarl. The bitch was laughing at him. Mocking his pain and humiliation. And in blind black rage he lashed out, his open palm cracking Sissy across the mouth, sending her stumbling into the closet door, blood spurting from her split lip.

'No! Sorry . . .' Steve reached out, tears springing into his eyes. 'No, I didn't mean – '

Sissy went rigid, screamed as his fingers dug into her bare shoulders. Terrified, she screamed again, and Steve clamped his hand over her mouth, stifling her, and with the girl struggling frantically in his arms he lost all control and struck her hard against the side of the head, knocking her to the floor. Grabbing a fistful of dark curly hair, he flung her onto the bed. Sissy squirmed away from him, uttering little tremulous cries of panic, and as she tried to escape Steve dragged the bedcover off her and flung it aside.

Her nakedness sent a shock-wave through him. Not sexual desire. A deeper, murkier, more unspecified emotion. Something like shame, mingled with the loss of what he had once been, and the unbearable reality of what he had become. A life, his life, once bright with promise, girls at his beck and call, wiped out and wasted by a sniper's bullet. Empty, futile, pathetic. Now there was nothing, and all he could do was stand and stare, trembling all over, the breath wheezing in the plastic tube, feeling the hot tears on his face as he broke down into helpless, uncontrollable weeping.

When Sissy slithered to the floor and wrapped the bedcover around her, his attempt to stop her was feeble and half-hearted, and he didn't even raise his bowed head when she ran to the door.

There was blood on his fingers, from Sissy's burst lip.

Steve blinked at it, swaying slightly, and he fell forward onto the bed, face buried in the rumpled sheets, his whole body heaving. In torment he rolled onto his back and stared up at the blurred ceiling. '*Steve* . . . oh Steve,' a hoarse, agonised whisper, as if calling to himself.

It wasn't a woman he wanted, not a woman, there had been too many, no one special. He was never with one long enough to give them any serious thought, or care if he saw them again, he was too young, had been too young to think about settling down, having a wife, kids, raising a family, he didn't ache for that. He cried out for the Steve that was always the centre of attention. The Steve that nudged and winked and said, 'I'll have the blonde' – or the redhead – the one every bloke was trying to get their hands on, he didn't cry for that or call out his name for the loss of pulling a chick. He cried out to the Steve standing up on the table in the bars and clubs, the Steve who jumped up on the stage and took off Tom Jones, the Steve who could sing himself hoarse, to the cheers and catcalls of his mates. He ached for the Steve everyone liked, the joker, the guy everyone made sure was along for the piss-ups and the curries, because if Steve was around, you'd have a good time, and if Steve was pissed, he'd get up and sing. He'd always fancied himself fronting a band, and with a beer bottle as a microphone he looked the business, *was* the business, but that Steve Harris was someone he had known a long time ago, in another lifetime, now he ached for the loss of himself, the Steve Harris who was never coming back.

19

The light was ebbing away, a few faint early stars sprinkling the darker sky to the east, and a pallid segment of moon creeping up behind the brow of the hill, directly ahead. Steve wasn't drunk yet – so far just three or four pulls from the bottle of Teacher's – but that was his aim, pure and simple. Blind stinking into sweet oblivion. It wasn't the answer, he knew that, but it was the only answer he had.

Bordered by thick hedgerows, the lane wound upwards, curved back on itself before rising above the treeline and most of the surrounding countryside, then dipping down into the next glen. Steve unscrewed the cap, treated himself to a good belt, felt the ball of heat expand from the pit of his stomach and radiate outwards. Wiping his mouth with the back of his hand, he went suddenly still, his meandering eye caught by a flurry of activity further down the hill. The light wasn't good, but Steve had 20/20 vision. Two caravans were parked under the trees, half-a-dozen men moving about, and at first he thought it might be a gypsy encampment until he spotted the scrambler bikes being wheeled from the back of a van. That didn't seem right.

From the top of the bank he had a better view, and it definitely wasn't right. A large panel-sided truck with a fretwork of aluminium refrigeration tubes above the cab was being backed out onto the road, chugging blue diesel smoke. One of the men appeared round the side of the caravan and went up to the passenger side window and handed something up. At this distance and in this murky light Steve couldn't be sure – not absolutely – but it looked to him like a double-barrelled shotgun.

'Take it easy, come on, breathe slowly,' Dillon said,

holding Steve by the shoulders to steady him. The lad was done in, sweat pouring off him, the neckerchief soaked through. He tried to speak, but all Dillon could get were gasping croaks and gurgles. The other lads, sprawled on the grass outside the hide, eating out of mess tins, couldn't have given a toss. The useless pillock in one of his usual drunken flaps, so what else was new?

'Easy now . . . slow . . . what's up, Steve?'

Dillon listened close as Steve finally got a word out. *Poachers*. And then in a burping, gulping rush, he got the rest of it. Dillon patted Steve on the back, well done, and turned to the others.

'Six men, two scrambling bikes – and they'll be armed.' He leaned nearer, nodding, as Steve burbled on. 'Yeah, yeah, okay . . .'

'Good double act you two've got going,' said Jimmy sardonically, glancing round the circle.

Dillon was stung. 'We're going to have to have a good act, because if they're armed to the teeth I'm not prepared to endanger any one of you,' he told them all straight.

Harry wiped a residue of cold baked beans from his moustache. 'What about Malone?' he asked, belching softly.

'Malone is going to be right in there – ' Dillon jabbed his finger at the turf-covered hide ' – out of our way!'

That was Plan A. Plan B Dillon was keeping under his hat, at least for the time being. Within the half-hour he had his lads deployed: sending Jimmy, Don and Steve down to the salmon tanks while Cliff and Harry kept watch through night binoculars. Illuminated by two large battery arc lamps, the compound seemed peaceful enough, the large steel tanks clearly visible under their wire-mesh netting. The police had turned up, and through the binns Cliff could clearly see Jimmy gabbing away to two young uniformed officers, who seemed to need a bit of persuading.

'Come on, cut the gas, Jimmy,' Cliff muttered, sharpening up the focus. Then he grinned and reported, 'They're trotting back to the Panda, radioing in . . . we just scored out.' Glancing round at Harry, already on the move, two flak jackets under his arm, he called out: 'We need their caps as well, and get the car hidden.'

Harry gave the thumbs-up and went off through the heather.

Malone was squatting by the radio, headset on, when Dillon poked his head inside the hide. Spread across his knees a 1:50,000 Ordnance Survey map squared up with red lines, which he was marking with pencil crosses. 'Who've I got on the south ridge, Alpha Three? Ahh, yeah, got it.' He made a cross, spoke into the mike, 'So we've covered the entire area, okay, okay . . . I'm all set.'

Malone couldn't organise a piss-up in a brewery, Dillon thought, but if he had delusions of grandeur that he was running the show, then let him. As long as the bastard stayed put and didn't get in their way.

Dillon gave him a level-eyed stare. 'An' we're depending on you — these guys could be armed and we've got nothin' but a few pickaxe handles. So we keep in radio contact at all times.'

Malone nodded, sure, no sweat, and watched with hooded eyes, waiting until Dillon had scrambled out before easing over and flipping back the corner of the blanket. Grinning, he touched the polished stock of the large-bore shotgun and ran his fingers along the blue-black barrel. Sure, Dillon, old buddy, no sweat.

Dillon had all the angles covered. At least he hoped to God he had. With the type of refrigerated rig Steve had described, it was obvious that these guys were tough, committed professionals. They'd invested thousands, knew where to lay their hands on the right equipment, had done their homework, and were playing to win. Well, so was he: Plan A the shop-window dressing, Plan B the sucker punch; come the dawn he'd know if his pass with distinction in tactical battlecraft at Pen-y-Fan in the Brecon

160

Beacons was all it was cracked up to be, not just a scrap of paper with his name in fancy scroll letters.

3.29 a.m. Silent as the grave, the pale sliver of moon now riding high behind thin trailers of cloud scudding in from the west.

3.30 a.m. The peace suddenly shattered by the roar of engines – the white truck careering along the narrow lane, headlights blazing, picking up speed on the slight downhill slope leading to the main gate, the two scrambler bikes close behind like flanking outriders.

Reinforced with steel bars to take the impact, the truck smashed through the gate, immediately tripping the wires and setting off the sulphur flares which zoomed up and burst with dazzling brightness over the compound. The raiders had planned it to the split-second. Even before the truck had slewed to a stop alongside the first tank, the rear doors had been flung open. Two men in balaclava masks leapt out, shotguns in their hands. Up front, the driver jumped down and ran round to assist his companion, the gang's leader. He was already up on the wooden walkway, hauling back the covering mesh. Two men working the tanks, the other four forming a shield around them. It was that simple.

Don ran forward, holding the dogs on a long leash. The Alsatians were going crazy, snapping and snarling. About to release them, Don hesitated. He cared for the animals, and he'd seen the shotguns the raiders were carrying. Even if the dogs got one man, two at the most, they'd still get blasted. Halfway across the compound, he met the first masked raider head on. Only his eyes could be seen through the ragged slit, bulging, bloodshot in the corners. Shotgun at the hip, finger on the trigger, the raiders snarled. 'Get the dogs in, leash 'em before they get their heads blown off!' He jerked the weapon. 'Come on! Come on, you wanna die?'

At Don's word of command, the dogs immediately quietened, heads down between their paws. The raider swung up the shotgun, indicating a wooden post next to the office. 'Tie 'em up. *Move it!*'

Shortening the leashes, Don obeyed, then put his hands on his head. He hoped the gesture might be conciliatory, but it wasn't. For his trouble he got the butt of the shotgun in his ribs, a gentle warning not to try anything as the raider frisked him for weapons.

The low whine of an auxiliary power unit started up, increased to a high-pitched howl. Swinging the plastic suction hose into position, the leader dipped it into the first tank. The driver reached inside the cab and threw a switch. The water churned. Under the powerful force, the thousands of swarming salmon were sucked into the large nozzle. Their flashing silvery bodies shot down the transparent tube and into a square plastic container supported by a metal framework, on the ground next to the rear doors. Layer by layer, the fish piled up inside, packed solid.

The two young police officers, now wearing flak jackets over their blue shirts, were being herded out of the bushes. One had foolishly tried to use his personal transceiver, attached to his collar. It had been torn off and stamped into pieces, and now he found himself staring into the business end of a shotgun.

'*Move* . . . come on, and get face down!'

'We are police officers,' the other one bravely tried. 'Put down your – '

'Yeah, an' I'm Sylvester Stallone, pricks.' The raider prodded them forward with savage jabs in the back. 'Down . . . *get down on your faces!*'

The two policemen lay down, hands stretched out in front of them. The other raider came up, pushing Don ahead of him, his hands clasped behind his neck. One of the officers tried to get up. The raider smashed a boot into his back and stuck the shotgun barrel into the nape of his neck. Don, forced down on his knees, his hands being roughly tied behind his back, yelled at the two young coppers. 'Just do what they want, *do what they tell you!*'

The raider swung the butt, gave Don a crack across the head that sent him sprawling, semi-concussed.

'Thanks,' the raider grinned. ' – You heard him, keep it shut, all of you.'

From his station on the rough ground overlooking the tanks, Steve dodged from bush to bush, hoping to sneak in on their blind side. But it was too late, he'd been spotted. One of the scrambler bikes came bucking up the hillside towards him. Steve broke from cover, wielding a crowbar. The rider charged straight for him, and Steve swung the crowbar over his shoulder, ready to swipe him from the saddle. Almost on top of Steve, the rider slammed on his brakes, flipped over the shotgun strapped to his back, cocked it and aimed it. He knew how to handle it, and he was in no mood for funny business.

'Start heading to the tanks,' the rider barked, *'move!'* And as Steve took a few steps forward, growled out, *'Chuck the spanner, sunshine.* Hands on your head – get down to the tanks!'

Steve tossed the crowbar down. Hands on his head, he moved down the hillside, the rider revving a few yards behind. He'd done his best, feeble as it was; now it was up to Dillon and the lads – and Plan B.

Malone had an ace up his sleeve – or so he thought. Having crept out of the hide and circled round, he suddenly leapt out, shotgun blasting, doing his Clint Eastwood act. Reacting too late, he heard the stuttering roar of an engine behind him. Before he knew what was happening, the second bike rider rammed him in the legs. Malone went tumbling, arse over tip, the shotgun spinning from his hands. He scrambled up, wild-eyed with panic, sense of direction gone. The rider skidded over the steep rough ground, trying to make a turn. The bike went out of control, lost traction, and bike and rider went slithering downhill, sideways on.

Sweating with fear, Malone legged it up the hillside. The perimeter fence lay ahead, but he knew of a gap, and once through it he'd have the sheltering woods to hide in.

Malone didn't intend getting a bullet in the gut for a few stinking fish. Nor for the benefit of that upper-class twit Griffiths, no way. The idea that he was also leaving his mates behind didn't even enter his head.

Herded forward by the bike rider, Steve stumbled towards Don and the two policemen, lying face down, hands and legs tied. One of the men guarding them kicked Steve's legs from under him, the other dragging his arms behind his back and tightly knotting his wrists together. The second bike rider came bouncing down the slope, steering with one hand, the other clutching the knee he'd injured in falling.

'Hey, come on, over here – we need help!'

The leader waved his men over. Two of the three plastic containers were packed to the brim, ready to be lifted into the back of the truck. The third was half full, the driver up on the walkway suctioning out the last tank.

Leaving one man to watch over Steve and the others, the two bikers gunned their machines across the compound, the second raider following at the run. Together with the leader they heaved two of the containers inside the truck. With the third not yet full, the leader ordered them to pack up. Unhooking the suction tube, the driver jumped down, and while the others manhandled the third container into the truck, he stowed away the equipment. As the bikes were handed up, the driver was already in the cab, revving up, ready for off.

The raider standing guard hung on until the very last moment, waiting for the truck to reverse. But he was getting jittery, and finally as he raced across, burst out yelling, 'Come on, come on, move it, move it!'

He leapt up and was dragged inside by three pairs of hands. Engine bellowing, the white truck sped towards the gates. rear doors swinging and banging, and roared off in a cloud of blue diesel smoke.

20

'What did I tell you?' Ripping off his mask, the leader tossed it onto the windscreen ledge. He lit up, sucked in a deep lungful, the flare of the match lighting up his grinning features. 'Like taking candy . . . Yeerrsss, beautiful, even more than I thought. Bloody beautiful . . .'

The driver nodded, concentrating on the narrow lane in the splay of headlights, anxious to keep clear of the deep ditches on either side. He slowed for a bend, and as they came round it, the leader sat up sharply, staring through the windscreen. 'Shit, what the hell is this?'

A police Panda was tilted over, one wheel in the ditch, headlight beams shining into the undergrowth. The officer behind the wheel was obviously trying, without success, to back it out. Another uniformed policeman in a flat cap stepped into the centre of the lane and flagged them down with his torch.

A scared voice from the back of the truck hissed through the grille, 'For Christ's sake, drive on, keep moving!'

The leader snatched his mask from the ledge and stuffed it under the seat. 'Get your masks off,' he ordered curtly, 'guns out of sight.'

He wound the window down as the policeman approached, flashing his torch. Leaning out, all smiles, the leader said, 'Trouble, officer? You want us to give you a hand?'

The officer came right up to the open window. The face underneath the checked cap was lean and hard, with a dark moustache, a thin vertical scar on the left cheek.

'Had a blow-out, deer ran straight into us,' Dillon said. 'Might need you to haul us out of this ditch.'

Inside the truck, crammed between the plastic containers packed with salmon and the two scrambling bikes, the

165

four raiders stood in darkness, waiting tensely. One of them raised his shotgun, cocked the hammer. A hand gripped his wrist, warning him to stay quiet.

At the open window, Dillon casually looked back at Cliff sitting behind the wheel of the Panda. He gave the signal with his torch. Cliff put the car in reverse, and the Panda, far from stuck, shot back into the lane, blocking it.

'Must be your lucky night,' the leader said, still faking his sunny smile.

Dillon said, 'But it's not yours, mate,' and rammed the torch in his face. The leader jerked back, shocked by the light in his eyes and the blow in his teeth. Dillon chucked the torch away, and reaching right in, he got a lock on the man's throat, crushing his windpipe. Cliff was at the door opposite. He yanked it open and dragged the driver onto the road.

Behind the truck, Harry came out of hiding, and signalled along the lane. With Jimmy driving, Steve and Don in the back, the jeep screeched up and stopped a couple of yards away, completing the ambush. The men jumped down and formed a semi-circle round the rear doors, pick-axe handles at the ready.

Still holding the man by the throat, Dillon yelled back, 'Nobody goes in . . . wait, *wait*!'

Dillon jerked the leader forward until their faces were practically touching. 'You got three seconds to get them to lay down their guns. I want them out, hands on heads.'

His fingers dug harder into the windpipe, throttling the man.

'One . . . two . . .'

The leader flailed his arms, banging the back of the cab with his fist. A voice from inside yelled, 'Okay, okay . . . we're coming out!'

Malone was laying into Griffiths, as if holding him personally to blame. Standing outside the estate office in the grey light of dawn, they were toe-to-toe, Malone stabbing his finger in Griffiths' chest, then jabbing it towards the tanks.

'They cleaned 'em all out . . . *no* weapons you said, you got *no* friggin' fish now!'

Griffiths cupped his forehead in his palm. 'Oh Christ . . .' he murmured wearily, totally beaten.

The blast of a horn made them both whip round. Malone's jaw dropped. Griffiths just stared, blinking incomprehendingly.

With Don at the wheel, Dillon beside him, the white truck drove into the compound and pulled up with a gasp of compressed air. The jeep was right behind it, horn tooting, the rest of the lads aboard, standing up and yelling their heads off.

'Morning, sir,' Dillon greeted Griffiths cheerfully, jumping down. He gestured with his thumb. 'Salmon's ready for collection, save the buyers getting their hands wet. We've got them all on ice, ready for the weigh-in.'

Malone pointed at Dillon, neck pumping. 'That bastard set this up with the gippos – '

Dillon jerked his head at Steve, who reached into the jeep and took out a shotgun. He tossed it to Dillon. 'What's this, Malone?' Dillon hefted the shotgun, his eyes flat and cold, his voice scathing. 'Only one of us was armed, and you still turned tail and ran . . .'

Griffiths was still having trouble taking all this in. He went to the back of the truck, where Don opened the doors and proudly showed him the containers of salmon inside. Malone knew something was in the wind. Something stank, and it wasn't rotten fish. It was starting to look bad for him, and he wasn't going to stand for it. That bastard Dillon was behind this, he felt it in his water. He strode after the estate manager, anxious not to have his nose pushed out. And sure enough, Griffiths was smiling, clapping Don on the back. Malone was about to lay into him when Dillon strolled up. White to the lips, Malone turned on him instead, almost incoherent in his fury.

'Guys like you, Dillon, are bein' churned out into civvies

167

every day of the week . . . an all of them thievin' bastards.'
He pointed at the back of the truck. 'You set this up!'

Dillon squared up to him. He'd had as much as, and
more than, he was ever going to take from Malone. But
his tone was quiet and calm, and he was in total control.

'Okay, Malone,' he said evenly, 'in front of witnesses.
We want that five hundred quid you nicked from us. If
you want to make it double or quits, now's the time.'

Malone got his meaning loud and clear. It wasn't just
the money Dillon was on about. Something more important had to be settled, once and for all. It almost amounted
to a blood feud between the two of them. Like a festering
boil of bitter black hatred, it had to be lanced. The wound
had to be torn open, the gangrene exposed and gouged
out.

Griffiths, as well as any of them, knew what was about
to take place; he sensed that it was inevitable, and no
matter what he said or did it was bound to happen. But he
wasn't prepared for its raw brutality, for its sheer animal
ferocity.

But then, he'd never witnessed a one-to-one brawl
between two ex-Paras before.

Malone didn't wait for the off. He charged straight in,
head-butting Dillon, opening up the old sniper abrasion
above his right eye. Blood spurted out, running freely
down Dillon's face, soaking into his shirt collar.

Leering, Malone raised both hands, waving him on.
'Come on then, Dillon, you been beggin' for it, come
on . . .'

Still dazed, Dillon shook his head to clear it. He looked
at the blood on his fingers, and then stripped off his
camouflage smock.

Although both men were expert in the techniques of
unarmed combat, they'd had their share of dirty street
fighting too, and that's what this turned into. It was ugly
to watch. Clawing, biting, scratching, kicking, each sought
to disable his opponent by any means possible. Malone,
bigger and heavier, could have beaten Dillon in a test of

168

pure physical strength, but Dillon wasn't going to give him that chance. He kept in close, fingers clawing at Malone's eyes, trying to rip off his ears. Malone bit into Dillon's forearm and it took a knife-edged open palm across the bridge of the nose to make him let go. Then a savage kick swept Dillon's legs from under him. Down he went, dragging Malone with him, the two of them rolling in the dirt, using fists, elbows, knees to inflict maximum damage.

Appalled, Griffiths watched as the two men grappled with each other, tumbling and rolling across the compound towards the stables and the fodder barn. The lads kept pace with the action, crouching, fists clenched, cheering Dillon on. It was a fight to the finish, to the bitter end; no truces, no split decisions; one victor, one vanquished.

Scrambling up, Malone grabbed a rake, swinging it viciously at Dillon's head. Ducking low, Dillon dived for a pitchfork leaning against the barn door. The two weapons clashed together, striking sparks. Dillon twisted the pitchfork, snapping the rake in two, then jabbed at Malone's stomach, forcing him inside the barn. The lads crowded in the doorway, yelling Dillon on. Half-blinded with blood, his face and neck covered in cuts and bruises, Dillon was eking out his last few precious ounces of strength. Malone sensed it. He waited, arms spread wide, for Dillon to jab again, then wrenched the pitchfork out of his grasp and turned it back on him. Dillon tripped, went sprawling backwards onto the straw-covered floor. With a snarl, Malone thrust downwards at Dillon's head, the four sharp tines burying themselves in the earthen floor as Dillon squirmed out of the way. He made a grab at Malone's leg, bringing the big man down – *splat*! – in a heap of horse manure.

'Good one, Frank!' Harry's usual florid complexion was shining beetroot-red. He pumped his fists like pistons. 'Go for it, finish him off, Frank!'

Smeared with horseshit, Malone pulled a fire bucket off its hook and hurled sand in Dillon's eyes. As Dillon backed away, temporarily blinded, he followed up with a kick to the groin that made every man there's eyes water. Dillon went down clutching himself, doubled over in agony.

'For God's sake,' Griffiths cried out, ashen-faced, 'someone had better stop this . . .'

Cliff raised an eyebrow. 'You want to get between them sir?' he inquired.

Malone spun a tap above a metal drinking trough and sluiced his head, shaking water out of his eyes. He pushed his hand through his glistening black hair, alert once again, ready for the final round.

'Look, Dillon, call it off,' Griffiths begged, wringing his hands. 'I'll make up the five hundred he owes you, this has gone far enough.'

Dillon spat out a mouthful of sand. He was back on his feet, but none too steady, and even after Harry tipped a bucket of water over him, he seemed dazed, blinking at Malone as if unable to focus. Chest heaving, water dripping off him, Dillon looked exhausted, all but done in.

'You quittin', Dillon?' Malone taunted him, teeth bared in a sneering grin. 'Want to quit, Dillon . . . ?'

Dillon wiped his hand down his face. When it came away, his eyes were staring. He was seeing Malone all right. The big square face, the black bar of his eyebrows. But Malone wasn't grinning. His face had a sickly grey pallor. His eyes were rolling, the whites showing, his mouth slack and quivering, as he burst from the toilet cubicle in the side passage of Hennessey's Bar . . .

'Come on Malone, get back in there!'

After swearing the pub was clear, the bastard was trying to do a runner. Didn't have the guts to stay and help. Only interested in saving his own yellow skin. Throwing Dillon off, barging his way into the crush of people jammed in the narrow passage, pushing bodies aside in a frantic effort to get out.

Still staring, Dillon said, 'Like the way you ran out on my lads?' He shook his head, his breathing hoarse. 'I'm not quitting!'

Malone lunged forward. Dillon hit him. Once. A sweet

right hand, smack in the teeth. Malone went cross-eyed. His legs buckled and he sank, very slowly, to his knees and toppled over.

'You had that coming for a long time, Malone,' Dillon panted, and with a smile at the lads fell down flat on his face.

'Just keep still . . . you're gonna have a beaut, split open like a tomato, mate.' Harry dabbed with a red-speckled towel, then stuck a plaster across Dillon's right eyebrow. Cliff stood nearby with a bloody sponge and a bucket of rose-tinted water. 'How's your ribs?' Harry asked.

Dillon eased himself into a sitting position in the back of the jeep. If his eyebrow was like a split tomato, the rest of his face resembled a blue and purple pumpkin. He pushed Harry's hand away. 'Gerroff me . . . you're makin' it worse!' Groaning, Dillon gingerly touched his cheek-bone. 'I feel terrible . . .'

Jimmy bounded up, grinning fit to bust. 'How's about this to make you feel on top of the world, mate!' He waved a thick bundle of notes in the air, licked his thumb and peeled through the twenties. 'Two weeks' wages, plus – you won't believe this, but his Lordship thought you took a beatin' from the poachers – bonus – one grand!'

Cheers and shouts from the lads clustered round the jeep. 'No, wait,' Jimmy held up his arms, 'plus, plus – Malone is out, and . . .' He wrapped his arm around Don's shoulder, who gave him a shy, quizzical smile. 'Don-boy here is now head keeper!'

Don went beetroot-red, stuttered, thank you, thanks, nodding his head up and down. Afraid to show how much it meant to him, he did a runner, running like the deer he loved, and they watched him running, watched him take a flying leap into the air, then they heard him whooping at the top of his voice, arms above his head, fists clenched.

Jimmy laughed. 'Well, he seems happy enough! Guy's a real fruit!' Then he leaned closer to Dillon, whispering. 'Eh, what you say Frank, we can make it a nice round

171

figure . . .' He flicked the wad of notes and slipped his arm around Dillon's shoulder, 'We could take him tonight, drive the carcass to Edinburgh, with nature boy owin' us, he can turn a blind eye, what you say Frank?'

'Forget it!' Dillon shrugged him off. He called out, 'Come on, let's get home.'

'Why? Who's to know it was us?'

Dillon didn't think it needed explaining, but obviously it did.

'Because he's free, Jimmy, don't let some bastard nail him to a wall.'

'Dillon!' Malone shouted.

As he came towards them, Jimmy whispered nastily, 'Okay, we'll nail this bastard instead . . .'

'Just stay put!' Dillon said.

Malone stopped a yard away, looking anywhere but into Dillon's face. He hesitated, then in a mumble, 'Rumour has it you and your lads are startin' up your own security firm.'

'Yeah, we're thinking about it.'

Malone took a thick buff envelope from his inside pocket and held it out. 'You won this, take it, it was double or quits, right?' He cleared his throat. 'It's a grand, Frank. Cash.'

Dillon took the money, handed it to Jimmy. He didn't say anything, just watched Malone's lowered head, the Adam's apple jerking in his throat. Dillon thought he was going to turn away, but then Malone said in a rasping voice that was full of torment, 'I checked out that pub, Frank, I swear before God . . .' His choking voice faded away to a whisper. 'Those lads that died . . . it wasn't my fault.'

Not his fault. That was all right then. Big fucking consolation.

Dillon said, 'Thanks for the dough.'

The jeep drove out. Malone stood watching until it was gone from sight. As if to himself, he repeated. 'I checked out that pub, Frank, I swear before God . . .' but no one

172

heard, he was alone with his guilt, as he had always been, feeling it eating into him, seeing the bodies lined up outside the charred remains of the pub, seeing those six young lads Dillon had strode in with, seeing their faces hideously disfigured, their bodies twisted. He had never forgiven himself, would never forget their six pitiful bodies, the bodies of the women and young blokes. They stayed locked inside his big barrel chest, locked inside his bullish head, and when the memories squeezed out in his night-mares, when he woke up sweating, he always saw Frank Dillon's face, his blue eyes more brilliant, like ice shafts in his smoke blackened face, that accusing vicious face haun-ted him like the dead. Malone knew why Dillon hated him, knew it, took it, and no matter how far he tried to hide himself, even to a bloody salmon farm in Scotland, Dillon caught up with him.

'I checked out that pub, Frank, I swear before God . . . it wasn't my fault.'

21

Dillon went up the steps of the Clyde Hotel, calling back to the lads in the jeep. 'I'll be five minutes!'

The lads exchanged knowing grins, and a chorus of whistles and cat-calls followed Dillon inside. From reception he glimpsed Sissy at the top of the stairs. She saw him and quickly turned away.

'Sissy . . . Sissy wait. I wanted to say goodbye, me and the lads are on our way home.' As Dillon mounted the stairs, Jimmy came in behind him and nipped through to the bar. Dillon went up, attempting to explain, 'I don't want them boozed up for the drive . . . Sissy?'

She was in her room, sitting on the bed, her face to the window.

Dillon knew at once. Even though Sissy wouldn't say anything, or even look at him, Dillon knew the instant he saw the angry bruising on her cheekbone, the puffy lip where it had been split. He knelt on the carpet, his stomach trembling, and gently took her face in his hands. 'Steve did this to you?'

'I didn't call the police, or anything, he – ' Sissy swallowed, her eyes downcast. 'I even feel sorry for him, he's sick . . .'

'Yeah, everyone always feels sorry for Steve,' Dillon said, his eyes hard as stones. 'Makes excuses for him. But this is different.'

A sob came up and Sissy squeezed her face with both hands, shoulders hunched and shaking. Dillon fished for a handkerchief. Sissy pointed to a box of tissues on the dressing-table. Dillon took one and knelt before her, wiping her wet cheeks.

Sissy blinked tears away. 'You look terrible,' she told Dillon.

174

'Had a bump into a tree.' He smiled and traced the outer corner of her lip with his finger. 'It won't scar . . .'

He cupped her face and brought it closer, and gently kissed her, away from the swelling. A discordant chorus of *Why are we waiting . . . oh why-eye are we waiting . . . ?* sailed up from the forecourt below.

Dillon stood up and went to the window. He stared out at the curve of moorland beyond the trees. There was a deep angry stillness about this man, Sissy thought, that she recognised but did not understand. As if he was waging a continual battle to keep a welter of seething emotions under iron control. A dark, brooding mystery to him that both baffled and attracted her, sensing that Dillon had lived several lifetimes already, and she hadn't yet lived one.

Sissy got up and went to him, pressing her body to his back, her head resting on his shoulder. The singing beneath the window faltered, died away.

In a small, faraway voice, Dillon said, 'You know the stag? When we found out how much he was worth we thought about knocking it off. Five grand's a lot of cash. But . . .' He gave a tight shake of the head.

'But?'

'He makes you think about freedom,' Dillon said, deep within himself. 'None of us has had too much of that, it's not the way the Army trains you. Everything is ordered, you live by rules and regulations.' Leaning against him, Sissy could feel the muscles in his arms tautening, then going slack, then going taut again.

'You don't know it's happening to you,' Dillon went on in the same quiet, charged voice. 'When you're on leave it's short-lived, you need booze and more booze to loosen you up, like you can't handle not having anyone watching your every move . . .'

He turned and laid his hand gently to her cheek. 'I did five years in Belfast, I hated the city . . . the kids spitting in your face, old ladies looking at you with hatred. Hate. You can feel it, but you act as if nothing is happening – '

175

A tremor passed across his bruised face. He seemed to physically shake it off, but the effort left his eyes unnaturally bright, moist in the corners. Sissy could hardly bear to look at him.

'You call low-life "sir" . . .' The words stumbled out. 'the players – we call the IRA suspects players . . .' The dam on the point of cracking, breaking, bursting open. Dillon shut his eyelids tight, wetness squeezing out. 'But in the end, the game's been on us . . .'

Sissy let the moment prolong itself. The pain ebb away. She said, then, 'Do you have kids?'

Dillon opened his eyes and looked into Sissy's. He nodded. Raucous shouts rang out from below, 'Frank! . . . *Come on, Frank* . . .'

'It's time I went home,' he said. And then, for only the second time she could remember, Dillon smiled. 'God bless, love.'

There was a cheer as Dillon came out. A long drive ahead of them, and the lads were eager to be off. Dillon walked to the jeep, hefted Steve's holdall from the back, dropped it on the gravel. He jerked his thumb. Out.

Steve slowly climbed out. Dillon took a fistful of money from his pocket and offered it. Steve backed away, fear in his eyes. Dillon gripped his lapel, pulled him close, and without even bothering to look at Steve, stuffed the money in his top pocket.

'Take it! You're on your own, Steve.'

Steve's face was white. The fear in his eyes was now mingled with the abject, cringing look of a whipped dog. He hesitated, then reached out a trembling hand, tried to catch Dillon's arm. Dillon jerked his arm free. He climbed into the passenger seat next to Jimmy, looking straight ahead.

The jeep backed away from the front of the hotel, wheels churning gravel, and shot off down the driveway. Lashed to the radiator was a stag's head – old MacFarland's stag's head – that Jimmy had swiped from the bar. Steve saw

176

the spread of its antlers above the hedgerows as the jeep sped along the lane, heard the bellow of a song floating back on the breeze, gradually fading, fading, fading away.

'Ten green bottles
Hanging on a wall,
And if one green bottle
Should accidentally fall . . .'

The stag's head went up, antlers raised high, scenting danger. It stood poised on the crag, all senses alert, its massive tawny flanks quivering slightly.

High up on the facing southern slope, Steve lay cushioned in the coarse grass, hidden by the waving fronds of heather. The wooden stock of Jimmy's L42A1 sniper rifle, fitted with a cheek rest, nestled against his shoulder. 7.62mm calibre shell, muzzle velocity 838 metres per second. Effective range 1,000 metres plus.

Steve squinted through the sighting telescope.

Beside him lay his empty holdall, his kit neatly spread out on the grass. Next to his wallet, a single photograph of Steve in his parade uniform. Face shining, smiling into the sunshine. Silver badge of winged parachute, crown and lion on his Red Beret. The Red Beret he was wearing now, with his jeans and denim shirt and the neckerchief swathing his throat.

Clearly outlined on the ridge, the stag slowly turned its head. Poised, muscles tensed, nostrils twitching, it looked in Steve's direction, seemed to stare directly into Steve's eyes.

The crack of the rifle shot scattered the peace of the valley. Screeching birds scattered, wheeled into the sky. Before the first echo had died away the stag was leaping down, crashing through the bracken, seeking the safety of the wooden glen.

On the grass, Steve's kit lay undisturbed, the photograph spotted with three splashes of blood, the largest one obscuring the smiling face. The impact had thrown the body backwards, arms flung wide. The rifle rested between his legs. Some distance away, the Red Beret lay on the grass, unmarked, pristine, cap badge shining bright.

JIMMY HAMMOND

22

Dillon stood in his boys' bedroom, looking over their board with all the photographs. There was one in the centre of Steve, his arms wrapped around Dillon laughing, there was another with his trousers dropped mooning to the camera. Dillon removed the picture of the two of them, touched Steve's smiling face. He whispered softly, 'Goodnight Steve, sleep quiet . . .'

Jimmy barged in carrying a black plastic rubbish bag containing all of poor Steve's possessions. He seemed completely unaware of what Steve's suicide meant to Dillon.

'We best get a move on. What you want me to do with his gear?'

Dillon shrugged, said there was no one to collect it, give it away, anything but he couldn't deal with it.

'What about his mother?'

Dillon shook his head, didn't want her to see Steve's few pitiful belongings, knew it would hurt her. She had his medals, she had those to remember Steve, that was better than sweat-stained T-shirts, old sneakers and a baggy coat.

'Okay, but we should get going, got a busy day.' Jimmy said impatiently.

Dillon nodded, wanting Jimmy out, needing him to go and leave him for just another second, but then he turned and followed him down the stairs and out into the court-yard. Jimmy tossed the black plastic bag into the bins. Dillon said nothing, he couldn't, he just touched the pocket where he had slipped. Steve's photograph, touched it, as if to say, it's okay, I cared, I care Steve.

'I want to go to the crematorium.'

'Shit, we already been there!'

'I want to go again, ALL RIGHT? THAT ALL RIGHT WITH YOU?'

Jimmy slammed the door shut. 'Fine, that's where you wanna go, that's where we go . . .'

They drove in silence.

It was a simple plaque, set in a small square plinth of smooth grey stone. Wreaths of clustered dark green leaves and flowers wrapped in clear cellophane, each with a message of condolence, were placed beneath it in a bed of red stone chippings. The biggest wreath had the Regimental crest as it centrepiece, with the motto *Utrinque Paratus* woven below in tiny white flowers.

Clad in his worn black tracksuit and his wrinkled Pumas, Dillon crouched on his heels, surveying the display of grief. He looked at the motto, and his lips silently mimed the words, 'Ready for Anything.' Anything but civvies, Dillon reflected bitterly. First Taffy, now Steve. A roll-call of battle honours, in reverse. Which one of them next? Jimmy? Dillon gave a small sour grin. Definitely not Jimmy, Mr Jim'll Fixit – not if Jimmy had anything to do with it. More likely himself. Much more likely . . .

He stood up as a middle-aged woman in a straight fawn coat with large round purple buttons approached along the path. For a long moment she gazed at the plaque with sad brown eyes, then rested her gloved hand on Dillon's arm.

'I never had the chance at the service to thank you. I'm just going to keep . . .' Mrs Harris made a vague gesture towards the condolence cards. 'My poor boy, he – he lost his way. I couldn't help him, but I know you tried.'

'Frank – hey, Frank!' Jimmy hailed him from the gated archway to the crematorium, beckoning urgently. No respect for the dead; not much for the living either, come to that.

Ignoring him, Dillon said, 'Me and a few of the lads are starting up our own company, security work.'

182

'That's good, good.' Mrs Harris nodded emphatically, large brown eyes fixed on him. 'You stick together.'

Dillon gave her a quick, tight hug and hurried away. Jimmy was sitting in the jeep at the kerbside. As Dillon got in, he said, 'It was on the cards, Frank.' There was contempt in his voice. 'If he hadn't topped himself some bugger would have done it for him. He was a waster!'

Dillon didn't respond. He wasn't sure who he was most angry with – Jimmy, Steve, or himself. In the early spring sunshine they drove through Bethnal Green and up into Hackney. Somewhere near the London Fields mainline station Jimmy took a left off Mare Street, and in a few minutes drew up outside a row of rather shabby-looking shops and basement offices. There was a betting shop, greasy spoon café, and a travel agent's – SUPER SHINE TRAVEL AGENCY – with flyblown posters in its grimy windows. Dillon wasn't impressed, and even Jimmy's breezy enthusiasm failed to dispel his doubts.

'It's not the greatest, I know, but it's a start. Lick o' paint here an' there . . .' he swept out his hand as if unveiling the find of the century, '. . . we're in business!'

Jimmy skipped past a couple of overflowing dustbins and a small mountain of black plastic bags spilling rubbish onto the pavement and went down a short flight of stone steps bordered by rusting iron railings. 'Come on, follow me, sunshine . . .'

Inside, the dark passageway smelled of vintage cat piss. It was littered with bricks and half-empty cement bags gone hard, and everywhere thick with dust. 'All this'll be cleared,' Jimmy assured Dillon, bustling ahead. 'Harry's gettin' a skip, right . . .' He produced a key and unlocked a door that a puff of wind would have blown off its hinges. 'Here we go!'

Dillon nodded dubiously to the floor above. 'That Super Travel place looks like a knockin' shop,' he said, following Jimmy into a small dingy room with a plain wooden desk and few hardback chairs. The filthy window gave a grand view of the iron railings, rubbish tip, the legs and ankles of pedestrians. Above the bricked-up cast-iron fireplace, Jimmy had nailed the stag's head to the bare plaster.

'We got it for one hundred a week, plus there's a bog outside, washbasins, and – ' Jimmy threw open the doors of a cupboard with a flourish. 'Ta-rrraaaaaaa!'

'Christ!' Dillon exclaimed, goggling at the two shelves of office equipment – telephones, answering machine, Xerox, fax, computer and laser printer, all brand-new, still in their boxes. 'Where did all this come from?'

'All legit, it's bankrupt stock,' said Jimmy smoothly, and before Dillon could even draw breath, he was onto the next item on the agenda, fingers clicking, busy-busy-busy. 'What you think? White walls, get some pictures up, carpet down – be a palace!'

Harry Travers blundered in carrying two four-litre drums of paint, two smaller cans under his arms, paint-brushes and rollers stuffed in his pockets. Jimmy did a double-take on the labels, glared at Harry.

'Pink? *Pink*?'

Harry shrugged. 'The white was double, an' we got one gallon free. Whack it over that corridor . . . it's not a bright pink,' he reassured them earnestly, 'it's soft shell . . .'

Dillon, wearing baggy blue overalls spattered with paint, trudged up the steps and heaved three bulging black plastic bags into the skip that was half on the pavement, half in the gutter. Cliff was sweeping up with a broom, his black face and short wiry black hair covered in a film of cement dust. Glancing left and right with a pugnacious frown, he said, 'Every bugger in the street is tossin' their rubbish on – I go inside for a minute an' . . . look,' he burst out angrily, 'that's not ours, that armchair.' Dillon turned to go back down. 'Hey, Frank, how's it lookin'?' Cliff asked.

'If you got a pair of sunglasses, I'd wear 'em,' Dillon advised.

He went along the passage, eyes half shut in a painful squint. The pink couldn't have been pinker. It coated every surface – walls, ceiling, skirting boards, including the wires

running up by the door frames and across the ceiling. Even
the cast-iron electric box Jimmy was working on, standing
on a ladder, a screwdriver in his teeth. Holding a torch,
he was poking round inside, a spaghetti of coloured wiring
trailing down.

'You know what you're doin'?' Dillon asked him appre-
hensively.

'We got the telephones all connected, no charge,' Jimmy
mumbled past the screwdriver.

'Until the GPO suss us.' Dillon sighed, wagging his head.
Everything was moving fast, too fast. He wanted time to
stop, to think, to consider, and Jimmy was charging on,
as only Jimmy could, full steam ahead. Throwing caution
and everything else to the winds.

'Ah!' Jimmy chortled triumphantly, and threw a switch.
The fluorescent striplight in the passage buzzed and came
to life. Dillon shielded his eyes against the shrieking pink
glare. *Jesus Wept*. Like a bleeding boudoir. Or a Bangkok
cathouse.

Jimmy hurtled past him, yelling excitedly, 'Cliff – Cliff,
is the sign lit up?'

The four of them gathered on the pavement, grinning a
bit self-consciously, looking up proudly at the glowing
neon sign, a red arrow strobing the way down to the
basement.

STAG SECURITY COMPANY

No one but a Para would know it, Dillon realised, but the
name was sort of appropriate – 'stag' being the term for
sentry duty in the Parachute Regiment. Thus: 'stag on –
stag off,' alternate periods on guard and standing down.

'Well, we got the premises, we got the phones,' beamed
Cliff. 'How we doin' with the kitty, Frank?'

It was an innocent question, but it stung Dillon on the
raw. He felt he was on a treadmill that was spinning faster
and faster, and he couldn't keep pace, couldn't even pause
to catch his breath.

'Still got a few quid!' he snapped irritably.

'Few quid?' Harry's eyebrows shot up in his big beefy face. 'What we gonna drive – dinky toys? We've not even got a motor, never mind a security wagon – '

'Friend of mine's got a garage,' Jimmy winked. Of course, Dillon thought, rely on Jimmy to have a friend who just happened to own a garage. 'He's got somethin' to show us,' Jimmy said, already vaulting into the jeep. He bashed the horn. 'Come on you dozy buggers!'

The treadmill was spinning out of control.

The 'garage' turned out to be more of a wrecker's yard. Half an acre of quagmire piled six-high with junked cars, vans and lorries. But Jimmy was confident that his mate Fernie would have just what they were after. He shoved open the double doors to the main workshop and disappeared inside, his voice echoing from the cavernous interior: 'Oi, Frank, come an' look over this baby, it's a cracker . . . armour-plated. *Frank*!'

Dillon stood with Harry and Cliff peering into the open bonnet of a metallic-gold Ford Granada with crimson stick-on speed stripes, Y reg, 94,000 miles on the clock. He glowered at the open workshop doors as Jimmy kept yelling for him to come take a look-see.

'I dunno, Frank,' said Cliff doubtfully, bent right over, his nose nearly touching the spark plugs. 'A lot of oil in here . . .'

Harry said scathingly, 'There would be, you soft git – that's the engine.'

A sudden shattering, stuttering roar, accompanied by a series of farting backfires, made them all spin round. An old rust-streaked security wagon, dents and scratches in every panel, radio antenna dangling over the smeared windscreen like a broken reed, chugged into the open, surrounded by a miasma of blue fumes. Jimmy leaned out, waggling his thumb. 'Hey, Frank – look at this mother!' He jumped down and at the third attempt managed to slam the door shut.

'It's a bargain!'

The three of them looked at it in silence, and then at

each other. Dillon scratched his head. Bargain? More like a death-trap on four bald wheels.

He fretted about the money situation all the way back to base. They needed ready cash to buy transport, and they needed transport in order to make some ready cash. Which came first, the chicken or the egg? Jimmy had something cooking on the back-burner; but why was it, Dillon brooded, that Jimmy's cooking always had a bit of a niff to it? They bought two six-packs of Red Strips at the local off-licence and sat in the pink office with the stag, two silent telephones, and an empty filing cabinet for company.

'I see the toothpaste and sleeping bag's still here,' Jimmy said, returning from the lavatory, zipping up his flies. He gave Harry a meaningful look. 'You not found a place to kip yet?'

'It's tough with no dough!' Harry protested.

Jimmy put his jacket on. At the door he said to Dillon, 'If you want to think about it, call me later. But it's money in the hand, enough to put down on the Granada and the wagon.' His tone said, if you can't shit, get off the pot – let's do it!

Dillon finished off the can, crumpled it in his fist. 'You known why!' he said, spots of colour appearing in his cheeks. 'I want us to be legit – we start off doin' dodgy runs, and we screw up – '

'How?' Jimmy leaned over the desk, arms spread wide. 'Tell me how? It's carryin' gear from A to B, and it's five grand cash!'

'Nobody gives nobody nothin' for free, Jimmy. An' I told you, anything to do with this Newman sucks.'

Jimmy made a dismissive gesture, as if wafting away five grand. 'Fine, say no more . . .'

'So how dodgy is it?' asked Cliff. 'I mean, what is this A to B crap? What do we have to do?'

Jimmy sighed and chanted off, 'We pick up gear from Heathrow Airport warehouse and we take it to the East End. How can it be dodgy? It's all been through Customs.'

He tapped his open flat palm. 'Five grand cash, in the hand . . .'

Harry perked up, sucking Red Stripe from his moustache. 'Sounds the business to me! What's your problem, Frank?'

Dillon closed his eyes, rested his forehead on the tips of his fingers. 'Okay,' he said wearily, 'let's go for it.'

23

Dillon emerged from the bathroom, a towel wrapped around him, still faintly steaming from the shower. He explored the cleft in his chin where he'd nicked it while shaving, and looked at his fingers for blood. From the tranny downstairs in the kitchen the Radio 5 weather-woman was cheerfully telling the nation to expect sunny spells and the chance of showers, and above her voice he heard Susie calling, 'Frank! Frank, are you coming down?'

She ran halfway up the stairs and caught him on his way through to the bedroom. 'Didn't you hear me? Mr Marway's here with Jimmy. Come and meet him.' Suddenly her face lit up in girlish exuberance. The job with Marway's MiniCabs seemed to have released fresh reserves of energy, renewed her zest for life. She'd been and had her shoulder-length russet hair layered and re-styled, and wore make-up every day, not just at weekends. But Dillon wasn't charmed by this new, younger, liberated Susie; the world was uncertain enough without finding you'd swapped an old reliable model for an updated, streamlined version with a fresh paint job.

'I did a perfect three-point turn!' Susie beamed at him, and beckoned with red fingernails. 'Come and say hello to Mr Marway . . .'

Dillon opened the towel. 'Like this.'

Susie rolled her eyes and went back down.

In the living-room Jimmy was sitting in an armchair, little Phil on his knee, listening raptly to Marway. Success always impressed Jimmy, and it was obvious that the Sikh businessman had achieved it, in the way he dressed, his refined voice, most of all his sense of composure, perfectly at ease with himself. And he seemed quite happy to pass on the secrets of his success.

189

'If you can prove you'll employ more than six men, then you'd be in line for a government small business loan,' he was explaining, and added frankly, 'That's how I started.'

Free money. Jimmy was interested. 'How much are these loans?' he asked.

'Depends on your collateral,' Marway smiled. 'But anything up to fifty thousand . . .'

Jimmy pursed his mouth in a silent whistle, more impressed than ever. Fifty Big Ones. Worth investigating.

'You ready?' Dillon said to Jimmy from the doorway, shrugging into his leather jacket. He jerked his head and turned to leave.

Susie stood up. 'Frank, this is Mr Marway – '

'How ya doin'?' Dillon gave a distant nod without looking at the elegant businessman in the pale cream silk turban. And with a curt 'Let's go,' he was on his way out. Jimmy ruffled Phil's cropped thatch, jet-black as his Dad's, and went after him.

Technically the security wagon was 'on trial', and rusty old crate that it was, at least it was transport. Jimmy drove them up to Hackney, while Dillon stared sullenly out, grousing, 'What does he know he's just givin' the wife drivin' lessons!'

'Way you carry on, you'd think he was givin' her a lot more than – '

Jimmy nearly swerved into a bus as Dillon cracked him one across the knuckles.

'What in Christ's name's the matter with you . . .! I was jokin' – an' he seemed an all right guy.' Jimmy glanced across at Dillon's stony profile. 'We should try this government loan gig. He said – '

'I'm not interested in what he said.'

Jimmy snapped at him. 'Well you should be. He's in the same business. We can use him – and Susie can palm us a few jobs.'

'She won't be workin' for him long,' said Dillon, more a dire threat than a vague promise. He had to brace himself against the dashboard as they pulled up outside Stag Security. Jimmy blasted the horn, then slammed the door as he got out. His portable telephone beeped. He went over in a huddle next to the basement railings. Harry thudded up past him and opened the passenger door.

'Where's Cliff?' Dillon asked.

'He rung in, he can't make it. Somethin' to do with that mealy-mouthed chick of his . . .'

Dillon glared. 'He's gettin' married to her!'

Harry was somebody else not exactly overflowing with the milk of human kindness this morning. 'I don't care if he's workin' out with Sylvester Stallone − he should be here!' Squashing his big arse in next to Dillon on the bench seat.

Jimmy came round the front of the wagon, folding his portable phone, and climbed in. 'Little change of plan . . . we hold the stuff here until the morning. Newman's not got the space cleared yet.'

Dillon punched the windscreen, which visibly shifted in its rubber mounting. 'This stinks already!'

Jimmy twisted the key to start up, and as the wagon moved off in a haze of swirling blue smoke, he said tightly, breathing through his nostrils, 'I'm just tryin' to get things organised, Frank . . .'

Nine large tea chests, which at Dillon's conservative estimate must have weighed two hundred pounds apiece. While Jimmy signed the release dockets under the watchful eye of two Customs officials, Dillon and Harry slid the last one into the back of the wagon, already sagging down to the axles. 'That Cliff's a connivin' sod, I'm knackered!' Harry grumbled, mopping his face. Dillon said so was he, and told him to belt up. Back at base they had it all to do over again, in reverse. It was after six when they'd finished, the crates overspilling the passageway into the office, and now they really were knackered.

'Okay, that's the last,' Jimmy said, ticking it off. 'Want me to lock up?' he asked Dillon.

Harry answered. 'Naaa, I'm dossin' down here.'

Slumped on a crate, fanning himself, he looked up and down. 'If I can find room for me sleepin' bag.'

Footsteps coming down from the street, and Barry Newman walked in, bringing the bracing tang of Gucci aftershave into the ripe sweaty atmosphere. His minder, the thickset guy with the widow's peak that Dillon had seen in Newman's office, lurked by the door.

Newman wore a dark-blue double-breasted overcoat and held a thin black cheroot in his gloved fingers. 'Any problems?' he asked Jimmy in that soft, silky voice that had been soaked overnight in Dettol.

'No.' Jimmy was suddenly all bright attention, doing his three-bags-full act. 'You know Frank, and this is Harry Travers.'

Newman ignored Harry. He slid his hand into his over-coat pocket and took out five grands' worth of brown envelope. 'I appreciate this, Frank.' He indicated the crates with the envelope before tossing it over. 'Be off your premises by the morning.' Faint glimmer of a glacial smile then, and the narrow, deepset eyes roamed up to the ceiling. 'My girls upstairs'll give you a special rate . . .'

Dillon's face changed. His eyes went from Newman, bored into Jimmy. 'Outside. Now.'

As he strode out, Jimmy behind him, Harry wore a delighted grin. 'It's a knockin' shop upstairs, isn't it? I knew it, what did I tell you . . . ?'

Dillon was standing stiffly on the pavement, one hand clenched round an iron railing. Jimmy bounded up, saying brightly, 'Frank, listen – ' and Dillon cut him off, eyes blazing. 'This is his place, isn't it?' he said, low, throaty.

'He owns the building, yeah,' Jimmy admitted, shrugging, a bit sheepish.

'What's in the crates? And don't give me the Indian artifacts crap – '

'Frank, he's opening market stalls . . .'

Before Dillon could respond to that load of bull, Newman came up the steps, trailing cheroot smoke. In his arms he carried a large glazed Indian elephant with an ornate woven headpiece of gold, black and azure blue, set with beads in the shape of pearls, diamonds and rubies of coloured glass. He plonked it on Dillon.

'Give it to the wife, Frank.' Newman removed the cheroot and blew out a plume of smoke, not quite in Dillon's face. 'Tell her it's a gift from an old friend.' He nodded to Jimmy. 'Thanks, son.'

'I couldn't get out of it, Frank – I mean, with the weddin' comin' up we got to get the place fixed up. This yours, is it?'

Cliff was studying with interest the monstrosity of an elephant on the kitchen dresser, where Dillon had dumped it the night before and not looked at it since.

Dillon sat at the table, a frown on his face, an open accounts book and wads of notes, neatly separated into three piles, in front of him. Through a mouthful of toast, Flora and marmalade, he said, 'Have it as a weddin' present. We got half a ton at the office.' He slipped rubber bands on the money, stood up wiping his hands on his jeans. 'Okay, let's pick up the Granada, put the deposit on the wagon . . . Cliff, you set?'

Cliff nodded, dead chuffed, the elephant tucked under his arm.

By the time they'd collected the Granada and done battle with the rush-hour traffic it was gone half-ten; even so, Dillon was surprised to see the crates had been moved, Harry sweeping up straw and polystyrene bubbles in the empty passage. Jimmy was leaning in the office doorway, leafing through a sheaf of pamphlets, every pastel shade under the sun.

'You got any collateral, Harry? Harry?'

Harry leaned on his broom. 'What do you mean?'

'You own anythin' – flat, house – you can borrow against?'

Dillon stood with the log book and car keys, taking it in.

193

Harry considered, scratching his moustache. 'My Auntie left me a house in Manchester, but me sister lives in it . . .'

Dillon jangled the keys. 'Got the Granada, put the deposit down on the wagon. Elephants out?' he said, eyebrows raised. 'Where you goin'?' he asked Harry, who had propped up his broom and was putting his jacket on.

'Get movin', Jimmy said to Harry, jerking his thumb, and to Dillon, 'Few cards I got made up, stick 'em round the pubs, clubs.' They went into the office, basking pinkly in the slanting sunlight. 'Me and Harry shifted the crates first thing . . . Here, present.' Jimmy took out his cordless phone and placed it on the desk. 'My contribution, nothin' to do with Newman. Where's Clifford?' He bellowed past Dillon's shoulder, 'Go on, Harry, don't hang about!'

Like a bleeding puppet-master, Dillon thought. Did he never let go the strings, never ever let up, not even for a second?

'What you want the deeds of Harry's house for?' Dillon asked, pinning up a large-scale street map of central London.

'Collateral. An' I got these forms from the bank, to apply for a government grant.' Jimmy tossed the pamphlets on the desk. The phone rang, and it was as if they were both frozen for a moment, stunned with the shock of it actually ringing.

Jimmy picked it up. 'Stag Security and Chauffeur Drive . . .' He listened, nodding, then glanced at Dillon, giving the thumbs-up. 'I'll just see if we have a car available.' He covered the mouthpiece. 'Taxi . . .'

Big ecstatic grin from Dillon, who grabbed a notepad and pen, shoved them across the desk.

'We have a Ford Granada available, yes . . . and the address? Yes . . . destination?' Jimmy scribbled. 'Fine . . . be with you in ten minutes.' He put the phone down and stuck out his hand for Dillon to shake. 'We're in business – that's our first fare! See? It's workin' out – Oi, Cliff!' Jimmy tore off the sheet, handed it to Cliff as he came in the door. 'Can you pick up at 12 Thresherd Street, a Mrs Williams, going to Bond Street.'

Jimmy was fizzing like a Roman Candle. Tossing the car keys, reaching for the cordless phone, mouth working overtime.

'Use the Granada, an' take this, it's a portable. You got money for petrol?' Snatched aside to Dillon: 'We'll have to get a kitty box organised, all receipts, etcetera . . .' And even while Dillon was patting his pockets: 'Okay, Frank, I got it, here's twenty.'

Cliff stuffed the noted away, and as Dillon went past him, 'Where you off to, Frank? We need the phones manned . . .'

'Takin' a leak,' Dillon said, not looking back, 'if that's okay with you, Jimmy!'

The puppet-master stared after him, but for once kept his trap shut.

24

Having got the boys sorted, sitting in front of the telly watching *Neighbours*, plates of fish fingers, beans and potato waffles on their knees, Susie went into the kitchen to the smell of burning bacon. On top of a long, hard day saying 'Marway's MiniCabs' ten thousand times, it was just what she needed. 'I told you to watch the pan!' Idle bugger hadn't even budged, elbows on the table with his back to the stove, a can of Tennents Export in his hand. Susie took it out on the eggs, cracking three into the hot fat, breaking one yolk.

'You're not workin' for that Paki any more.'

'Oh no? That an order is it?' Susie looked over her shoulder, teeth pressed together. 'You think you could get yourself a plate, knife and fork?'

Dillon's chair scraped as he got up. He made a performance of slamming open the drawer, clattering inside, grabbing a plate from the draining rack.

Susie counted to ten but only got to five, unable to help herself.

'The rent is due! The milk bill, the kids need new gym gear. Got the money, have you, Frank?' She slid two rashers and the two unbroken eggs onto his plate, then did her own. She stood holding the empty pan. 'There's no money coming in from you, Frank . . . who you think's been paying the bills while you were gallivantin' all around Scotland?'

Dillon stared down at his plate, decided he was too hungry to pick it up and hurl it at the wall. It hadn't been a good day up to now, and he could do without Susie rubbing salt into an open wound. Two calls they'd had so far. Two measly, stinking calls. All afternoon they'd sat around the office, dozing, scratching their arses, waiting for the phone to ring. Finally, Jimmy had suggested putting in a call to Newman. Work was work, another five grand in the mitt, just for doing the airport run . . . What about it, Frank?

Dillon folded a slice of bread, dunked it in the eggs. 'I was workin' in Scotland, started up the business with the cash,' he reminded her. He took a bite, chewed, glared at the Daddies Sauce bottle. 'Not that you've shown any interest. Not even been to see the place . . .'

'I'm not actually flushed for time, Frank,' Susie said, attacking the bacon. 'I shop, cook, clean the house, as well as washing, ironing. You think your shirts walk into the wardrobe?'

'I don't want you workin'.'

'We *need* the money from Marway – '

Dillon swiped his plate off the table, along with the cutlery, salt and pepper, sauce bottle. He wrenched a bunch of crumpled fivers from his pocket and flung them on the table, white to the lips.

'Take it, take it – an' get on that phone, tell your Mum, tell her *not* to come, I want you here lookin' after my kids!'

Jimmy pulled up in the metallic gold Granada just as Susie was leapfrogging across the central courtyard in an L-plated Nissan Micra, gripping the steering-wheel in both hands, a frown of concentration on her face. Marway sat beside her, composed and calm as ever.

Grinning, Jimmy did a sweeping bow, ushering Susie on her way. 'Left hand down a bit, love!' he laughed, and then caught a glimpse of Dillon in the flat above, lurking behind the bedroom curtains.

'Big Brother's watchin' you, Susie!' Jimmy waved. 'Hi, Frank!' and hooted again as Dillon ducked out of sight.

Dillon was livid. Susie had paid no attention to the 'I will be obeyed ' act and it pissed him off. She had started getting at him, not listening to him, and he felt inadequate. She'd even got her ruddy mother coming over even though

197

he told her that he didn't want her in the flat, but the frustrating thing was, deep down, he knew Susie was right, they did need the money. He just hated feeling impotent.

The boys were in the bath, and Jimmy got roped into towelling them down while Dad sorted out clean pyjamas. He emerged from the bathroom carrying young Phil wrapped in a towel, bouncing him up and down.

'Second one all clean an' ship-shape, Sergeant! Where you want him?'

In the boys' room he found Dillon, wearing a plastic apron and a scowl, wet shirt sleeves rolled up, buttoning Kenny's pyjama top. The doorbell shrilled, and Dillon said, 'That'll be your Gran . . . get 'em in their bunks, Jimmy, then we gotta get a move on.'

He was halfway along the landing on his way to answer the door when Jimmy's mocking voice floated from the bedroom. 'Don't forget to take your pinny off, Freda!'

Dillon dragged it off and furiously flung it over the banister. After all he'd said – after giving it to her straight, and she hadn't taken a blind bit of notice. Well, we'll see, he thought, thumping down the stairs. We'll bloody well see about that.

'Awww shit! These bloody elephants are givin' me a hernia!'

Sweat running down his neck, Harry staggered through the doorway into the passage, a tea chest clasped in his arms. He nearly tripped, grazed his elbow on the pink wall, and lost his grip. The corner thudded against one of the tea chests already stacked there, the side split open, straw and plastic bubbles spilling over the floor.

'. . . five, six, seven,' Dillon counted, checking them off on his clipboard. Jimmy and Cliff panted in, carrying one between them. 'Eight,' Dillon said. 'This the lot, Jimmy?'

'Yeah, this is it . . .' Jimmy mopped his face, then noticed the gaping split. 'Which cack-handed twat did that!'

'I just dropped it,' Harry said lamely. 'Weighs a ton . . .'

'You're tellin' me!' Jimmy used the side of his foot to

tidy up the straw. 'Get it back together, come on, they'll be here . . .'

'I'm off,' said Dillon, handing over the clipboard. 'Check the cash, Jimmy. Knowing Newman, he's probably printin' it hisself.' And swapped Jimmy's dark look with an even darker one of his own. 'I don't wanna see him, okay?' He went out, banging the door.

Jimmy squatted on his haunches. An elephant with no nose was sticking through the tangle of straw bulging from the split. He yanked it out.

'Its trunk's off!'

Cliff leaned over. 'I got the same back at the flat. We just switch it over, they won't know.'

Jimmy jerked his arm out, pointing. 'Go an' get it – move! They'll be here . . .'

The panel buzzed, lights flashed. In her little plywood-and-glass cubby-hole Susie swivelled round in the typist's chair, mug of tea to her mouth. She put one on hold, flicked a switch. 'Marway MiniCabs. Oh, hi, where are you, Tom? I've got a fare holding.' She flicked over. 'Sorry to keep you waiting . . . Heathrow. Do you need a collection return service? Okay, thank you . . . right, about fifteen minutes.' She flicked back. 'Tom, 12 Ranleigh Crescent to Heath-row, basement bell, Mrs Dunley.' Buzzing, flashing. 'Marway MiniCabs . . . I'm sorry, I'll just check where the driver is – will you hold?' Flick of the switch. 'Car 14, come in, Car 14 to base, please.' Crackle. Hiss. Voice from Mars. *'Car 14, I'm in Edgware Road. There's an overturned lorry . . .'*

Susie laughed. 'Yeah, I'm sure. Can you get the fare in Ladbroke Grove or not?' She paused, her hand on the switch, as Dillon walked in, lightly perspiring in a red vee-necked sweater with no shirt under his black leather jacket. He came up to the counter, stood there, feet planted, and she didn't need to ask what mood he was in; his face was eloquent testimony to that.

199

The glass-panelled door to the inner office opened. Marway peered out. Dillon ignored him.

'Susie, get your coat.'

'Nothing wrong, is there?' inquired Marway, raising an eyebrow.

'Not yet!' Eyes front and centre, voice deadpan.

Susie didn't move, watching him carefully, waiting for the eruption. Instead Marway said in his pleasant, modulated voice, 'I've got some details of insurance companies for you.' He indicated behind him, a graceful wave of the hand, gold cuff-link glinting. 'You want to come upstairs?'

Dillon shot a glance at the Sikh. His eyes clouded, more in confusion than anger. Susie didn't know what he would do next, and neither, she realised, did he.

Shirley was up a ladder, paste brush in one hand, scissors in the other, when Cliff arrived at the flat. He stepped round the furniture, draped in dust sheets, the trunkless elephant under his arm, giving his fiancée's endeavours the once-over.

'That bit over there's crooked,' he said, and started rummaging amongst the paint cans and decorating paraphernalia on the newspaper spread over the floor. 'Where's the strong glue?'

'Crooked?' Shirley backed down the steps, her long legs and shapely rump camouflaged under a baggy check smock. 'You'll get this brush wrapped around your head ... Ahh!' Seeing the elephant, she gave a cry of anguish. 'Did you break it?'

'It's just the trunk,' Cliff reassured her, prising the top off the small plastic tube. 'I'll fix it.'

'That's not the same one −!' Shirley bent down for a closer look. 'That's got green eyes, the other one had brown. I don't like that one! Where's the other one?'

Cliff applied epoxy double-strength quick-drying glue to both surfaces and pressed the trunk back into place, using his finger and thumb as a clamp. 'I had to take it back.' He waited a couple of moments and then tried to let go. 'Oh!' Stuck. 'Shit!'

'Which colour do you like?' Shirley opened a sample book of curtain material, marked with slips of paper. She held it up to the light. 'This one . . . or that one? I like this one,' tapping a lemon polyester with faint green stripes.

'Yeah, great.' Cliff said through his teeth, attempting to unpeel himself from the elephant. He yanked hard, bringing tears to his eyes. One intact elephant. Minus two fingerprints.

Mrs Marway poured tea into bone china cups from a silver teapot with an S-shaped spout. She leaned across the low table, and with a smile handed Dillon his tea, a bracelet of gold inlaid with lapis-azuli on her slender brown wrist, matching the heavy necklace displayed against her cashmere sweater. Perched on the edge of the sofa, Dillon tried to get his finger through the S-shaped handle, and couldn't, so he gingerly held the cup in both hands, scared to death of dropping it.

Susie, seated next to him, watched with bated breath. She nodded and smiled at Mrs Marway, who nodded and smiled back. The room seemed very warm, almost claustrophobic. It was lavishly decorated, with embossed wallpaper and fringed wall hangings and framed prints, rich fabrics and furry rugs everywhere, cabinets with built-in spotlights showing off shelves of china, crystal and copperware. Expensive, quite impressive, but a bit overwhelming for Susie's taste.

'He's been fair to me from day one,' Marway was telling Dillon frankly. He leaned back at ease in his winged armchair, fingers clasped together, legs elegantly crossed, a crease in his trousers that could have sliced cheese. 'And if you open an account, show a good cash flow . . .' He spread his hands. No problem. Plain sailing.

'We made over five grand, first week,' Dillon revealed after a slight hesitation. '. . . No thanks,' he said politely, refusing the small silver tray of cakes and biscuits proffered by their hostess.

'That's good, just one car.' Marway was impressed. 'Word of advice. Don't ask for just the amount you need, you'll have to give yourself manoeuvrability. If I were you, I'd specialise. With the army experience your men all have, terrorist training . . . make that your speciality.' He pursed his lips, eyes gazing meditatively at a hanging brass lantern. 'At a low, thirty. But try for forty.'

Dillon nearly dropped his cup. 'Thousand?!'

Marway nodded. 'But you can't have my receptionist.'

Dillon's head went forward at that, and Marway's grave face broke into a smile. 'Just joking. But I believe one of the reasons my business runs smoothly is because I use my family – my three brothers, a cousin, two uncles – all drive for me. It's a family concern.'

Dillon finished his tea and gratefully put the cup safely back in its saucer. 'My lads are my family,' he said, standing. He put out his hand and Marway got up to shake it. 'Thanks for this,' Dillon added, meaning it, 'and for . . .' He indicated Susie. 'She driving yet?'

'Test next month, isn't it, Susie?' Marway said with a smile.

Dillon looked quickly at Susie, gawking a little. Susie smiled at the carpet, flushing.

Later, as they were undressing in the lamplight, Dillon said, 'So you think you'll pass?' His feelings were at sixes and sevens, not sure whether he felt proud, or threatened, or what.

'I don't know.' Susie crawled into bed and lay down on the pillow, eyes closed. 'I can still have lessons then?'

'I'm sorry . . . he's an okay bloke.' Dillon sat on the edge of the bed in his jockey shorts, elbows on his knees. 'Things have been getting on top of me – well, Jimmy. He means well.' He sighed, shaking his head. 'It's just so easy for him, he's been out longer. Well, to be honest,' Dillon

202

admitted in a rare moment of confession, 'he's arranged most of it . . .'

'What about the others – Cliff, and, and – ' Susie yawned.

'Harry. Harry Travers. He's okay, and Cliff. It's just . . . Jimmy.' Dillon picked at some loose skin on his thumb. 'There was a night, in Northern Ireland, there were ten of us, me and my lads, and we were . . .'

A soft snore made him look round. Dillon reached over and drew the bedcover up around his wife's shoulder. He gently touched her cheek. He said in a whisper, 'I'm trying, Susie.'

By shoving the desk forward a couple of feet and pushing the chairs to the wall, Harry had found a space for his doss bag. With a chicken vindaloo, mushroom pilau and two brinjal bhajis keeping the lid on five pints of bitter and two large Jamesons, he was well away, snoring loudly. From above, the faint sound of Annie Lennox, the murmur of voices and laughter, but Harry slept on.

Two shapes slid past the window, silhouetted in the streetlight. The clink of something metallic, the protesting groan of timber, and then a sharp crack as full leverage was applied.

Harry stopped a mid-snore. His eyes came open. He held his breath, listening. The splintering of wood from the passage confirmed it; he hadn't been dreaming. In one movement he slid out of the sleeping bag, kicked it under the desk, rocked himself up. Barefooted, wearing his old maroon tracksuit with the blue regimental crest and the word 'Airborne' on the left breast, he moved to his bergen and from a side pouch slid out a nine-inch iron bar with a bulbous end.

A slit of light appeared under the door as someone flashed a torch.

Harry crept round the desk, flattened himself against the wall. Torchlight fanned out under the door. A floorboard creaked. Harry raised the iron bar. The knob twisted and the door slowly opened.

Harry waited just long enough to check out there was more than one, and as the torchbeam swept the office, let the first man have it, downward smash, on the back of the head, knocking him cold. He swung round to face the second man, a big sod, framed in the doorway, and beckoned to him with a smile.

'Come on, you bastard . . . come on!'

The man lunged. Something glinted in his hand. Harry pivoted on the balls of his feet, chopped the wrist as the blade went for him, and heard a clatter of metal. The man stumbled forward under his own momentum. Harry clipped him with the iron bar, and the man collided with the desk, sending it crashing over. He was up fast, hurling the telephone, a chair, anything he could lay his hands on. Then it was Harry's turn. He saw the right hook coming, parried it with his left arm, brought up the iron bar and clouted the man across the ear. The man staggered, nearly fell, regained his balance. Harry followed in with a heel to the knee-cap and finished it off with a head-butt. It was a job well done, neat, tidy, professional, and Harry, softly rifting vindaloo fumes, felt quite pleased with himself.

25

Cliff's jaw sagged as he took in the shambles. 'Bloody hell, does Frank know yet?' he asked, stepping over a broken chair. He looked round, shaking his head, and then saw the two figures hunched against the wall, shirts pulled up and knotted over their heads, arms between their knees, hands and feet tied together.

Harry leaned against the overturned desk. One sleeve of his tracksuit was rolled up, his forearm bandaged and taped. He straightened up as Dillon walked in and stopped dead in the doorway, staring. Susie appeared behind him, peering round his shoulder.

Scratching his head, Harry launched in, 'They broke in last night. I didn't even feel it,' pointing to the bandage, 'but one of 'em slashed me arm, so when I done the business . . . Hello, love,' he greeted Susie, 'I went to the hospital. I just got back.'

'I'll go,' Susie said. She looked up into Dillon's face. 'I thought it all sounded too good to be true.'

'Susie!' Dillon called as she stumped out. He half-turned to go after her and changed his mind. He looked at the wrecked office and then at the two men, trussed up like IRA suspects. 'You didn't call the police?'

'No.' Harry moved across to them. 'I might have been a bit nasty, I gave 'em both a hell of a whack . . .' It sounded more apologetic than boastful. 'And then when I turned the lights on – ' reaching down and yanking up one of the shirts ' – I recognised him!'

So did Dillon. It was Newman's minder, Colin, the one with the widow's peak and the permanent five o'clock shadow, only now it was a nine o'clock shadow the morning after. His hair was matted with blood, and it had caked down one side of his face. There was a sock stuffed in his mouth, which was why his bulging-eyed fury was restricted to apoplectic gurgles and choking grunts.

Dillon was puzzled. 'What did they want? Did they get our cash? I mean – why wreck the place?'

'Ask him! Or whichever – ' Harry tore off the shirt, revealing the other man's head, which had an open gash along the jawline and two bloodshot eyes separating a yellow bruise ' – you want!'

Jaunty steps down to the basement and Jimmy breezed in, whistling. As the whistle died away to silence, the phone rang. Jimmy kicked the broken chair aside. 'What the hell's been goin' on?'

Dillon threw his hands up. He snapped irritably, 'Answer the phone, Cliff!'

'I'm lookin' for it, all right?' Cliff said, down on his hands and knees, crawling through the wreckage. He found the wire and traced it hand over hand to the corner behind the filing cabinet.

Dillon pulled the sock out of Colin's mouth and narrowly avoided being spat in the face for his trouble. The man was berserk, frothing at the mouth, eyes rolling.

'You bastards! I'll have this place torched! You bastards – crazy bastards – '

'Hey Frank, Frank,' Cliff yelled. 'This is business, it's Shirley . . .'

'Get rid of her.' Dillon clamped his hands to Colin's face. 'You shut it!' he snarled.

Cliff was still yelling. 'Jimmy, can you get your hands on a roller for a weddin'? It's Mavis's sister, friend of Shirley's, she's been let . . . *Jimmy?*'

'You make your soddin' weddin' plans another time,' Dillon shouted. 'Get off the phone!'

'It's not my weddin – it's a job!'

Jimmy whirled on him. '*Say yes, get off the phone!*'

'Order a hearse, you're gonna need one,' Colin muttered, dark murder in his eyes. Dillon used the back of his hand to smash Colin's head against the wall.

Cliff had finished the call and hovered near the door. 'Burt it's tomorrow, Frank . . . they want a Roller.'

With a glaze over his eyes Dillon grabbed Cliff by the collar, shoved him into the passage and slammed the door, screaming, 'Get off the fuckin' phone!'

He turned back. Harry was swinging his leg. His toe thudded into Colin's ribs. Colin, already hunched over, hunched deeper, howling. Dillon said, 'You got ten seconds. What you after?'

Colin's strained, agonised face came up. 'He just wants the bloody elephant back . . .'

Dillon went down on one knee, gripped Colin by the throat, fingers digging in. His voice was lethal.

'You tell that prick Newman – he wants somethin' from me, then all he had to do was ask!'

He stood up, eyes glittering, yanked his jacket straight, and went to the door, jerking his head for Harry to follow.

'What you doin'?' Jimmy asked, confused.

Dillon said coldly, 'They're your friends, take 'em to Newman!' and went out.

Shirley was doing the tricky bit round the window frame when Dillon and Harry showed up. She let them in and went back to her scissors, straight edge and paste brush. 'Did you get that Roller organised?' she asked Dillon, who was standing near the door, looking round the room. It took him a second to cotton on.

He nodded, lifting a dust sheet. 'Cliff's handling that personally.'

'Well that's all right then.' Shirley peeled away the edge of the wallpaper, snipped three times, pressed it back. '. . . Mavis is givin' me my dress at cost price, if Susie wants anythin' run up, shirts, blouses, she'll – '

Dillon spotted it, under a sheet of newspaper on the sideboard. 'We've just come to pick up the elephant.' He grabbed it, stepped over paint cans on his way to the door.

'Oh!' Shirley glanced round with a surprised smile. 'Can you change it?'

Dillon looked at her and then looked at Harry, who shrugged. What's she on about? Down in the street, Harry opened the rear door of the security wagon and they climbed in. Sitting opposite one another on the steel benches, Dillon held the elephant in both hands and gave it a gentle shake, then a harder one.

'Is it hollow?' Harry sucked at the fringes of his moustache. 'You don't think it's drugs, do you?'

'It's not hollow, doesn't sound hollow.' Dillon snapped the trunk off where Cliff had fixed it and tapped the solid part with his fingernail. He held the elephant up, turning it this way and that. 'Can you see joins?'

Harry had a brainwave. 'Ivory, it's illegal – he's bringin' in ivory! Is that ivory, the tusks?'

'Harry,' said Dillon wearily, 'the tusks are an inch long – he'd need twenty tons of them. Come on, let's get back to camp.'

Harry reached for the handle that wasn't there; the inside of the door was smooth welded steel with a horizontal slit near the top.

'Ohhh shit! You can't open the doors from inside,' Harry suddenly remembered. 'It's a security device . . .'

Dillon closed his eyes.

'It's okay,' Harry said, peering through the slit. He whistled. 'Oi . . . Oi, Shirley!'

About to dump a black plastic bag in the bin at the garden gate, Shirley looked round. Harry's eyes squinted at her through the slit.

'Can you just open the door, Shirley . . . we're locked inside.'

Shirley doubled over, shaking with laughter. 'Call yourselves a security firm . . . !'

There must have been ten thousand items in the warehouse. Rack upon rack of carved wooden figurines, brass ornaments, beaded cloths, ashtrays, beaten copper tea trays, ebonite letter openers, brass wind chimes, pregnant fertility goddesses, tigers, elephants and snakes of baked terracotta with bits of coloured glass for eyes. The peoples of the Indian sub-continent were paid starvation wages for churning out the stuff. Barry Newman imported it by the container-load and slapped on a mark-up of twelve hundred per cent. It was what was known as enterprise initiative.

Newman moved along the racks, his gaunt, hollow face as stiff as one of the carved heads. Jimmy walked behind him, stepping lightly as if he were treading on eggshells. 'Frank said you gave it to him!' Jimmy protested, not liking the wheedling tone of his own voice, especially after the third or fourth time.

Newman stopped. Seized by a sudden fit of rage, his bony hand shot out, sent one of the metal racks toppling, hundreds of cheap and nasty artifacts and ornaments crashing to the concrete floor.

'I am gettin' tired of repeating myself, Jimmy,' Newman said flatly, not even raising his voice above the clattering echoes. 'He was given one from the first shipment, but the missing one came from the second! What did he do? Switch them?'

Jimmy backed away, hands raised. 'It's just a mix up, leave it with me and I'll sort it. You'll have it tonight!' he promised.

He turned and hurried out as two of Newman's men started to clear up the debris. What bloody game was Dillon playing? Messing with Newman, he wanted his bumps feeling. Newman had been mates with the Krays and had picked up one or two of their nice little habits. And added a few neat twists of his own. Like carving his initials in people's faces, using knee-caps for target practice. Dillon wasn't part of the Maroon Machine any more, he was in civvies, and if he didn't wake up quick to that fact, he'd soon wake up dead.

'Go on,' Dillon urged Harry, who was standing over the elephant with a hammer. 'Smash it!'

Jimmy walked in and saw the elephant on the desk. He

said in a relieved voice, 'Frank, you got it!' and then saw Harry, hammer raised high. 'No! Wait . . . !'

Horrified, he watched as Harry clouted it one, smashed off a chunk and knocked the elephant to the floor. Dillon picked it up, set it back on the desk. 'Hit it again . . .'

'Come on, don't mess around,' Jimmy said, frantic. 'Give it me!'

Harry brought the hammer down, this time the arse-end and one of the back legs fell off. 'It's solid, Frank,' was Harry's considered opinion.

The phone rang, over in the corner. Distracted, Jimmy looked round and saw it was on top of the filing cabinet where Cliff has left it. He snatched up the receiver, eyes fixed on Harry, who was hefting the hammer for another crack.

'*Yeah*?' Jimmy almost snarled into the phone. '*What*? Shit . . .' He covered the mouthpiece. 'It's a geezer wantin' a cab to Gatwick . . . Don't smash it, Harry!'

Jimmy flapped his arm desperately. '*Harry – wait*!'

Too late.

'I need it by eleven in the morning, but it's got to be white,' Cliff said to Fernie. They were standing outside the main workshop doors, a weak sun playing hide-and-seek behind some threatening clouds.

Fernie wiped his hands on an oily rag, looking round the yard. 'That's all I've got,' he said finally, pointing a black-rimmed fingernail. Cliff goggled. It was a hearse. Chromium-plated cherubs supporting the coffin guide-bars in the long rear window.

'I can put seats in the back,' Fernie offered helpfully.

The portable phone beeped on the Granada's dash-board. Cliff reached inside to answer it. 'Who? What? Gatwick?' He frowned into the phone. 'But I'm out of gas! Hang on . . .' He patted his pockets, pulled out an Oddbins receipt, and turned to Fernie. 'Can you lend us twenty quid till tomorrow?'

Fernie just stared at him.

The last of the stragglers were heading off home when Susie arrived at the schoolyard. She went through the gates, struggling with two Tesco carrier-bags laden with shopping, a skirt she'd just collected from the dry cleaner's in a plastic wrapper under her arm. Stupid woman had got the tags mixed up, which was why she was late. The last of the kids had gone by now, the yard empty except for two boys aimlessly kicking a football about.

She went over to them. 'Do you know Phil and Kenny Dillon?' One of the boys shrugged, while the other simply ignored her, balancing the ball on his instep.

The caretaker came out with a bunch of keys. Same question, and pretty much the same response. Susie trailed back to the gates, a breathless, fluttery sense of panic in her chest. But they couldn't have gone far, they'd been told time and again not to wander off. They were good kids really. She looked worriedly up and down the street . . . just wait till she got her hands on the pair of them!

One of the boys called out, 'They were picked up, 'bout fifteen minutes ago.'

Frank? But he was working. Then who? Susie started running.

26

The pressure was on. Dillon felt he was in the middle of a Marx Brothers movie, not sure whether he was Groucho, Chico, Harpo, or Karl. First Cliff rang in: transport for tomorrow's wedding job sorted, which was one headache less, at least. The instant Dillon put the phone down it rang again. Marway. Appointment with the bank manager fixed up. Could they make it for ten in the morning, on the dot? 'Yeah!' Dillon was excited. 'Yeah, we'll be there . . .'

With the elephant under his arm, Jimmy was halfway to the door.

'Wait . . . !'

Harry, who was on his way out, came back in.

'Not you, Harry, go on, get out – put that back!' Dillon said to Jimmy, pointing at the desk. He spoke into the phone. 'Sorry, Mr Marway . . . yes, okay, and thank – thank you very much.'

He banged the phone down and darted for the door, yelling, 'Harry! *Harry – wait!*' and caught up with him in the passage. 'We got an appointment at the bank with the manager.' Dillon counted the tips of his fingers. 'Now, we'll need all your deeds, an' all our commendations from the Army, an' – '

The phone rang. Jimmy shouted from the office, 'Frank, it's Susie!'

'Ask her what she wants,' Dillon called, not quite through. He was still on his third finger, trying to remember what it was. Somebody knocked on the door, making him forget completely. 'See who it is, Harry,' Dillon said, turning back.

'Bloody hell, what you think I am, a yo-yo?' Harry grumbled, opening the door. 'Tell me one thing, then – '

Two engineers in trim grey overalls, British Telecom logo

212

on their breast pockets. 'Frank!' Harry yelled over his shoulder. 'Hey, Frank, better come out here . . .'

Halfway through the door, Dillon swayed back from the hips, got a peek, and dived into the office. Jimmy was saying into the phone, 'He's just comin' . . . what? No, we bin here all afternoon.' He held out the receiver to Dillon with one hand and picked up the elephant with the other.

'Put that back!' Dillon ordered, grabbing the phone off him. He jerked his thumb. 'There's two blokes out there from the GPO, take care of them!' Jimmy opened his mouth as if to protest or perhaps explain, but Dillon wouldn't give him the chance. 'I warned you about connecting the phones – just sort it out.'

Reluctantly, dawdling, Jimmy turned away.

'Sue?' Dillon said. And then through his teeth: '*Give that here, Jimmy*!'

Sighing, Jimmy put the elephant down on the desk. The engineers were just outside the door, looking up at the electric box. One of them unclipped a pencil torch. 'Is there a problem, mate?' inquired Jimmy heartily. He glanced behind at Dillon and pulled the door shut. 'Only we just moved into the premises . . .'

Dillon sat on the edge of the desk, frowning at the elephant, what was left of it, with its decorative head-covering of tiny beads and glass baubles, vaguely trying to concentrate on what Susie's agitated voice was saying.

'Sorry, love, what . . . ?' Not drugs, the thing wasn't hollow. Not ivory. He couldn't think what else. He said, 'Aren't they with your Mum? Well – I'd have told you if they were with me.' He listened, nodding, pushing a hand through his hair. 'Okay, call me back.'

Dillon put the phone down, still gazing at the elephant, now wondering about Kenny and Phil. He wasn't unduly worried, not at this moment, but it was yet another niggle he could do without, on top of this weird Nelly the Ele-phant business, the bank appointment in the morning, and now the damn GPO snooping around. He'd warned Jimmy, but Jimmy wouldn't be told. He knew all the

213

angles. Which corners to cut. How to bend rules and regulations, con the VAT-man, dodge standing charges. Always shading the odds in his favour, living by his wits and a winning smile. Dillon looked at his hands, flexing his fingers. That's what Jimmy was to him, Dillon thought, like one of his own vital, indispensable hands that had turned rogue. Jimmy Hammond. His Bad Left Hand.

Jimmy pushed the door open with his own left hand, edging in backwards. 'They were already connected, we just got the one line,' Dillon heard him telling the engineers. 'I mean, why do we have to pay a connection fee if we're already connected?' Puzzled, querulous, an innocent child falsely accused.

He sidled round the door, and with a guarded look at Dillon, shoved one of the telephones into a drawer. Dillon slammed it shut. He hissed at Jimmy, 'We got to get all our references, we're in the bank ten sharp for the loan.'

Jimmy's face registered disappointment, even hurt. 'I was gonna set that up . . .'

'Well I've done it. So you sort them – ' jabbing towards the passage. 'If we have to pay, then pay up.'

Having given an order, Sergeant Dillon marched out, double-quick time, the elephant under his arm.

He walked through his front door to hear Helen's voice from the living-room going on about calling the police or something. Then Susie rushed into the hallway, her face white as a sheet. 'Frank! Are the kids with you?'

'No, why?' Dillon said, the telephone receiver in his hand. 'The ruddy phones in the office are off, I've got to contact Cliff – '

It all came out in a rush.

'They've been missing all afternoon Frank I've called everyone I don't know what to do Frank I can't . . .'

'Al right, love.' Dillon went very still. Carefully he put the phone down. His voice was calm, his movements unhurried, even gentle, as he led her into the living-room. '. . . All right, I'm here now. How long they been gone?'

214

There was a knock at the door. Susie tried to pull away from him but Helen got there first. Jimmy came in – 'Hi, Frank, you still got it?' – his gaze fixed on the elephant, which Dillon had placed on the sideboard.

Susie burst out, 'Nobody's seen them since four, a lad said they'd been picked up,' while Helen broke in, 'I been round the estate and back to the school three times – '

'One at a time, Susie – picked up by who?'

'What?' Jimmy looked quickly from one to the other. 'Somethin' happened to the boys?'

'I don't know . . .' Susie bent forward, hands clenched, and screamed at the top of her voice, '*I don't know*!'

The phone rang. Dillon held up his hand as Susie made a move. 'I'll answer it.' He went into the hall.

Susie watched him, her eyes large and bright, her body straining forward as if waiting for the starter's pistol. 'Oh please dear God, please let it be them . . .' She saw his shoulders tense. He turned then, and when she saw his face, rigid, the muscles twitching in his jaw, Susie nearly had heart seizure. Barely moving his lips, she heard him say, 'You touch a hair on their heads an' I'll swear I'll – '

'What is it? Frank? *Frank*?'

Dillon put the phone down. His teeth bit deep into his lower lip, forcing the blood out, while his dark hooded eyes bored into Jimmy's with an intense smouldering anger. He said hoarsely, 'Jimmy and me'll bring 'em back.'

'Where are they . . . ?' Susie whispered. '*Frank*?'

'Stay put, Susie, it's just a misunderstanding . . . *stay here*! Mum, look after her!' Dillon slowly brought his hand up and pointed at Jimmy. 'You, with me. Move.'

Down on the second landing, Dillon said, 'That bastard's got my kids, Jimmy. He's got my kids.'

They reached the courtyard just as the black Jaguar Sovereign was ghosting in from the street, Newman's chief minder Colin in the passenger seat, his bruiser's mug bearing the marks of Harry's night ops. Kenny and Phil waved through the rear window, loaded up with Indian temple

215

bells, papier-mache masks, brass candlestick holders and sundry other Third World trash.

Colin stood by the open door as they tumbled out with their spoils. 'Mr Newman just wanted to show you how easy it is, Frank.'

Dillon stepped forward, fists bunched, and Colin held up his hand, smiling. 'Not in front of your boys, Frank . . .' He got back in the car, slid the window down. 'You've got something that belongs to our Guv'nor. Hand it over – simple as that.' His eyes shifted from Dillon's face. 'Tell him, Jimmy.'

Dillon stood between the boys, hands on their shoulders, his face carved from stone. 'You tell Newman I'll bring it to him,' he said as the car pulled away. 'Personally.'

Harry was trying for his good housekeeping badge, tidying up what was left of the office, when Dillon and Jimmy walked in twenty minutes later. Dillon got the tool box from the bottom drawer of the filing cabinet and took out a hammer, chisel and screwdriver.

'I got me sister faxin' all the details direct to the bank,' Harry told them, sweeping rubbish into a nice neat pile in the corner. 'Cliff's out buyin' weddin' bells.'

'If that bank manager was to come down here,' said Dillon grimly, 'we'd not get a post office savin' book, never mind a loan.' He gripped the hammer, a frown of concentration on his face as he stared at the broken elephant. 'Newman kidnapped my kids for this . . .'

'For chrissakes, Frank,' Jimmy panicked, 'he just wants the bloody thing back!'

Dillon angrily shook off the restraining hand. 'Nobody threatens me, nobody gets my kids, frightens my wife, and I just take it!' His fierce glare made Jimmy back off. 'What went down when you saw Newman, Jimmy? And don't give me any bullshit – '

'Frank, I told you, I swear.' Jimmy held out both palms towards the elephant. '*He just wants that.*'

Dillon raised the hammer, ready for an almighty swing,

216

and then slowly lowered it. He blinked, and his jaw dropped. 'Oh man . . .' he said softly, almost mouthing it, '. . . it's staring at us in the face. Newman deals in gems, right? What if these were real?' He tapped the beads and coloured glass woven into the headpiece. 'Look at the bloody size of them.'

Taking the screwdriver, he prised out one of the fragments, a cold blue fire in its depths, and placed it in the centre of the desk.

'Okay, Harry – hit that with the hammer!'

Gripped in both meaty hands, Harry brought it down with all his eighteen stone. The desk split across the middle and caved in. All three down on their knees, muttering and cursing, scrabbling and searching. A glint amongst the debris. Dillon plucked it out and with a grin of triumph held it up – intact.

'Bingo!'

The warehouse was in darkness but there was a light burning in Newman's office. Dillon walked in without knocking. Under his arm he carried a shapeless parcel wrapped in newspaper. Jimmy stayed by the open door, trying not to look at anything specific, in particular Newman's face, a pale, gaunt death mask in the light of the desklamp.

Colin uncoiled from his chair, and Newman made a tiny fluttering motion with his fingers. 'S'all right.' He motioned the minder to leave. Colin went out, giving Jimmy a hard stare, and shut the door.

'Sit down, Frank. Want a drink?'

Dillon placed the parcel in the middle of the blotter and folded his arms. Newman unwrapped it. His face didn't alter when he saw the battered elephant, nor even the empty headpiece, the stones plucked out. He merely sat back in his chair, his pointed tongue flicking out across the wide slit of his mouth.

Dillon took a small canvas bag from his pocket and dangled it.

'Eight crates. That was a big shipment, Mr Newman. Very decorative.'

'Very lucrative.' Newman reached out. 'Hand them over, Frank.'

'Five grand?' Dillon's face went ugly. 'We been caught, we'd have got more than five years *each*.'

'I can pick your kids up any time, Frank – understand me?' The soft voice, dipped in acid, was back. 'This isn't some two-bit racket, this is an organised – '

Enraged, Dillon said venomously, 'And I can have the law pick you up – *Mister Newman* – *any time*. You want to play it that way . . .' he nodded, 'fine by me. If I'm not out of here in ten minutes, I got one of my lads waitin' by a phone.' He held up the canvas bag, clutched tight. 'An' if you want to try an' get these by force – ' Dillon lifted his head and bellowed, '*Harry*!'

The door was kicked open. Framed in the doorway, Harry and a mate of his, built like a brick shithouse, had a furious, struggling Colin pinioned between them. Newman stared at Dillon, tight-lipped with fury, a tiny muscle twitching near his left eye.

'How much?'

Dillon sat down and leaned forward, forearms flat on the desk.

'I want a legit lease on the premises – four years'll do. We'll pay you a fair rent.' Newman tried to interrupt. 'I'm not finished. Plus, we want it re-wired, telephones installed, and an agreement to run a business on the premises. Then the damages to the furniture, re-decoration . . .'

'An' that's it?' Newman said after a little silence had collected. He reached for a cheroot and moistened the end of it.

Dillon nodded. 'One more thing,' and the husky softness in his voice made Newman pause in the act of lighting it. 'I see them near my kids – ' Dillon turned his head and looked deliberately into Colin's face and deliberately back again ' – then it becomes personal. I'll do ten for you, Newman, understand?'

27

I'll do ten for you, Newman, understand?

He'd understood all right. In the flare of the match as he lit his cheroot, Dillon had seen it in the flat grey eyes. And Dillon had meant it. Not big, empty words, running off at the mouth, but the complete, literal truth. One more move like that and he'd gladly, willingly, definitely do for the bastard.

Dillon blamed himself. Everything Newman touched was corrupt, rotten, and yet he'd allowed Jimmy to get them involved, given way easily and weakly just at the moment when he should have toughed it out. Better to go to the wall, jack it all in, than sink into Newman's pit of slime. He wanted nothing more than to provide for Susie and the boys, but he'd be doing them no favours stuck in a prison cell for five years, Barry Newman's prize mug and fall guy for one of his crooked enterprises. And that's what would happen, as inevitable and predictable as clockwork.

He was still tensed up, an odd mixture of anger and elation jumping inside him, when he arrived back at the estate just before midnight. Driving into the courtyard, Dillon saw Jimmy sitting in the jeep. He was slumped down in his seat, as if he'd been waiting for some time, holding a quarter-full bottle by the neck. There was something going down; Dillon didn't know what, and he wasn't keen on finding out. His skin felt prickly, as if charged with static electricity, his chest tight. He locked the Granada, taking his time, and strolled across.

'I just dropped Harry off, then went to see if Cliff's all clued-up for the bank manager.' Dillon snorted ruefully. 'He's at his soddin' weddin' rehearsal.'

Jimmy wasn't pissed. He'd drunk himself beyond that,

into a kind of sullen, dead-eyed edginess, just this side of hysteria. His voice wasn't at all slurred, but it was sneering.

'Ah ha! Cliff goin' into the bank, is he? I don't believe it. I get the premises, get everythin' set up . . .' He stared. 'Why, Frank? It should just be you and me at the bank, those two assholes'll screw up!'

He jumped out, suddenly manic, jabbing his finger into Dillon's chest. 'This was us – partners.'

'The deal was the four of us, Jimmy. We're in it together, but we want it legit – no scams.'

'You came out on top, an' you could have asked ten times the amount.' Jimmy's tone was scathing, as if talking to a cretin. 'Newman was laughin' – '

'You can't stay away from him, can you?' It was an effort, but Dillon kept his temper. 'Sooner or later you'll go down.'

Jimmy turned away, as if to get back into the jeep, then he hesitated. He didn't seem to know what to do, where to put himself, so he swung back, thrust out the bottle of vodka.

'No thanks.' Dillon watched him throw his head back, take a long swig. 'There's no easy money, no easy way, we got to do it by hard graft,' Dillon said. He looked into Jimmy's eyes, bloodshot in the corners. 'If it's not for you – '

Jimmy said nastily, 'Oh, I see – this is the kiss off, is it?'

Dillon's barely-controlled temper went up a notch or two.

'Nobody's kissin' anybody off. You want out, say so, you'll get whatever dough you put in.'

Jimmy swallowed hard, as if what he really wanted to do was cry. 'Have a drink with me, Frank.' Quiet, plaintive. '*Frank!*'

'No, Jimmy, not tonight.'

'When then? *When Frank?*'

'I'll see you tomorrow.'

'You won't, I'm gone,' Jimmy said. 'I'm out of here.' He hurled the bottle against the wall.

Dillon tried to take his arm. 'Don't be like this, Jimmy . . .'

Jimmy yanked free. 'Get off me! Go in to your screechin' wife and kids – ' He blundered forward swinging, a clumsy punch that knocked Dillon backwards. Jimmy's eyes were hot and wild, urging him to take a swipe, goading him on. Dillon wiped blood from his mouth. He said quietly, 'You're pissed, Jimmy.'

'Am I? What about just pissed off!' All of a sudden he seemed to cringe down, abject, pleading. 'I want you to have a drink with me.'

Dillon said nothing. He just shook his head slightly, as if his tolerance level had finally, at long last, been breached. He was as confused as Jimmy in a different way, feelings of anger, contempt, pity and compassion all jangled together, making no kind of sense.

As if realising he had overstepped the mark, Jimmy hesitantly reached out and touched Dillon's burst lip.

'I'm sorry . . . Frank, come on, you know, know I care about you. You need me . . .'

'No,' Dillon said, muted, 'you got it all wrong, I don't – '

He went stiff. Jimmy had his arms around him, hugging him. He was crying, sobbing, like a broken-hearted child. Dillon felt Jimmy's hot tears against his cheek, the scrape of his chin, and then the slobbering mouth as Jimmy tried to kiss him. Dillon stepped back, shuddering. He hit Jimmy open-handed across the face. Jimmy took it and stood, head bowed, tears dripping down, and Dillon slapped him again, as hard and viciously as he could.

'I've always covered for you, Jimmy, now I'm warnin' you, you're out. And don't you come anywhere near my kids.' He wiped his mouth where the blood had smeared. 'You sick bastard.'

Dillon turned his eyes away from the wretched sight and walked towards the concrete stairwell.

'It was a joke!' Jimmy called out pathetically, attempting

221

to laugh. 'No harm done, eh? I just wanted you to have a last drink with me . . .'

Dillon kept going.

'I've signed on the dotted line, Frank, I'm going to . . . *Frank*!'

Dillon entered the stairwell and started to climb.

'Stuff you – stuff the security crap!' Jimmy shouted. 'This time next week I'll be in Colombia,' his voice bouncing and echoing round the brick tenements and concrete landings. '. . . Frank?' Then raising both fists to heaven, he shouted with all his might, '*FRAAAAANK*!'

The echo boomed and died away. Jimmy let his arms flop down. 'I love your kids, Frank,' he said, wiping his eyes with the back of his hand.

On the second floor landing Dillon stood with his back to the wall, head resting against the concrete, listening to the jeep revving up in the courtyard below. It set off with a squeal of tyres and screeched round and round, like a lone dodgem car in a deserted funfair, headlights flashing against the buildings opposite, flashing this way as it turned, making a swirl of patterns on the underside of the walkways.

Flashing lights of ambulances and fire engines on the ceiling of the upstairs room in Hennessey's Bar. Smoke seeping through the floorboards. Downstairs an inferno. Taffy, Jimmy, Steve, Harry, Dillon's lads, crawling through the smoke and flames, searching for the injured. Taffy lifting a beam to let Steve get through with Billy Newman. Harry holding up a table while Jimmy dived underneath to get the girl clear. All of them risking their necks, laying their lives on the line, not because of duty, not because of Queen and Country, but because that's the kind of blokes they were. While the Malones of this world shat their pants and scarpered, this breed of men put their bollocks in a vice and got the job done. It was a privilege to know them, an honour to have served with them, a matter of pride that he was one of them, his mates, his lads. Nothing could ever break the bond, whatever the crap Civvy Street threw at you. Nothing was worth breaking it for.

Dillon was running. He leapt down the stairs three, four, at a time. He cleared the last flight in a single flying jump and came charging into the courtyard as the jeep rocked on its springs in a last crazy turn and shot off into the street and vanished into the night.

Dillon heard it screeching far, far away in the distance. Jimmy Hammond. His Bad Left Hand. But he would sooner have cut off his own right hand than lose him.

'Jimmy . . . ah! Jimmy,' Dillon said, staring into the darkness, his face wet. 'I didn't mean it.'

Dillon waited in the hope Jimmy would make one last trip back, wanting, needing to tell him, he didn't mean it. The jeep never came back, and Dillon sat on the wall and looked at all the graffiti. He lit a cigarette, and inhaled deeply, letting the smoke slowly drift out of his lungs. He wondered if Jimmy would just forget it, waltz in the next day, give him that wink of his . . . Dillon knew that telling him not to see his kids would have cut into Jimmy's heart, he did love them, half the postcards on their board were from Uncle Jimmy. Every Christmas the gifts came, he never forgot one of their birthdays. Jimmy truly loved Frank's boys, maybe because he knew he'd never have any himself.

Dillon pulled on his cigarette and wondered if he should call Jimmy until it dawned: he didn't even know where he was shacked up, but that was Jimmy, his private life was always kept well out of access. It has been a strange sort of agreement they had made, even though it had been years ago.

'What you do in the privacy of your own time Hammond, is your business, but, I don't know about it, I don't want to know about it, and no one else is gonna know – well not from me!'

Jimmy had stood with head bowed, his thick thatch of blonde hair as always immaculate, he stood as if expecting

Dillon to say more, but when nothing else was said he slowly raised his head, looking directly at Dillon. There was no shame in his eyes, almost an arrogance. 'I am what I am, Frank.'

'I know, but don't let the blokes get so much as a whiff or your career's out the fuckin' window.'

'Yeah, I know.'

Jimmy, the bloke with no fear, the first man to volunteer to defuse a bomb, the bigger, the more dangerous the better, as if he liked the adrenalin, needed it. Jimmy, the soldier all the blokes reckoned was gonna roar through the ranks, Jimmy Hammond earmarked for officer material, if it leaked he was a queer, he would be out, and Dillon was the only man who had sussed him. It hadn't been so much as sussed, he'd had a complaint from a recruit who never even made it through the training. Lucky for Jimmy, but it had been Dillon's job to call it . . . At first Jimmy had denied it, called the young bloke a wanker, but then when told if he didn't shut the fuck up and listen, it would go further, he had stood head bowed.

'The kid's useless Jimmy, he's out of here, that's why I am giving you this opportunity to come clean with me, to admit, admit whatever your kink is – and to keep it out of the barracks. Out . . . understand?'

Jimmy had given his odd smile, as if he still felt it was all a load of bull, but Dillon wasn't going to let him bullshit him as he was able to do everyone else. 'He was telling the truth Jimmy, he wanted to go over to medics, you beat the shit out of him, so don't fuck around with me . . .'

Jimmy crossed to the window, again showing not a sign of what he was feeling, no body language gave him away, he was seemingly relaxed and almost joking. 'Yeah, yeah, I'm an iron . . . what you want me to do, go to the CO, tell him, get chucked out?'

'You're not hearing me right Jimmy, I reckon you're one of the best men I've ever worked alongside, I don't want to lose you, this is just a warning, one between you and me, won't go any further. I'm just telling you to keep your private life private . . . that's all, nothing else.'

Jimmy remained standing with his back to Dillon. 'Na! I'll quit, I'm not having that bunch start screaming woofter at me!'

Dillon wanted to hit him. 'I'm not gonna spill the beans, like I said this is just between you and me, understand you great thick-headed bastard?'

Jimmy turned to Dillon then, there was a strange expression on his face, as if he was surprised, almost stunned. 'You'd do that for me?'

'You're one of the best, Jimmy, I'd go out on a limb for you, that's what I'm saying.'

'Well thanks, Frank . . .'

Dillon nodded, and was about to leave, when Jimmy laughed. 'I suppose a fuck's out of the question.'

Dillon turned, couldn't help but laugh, he gave Jimmy a light punch, then clasped him in his arms. 'Watch yourself eh? . . . This is just between you and me?'

They shook hands, and in all the years the subject had never been brought up again between them. Nobody ever did suss that Jimmy 'Fearless' Hammond, was an iron, nobody would have believed it and Jimmy took Dillon's confab to heart, he never at any time referred to or discussed his private life. It remained his secret, and after he returned from any leave, he was the one with all the stories about how many women he had laid, only occasionally would he cast a hooded look at Dillon, but even that was a little furtive, as if he knew not to take it any further.

Dillon had nicked Jimmy's CV from headquarters, read that he had been brought up in a children's home, but that was about all the background anyone ever really knew about Jimmy Hammond. What the file did contain was his recommendations, his qualities as a soldier always written up in glowing terms. Hammond was very much earmarked for officer material, although he was aggressive and was often in brawls with his superiors, but his ability in combat, especially in the Falklands, had been noted.

There was even a special recommendation from Frank Dillon.

Dillon tossed the cigarette down and ground it out, walking slowly up to his flat, up the stone steps, past the graffiti, and on to his own flat's corridor. He leaned on the railings, staring into the darkness. He would probably never understand the Jimmys of this world, or their sexual predilections, they were an alien species. Dillon could never even contemplate the fact that Jimmy Hammond was obsessed with him, loved him deeply, and wanted him to himself. All Dillon knew was that he had hurt Jimmy, said something he knew would hurt, and that he was sorry for that, but it had to be said. Jimmy was dragging them into Newman's world, and it was a world Dillon knew would be destructive. He went back into the flat, more at ease with himself, sure he had done the right thing, but deep down he sort of suspected Jimmy might not come back. He had in the end overstepped their rules, even though they were now in Civvy Street. Jimmy's pitiful attempt at an embrace had broken the agreement; in a way it was a relief, a sad one, but nevertheless Dillon was relieved and, unlike Steve, Jimmy was a winner, he wouldn't do anything crazy like top himself, he was too cool for that. Jimmy'd land somewhere, someplace on his feet, probably with a machine-gun in his hands, needing the rush of adrenalin, loving the edge of danger that cloaked in fury the small, abused, loveless child, who constantly searched for the father figure he never had. Not the mother, because it was his mother who had abused and beaten him, his mother who left him starving in a squalid bedsit for two weeks. Jimmy had been in care since the age of four in eight different institutions. His army records simply stated that he had been brought up in children's homes.

28

The meeting the next morning with the NatWest bank manager wasn't exactly 'an interview without coffee' – Para slang for a telling-off by the C.O. – but it didn't bode well, not in Dillon's estimation. Along with Harry and Cliff, freshly shaven, all three tarted up in their best suits, he did his level best to present an image of sober respectability allied to a keen business brain. The only thing he lacked was the Masons' secret handshake. Whether the bank manager was taken in by the act was doubtful, but at least they were given coffee and biscuits.

Coming out into the street, though, Harry was cautiously optimistic, a bit puzzled by Dillon's obvious dejection.

'Well, he said he'd put the wheels in motion. I mean, that's something, isn't it, Frank?'

Dillon wrenched his tie loose, striding along with the buff document file jammed under his arm. He snapped irritably, 'Harry, without a guarantor we don't stand a chance in hell!'

'Should have had Jimmy with us!' said Cliff vehemently, and it was all Dillon could manage not to blow up at him too. 'I mean,' Cliff went on, 'who do we know that's got that much clout?' He stopped suddenly, smacked his forehead with his hand. '*Christ*! . . . I forgot!'

Dillon's eyebrows shot up. 'You know someone?'

'The bloody weddin'!' Cliff broke into a trot. He flagged his arm frantically. 'Come on, follow me . . . I'm in the NCP car park!'

Dillon and Harry exchanged a look that would have bored holes in galvanised steel and set off after him.

Five minutes later, standing by the Granada, Dillon impatiently checked his watch, reckoning they might just make it by the skin of their teeth if Cliff didn't take all day getting the white Rolls-Royce. Harry sat behind the wheel, keeping the Granada's engine ticking over, ready for the off.

They both looked up at the sound of squealing tyres. But neither one could believe their eyes. Dillon actually thought he was suffering from a bad case of the DTs. Down the concrete ramp came Cliff, driving a long, black Daimler hearse tricked out with silver horseshoes and plastic wedding bells, pink and white ribbons fluttering from the radio aerial. As the Daimler bounced into the street, Dillon clasped his face in both hands, eyes bulging.

'You pillock! What the hell are you drivin'? White Roller . . . *white*!'

Cliff scowled out pugnaciously. 'I know the difference between black an' white, mate! This was all I could get.' With a horrible clashing of cogs, he rammed into first. 'Now follow me, we're late!'

Dillon leaned weakly against the Granada's bonnet. Harry stuck his head out, blinking as he watched the disappearing Daimler. 'Hey, Frank,' he said, scratching his chin. 'That's a hearse . . . !'

Dillon slowly turned his head to look at him. Why, with his crown of thorns, was he surrounded by pricks?

The bride, her three bridesmaids, her mother, sister-in-law, her father, and the best man, who had returned from the church in a panic as the bride was over half an hour late, were standing in hysterics looking up and down the street.

The bride burst into floods of tears, as the chief bridesmaid went inside the house to call for a taxi. The bride's father was ready to kill, fists clenched he threatened and shouted, as rows of neighbours stood looking up and down the road. The cheer went up as, the car horn blasting, Dillon and Harry hurtled into view in the Granada the white ribbons already trailing the floor. Harry had been in such a hurry to stick them up, now they had blown loose.

The bride almost fainted with relief, the best man was shouting for the chief bridesmaid to stop calling the taxi when round the bend, at the top of the road, and hot on the heels of the Granada, with silver bells, bows, streamers of white ribbon, horseshoes and large strips of Christmas decorations the shop had thrown in for free, came Cliff, hat rammed on, car horn blasting. It's tough to actually disguise a hearse, even covered in decorations and two seats rammed in the back! As Cliff stepped out, trying to appear nonchalant, the father of the bride, already in a state of hysteria, lunged at Cliff.

'That's a fuckin' hearse!'

Cliff sat in the office, his head bent back, holding a bloody tissue to his nose. The bloody nose was a present from the bride's father. Occasionally he closed his eyes and uttered a low moan.

'Don't be a wimp, it's not broken,' Harry growled, leaning over for a look. He flopped down and sucked fresh life into the fat cigar he was holding – a present from the best man. 'It was just that you were drivin' the hearse,' he said by way of comfort.

'We got her to the church on time!' exclaimed Cliff furiously. 'Wasn't as if she had to lie down . . .'

'He apologised, didn't he?' Harry said. He gave Dillon a look. 'But if Jimmy was here he'd have a fleet of Rollers – ' snap of the fingers ' – like that!'

Dillon flicked confetti off his shoulder. 'Jimmy's got us into enough crap. We're better off without him.'

'You think he really signed on then?' Harry blew smoke and watched it billowing up past the stag's head. 'I've often thought of doin' a mercenary stint meself, but some of 'em are crazy bastards. He should watch out – '

'He'll be okay,' Dillon interrupted sharply. He stared off somewhere. 'You know Jimmy . . .'

'Nobody ever knows Jimmy.' Harry ploughed on

229

regardless. 'He's one of those weird guys – he was demoted more than any other bloke. He was officer material, could have gone right to the top, but . . . you know what he is?' His blue eyes sought Dillon's.

'I don't want to talk about Jimmy,' said Dillon, tight-lipped.

'Just gonna say he was a – '

'Shut it, Harry!'

'Kleptomaniac,' Harry said, puffing on his cigar.

Dillon cackled a sour, hollow laugh. The phone went, and with a tremendous, grudging effort he reached over to answer it. Newman had delivered on that much, at any rate, had BT reconnect the line. 'Stag Security,' he mumbled into the receiver.

Cliff sat up and threw the bloody tissues into the waste basket. 'That weddin' cost us the last of the kitty . . . maybe if I'm broke, unemployed, it'll get me out of me own weddin'.'

'Well it was good while it lasted!' Harry said, the wise, ancient philosopher. He gave out a long sigh, suddenly dejected, and slumped down in his chair. 'I'm goin' to miss old Jimmy.'

Dillon had finished the call. He sat with his head in his hands, staring unseeingly at the desk-top. He said to no one in particular, 'I don't believe it . . .'

'It's not Jimmy, is it?' Harry asked quickly.

'No,' Dillon said. 'No. No.' He arched back in the chair and then slammed his fist down on the desk. The other two looked at him, alarmed, but his face was alight, positively glowing.

'I think we're in with a chance for that bank loan,' Dillon said, eyes dancing. 'We got a guarantor . . .'

Harry sat up. 'You jokin'?'

'Thirty thousand quid.' Amazed. Incredulous. Gob-smacked. 'It's Marway.'

A movement above Dillon's head had caught Harry's eye. He said, 'Hey! Frank – !'

'No, listen – we're in business!'

The massive stag's head was ever so slowly tilting forward from the chimney-breast, its huge weight dragging
the nails out of the plaster.

'But Frank – !'

'Shut up, because you know what?' Dillon exalted,
dreams filling his eyes, words bubbling out of him. 'We're
gonna make it the biggest, the most successful – ' arms
up, fists clenched, ' – Taxi! Chauffeur! Security Company!
– in London. *Yesssss . . . we're gonna make it, I know it,
I feel it*!'

The stag's head jerked. With a quick nod to Cliff, Harry
tossed his cigar butt to the floor, the two of them jumping
up. Dillon bent down to pick up the discarded butt.
Directly above him the stag's head came loose and toppled,
grabbed by Harry and Cliff in the nick of time.

Puffing away, Dillon strolled forward, airily sweeping
out the hand holding the cigar, the mogul at his ease,
business tycoon of the year. He turned to find Harry and
Cliff, red-faced and straining under the weight of the massive stag's head, holding an antler apiece. If it hadn't been
for their quick thinking it could have crashed down on
Dillon, and killed him.

Unaware of the near miss, Dillon turned. 'No, leave that
up, lads,' he said, wafting a hand. 'It's lucky.

HARRY TRAVERS

29

They were standing in a row, like statues. All three wore new grey suits, peaked chauffeurs' caps of the same grey material tucked under the left arm, shiny black shoes. Completing the ensemble, crisp white shirts and the Regimental maroon tie patterned with the winged parachute motif in dark blue. Behind them, in vee-formation, a gleaming silver Mercedes stretch limo with tinted windows and the metallic-gold Granada, polished to within an inch of its life, sporting a new radio antenna. And behind these, square on, the resprayed and refurbished wagon with a new set of wheels, new windscreen, and emblazoned on its side panel, STAG SECURITY COMPANY, in the Para colours of maroon and dark blue.

Across the yard, Fernie in his baggy, greasy overalls leaned against the workshop doors, arms folded, looking on. Last month, he reflected, these geezers had to cadge twenty quid off him for gas. Now they were done up like a dog's dinner, with their own transport fleet fitted out with cellular radio links. Funny old world.

Harry's neck chafed inside his size-fourteen collar. He had an itch just below the privates department where the suit material was rubbing him. His bloody feet hurt too, cramped inside the stiff new shoes. From the side of his mouth he muttered at Dillon, 'How much longer is he gonna be!'

'Shut it,' Dillon said, turning his head just as the flash went off.

The photographer looked up from the tripod camera, a pained expression on his face. 'Can you hold your positions, please!'

All three looked to the front, legs slightly apart, hands clasped in front of them, motionless as zombies. The camera flashed three time and the ordeal was over. 'Okay, that's it . . . thanks very much.'

Susie opened the flaps of the cardboard box, took out wine glasses four at a time and lined them up on top of the new dish-washer. Helen was at the kitchen table, unwrapping cling film from plates of sandwiches, pork pies, sausage rolls and Marks & Spencer quiches. Harry was sorting out the beer. He'd wedged the eight-gallon aluminium cask on the draining-board and was screwing in the brass tap. One of Harry's mates, Tony Taylor, humped in a crate each of Newcastle Brown and Czech Budweiser, stacked them next to the Hotpoint tumble-dryer which still had the Rumbelow's label, and the guarantee card in a clear plastic sleeve, stuck to its side. From the living-room came raucous bursts of music – a snatch of Tina Turner, rasping Little Richard, Donna Summer on heat – as Cliff got the stereo system set up. Several other anonymous bodies that Susie didn't know from Adam wandered in and out, bringing in more crates, bottles of Thunderbird, six-packs of exotic foreign beers. My God, she thought, they had enough booze to float the *Titanic*.

The guests had already started arriving. Every few seconds the doorbell would go, laughter and loud voices as newcomers spilled into the hallway. Somebody must have been answering the door, though Susie hadn't a clue who. She heard Cliff yelling, 'One speaker's not workin' . . . hang on,' and by Christ it suddenly was, as Eddie Cochran's *Twenty Flight Rock* nearly ruptured her eardrums. Above it Harry bellowed, 'Somebody answer the door!' as the doorbell drilled away in the background. Susie glanced across at Helen, slicing ham and mushroom quiche into quadrants, mother and daughter exchanging looks of alarm and foreboding . . . and the party hadn't even started!

236

Wearing a broad pleased smirk, Dillon was standing next to the microwave, several folded newspapers under his arm, one held open at arm's length. He was telling Wally with smug pride, 'I'm gonna have this framed – good publicity. Get the stack sent to the barracks, wait till they see this!'

Wally put his mouth close to Dillon's ear, yet still had to raise his voice above the bustle, the music, the ceaseless doorbell.

'Hey, Frank! I got some info. Important. Those two bastards your lads were after, word is – '

'Not now, Wally, eh?' Dillon held the paper up. 'You seen this, second page? Merc . . . looks good, very impressive, eh . . . ?'

'I told Harry,' persisted Wally, 'it's a reliable tip-off. Those bastards are here, Frank, in London.' He looked to Harry, who was wiping his hands on the tea towel, and Harry returned a slow, conspiratorial wink. But Dillon wasn't in the mood to listen; with an edgy, abrupt movement he folded the newspaper and slid it onto a shelf with the others.

'Not tonight, Wally,' he said. 'This is a celebration.'

Harry gestured around with his thumb, 'Now's the time, Frank, with all the lads arrivin' – ' And just then, to add weight to it, the doorbell went again. 'We can get a dozen – '

'Leave it out,' said Dillon shortly, and turned away to grab himself a bottle of Czech Budweiser.

'My God, we've got enough food for an army!' Helen exclaimed, surveying the laden table.

'You might just be seein' one,' Dillon grinned, his high spirits soon back, 'the lads from the caterin' corps did all this. Have you seen the paper?' He knew damn well she had but he wanted to chalk one up, gloat a little.

'Well, I hope to God they like pork pies, or we'll be eatin' them for months.' Helen was having trouble finding fault, and the best she could manage was a tart, 'You're

237

wearin' your eyes out lookin' at that newspaper . . .' But all she got from Dillon was another broad grin.

Harry clapped his hands. 'Right, I done my share, I got to go an' pick up Trudie.' He went out, cuffing Wally on his bald head, who was handing bottles from the crate to Dillon, who in turn was lining them up next to the cask on the draining-board.

'Tell everyone, coats upstairs,' Dillon called after him, the doorbell competing now with Chuck Berry who had no particular place to go. Dillon frowned at Wally. 'Trudie?'

'She's the manageress from the travel agency.' Wally's eyes rolled. 'An' she's bringin' a few of her friends . . .'

Dillon nearly said something, but Susie was at his elbow, bottle of red, bottle of white, in either hand. 'Frank, you should answer the door!' she reprimanded him, anxious to keep up the proprieties.

Dillon kissed the tip of her nose and meekly did as he was told.

By nine-thirty the place was jumping. Susie reckoned they had half the battalion there, plus wives, girlfriends and assorted hangers-on. Some of the men she knew by sight, from the early days in married quarters when Dillon was based at Montgomery Lines, as the barracks were known. But most of the faces were young and strange, Toms who'd joined since the Falklands and come to know Dillon as their Sergeant PJI, Parachute Jumping Instructor, during their three-week Basic Para training at Brize Norton

Clutching a glass of wine, Susie squirmed through into the living-room. She hoped the neighbours wouldn't complain. The stereo seemed to be permanently at top whack, even though every time she went by she tweaked it down – obviously somebody immediately tweaked it up. Above the heat and noise and swirling cigarette smoke, Kenny and Phil peered through the banister rails, huddled together to make room for the constant flow of people traipsing up to the bathroom. Helen was standing on the bottom step, pointing a stern finger.

238

'Bed you two – you've been told twice! Now come on . . .'

Susie stepped over somebody's legs, got bumped in the rear by a jiving girl, and steadying her glass called up, 'Do as you're told, you two! You got a drink, Mum?'

Helen pushed the boys ahead of her. She leaned over the banister, face like a thundercloud. 'I want a word with you! Come up, come on!'

On the landing, having got the boys inside, Helen kept her hand on the doorknob, holding the door shut. She turned to her daughter with wide, outraged eyes. 'There's four women down there,' Helen hissed, 'an' if you don't know what they are, then – '

Susie half-closed her eyes. 'Mum, just don't start . . . they're celebratin'. I dunno who half these people are.'

'Tarts,' Helen said in a furious whisper. 'You got tarts down there! Never mind half a ton of pork pies . . .'

And when Susie couldn't help it, burst out laughing, Helen did her Mrs Disgusted of Tunbridge Wells act and flounced into the bedroom and slammed the door. A tall, slender black girl came out of the bathroom. She gave Susie a bright smile. 'Hello, I've not been introduced, but I'm Shirley, Cliff's fiancée.'

Susie said hello and they went down together to join the fray. Fifties rock 'n' roll was in favour at the moment, Elvis in his prime, never as good again, with *My Baby Left Me*, Bill Black's thudding bass making the backbone shudder.

The two women eventually made it past the whirling bodies into the kitchen. A dozen or so ex-Paras had done a flanking move and set up base camp around the beer keg. In the middle of them was Harry, foaming pint in one hand, the other clamped to the ample waist of a blonde woman who was more than well endowed everywhere else. She clanked with jewellery, from earrings in the shape of swinging dragons down to a gold anklet laden with chunky gold star-sign charms. Probably a social worker,

239

Susie decided charitably, which wasn't far wide of the mark.

In expansive mode, Harry was giving with the gab to some of the younger blokes. 'We got an armour-plated security wagon. We got a stretch Merc used to belong to some Iranian, Ford Granada an' – he took a swallow, sucked his moustache ' – suite of offices. You need a job mate – ' belch ' – give us a call.'

Wally flagged Dillon over, draped his arm matily around Dillon's shoulder. 'Hey Frank, you met Kenny Hill, he was in the Gulf, he's just got out . . . any chance of him joinin'?'

Fishing in the breast pocket of his shirt for a card he didn't have on him, and was too pissed to find if he had, Dillon said grandly, 'Give me a bell – you got one of our cards?' He pulled away from Wally and did a Wagons Roll wave of the arm. 'Come on, lads, move into the other room . . . *in – the – other – room – !*'

As the group began to move, Cliff was excitedly telling them, 'We went into the bank manager, showed him our references. We got the loan an' we got more business than we can handle!'

Helen came through, manoeuvring past them with two handfuls of dirty plates and glasses. Susie was pouring a glass of wine for Shirley. Helen stacked the plates in the dish-washer and put the upturned tumblers and wine glasses in the top tray. 'Go for one of these, love,' she advised Shirley. 'They don't half make the glasses sparkle.'

Shirley took the wine from Susie. 'It was a toss-up whether I got one of these or a microwave,' she said, big brown eyes everywhere, taking everything in. She spotted Cliff just inside the living-room door, and at the third shout, because the music was blasting out, he got the message and came over.

'They got a new washing machine, tumble-dryer, dish-washing machine, an' a fridge.' Practically the same height as Cliff, Shirley looked at him, quizzical, and nudged him with her elbow. 'So you tell me, how much you been given?'

Cliff touched a finger to his lips and winked.

Susie rushed past them, having caught a glimpse of her boss and his wife, all at sea in the crowd. Marway was smiling as she brought them through to the relative calm of the kitchen, but his wife had a wincing expression, unaccustomed to a sweltering roomful of burly sweating men, some interesting looking women, and *Green Onions* at sixty-five decibels.

30

'I said, for that much, love, I'd swing from a chandelier naked! An' that's how it started, like it was just a laugh, you know . . .'

Trudie threw back her blonde head and laughed, everything shaking and jiggling, including the dragons dangling from her earlobes.

Wally was well into another of his interminable tales that never seemed to have a point or a punchline: '. . . an' then the C.O. caught us red-handed — what you two friggin' think you're playin' at? We're collectin' information on the opponents' military capabilities, sir!'

'So we raided the house, small terraced job, opposite the suspect IRA house.' A Full Screw — corporal — from 3 Para was holding two young Toms enthralled. 'An' we get into the loft, then we get a slate off, use the old elastic band gig, an' we . . .' he crouched down, using his hands for binoculars '. . . were stuck in there for fourteen fuckin' days!'

'No, listen,' Harry said, hanging onto the bloke next to him, because if he didn't he'd fall over, 'Harris — Steve — he turns to the arsehole, says to him — Sir, I wasn't doin' any field signal, I was tellin' that bugger behind me to get a friggin' move on! Laugh . . . !'

Dillon, in the middle of five, had one of his best stories rolling. He'd gone from keg bitter via Newcastle Brown, with a brief detour for a Grolsch or three, to Famous Grouse, and he was feeling on top of the world, no muzziness, no whirling pit, dandy, just great, fantastic.

'. . . so Jimmy says, Sir, I know how we can get our bearings — compass was lost, see — so he takes out this razor blade, starts stroking it against the palm of his hand, an' this prat of an officer looks on. What the hell you doin', Hammond? Magnetising the razor, Sir. He ties this piece of cotton round it, and it worked. Next day there's this prat with a bandaid round his hand – an' we know . . .' Dillon broke off, gasping with laughter '. . . we know the stupid bastard's gone an' tried it!'

From the kitchen doorway, standing with Helen and Shirley, Susie watched her husband's face. His eyes had nearly gone, that was easy to tell, but she didn't mind. It was the first time since he'd come out that he'd allowed himself to relax, really let go. She knew the strain he was under, trying to make a go of things. Things had been tough at first, no proper job to slot into (not much call in Civvy Street for Fieldcraft – weapons handling, camouflage and concealment, surveillance of enemy firebase), and on top of it, the trouble with Taffy and Steve. But now, fingers crossed, things were looking up. Not just a job, any old job, but his very own *business*, and money to back it, thanks to Mr Marway. Feeling a bit guilty that she was neglecting them, Susie looked round for the couple, but they seemed to have drifted off somewhere. Hardly surprising in this bedlam. Her own head was starting to throb, and a fixed look of long-suffering exhaustion was stamped on Helen's face, like one of those TV adverts for pre-menstrual tension.

Tina Turner had replaced Buddy Holly, her raucous, strangulated voice belting out *Simply the Best*. A drunken chorus took it up, and Dillon was hauled onto a chair, glass in hand, to lead the community singing. Halfway through the mind-blowing din, Harry turned the sound low and gave Dillon a broad sweaty grin and the thumbs-up.

'Thanks – thanks for coming . . .' Dillon beamed down on them, on top of the world, his voice hoarse with singing and the emotion of the moment. 'This is a big day for me, for Stag Security – so pass it on to any of the lads comin' out into civvies – *we got work for 'em*!' He stuck his fist in the air, pumping it in a victory salute. '*We're simply the best*!'

Cheers and shouts turned into a chant of 'Dance! Dance! Dance!' which was all the encouragement Dillon needed, if he needed any. A space cleared, and Dillon and Tina went for it, a circle of clapping hands and stamping feet, the singing almost loud enough to drown out the stereo.

On the fringe of the crowd, Susie shrank away, embarrassed at the spectacle Dillon was making of himself. He was gone, in a world of his own, shirt stuck to his body as he spun round and round, arms up, fingers clicking, hips swaying, performing fancy side-steps and sensuous shimmies. Then she thought, he's not at all bad. In fact he was good. Hellfire, he was brilliant!

Helen had had enough, both of Dillon's gyrations and Tina Turner's shrill vocals. She leaned over and shouted in Susie's ear, 'Can somebody change that bloody record! You know the neighbours have been at the door – next thing they'll call in the police. Turn it down!'

Susie nodded, put her glass down on the sideboard and slid open a drawer; she had something else in mind. Frank was enjoying himself and she wasn't going to spoil his fun, not tonight of all nights. She knew it was here somewhere, amongst their collection of EPs, some of them as old as the Ark. Rummaging through, she pounced, triumphant.

'Found it!' She held up the record in its tattered paper sleeve for Shirley to see. 'This used to be his favourite – he's always loved dancing to it.'

There was no way she could get near the stereo. 'Harry!' Susie waved to attract his attention, handing the record to him over the heads and crush of bodies. 'Will you put this on, it's his . . .' pointing to Dillon, still lost in the music '. . . it's his favourite.'

Harry yelled, 'Cliff! Cliff!' and passed the record on to Cliff at the turntable, then went back to his monologue on the art of warfare that even Tina Turner couldn't disrupt: 'I mean, a stun grenade, mate, it's what – fifteen centimetres high and ten centimetres round, weighs 250 grams, you pull that ring, you get one helluva bang that

244

ignites the magnesium – that's what creates the flash-bang effect . . .'

Cliff had missed his way as a deejay. There was barely a break in the music. One moment Dillon was whirling and singing along to *Simply the Best* in the middle of a bopping, heaving crowd. In the very next, four heavy pounding piano chords pummelled the air.

BAM-BAM-BAM-BAM!
You shake my nerves and you rattle my brain –
BAM-BAM-BAM-BAM!
Too much in love drives a man insane –

The crowd bopping and heaving around him, Dillon stood frozen to the spot, hair plastered to his scalp, sweat dripping off him. Something in his face seemed broken. His throat worked. Wild-eyed now, his expression ugly, demented, Dillon barged forward, roughly thrusting bodies out of the way. He reached out, hands like claws, swiped the playing arm, an horrendous *screeeeech* as the stylus skidded across the record.

'Which bastard put this on!' Panting, staring round, eyes out of kilter, mad-looking.

Harry was there in a trice, a bulky, comforting arm around Dillon's shoulder. 'Outside, come on, old son. Let's have a breather . . .'

Numbed by the suddenness and shock of it, Susie watched her husband being led away, shoulders hunched under the protective shelter of Harry's arm. As for the third or fourth time that night Tina Turner began yet another rendition of *Simply the Best*.

Some of the crowd had spilled from the flat onto the outside landing. They were getting to the silly stage, fizzing up bottles of lager and squirting one another, laughing like drains. Farther along, neighbours were poking their heads out, and when they didn't get much change, slamming back inside.

Harry sat on the concrete steps. He offered a cigarette to Dillon and they both smoked for a while, the thump of

245

music, shouts and screams of laughter issuing from the flat. Leaning against the brick parapet, Dillon stared off into the darkness, a million light-years away. He hardly heard Harry's angry, 'I'll whop that idiot Cliff! Guess he didn't know, Frank.'

As if voicing a private thought, Dillon said, 'I don't understand, it's only since I been in civvies it keeps on comin' back . . .'

A bottle went over and splintered in the courtyard below. From somewhere, a man's enraged shout about this time of night, pack it in or else. Dillon dragged deep, let the smoke out with a sigh. 'Yeah, I know, you think I want to get involved?' he said. The question was addressed as much to himself as to Harry. 'He says they're in London.'

'Yeah, an' maybe Wally's contact's a load of crap,' Harry said. 'Right now, we got an opportunity to give a leg-up to our lads comin' out. They all need work.' He stood up and flicked his cigarette end away, the red ember sailing off through the dark air. 'Let's go back in, I don't want one of those buggers pullin' my blonde.'

The music was even louder now, hysterical screams mixed in with it. Another bottle went crashing down. The men outside the flat were booming out *'Here we go here we go here we go. Here we go here we . . .'* full-throated baritones and basses.

Dillon made a small gesture. 'Yeah, go on, gimme a few minutes.'

Harry moved off. He looked back over his shoulder. 'Not our war any more, Frank,' he said, and carried on, shouting at the drunken scrum outside the flat to bloody well keep the noise down.

From the landing below a woman's voice screamed up, 'I'm gonna call the police! You hear me? I've got two kids tryin' to sleep, *you got no right! Stop it!*'

She was standing in the concrete stairwell, built out from the main block, strained white face staring up. A thin woman with straggling hair, she clutched the fur-

246

trimmed collar of a long coat to her throat, a night-dress underneath, fluffy slippers on her bare feet.

She spotted Dillon at the parapet and shook her fist at him. 'You bastards think you own this estate! I got two kids scared out of their wits . . . !'

Dillon stared back down into the venomous face, pinched with fury. He was used to faces like that, women's faces especially. And their eyes. It was their eyes that haunted him. Eyes that looked at him as if he'd crawled out from under a stone and left a trail of slime behind him. As if he wasn't even human. As if he wasn't any kind of life-form at all.

Border checkpoint. County Tyrone. October 1987.

It is dusk, the poor light made worse by the drizzle sweeping in across the fields and the isolated clusters of farm buildings, their red corrugated roofs shining slick-wet. A line of vehicles, cars and vans, most of them old and beat-up, all of them mud-spattered, wait at the striped barrier. The squaddies are in no hurry. They are here till changeover at twenty-one hundred, so it makes no difference to them. Four men form a semi-circle round the car at the barrier. They wear flak jackets over their DPM uniforms, with special non-slip shoulder pads for their rifle butts. At the hip, trained on the leading vehicle and ready to fire, they hold L1A1 rifles, fitted with thirty-round magazines. The sling of the weapon is attached to the right wrist so that it can't be snatched off in a scuffle.

While these four keep watch, three men and a corporal search the car and its occupants. In this instance, a single occupant, a young man of about twenty, twenty-one. Suspect age group, late teens, early twenties, so he is made to stand, hands on head, just a shirt and pullover, in the grey drizzle. Two soldiers check the inside, one has a sken in the boot. As they re-group the young man mutters under his breath, 'You bastards do this, ya know it's the grey-hound meetin'. You do this every meet.'

The squaddie nearest him raises his rifle and smacks the

butt into the side of his head. That shuts him up. The young man bends over, hands on head, cowering. He is bundled in the car, the door slammed shut on him, waved on. The next car takes its place at the barrier.

Dillon and his squad — Jimmy, Harry, Taffy and six Toms — stand next to the guardpost, watching. They've been out for four hours, 'tabbing around the cuds' as the Paras call patrolling the countryside, and they are good and wet and miserable, and to add further insult, the Bedford RL hasn't shown up, which is a real pisser.

Dillon glances at his watch, unnecessarily, for the third time. The truck is two minutes later than it was the last time he looked. He says to Jimmy, 'Go check where our ruddy transport is, it's half-past seven!'

The next car is a real old banger, more rust than body-work, two teenagers inside. Same procedure as before. Made to stand, hands on heads, away from the vehicle, four rifles trained on them while the search team go to work. To vary the monotony, however, this time they decide to chuck everything inside the car, including cloth-ing and personal belongings, onto the muddy road. A green plastic holdall is tipped out — gym kit, Adidas trainers, bodybuilding magazines, CDs, videos, a Japanese com-puter game and cassette tapes. The glove compartment is swept clean, the boot emptied. Then the boys are shoved up against the car, arms spreadeagled on the bonnet, legs kicked apart, while they are body searched.

The drivers waiting in line are becoming impatient. One or two hanging out, waving and cursing, others sounding their horns. This makes the same difference as before, which is nil. Twenty-one hundred hours is approaching at its own sweet pace, and a few curses and car horns won't make it get here any quicker.

One of the teenagers says something, or is thought to have said something, or perhaps he just happens to have that kind of face. He gets a rifle butt in the kidneys and slumps to his knees, clutching his back. The three soldiers stand in a tight circle around him and his companion, crowding them a little, as if egging them on, as if eager for an opportunity, waiting in hopeful expectancy for a show of retaliation, no matter how feeble. Meanwhile the drizzle comes down, the light fades by the minute, the car horns toot, and Dillon and his lads stamp their feet to keep the circulation going.

Jimmy returns, a sour expression under the streaky brown camouflage cream on his face. 'It's broken down, 'bout five miles back,' he tells Dillon disgustedly. 'We can start on foot, they'll pick us up soon as they got a replacement.'

'Shit!' Dillon shakes his head. 'Okay, right lads, fall in.'

Moaning and cursing, the squad forms two lines and moves out from the guardpost. As they pass the soldiers on duty, a barrage of friendly, filthy insults is exchanged; there isn't much love lost between the regular infantry and the Paras, but they have to keep up the appearance of unity for the sake of the locals.

Bringing up the rear, Jimmy bends down and lets the air out of one of the car's front tyres, gives the two boys a cheery wink, and goes on his way.

31

Capes glistening, the squad trudges on, rifles at forty-five degrees pointing to the ground, gloved hands curled round the trigger guards, ready for action. The gloves have padded knuckles and fingers, except for the trigger finger, to allow maximum feel and sensitivity. There is dissension in the ranks, grumbles and moans, and Dillon is getting a mite fed-up with it. He bellows over his shoulder:

'It's not my fault the ruddy truck's broken down – we just gotta head back to base, there's no changeover!'

He's ready for a shower and a hot meal as much as any of them, but if they've got to tab another five miles, that's all there is to it. No point the fat knackers grousing.

Peering ahead into the gloom, Dillon raises his hand, makes a gentle up-and-down motion. In taking a corner too fast, a dilapidated old farm truck with a few bales of hay in the back has skidded on the muddy road and got its front offside wheel bogged down in the ditch. A coat held over her head, a woman stands watching two young lads stuffing their sodden jackets under the wheels to provide traction. She gets up into the cab, and with a grinding of gears, revving like crazy, tries to reverse onto the road. The wheels spin, mud flying, and it's clear that if the woman perseveres till Doomsday, she's not going to make it.

Dillon inspects the hedgerows on either side of the lane. He fans his arm, and the squad splits into two.

'Just check it out, lads. If it's okay we can bum a lift back. Jimmy, take the rear.' Dillon waves Harry on. 'Left side . . . you lads to the front.'

The two young farm boys turn as the squad warily approaches. Hair stuck to their heads like shiny black caps, they stare at the men with flat, expressionless eyes.

Dillon walks past them to the cab. He waits for the nod from Harry, gets it, and the thumbs-up from Taffy. All clear. The woman looks down at him. She has long greying hair, darkened to the roots by rainwater, limp strands trailing over the collar of her saturated coat.

'You want a hand, love?' Dillon holds up four fingers, motions four of the Toms to the front of the truck. Two down in the ditch, two on the road, they put their shoulders to it, the woman pressing down hard on the accelerator. The truck shifts a few inches, rolls down again, and with a final heave judders out of the ditch and onto the road, belching blue smoke.

If Dillon is expecting a nod, or even a word of thanks, he is sadly mistaken. The woman jerks her head to the two farm boys, holding their sodden jackets like bundles of wet washing.

'Can you give us a lift, about five miles up the road, love?' Dillon asks, pleasantly enough.

The woman ignores him. 'Get in,' she tells the boys. 'Now!'

'Bitch!' Jimmy says, standing at Dillon's shoulder. And as the two boys move to the cab, gives a muttered, 'Frank, you see their drivin' licence?'

Dillon puts his hand out, restraining one of the boys as he's about to climb aboard. 'Just a second, son, how old are you?'

The boy tenses, looks down at Dillon's gloved hand. For a moment nobody moves, the clinging veil of drizzle shrouding the motionless figures of the two boys and the soldiers in grey murk. Nothing is said, no overt action taken, but a change has taken place. Everyone senses it. The farm boys are edgy, eyes flickering nervously. The Toms have spread themselves out in a circle, weapons raised, training them on the truck. This is bandit country and the enemy is everywhere, and it doesn't pay to forget it, not even for an instant. As NITAT training for a tour of the Province has drummed into them so they can recite

251

it in their sleep: 'Why learn from your own mistakes when you can learn from the mistakes of others?'

Stepping back, Dillon makes a sign. It is a standard drill, and the men perform it as an automatic reflex. It is rapid, short, brutally efficient. Without ceremony the boys are manhandled against the side of the truck, faces bashed into the wooden slats, arms twisted behind their backs, legs kicked apart. Dillon steps back in, grabs a full fistful of hair, yanks the boy's head around.

'Check inside the truck,' he orders Jimmy, and to the boy, whose terrified eyes are rolling in their sockets, showing the whites, 'An' you look at me, *look at me*! Name, age, address. *Now*!'

Dillon unhooks his thirty-four-centimetre long metal flashlight and hits the boy in the face with it, then shines the light directly into his eyes

'Leave him alone, dear God!' the woman screams from the cab. She leaps down, coat billowing around her. She kicks out at Dillon, face twisted in a rage of anguish that is pitiful in its sheer helplessness. 'Dear God, just leave us alone, they're just kids . . .'

Dillon lets go of the boy and with the back of his hand slaps the woman so hard across the face that she is knocked reeling into the side of the truck. He grabs the boy by the collar, drags him to the front of the truck. Harry and Taffy are sorting out the other one. They have him pinioned between them, a shrimp between two whales, an arm apiece, their two faces an inch either side of the boy's, shouting into his ears, '*Name age address, Name age address, Name age address.*'

Dillon has the young boy bent backwards over the mudguard, arm across his throat. The boy is choking, turning blue. In a croaking whisper he gasps out, 'Lee Farm, I'm sixteen . . . what have I done, leave us alone . . . Ronan . . . me name's Ronan Shaw . . .'

With two Toms covering him from the road, Jimmy has climbed up into the back of the truck. Rifle up in the firing position, he unclips his flashlight and shines it over the bales of straw. He crouches on one knee, directing the beam into the gaps underneath and between the bales. Jimmy stiffens as he sees something move. Not a trick of the light, not just a shadow, he's damn sure of that. Vaulting backwards off the truck, Jimmy rams the rifle butt into his shoulder and pumps off half a mag. The shots crack and reverberate over the empty dark fields, rolling away like distant thunder. Something shrieks.

Dillon appears at the run, eyes dark, glittering, under the leather rim of his Red Beret.

'Jimmy? . . . Jimmy?!'

A thin, shrill yelping sets their teeth on edge. Holding onto the side of the truck, the woman swings her face towards them, mouth bleeding, and starts screeching, 'Bastards, *bastards*, it's the dog, you filth, you scum, it's the dog!'

In the flashlight beams the long narrow head lifts up and falls back. It tries again, gets its head up, paws scrabbling feebly, and slides down again, slipping in its own blood. The rough rope halter around the dog's neck, tied to the back of the cab, gleams wet and dark red.

'It's their dog, Jimmy,' Dillon says in a low voice. 'What the fuck have you done?'

'It moved!' Jimmy retorts indignantly. 'It was hidden under the straw.'

'Put it out of its misery. Do it!' Dillon glares at him, and then his grim face suddenly cracks in a smile. 'They should've given us a lift, so sod 'em.'

He walks back to where the woman is tending to the farm boys, dabbing at their cuts with a soiled rag. Both are scared witless, both crying openly. The woman gives Dillon a look of venomous hatred. He shoves her towards the cab, signals the three of them to get in. From the back of the truck the piteous whimpering of the dog is cut short by a single shot. Dillon wafts his hand. 'On your way, go on, get moving.'

The engine roars, and as the truck moves off, the woman leans out. Her face has a wild, tortured look, framed by long grey hair straggling in the breeze. 'I hope you all die of cancer,' she says into Dillon's eyes, and spits at him.

Dillon runs alongside the truck, keeping pace, shouting up at her, 'I remember your face, bitch! You hear me, *move*, go on, get out!'

The truck disappears into the gloom, its single faulty tail-light flickering dimly. The squad trudges on through the heavy drizzle. Only four miles to go. Jimmy catches up to Dillon. After a minute or so, sloshing side by side through the mud, he says, 'They must have been headin' for the Lifford.' Dillon looks at him. Jimmy nods, an impish smile lurking at the corner of his mouth. 'The dog, it was a greyhound!'

'Be in their stew tonight,' Dillon says, eyes straight ahead, ploughing on. 'Animals all of them.'

Ten minutes later the best sight of the night, a Bedford RL lumbers into view. Everybody yells, fists in the air, Dillon included, and all give the driver their choicest repertoire of foul abuse as he rumbles up, flashing his lights.

Clutching her fur collar, the woman stared up into Dillon's face. She was visibly shaking, hair bouncing on her shoulders. 'You dirty bastards, they're pissin' over the railings, *animals . . .*'

'I'm sorry, okay.' Dillon held up his hand. 'I'll go an' quieten 'em down.'

'I know who you are, Frank Dillon!' the woman suddenly said. She pointed an accusing finger. 'I'm gonna call the police.'

Shaking his head, and feeling it start to spin, Dillon moved to the top of the stairwell. Holding out both hands in appeasement, he stumbled down a step or two, and the woman dodged back as if a pan of boiling water had been tipped over her foot.

'Don't come near me!'

Dillon swayed on the steps the lethal mixture of keg bitter, brown ale, lager, Scotch and Tina Turner combining and igniting in his brain like nitroglycerine. He tried to turn back, missed his footing, and slumped instead against the wall, his face scraping the concrete. Down on his knees, cheek pressed to the wall, Dillon whispered in a voice near as dammit to weeping, 'I got two kids . . . I got two kids.'

32

Falls Road District. Belfast. March 1988.

It is night, the streets are quiet, the pubs and clubs emptied and dispersed nearly an hour ago. A cold wind blows along the street of terraced houses, each with its tiny square of garden bordered by a low brick wall, rattles the chip papers in the gutter. A garden gate creaks, four hunched shapes scuttle in, flatten themselves like limpets to the front wall of the house. A light burns above behind floral bedroom curtains, a glow from the hallway through the stained-glass fanlight above the door. Crouching close to the wall, the brick is chill and damp against Dillon's cheek. He checks the illuminated dial of his watch. The green second-hand creeps into the third quadrant. Very slowly he eases himself up and looks back to the corner of the street. A single ruby-red light winks from the driver's aperture, telling him that the APC is in position, ready to move in.

Once more Dillon looks at his watch, for the last time. The green hand sweeps away the final seconds. Dillon gives the signal.

Jimmy steps up and with one swing of the sledgehammer smashes the front door open. The armoured personnel carrier is already at the gate, the rest of the squad piling out, the alsatians straining on their short leashes, soldiers in visored helmets deploying along the street. At the kerb, a lance-corporal speaks into a shortwave walkie-talkie, confirming to the 21/C that entry has been effected.

The hallway of the small terraced house is suddenly packed with bodies. A woman with cropped dark hair and a narrow pinched face stands screaming at the foot of the stairs, arms held wide barring access; a pregnancy in its seventh month makes a bulge like a bowling ball in her quilted housecoat.

'No, please, dear God no!' The woman retreats one step up but keeps her scrawny grip on the banister. 'Oh, God help me please, don't harm my kids ... there's just children upstairs.'

'How many upstairs, who's upstairs?' Dillon barks at her. He grips her arm tight, shaking her. 'Gimme their names, ages, come on!'

From the living-room and kitchen, the sounds of drawers being wrenched out, cupboard doors flung open, their contents scattered, ornaments swept off shelves, crockery breaking.

'I swear before God it's just my kids,' the woman weeps, her eyes pleading with Dillon.

Jimmy comes through waving a family allowance book.

'She's got seven bastards, eldest is seventeen, one fifteen, an' two twelve-year olds, rest are girls.'

'Get away from the stairs.' Dillon twists her arm, prising her grip from the banister. 'I said *move it!*' He turns, gives a curt nod to the four Toms crowding in through the front door. 'Back up, move up.' Roughly shoving her aside, Dillon cautiously mounts the stairs, clicking the firing control of his rifle to automatic, a live one up the spout, ready to fire.

'You got any lodgers, eh?' The woman lies slumped on the stairs, stretched out. 'Answer me!'

The woman shakes her head, tears streaming down her cheeks. Feebly she tries to grasp hold of Dillon's trouser-leg. He kicks her away without looking. In a broken voice she pleads with him, 'Ah no, please, they're just children. Please don't, they've done nothing wrong ...'

Jimmy laughs, dangling the family allowance book in front of her. She makes a grab for it. Holding it tauntingly out of reach, he rips it to shreds and sprinkles the scraps over her.

'You scum!' The woman's face breaks out in ugly red blotches. 'I got seven kids to feed, how long you think it's

257

gonna take for me to get that renewed . . . *please why don't you tell me what you want, please!*'

From up above comes the sound of doors banging, scampering feet on the bedroom floor, the terrified screams of children. Furniture is being moved, wardrobe doors crashing open, the tinkling of breaking glass.

Harry wanders in from the kitchen, shaking his head. Jimmy gives him the nod. 'Out in front, get the flagstones up.' He shouts upstairs, 'Everything kosher down here, Frank!'

Dillon leans over the banister. 'Get the bitch up here!'

Jimmy grabs the pregnant woman under the armpit and force-marches her up the stairs, practically dragging her on her knees the last few steps. The front bedroom has been ransacked, the mattress ripped apart, bedding thrown into a corner. The contents of the dressing-table and wardrobe are strewn over the floor. A little glass shelf and its collection of religious pictures and icons lie broken and trampled behind the door.

Jimmy crunches through the debris, his bent arm hooked under the sobbing woman's arm, half-supporting her. Harry comes in behind, his square bulk filling the doorframe.

Dillon points. 'Get the baby out.'

In its crib, an eighteen-month old baby with a halo of golden curls, thumb tucked into its rosebud mouth, sleeps peacefully through it all.

'Leave her be, you scum!' The woman flails her arm helplessly, but Dillon is well out of range. 'There's nothin' here – leave her! *Don't you touch her!*'

Jimmy swings her forward. 'Do what he says, tart! What are you, a breedin' machine, a real slag, aren't you – get the kid out.'

'I'll get the police, you soldiers you got no right, no right to do this!'

Dillon beckons Harry over and together they approach the crib. Jimmy restrains the woman, who wants to scream yet daren't, for fear of waking the child. Harry looks

258

underneath and round the back of the crib while Dillon feels gingerly along the edge of the mattress. He eases the covers back. The baby's eyes open, she blinks and focuses, and starts to bawl. The mother screams and claws to go to her. Jimmy hauls her straining body to the door. Harry lifts out the crying, wriggling baby and Dillon removes the pillow and mattress, prods and feels at them, tosses them down.

Out on the landing, Dillon says, 'Get a neighbour, we'll take the tart in for questioning.'

The rest of squad waiting in the hallway shake their heads as Dillon comes downstairs. Behind them they have left a wrecked house, and nothing to show for it. Stepping over the torn-up paving stones, Dillon gives the wipe-out signal. The soldiers deployed along the street start to gather in, the APC throttles up, the dog-handlers rein in the alsatians.

Two Toms lead the woman through the gate, still wearing bedroom slippers and quilted housecoat, her head bowed, both hands pressed to her swollen belly. Always one for a ready quip, Jimmy calls out, 'Sorry about this, tart, we were lookin' for a dead hunger striker!'

This gets a general laugh, slackening the tension, and Dillon says through a grin, 'Just hold her for an hour or so, get a photograph an' let her go.'

The woman is bundled into the back of a Land Rover fitted with Macralon armour and toughened anti-shatter windows. She leans out, her face distorted, so that it's hardly recognisably the same woman, with an intense, implacable hatred.

'You're animals, all of you!'

Walking by, Dillon ducks his head. 'Tarra! See you again some dark night! And Kathleen – ' he wags his finger ' – watch out for your kids eh!'

The Land Rover moves off, the woman turning to look at Dillon through the back window. She will never forget his lean, hard face with its vertical scar below the left eye, and Dillon will never forget hers, with its look of dumb, hopeless, helpless defeat.

A priest hurries across the street and pushes through the knot of soldiers waiting to board the APC. He pauses with his hand on the garden gate, grey-haired, slightly stooped, taking in the upturned paving stones, the wrecked front door. He turns to look at the soldiers, and then at Dillon, the streetlight glinting off his metal-rimmed spectacles. Stepping through the front door, he sees the shambles of the living-room, and looks up the stairs. On the landing, the younger children, three boys and two girls, in pyjamas and nightdresses, sit huddled together, crying, shivering with fright. The older boy stands behind them, an eyebrow split open, blood running from his nose, holding his baby sister in his arms. The little girl has stopped crying and is examining with curiosity the blood dripping onto her fingers from her brother's nose.

The priest has to close his eyes.

'Why? Dear Mother of God, why?'

'Frank!'

Wearily, Dillon opened his eyes. He didn't know where he was. He didn't know what time of day it was. Yes he did, it was dark, which meant it must be night. But he wasn't in bed, so where the hell was he? Susie's voice – shrill, hysterical – pierced through the tender tissue that was his throbbing brain.

'*Frank*, for God's sake will you get them out of the house, they're going into the kids' room, *Frank*! They're gettin' out of hand, throwing bottles over the railings, the neighbours have called the police . . . *Frank*!'

Dillon pushed himself up, crawling hand over hand up the concrete wall of the stairwell. Once upright, he shook his head blearily, and staggered past her up the steps. 'I'll get them out.'

'They're bargin' into the kids' room, terrifying them . . .'

Dillon halted on the landing. His head came slowly round to look at her over his shoulder. Susie had never

260

before seen such a dark welter of twisted demonic hatred on his face, much less turned upon her. As if he loathed her with all his being. Loathed *her*.

'Frank . . . ?'

Dillon turned back, a strange distant glaze in his eyes, and went on, head down like a charging bull, leaving Susie frozen to the spot.

Dillon kissed the boys, tucked in their duvets. 'Nothin' to be scared of, they're just havin' a good time!' Trying to make it sound hearty and jovial. 'You weren't scared, were you? Eh? Not big lads like you two? Nothing to be frightened of . . .'

Phil peeped out. 'They're drunk, one of 'em's been sick in the toilet.'

'I'll clear it up,' Dillon said. 'Now, go to sleep – tell you what, I'll sit here, keep guard, eh? So nobody comes in, how's that?'

He patted their shoulders and pulled up the small chair from Kenny's desk, sat down facing the door. Opposite him, the picture gallery of posters, postcards and photographs, the relics and mementoes tacked to the wall. High up in one corner, soundlessly circling on invisible strings, a camouflage-pattern C–130 with RAF roundels. Hunched forward, Dillon stared at the wall of memories, listening to the noise of revelry still going on downstairs. Music was still playing, and through it he heard Harry bellowing, 'Everybody out, come on now, lads, party's over. Come on . . . out now!'

The racket gradually diminished as people started leaving. Voices on the landing outside the window, laughter, the clatter of footsteps. The Beatles finished *Norwegian Wood*, followed by a silence that seemed to signal the end of it all, and then a pounding piano and *Great Balls of Fire* burst out once again. Dillon rested his forehead in his hands. Abruptly the music stopped. The front door banged.

From the window Dillon watched the lads climbing into

their cars. Drunken singing and shouting sailed up from the courtyard. Some of the cars drove round three or four times, headlights flaring, horns blasting. Dillon saw headlights shining through smoke, hoses trailing across a cindery patch of earth bordered by whitewashed stumps. Groups of people with blackened faces, shrouded in blankets and coats, gazing with shell-shocked eyes at the smouldering ruins of Hennessey's Bar. Harry, chin jutting out, saying *Come on, let's get back in there. I'm game!* Harry was game all right. Too fucking game. Because he'd nothing to lose. No wife, no kids. The Paras had been his entire life – wife, kids, family all rolled up into one, stamped in silver with a winged parachute, crown and lion. If coming out into civvies had been a shock to Dillon, it must have been traumatic for Harry, like being severed from the umbilical cord all over again. Suddenly finding yourself floating, rootless, in an alien world that didn't give a toss who you were or what you'd done. Just another useless fat knacker who hadn't had the sense to stop a sniper's bullet in the Falklands or in Ulster like some of his mates had. Isn't that why you joined the Army, mate, to get your fucking brains blown out?

The door was pushed open and Harry crept in. 'Cops arrived, but it's all under control. Just a few stragglers left.'

He went to the window and looked down, his broad, beery-red face relaxing into a fond grin. 'But they're on their way home now . . . okay bunch of blokes.' He patted Dillon's shoulder and turned to leave. 'I'll check out Wally's info – that what you want?'

'Harry, wait . . .'

Harry stopped, his hand on the doorknob. His face wasn't relaxed any more, the fond grin had gone. Now he looked tense.

'Like you said, mate,' he reminded Dillon, his voice low and angry, 'we made a pact! Jimmy's gone, Steve's dead, not a lot Taffy can do from inside, so it's down to you and me Frank . . . I'll check out Wally's info and get back to you.'

Harry shut the door quietly, not waiting for Dillon to reply. They had made the pact and there was no backing out of that, but without the others, without the backup – or was it without the army? . . . Dillon sighed, he was so screwed up inside that twisted emotions strangled each other – guilt, anger, grief. He had no fury left, he could not feel the hatred or the anger he knew he needed. What if Wally's information was sound, that these were the two dark-haired boys who were sitting at that table that fucking awful night, the two smiling boys who had downed their beers and offered Dillon's crowd their seats, those two, who had strolled out of the bar that night, knowing within seconds the place would be blown apart. They had to have known. Wasn't that why they had smiled?

There had been many weeks of checking and questioning everyone in or near the pub that night. A barman remembered the boys. He had never seen them before, they were not regulars, but he remembered them because one of them was carrying what looked like a carrier bag with booze brought in from outside. The disco attracted a lot of kids who'd slip in their own liquor to save a few bob, but then the two had ordered beers and sat at the table, the same table Dillon's lads took over.

No one had ever been arrested for the bomb attack. Months, even years after, the description of those two killers' faces was imprinted on, and in, each of the minds of those who survived. They would always mark the anniversary with one hell of a binge, and they had always sworn no matter how long it took, that they would each make it their responsibility to keep the hunt going, it was personal, not Army. The last anniversary, they had actually combined with a new recruit's birthday bash, but it didn't mean their pact was over. Yet thinking back, Dillon knew that in some way the fever was dying, life went on, other mates had been killed.

263

Dillon thought about Barry Newman and wondered whether maybe that was why he remembered so often now. It wasn't because of the music, the same song that was being played that night, that bloody *Great Balls of Fire*. It was Newman's son Billy. That was the connection or the memory and it was there like a dark cloud. Dillon stared at the wall of photographs. He closed his eyes to blank them out. 'Oh Christ,' he whispered, as he felt the dark insidious cloud creeping over him, felt the tremors of guilt, of anger, of grief and then the burning sensation, the fury. It was coming back, and he was afraid. Why was it that every time he felt as if he was breathing clean air, something, someone drew him back down? It was as if he was suffocating inside himself, but he had instigated that pact, and if there was only Harry and himself left then he would have to see it through.

33

Dillon came into the office to find Susie halfway through the invoices, a neat stack of typed envelopes, already stamped, ready for posting on the desk.

He said, 'Cliff not here?'

'No, he's gone home, felt sick, said it was the pork pie.' She rolled another blank invoice into the machine, gave him a look from under her eyebrows. 'He was just hungover!'

Dillon went to the board, hunting round for a piece of chalk. 'Good news is, we got the Embassy job – two weeks' work, bodyguard, driver for an official. The armoured Merc blew him away.'

Susie totted up figures on the calculator and started typing. 'Still not covering costs. What's the Embassy paying, and I'll log it.'

'Four hundred a day!' Dillon said, and when she didn't leap up and hug him, tell him well done, he said testily, 'Harry on a job, is he?'

'Mmm, could do with a few more like that . . .' Susie frowned, concentrating on working out the seventeen-and-a-half per cent VAT. Bloody stupid figure. She said after a moment, 'I don't think that car will pay for itself, you know. The Granada will, even the security wagon . . .' She glanced up. 'What did you say?'

Dillon tapped the board with the chalk. 'Who's crossed these fares out?'

'Do you know what your outgoing costs are?' Susie asked, resuming her typing. 'The hire purchase, insurance, the rent?'

Dillon waved her off. He couldn't be bothered with mere details. The phone rang. As Susie picked it up, Harry walked in. He gave Dillon a straight look. 'We got to talk . . .'

'Stag Security, Taxi, Chauffeur Drive.' Susie put her hand over the receiver. 'Are you free, Harry?'

'Yeah, yeah . . .' He plucked at Dillon's sleeve. 'Wanna word.'

Dillon didn't want to have a word with him. He knew where Harry had been, and it wasn't out on a job. He'd been cruising round in the Granada, checking out a certain address. Harry had his sights fixed, total tunnel vision, determined to see it through to the bitter end.

'Sorry to keep you waiting . . . yes . . . Aldershot? And the address?'

Harry reached out. 'That's for me!'

'What?' Dillon said sharply. Somebody calling from The Depot? What the hell was going down here?

'Wants to speak to you, Harry,' said Susie, handing the receiver to him. He sat on the edge of the desk, his back to them. 'Yeah, it's me, speakin'. Oh yeah, yeah . . . he told you what I'm interested in, did he? Okay, I'm on my way. Thanks.'

Harry put the phone down. 'I'm not free,' he said to Susie, and to Dillon, looking him in the eyes, 'I need the Granada.' He jerked his head towards the passage. 'Frank . . . !'

Sighing, Dillon moved to follow him. Susie threw down her pencil, arms folded tightly across her chest.

'Can we just sort a few things out first? One, you're going to have to stop using the limo for straight taxi fares, it costs *us*. Eats petrol. What do you want the Granada for, Harry?' Susie nodded fiercely at the telephone. 'Was that a job?'

Sitting there, Miss Business Efficiency got right on Dillon's tits. He burst out, 'Nothin' I do is right accordin' to you! An' don't start handin' out orders like you run the show – '

Susie interrupted. 'You keep the portable when you don't need it, or you do for phoning in your bets!'

'I don't call them in, I just go over the road!' Dillon told her with a nasty, leering smile. 'An' if you want me, that's where I'll be.'

'Then get somebody else to do this!' Susie was up out of her chair. 'I'll go back and work for Mr Marway.'

'You think I don't appreciate it?'

'Er, Frank . . . Frank?' said Harry uneasily, sniffing a storm force ten row brewing.

'Just a minute!' Dillon glowered at his wife. 'I'm sick of you shovin' that Marway down my throat.'

Susie snatched up her bag, really fuming now. Harry sidled to the door, the expression on her face convincing him that this was as good a moment as any to take a leak. He slipped out as Susie said very softly, the calm before the storm, 'I don't believe you said that. If it wasn't for him *you wouldn't have a business.*'

'I hear you – okay – *I hear you,*' Dillon snarled at her.

'If you go down, Frank, if you and your precious lads don't get this company working, then you will all fall flat on your faces.'

'You'd love that!'

'How can you say that? Don't you understand that if you don't show decent returns to the bank, they can review the loan – it is a loan, Frank, it's not a gift!' She added quietly, reasonably, 'You have to pay it back.'

'I know that,' Dillon muttered.

'An' if you blow it, Frank, then Mr Marway's liable for that loan.'

Here we go again, he thought. All roads lead back to Saint fucking Marway. He said bitterly, 'You want me to grovel to him? Thank him for lettin' my wife off early so she can give me a few hours . . .'

Susie yelled, '*He doesn't give you them, I do!*'

Dillon nearly tore the handle off opening the desk-drawer. He slammed the petty cash box down, grabbed a fistful of notes and coins and flung them at her. Susie looked quickly away, blinking back tears. She snapped her handbag shut and picked up her coat.

'I'll collect the boys, no need for you to bother yourself.'

She walked past him to the door. Without turning, Dillon said, 'I suppose he'll be givin' you one of his cars to drive around in next.'

'Oh – you knew I was taking my driving test, did you?' There was something in her voice, odd, strained, that made him turn to look at her. 'Well, I failed it, Frank – happy? I failed.'

Dillon put out his hand, some small gesture of regret, apology even, but Susie wasn't there to see it. Smacking his fist into his palm, he went into the passage, hearing the click of her high heels on the basement steps. He could have run after her and caught her easily, but he was damned if he would. At his own pace, in his own good time, he went outside and up the steps.

The lavatory flushed. The phone was ringing as Harry came along the passage. Cautiously he poked his head in and looked round the empty office. 'Frank . . . ?'

Cliff felt like death. He wished he was dead, actually dead, and then the awful sickly throbbing would cease. He was lying on the sheet-draped sofa, eyes closed, when Shirley arrived back at the flat. She dumped more fabric and wallpaper sample tomes on the table and hung up her coat.

'I've been sick again,' Cliff greeted her piteously. 'I've had aspirin, Disprin, Andrews . . . I've never had a head-ache like it.'

'I'm about to give you another,' Shirley said, taking off her silk headscarf.

'Have you been sick?'

'Yes, for the past five mornings.'

'Well, that couldn't be the pork pie,' Cliff said. 'Terrible pain right across my back, just here!'

Shirley stood in front of him and folded her arms.

'You know, sometimes I don't think the lift goes to the top floor with you. Didn't you hear what I just said, don't you know what it means? I'm pregnant, Cliff!'

268

Cliff closed his eyes again. 'Oh no!' he levered himself up. 'Oh shit!' The door banged behind her as Shirley went into the bedroom. Moaning, Cliff flopped back, something really to moan about now.

Trudie hung out of the upstairs window as Harry bounced down the steps of the Super Shine Travel Agency, to whop Cliff on the back.

'I just refreshed parts no beer can do justice to!'

Harry leaned on the railings staring down the street to the betting shop.

'I'm gonna be busy for an hour or so, you know Frank's takin' up residence in that shop, I'll catch him there.'

Cliff stood at the top of the basement steps. 'Shirley's pregnant!'

'Nothin' to do with me mate!'

'Ha ha, very funny, but I'm right in it!'

'Wrong son, I'd say she is!'

As Harry sauntered off to the betting shop, he paused by the strips of plastic curtains, watching Dillon looking at a newspaper, jotting down his runners, then flicking looks to a row of TV screens, clicking his fingers with nervous excitement. There was a nicotine smog that would have felled a carthorse.

'Skived off, did you?' With a grunt of self-satisfaction, Harry plonked himself down on the next stool. 'Cliff's back, Shirley's up the spout, not a happy man!' *More* than satisfied.

'We all got problems.'

'Yeah – marital! A situation I am glad to say I have successfully escaped from. In fact I'm becoming an endangered species – handsome, heterosexual, no strings, an' after the performances I've just administered, no problems with the old rod!' His smirk faded as he leaned closer. 'I'm just gonna meet up with a pal at Aldershot, you listenin'? I've checked out Wally's tip-off place, looks like it could be a safe house. Frank?'

269

Dillon nodded, eyes on the screen. 'I'm on a treble, this one comes in I'll be a rich man.'

'Wally's contact works in the Records Section. I mean, it might be out of the window, but on the other hand if those blokes are in London we'll need some ammo . . .'

'Go baby . . . come on, come on! Dillon was nodding, clicking his fingers. 'Yes, yes, look at that mother, yes . . . *yes!*'

Harry slid off the stool. He glanced briefly at Dillon's flushed face, body tensed, fists clenched, willing his horse on. With three furlongs to go, apparently the clear winner, the nag ran out of steam and didn't even merit a place.

'Bastard . . . Goddammit!' Dillon tore up his betting slip.

Harry was waiting at the door. 'You comin' with me or not, Frank?'

'Talk to you later,' said Dillon, already buried in the *Daily Mirror*'s racing page. 'I got a good runner in the three fifteen . . .'

Harry went out, stony-faced. Dillon ferreted in his pockets, came up with a crumpled tenner. He looked guiltily towards the empty doorway and then jerked his head back to the screens. Five minutes later, clutching a new betting slip, Dillon was on a roll again. He'd gone for a long shot, shit or bust time, and the little beauty was tearing down the final straight as if it has a red-hot poker up its arse.

'Yes . . . *Yes!* Come on you lovely bastard, yes . . .' Dillon clapped it home and stuck both fists in the air. '*YES!*'

34

'Okay, close your eyes . . . ready?'

Taking his wife by the hand, Dillon pushed open the bedroom door and led her inside. Laid out on the bed, a long flowing nightgown in pale blue chiffon edged in lace, with thin satin straps. Beside it, a leather handbag, a bunch of flowers wrapped in cellophane, an envelope inscribed, 'For Susie – XXX.'

'Okay,' Dillon said. 'Open your eyes!'

For a long moment Susie could only stand and stare. It wasn't Christmas, it wasn't her birthday, and even when it was, Dillon had never been so extravagant.

'*First*, open this.' He held out the envelope. 'I'm sorry you failed, I didn't know about your test. So – six lessons with a proper driving instructor, next time you'll pass.'

Hesitantly she touched the nightdress, as if at any second it might vanish in a puff of smoke. Childishly eager to please, Dillon said, 'That's for you – and this, it's all leather, inside and out. I was going to get shoes, but I wasn't sure of your size. Well? You like them?'

'I don't know what to say . . .' Subsiding onto the bed, Susie fingered three or four leaflets with colour pictures of cathedral spires and elegant country houses on their glossy covers. 'What's this?'

'Weekend away . . .' The phone rang in the hallway and there was the scampering of feet as one of the boys scurried to answer it. 'Well, they're just brochures,' Dillon shrugged, 'but you can pick any hotel, any place you fancy. Your mum will look after the kids.'

Kenny's voice piped up the stairs. 'Dad! . . . Dad, it's for you!'

Dillon went to the door. 'Try that on, I'll be right back.'

Susie gathered up the nightdress and ran her fingers over

the delicate lace neckline. The price tag was still attached. She looked at it in quiet wonder, slowly shaking her head.

It was Harry on the phone, as Dillon dreaded it might be. On his way back from Aldershot, he was calling on the portable, couldn't wait to tell Dillon the news. His pal in Records Section thought he could lay hands on a couple of mug shots, IRA suspects, for him and Dillon to give the once-over, see if they checked out. 'For chrissakes, you should have talked this through with me,' Dillon told him, exasperated. He got the feeling he was being steamrollered. Harry had plans, and whether he liked it or not, Dillon was included, a cog in the relentless, unstoppable machine Harry had set in motion.

Why now of all times, he fretted, on his way back upstairs. Why now? He sighed and went in.

'It was Harry. Nothing to worry about.'

Susie was sitting at the dressing-table, dreamily brushing her hair. 'That makes a change.'

'Don't you like this?' Dillon said. The nightdress was lying on the bed, a bit rumpled, as if it had been picked up and discarded.

Susie laid down the brush. 'I've got to run the kids' bath.'

'They're okay, they're watching TV,' Dillon said, looking at her in the mirror.

'But Kenny has to do his homework . . .'

Dillon put his hand on her shoulder. 'Susie, his homework can wait – '

'No it can't.' She came suddenly to life, stood up, agitated almost. 'If he doesn't do it now, then he won't at all.'

Dillon clumsily tried to embrace her. 'Susie, I haven't touched you for months . . .'

'It wasn't me drunk last night.'

'You always say you're tired . . . you've been tired since your started work.'

Susie pushed past him. 'Don't start in on that, Frank!'

After Harry, now this. When he'd gone to the trouble

272

of buying her stuff, hoping to make his peace with her, trying his bloody best. Dillon held onto his temper and tried again.

'I was going to say if it's too much working for me as well, then – '

'Then give up my job? *No,* Frank. *No . . . no!*'

Christ, this was hard work. 'I meant,' Dillon ground out, 'you needn't come and work for me. But you take it any way you want, an' I tried . . .' He spread his hands helplessly. 'I tried . . .'

'You tried what, Frank?'

He flared up at this. 'To reach you, talk to you!'

'Why don't you look at your face when you speak to me like that?' Susie pointed at the mirror. 'Go on, look . . . You want to reach me, talk to me, then start getting to know who I am – '

'Take a look at your own face, sweetheart! You think any man wants to come home to – ' He grabbed hold of her by the neck and thrust her head towards the mirror, 'That! Everythin' I do is wrong, I'm not good enough . . .' He let go, and the force of it sent her hands skittering through bottles and lipsticks, knocking them to the floor.

'Fine – you don't like this – ' Dillon had the nightdress in both bunched fists, ripping it up in long slow tearing motions.

'Frank, no, stop it . . .'

'You don't want to come away with me, fine!' The brochures went the same way, showered over the carpet. 'I'll find another bitch that does. You don't like this – ' He snatched the driving lesson vouchers off the bed. 'Fine!'

Susie plucked the envelope out of his hand, clutched it to her chest. 'Haven't' you wasted enough money for one day?' she said, not meaning it vindictively, more of a gentle chiding joke.

Dillon hit her. A terrible, vicious crack across the face. Susie crashed into the wall and slid down. She rubbed her cheek, the marks of his fingers glowing fiery red. In contrast the blood had drained from Dillon's face. In his eyes, the most mortifying pain. Hardly knowing what he was saying, he started burbling, 'I've got money, I'm earning good money, I got thirty grand . . .'

Susie got up, holding her cheek. 'You'd never have got that loan if I hadn't sobbed my heart out to Marway,' she said quietly, her eyes dry and hard.

Dillon took a step towards her. A vein beat in his neck. He curled his fist but Susie didn't flinch. He broke out hoarsely, 'You got a new kitchen!'

'It's not your money, and don't expect me to jump around like some stupid tart because you buy me this.' She swept her hand at the torn nightdress. 'I am sick to death of looking out for you, trying to make you see sense.'

There was volumes more she could have said; instead she stormed out onto the landing, and would have slammed the door if Dillon hadn't caught it on the swing. He went after her.

'That's what this is really about, isn't it? You want shot of me, need somebody else – '

Susie swung round at the head of the stairs and screamed in his face, '*Yes. Yes. Yes. I need – yes – all right?*' Huge tears welled up in her eyes. She turned her head away from him. 'And I wanted to pass that driving test so badly, I wanted to pass something . . .'

The smallness of her ambition moved him. That something so trivial, so petty, should mean so much. Dillon's throat went tight. He reached out to cover her hand on the banister rail and Susie jerked away, missed a step, and in trying to save herself lost her footing altogether and tumbled to the bottom of the stairs, landing with a heavy jarring thud he felt in the soles of his feet. Dillon heard something break. There was blood. She lay awkwardly, one leg bent underneath her, head twisted at an angle, and he thought her neck was broken.

Kenny skidded through the doorway, biting the fingers of both hands, Phil behind him screaming one endless, never-ending scream on a single high note.

'Don't touch here. Get away from her.'

274

Dillon knelt beside her. She was his wife, but he couldn't help her by being the hysterical, panic-stricken husband. Part of his brain clicked into automatic mode. He pressed two fingers to the carotid artery in the neck, checking the pulse, and ran his hand along the leg that was partly doubled under. Satisfied it wasn't broken, he eased it out and looked to the injuries to the head and face. Bruising to the left temple and a gash above the left eye, where the blood was coming from. Dillon rolled back an eyelid. Pupil constricted, which meant the nervous system was functioning okay. He cupped both hands under the head and very slowly brought it to a more natural position.

'Kenny, get pillows, cushions on one end of the sofa, bowl of iced water. Come on, lad, move it! Phil, out of the way, get the TV off.'

'Shall I call Gran?' asked Kenny in a quivering voice. 'Dad?'

'No, I'm here, I'll take care of her.'

'You pushed her down the stairs,' Phil said, snivelling.

'No, I didn't, son, she fell.' Dillon slid his arms underneath his wife. 'Now move away. Get out of my way . . .'

Phil's chin wobbled. He sucked in a huge gulp of air and his mouth opened wide.

'Phil, you stop that!' Dillon commanded, lifting Susie in his arms. '*Get out of my way!*' He carried her through.

In the tiny back room he rented above a Bengali food store just off Lower Clapton Road, Harry was preparing his evening meal. This entailed the removal from the Tesco bag of the dinner on a tray for one – chicken and mushroom pie, sweetcorn, mashed potatoes, gravy – and the insertion of same into the microwave which stood on the small varnished table. Set the timer for eight minutes, and hey presto.

While he waited, Harry busied himself. From his bergen he took out nine separate components wrapped in dark green dusters and laid them in a row next to the microwave. The 40-watt bulb in the bedside lamp gave him barely sufficient light to work by, not that it actually mattered. He could assemble an M16 Armalite AR–15 blindfold, and had, too many times to count. He loved the feel of the lightly-oiled precision-engineered sections, slotting smoothly and easily into place with a satisfying metallic click. Call the Yanks all you want to, but they knew how to make a bloody good weapon. Gas operated, rotary locking mechanism, the M16's small calibre 5.56 mm cartridge didn't suit all tastes, but it could stop a body stone cold dead in the market at anything up to 400 metres. And Harry intended being a damn sight closer than that. Like, say, ten feet.

He hefted the assembled rifle, just over three kilos unloaded, and balanced it on his broad palm. Lovely piece of machinery.

The bell pinged. Harry took out his steaming dinner, savouring the smell of hot gravy. 'Bloody marvellous,' he murmured, rubbing his hands together, reaching into his bergen for knife, fork, spoon.

The break was to the left forearm, the X-ray revealed, which considering that two inches lower it would have been the more complicated wrist alignment, was good news, so the doctor said.

The facial injuries looked bad, but they were superficial, he assured Dillon. Her arm in plaster, supported in a stockinette sling, Dillon pushed Susie in a wheelchair to the car, Kenny and Phil tightly gripping either side, Mum's personal bodyguard.

Back home he took Susie up first, made sure she was comfortable, and then got the boys bedded down. They were both dead on their feet, and Phil was off the instant his head touched the pillow. Dillon tucked the duvet round Kenny in the top bunk and switched off the lamp. Standing in the wedge of light from the landing, Dillon's gaze moved slowly over the wall of photographs. All his lads were there, singly and in groups. All the faces in all the places. Belize, Ulster, Cyprus, Oman, Falklands, Pen-y-Fan.

Jimmy Hammond, No. 2 Dress, lounging outside the NAAFI at The Depot. Dillon touched the photo, remembering the day, almost the minute, it had been taken. Two weeks prior to the Ulster Tour '87. The old sweet-talking bastard . . .

'Is he fighting again, Dad?' inquired Kenny through a yawn. 'Uncle Jimmy?'

Dillon unpinned the photograph.

'Yes, he is, he's joined up with mercenaries,' Dillon said. He unpinned several more, collecting a sheaf of them. 'They're freelance – still soldiers, they just get paid better!'

Lastly he took down one of Steve Harris, added it to the pile.

Kenny had pulled the duvet over his head, Phil was fast asleep. Dillon went out and softly closed the door. From within, he could hear the sound of Kenny's crying, muffled under the duvet. Dillon turned away, the sheaf of memories in his hand, and moved silently along the landing to where Susie was sleeping.

She was lying on her back, breathing rhythmically, the pale blur of the plaster cast resting on top of the bedclothes. After watching her for several moments, Dillon backed out, easing the door to.

'I'm awake, Frank.'

Dillon came in and closed the door. He groped towards the bed, the room in darkness except for a faint spray of light on the ceiling from the streetlamps below. He sat on the opposite side to her, slightly hunched, the photographs crumpled in his hand.

'Susie . . . ?' He hesitated and then went on, very subdued. 'I'm sorry for everything. The way I am, way I've been. Just that, I've had a lot on my mind . . . but, well, I made a decision, I'm going to put the past behind me because . . .' His voice sank to a husky whisper. 'You're the best thing that ever happened to me, and – and if I was to lose you – '

He bowed his head, face screwed up tight, tears squeezing out from under his eyelids.

'I don't want you to leave me,' Dillon said, weeping openly now, unashamedly. 'I love you, Susie.'

With her right hand she reached across, found his hand, held onto it.

Dillon wiped his face with his sleeve. 'Everything you say is right, I know it, and I guess I just, well, I won't listen because – ' A small rueful smile into the darkness. 'Takin' orders from a woman, you know, it's tough for a bloke like me. I never had nothin', I think I joined up because I was nothin' – never passed an exam at school.'

'I know.'

'I've acted like a kid, stupid.'

'You deserved the break, Frank.'

Dillon looked at her. 'It doesn't mean anything without you. You want me to sleep downstairs?'

'No.'

Dillon held her hand tight. He said softly, 'I'll just turn all the lights off.'

Susie nodded and smiled, hearing him creeping down the stairs, light switches clicking off, and waiting for his soft footfall to return to the bedroom. He eased the door closed, and from half-lidded eyes she watched him take off his clothes. She didn't say a word, he always folded everything up neatly, and was meticulous about clean socks and underwear, he stuffed his dirty clothes into a basket by the dressing table. He stood naked in front of the mirror, his taut muscular body with the shades of the many tattoos over his back, his legs, his arms, even his hands, and there was a heart with her name, and their two boys' names entwined with his own.

Dillon eased back the duvet and slipped in beside her, leaving just a few inches between them, but it was a while before she felt his body heat closer, closer.

'Are you awake?'

'Yes,' she whispered, and he leaned up on his elbow,

gently lifting a stray strand of her thick brown hair away from the bruise on her face.

'I love you, you do know that don't you?'

She met his dark eyes, and nodded, she could see him straining to find the right words to say. 'I . . . we lose each other a bit sometimes don't we?'

Again Susie nodded and he rested his head against her breast. 'I'm not hurting you am I?'

He could feel her heart beating, and he wanted her to hold him, but knew with her bad arm she couldn't.

'I can fix the nightdress, Frank, it'll look okay.'

He lifted his head, and gave the smile, the smile she so adored, childlike, innocent. 'Bugger the nightdress . . . all that matters is you and me, and we're okay aren't we?'

'Yes, yes we are . . .'

Susie had no knowledge of how long he lay close to her, or for how long he studied her face as the painkillers made her drift into a deep dreamless sleep. He scrutinised every pore, every contour of her lovely face, her lips slightly parted, her dark eyelashes, the same as Kenny's, thick, dark eyelashes, and her high sweeping cheeks, just like Phil's. His wife, their mother, his beloved. He knew it had to be over, he would start fresh in the morning, have a serious talk to Harry. It was not their business any more, and may God forgive him, he would bury the pact he had promised the dead boys, it was the living, his family, that mattered most in all the world to him, and he was not going to jeopardise their safety. He had almost lost Susie's love, he knew that, and to have used physical force on her was shameful, he would never do that again. He could feel that dark cloud lifting, perhaps it was just sleep slowly enveloping him, but he felt good, felt peaceful for the first time in many years.

35

Start afresh, don't look back, what's past is past. The bright new philosophy according to Frank Dillon. The past had fucked up, so dump it in the trash bin and given the future a fighting chance.

And Dillon meant it, more determined than anything he'd ever done or attempted in his life before to make it work. Which meant (Susie was right, he knew it in his bones) that Stag Security had to be run by the book. Get the business up on its feet and they were off to a flying start.

Anyway, the signs looked good, because the office had never looked better, Harry with the Hoover on the go, Cliff mopping down the basement steps when Dillon showed up. He got an earful soon as he walked in.

'Oi! Wipe your feet, I just Hoovered there – ' Harry jabbed a finger at Cliff, trailing in with a mop and bucket. 'An' you, take that bucket out into the yard.'

'Need new bog rolls,' Cliff put in. 'Stamps, coffee, tea and sugar, milk, an' we should keep a first-aid kit handy too. Aspirins, liver salts, stuff like that.'

Dillon was at the desk with a clean sheet of paper, pencil in hand. 'With Susie out of action I've got a bit of schleppin' to do with the kids, so I'm workin' out a rota.'

'I don't mind doin' nights,' Harry offered.

'Just a sec.' Dillon wanted to start another clean sheet. 'I reckon I've been throwin' me weight around, an' we're all in this together, okay? So if I say somethin' you don't agree with . . . well . . .' He gestured vaguely.

'You'll give us a sock in the gob!' Harry grinned.

Cliff laughed and clanked outside with his bucket. Harry looped the cable to the Hoover, watching him go. He said confidentially, 'Hey, Frank, about that other matter. I'm handling it.'

Dillon was writing. Without looking up he gave a small, tight nod. Start afresh, don't look back, what's past is past. The pencil dug into the paper. He looked up sharply.

'Harry . . . !'

At the door, Harry turned, Hoover in hand.

Dillon stared at him. He shook his head. 'Nothin'.' He went back to his writing.

He'd been heading up a blind alley but now he could see light ahead. Dillon's feeling that things were changing – for the better – grew stronger each day. Work was coming in, they were even building up a small core of regular clients. He had the sense that a watershed had been passed, and that with hard graft and a bit of luck they were going to make it.

The first encouraging proof came just over a week later, and he couldn't get home quick enough to tell Susie about it. She was in the kitchen, putting food away in the fridge. Getting rid of the stockinette sling gave her some freedom of movement, but the cast was still an encumbrance. Dillon waltzed in, waving a folder.

'We're in profit – it's paying the cars, the rent and wages – !'

He swung her round, hugged her.

'You mean you can start paying me a wage?' Susie asked him with an impish grin.

Dillon gave her a look. 'You not workin' for Marway?'

'Just Stag Security-Taxi-Chauffeur,' she said firmly. She gently punched him under the chin with the plaster cast. 'This'll be off soon.'

Dillon laughed and gave her a smacker. On his way to answer the doorbell he sang out, 'Give you my word, you won't regret it!'

His terrific good mood lasted until he opened the door and saw Harry's face. More exactly, its set, closed expression, eyes fixed on his, unblinking. 'I wanna show

281

you somethin'.' As Dillon's mouth tightened, Harry held up his hand. 'Hey, take it easy. Can I come in?' And when Dillon made no move, just stood there blocking the door, delved inside his jacket and produced two photostat images and held them up.

'These are the suspects. Take a look for yourself.'

Full face, left and right profiles, two men, early twenties, one with sideburns. Dillon barely glanced at them before shoving Harry onto the landing, well out of earshot. Harry caught his drift and had sense enough to keep his voice low.

'Guy on the second page, it's one of them, Frank. Wally's tip-off was legit.'

'Harry – I got to think about this.' Dillon rubbed his face, and then his head shot round as he heard Susie's voice calling, 'Is it Mum, Frank?'

He stuck his head in the door. 'No, love . . . just Harry,' and carefully pulled it shut.

Harry waited a couple of moments, studying Dillon's face. 'You don't have to get involved,' he said, slow, deliberate, the meaning made stronger because of it. 'But you started this, Frank, not me, you.'

'I dunno.' Dillon looked at the door. 'I don't know, I need time . . .'

'I don't have it, they could move on any day.' Harry had said his piece, Dillon knew the score, and he turned to go. Dillon grabbed his arm, pulled him round. His whisper was harsh.

'You know where he is?'

Harry looked into Dillon's eyes. He nodded. 'I just needed to be sure.' He thrust the photostats into Dillon's hand. 'Keep 'em, tell me tomorrow,' he said, and went down the stairway.

Dillon leaned against the wall. He rested his eyes for a minute, aware of his heart beating rapidly. Slowly he opened them and stared down at the two faces. Early twenties. Long dark hair. Sideburns. Leather jacket. Dillon leaned over the railings, waiting to see Harry across the courtyard below. He whistled and Harry looked upwards. No words passed between them, Dillon simply gave him the signal to wait.

The closing credits of a cops and robbers series were rolling up as Dillon popped his head into the living-room. He said brightly, 'I won't be too late. Kids are asleep!'

'What is it?' Susie asked, feet propped up on the couch. 'Security work?'

'Yeah!'

'Is it cash or . . .'

Dillon cleared his throat. 'Cash,' he said decisively. 'Night, sweetheart.' He went out, closing the front door so it didn't slam. Susie flicked the remote control. The chimes of Big Ben boomed out, *News at Ten* just starting.

Harry had cased the house that afternoon. Couldn't be more perfect, he assured Dillon. Run-down neighbour-hood, poor street lightning, gasworks wall at one end so there was no through traffic. Derelict place directly opposite, ideal for cover. They took up positions, peering across the darkened street through a window-frame with a few shards of glass in it. Both were kitted out for night ops: black sweaters, old combat jackets, black woollen ski hats, the faithful Pumas that had seen action on Heart-break Hill. And Harry had the Armalite, which had seen action with the Gurkhas in Brunei and the Far East. Dillon got the stomach cramps just watching him checking it over, as gentle and loving with it as a mother with her new-born babe.

'If there's anybody in there, they're crawlin' around in the dark,' Dillon decided, straining his eyes to see. He craned forward. 'No they bloody ain't – you see it, front room, right-hand side? Somethin' flickered.'

Harry was already on the move, rifle inside his combat jacket, held by the butt, pointing to the ground. 'Let's take a closer look,' he growled.

A child of six could have picked the back door lock with his Meccano plastic screwdriver. Dillon sidled in, ski mask down over his face, two ragged slits for the eyes. The kitchen was filthy and stank to high heaven. He had to watch where he stepped, there was all sorts of junk littered about the place. More a doss house than a safe house. Harry followed, treading with an incredible feline lightness and agility for such a big man.

In total silence they moved from the kitchen into the short passage leading to the front room. Blue light flickered under the door, and they could hear the muted burble of the television. Dillon touched his chest and pointed upstairs. Harry nodded. He flattened himself against the wall adjacent to the door, the rifle held slantwise across his body. Dillon went up, testing each tread before committing his weight to it.

He trod even more carefully on the bare dusty floorboards of the front bedroom, aware that a single creak would alert whoever was directly beneath him. There wasn't a stick of furniture. He knelt, and using hands as well as eyes, made sure he had it right. Three sleeping bags. A plastic holdall with a broken strap contained tee-shirts, underpants, socks, shaving cream, razor.

The bathroom was a haven for dirty towels. Two on the floor, two more stuffed over a rail, three or four in the bottom of the stained old tub. Lying in the greasy soap residue on the splash rim of the washbasin were three toothbrushes and one tube of toothpaste squeezed to within an inch of its life. He turned away and then paused, aware of a heavy subterranean thudding. It was his heart. His scalp was prickly with sweat. He hissed in a breath and crept out.

Harry hadn't moved a muscle. He stood flattened to the wall, watching Dillon slowly and silently descend. Then nodded as Dillon held up three fingers. With twenty rounds in the mag he could take out three Irish bastards and still have enough to spare for their slags and brats. Wipe out the Irish nation, that was Harry's final solution.

He went suddenly tense, and Dillon froze on the stairs. The man in the room hacked out a cough and did a couple of ferocious encores. Dillon counted to five and took another step down, letting go a breath, when the door opened and the man came out. In the poor light coming from the TV, Dillon registered only that he was young, with long hair, wearing a scruffy jacket over an open-necked shirt. He saw Dillon first, and started to backtrack into the room, grabbing the edge of the door to slam it shut. Harry sprang round from the wall, smashed the butt of the rifle into the door, knocking it back on its hinges. He swung the rifle round, levelling it. Dillon jumped the rest of the stairs. He landed in the hallway, arms up ready to dive forward and grapple with the man, when the rifle blasted. The man uttered no sound. There was a crash, a thump, and then, save for the TV burbling to itself, silence.

He was lying half on his side, face down to the carpet. One hand still clutched a grimy handkerchief. In falling he'd upset a little two-bar electric fire, a flex leading from it to the light bulb socket, which was why the room was in semi-darkness.

'He grabbed the bloody thing, Frank,' Harry complained. He ejected the empty shell, picked it up and put it in his pocket. 'Is it him?'

Dillon checked the pulse in the man's neck, but there was really no need to. His arm was flung out, away from the body, and there was a hole in the left armpit, right next to the heart. That's why he hadn't uttered a squeak.

'You've killed him.' Dillon pushed the body over onto its back. Slowly he straightened up. 'Oh my God,' he said, 'this isn't him. It's not him!'

Harry leaned over to see for himself. He squatted down on his haunches, supporting himself with the rifle. He glanced up. 'Where the hell you goin'?'

Dillon was at the door. He said, 'There were three sleepin' bags, they could be back.' He jerked his thumb savagely. 'Leave him, *just leave him*!' and was gone.

Harry laid the Armalite down. The dead man had nothing on him except a cheap wallet with a few quid in it. Harry put it in his pocket. He tucked the rifle under his arm and stood up, about to follow Dillon. He looked at the electric fire on its side. A thin wisp of smoke rose up where the bars had already singed the strip of carpet. With his foot, Harry pushed the fire closer to the dead man, and with a nudge, closer still, until it was touching. He reached down and picked up a bottle of Powers on the floor next to the armchair, about quarter full. He took a big mouthful, glancing towards the door, and spurted out a spray of whisky straight onto the bars. There was a whoosh of flame. The dead man's jacket sleeve ignited. Harry tossed the bottle on top of the funeral pyre and scarpered.

Dillon leaned over the washbasin, splashing cold water into his face. He blinked the water from his eyes and stared at his hands, shaking uncontrollably. His face in the mirror was ashen. He reached for the towel. From the office along the passage he could hear Harry's voice: 'Sorry to ring so late, Wally, but we're on an all-night job. Na! Bit of security work, they can't afford a dog.'

When Dillon came in, drying his hands, Harry was standing at the desk, laughing into the phone. On the blotter in front of him lay the photostats, the two images, full face, left-right profiles, stark under the lamplight. 'Just wanted to make sure you're on for some work tomorrow . . . yeah, G'night.' He hung up.

'You get shot of that friggin' rifle, take it back where it came from, just get the thing out,' Dillon said. He tossed the towel down and indicated the photostats with a curt nod, his eyes very dark in his pale face. 'No more. I mean it, Harry, and I'm warnin' you . . . Burn it, do it.'

'What's the matter, Frank, lost your bottle?'

'Yeah, maybe I have.' Dillon looked away, scowling. 'We just killed a bloke. I dunno how it makes you feel – '

'I feel fine,' Harry interrupted. He looked fine too, blue eyes bright, high colour in his cheeks, adrenalin surging through him. 'An' I sorted Wally, he thinks we're on an all-nighter.'

'Well I don't feel fine, I feel like shit. You want to keep going, then you get out of the firm. I got too much to lose, an' I'm not losin' it for you, for . . .' hardly hesitating '. . . my lads. It's over, Harry.'

'Over for you, over for them,' Harry said, a harsh edge to his voice. 'They were just kids – one of 'em, Phil, he'd only enlisted six months.'

Dillon went up, grabbed a fistful of Harry's combat jacket, his eyes blazing. 'You're using them, Harry, don't do this to me! We're in civvies, we got no right to take the law into our own hands.'

'This is Army business –'

'Bullshit. And we're not in the Army, we're in civvies.'

'They don't wear a uniform neither,' Harry said stolidly, the immovable object, the implacable force.

'But it's their war, it's not ours, not any more. It's over, and if you want to lose all this –' Dillon gestured round '– then we'll buy you out. I won't let you – or that scum – drag me down.'

Dillon stared into the blue eyes. Harry stared back. A moment's silence passed, which lasted several ages, until Dillon said:

'So I'm asking you, let it go.'

He couldn't or wouldn't. Or would he?

'I can't do it, Harry, I'm out, man.' The towel lay over the back of the chair, where Dillon had tossed it. Now he was throwing it in again, and he didn't care that Harry knew it, or that Harry might call him traitor, coward, betrayer. The lads were dead, let that be an end to it. *What's past is past.*

It took a long time, each word had to be dragged from his heels upwards, landing like lead in his chest, words that strangled him, he was so charged with emotion. Not weeping, they were not those kind of tears that trickled down Dillon's cheeks and glistened in the line of his scar, to Harry it was not even Dillon speaking, the depth of sorrow was like the aftermath of a hard punch in the gut.

'I want out Harry, let me go. I have too much to lose, I'm finished with this, God forgive me . . . I want out!'

Harry straightened his shoulders. He thought he knew all there was to know about Dillon, but he'd learned something more. Another depth to the man he'd never suspected, through all their years together. Another Sergeant Dillon entirely. He didn't know whether it was an added strength, or a hidden weakness, but none of that seemed to matter, and he clasped Dillon tightly in an embrace that said he didn't care, that it was over, done with, finished.

'You're the Guv'nor,' Harry said.

CIVVIES

36

Harry drove into the Roche Laundry Services' car park and parked the security wagon on the diagonal yellow stripes outside the main office. He put on his visored helmet and tightened the chinstrap, hoping, praying, that it might muffle or even, praise be, cut out Cliff's endless yakking completely. No such luck. Getting out and walking round to join Harry, Cliff kept it up.

'. . . I tell you, if I'd known what it was gonna be like, I'd never have agreed, she's goin' nuts. I'm workin', right, and I get back to bleat-bleat, you think she was the first woman to get pregnant. She keeps havin' fittings for the weddin' gown, rehearsals for the weddin' — terrified her Dad'll find out.'

'Well, they'll all know six months after yer weddin', she'll be in the maternity ward,' Harry said, for something to say. 'Why not just tell 'em?'

They went through reception to the Wages office, where the canvas sacks, fastened and sealed with dated lead slugs, were piled on a trolley awaiting them. They showed their IDs.

'Huh!' Cliff retorted. 'You think I want that bugger round — he hates me!' He shook his head, gave a long-suffering sigh. 'You got the right idea, Harry — stay single!'

One pulling, the other pushing, they wheeled the trolley out and started loading up. The sacks were heavy, and it was hard work, but at least it kept Cliff quiet for a while. Harry was grateful for small mercies.

Across the main road from Roche Laundry Services, on the second floor of what had been, pre-recession, the Streatham branch of a company supplying contract carpets to city offices, a man in a black boiler suit watched the loading operation through binoculars, speaking into a short-wave transceiver fastened with parcel tape to his right shoulder.

'*Right on schedule . . . stacking the dough . . . I count twelve sacks, no, thirteen, unlucky for some . . . okay, they're closing the doors . . .*'

'I've had more rehearsals than they have at an amateur dramatics,' Cliff grumbled, slamming his door shut and operating the dead-lock bolt. 'The bridesmaids are now up to seven, there's kids, pageboys, it'll look like a pantomime.' Harry pulled the wagon round in a tight turn, blue smoke bellowing. '. . . It's gonna be a real embarrassment. Frank's gonna be best man, she wants everyone in top hats . . .'

Harry halted at the gate, checked both ways, pulled out. He pushed the visor up with his thumb but kept the helmet on.

'*They're on their way, turning right, that means they'll be using the A23 route. Over and out.*'

At the next roundabout the wagon took the right-hand fork and slid into the flow on the A23 southbound. Harry filtered through into the fast lane and put his foot down flat to the floor.

'. . . I said to her, wouldn't it be a better idea if we took a honeymoon at a later date, like she's sick most mornings.'

Harry nodded, both hands gripping the wheel. Something Cliff had said ten minutes ago distantly registered, tickled him. 'You won't get Frank in a penguin suit – an' you'll look a right prat. They don't have toppers your size!'

Harry glanced over and laughed, more at Cliff's glum face than at his own weak joke. Serve him right, getting hitched. Dickhead.

At Thornton Heath he switched back down the lanes, ready for the Croydon turn-off. A convenient gap in front of a large removals van doing under fifty let him into the slow lane. As they were leaving the A23 a lorry loaded up with logs came down a slip road to their left and instead of stopping, kept on going, causing Harry to brake. He thumped the horn, gave a long blast.

'Stupid git . . . you see that? Cut right in front of us!'

'Hey!' Cliff was staring into the nearside wing-mirror. 'You got a big vehicle right on your tail, Harry – overtake!'

Harry flicked his indicator on, clocking the removals van in his wing-mirror. It was closing in. Then it flashed its lights, as if warning him not to overtake. The lorry in front had slowed down, the security wagon boxed between the two. About to swing out, Harry realised that the removals van was coming up alongside. It drew level. The open passenger side window was only a couple of feet away, a man with a ski mask covering his face leaning out, a sub-machine-gun cradled in the crook of his elbow.

'*Pull over . . . Pull over!*'

Harry eased down on the brake slightly, as if to show willing. The removals van did likewise, keeping dead level.

'Hang on, Cliff,' Harry muttered, and side-rammed the removals van with the wagon's armour plating. The van rocked but kept with them. Harry rammed it again, harder, and had the satisfaction of seeing the van sway alarmingly, lose speed and drop behind.

Cliff was bashing the horn, urging the lorry in front to get a move on. He might have been pissing into the wind for all the difference it made. He grabbed Harry's arm, as a warning, but Harry had already seen it. The tailgate of the lorry, attached by a rope to the cab, was suddenly released, the logs slithering out and tumbling into the road. Harry wrestled with the wheel as the wagon bounced like a bucking bronco. A log jammed under the front bumper, the wagon slewing left and right as Harry fought to keep on the road.

The removals van came up behind, gave them a terrific shunt up the backside. It came again, the wagon shuddering under the impact, its rear doors buckling. The log had worked itself up into the wheel housing, and there was a horrible grinding, splintering noise as the front wheels locked solid, bringing the wagon to a jolting halt.

Two men leapt from the back of the van and raced forward to the buckled rear doors, one of them lugging a holdall. The raider with the sub-machine-gun jumped down and ran up to Harry's window. 'Hands on your heads!'

Harry shoved Cliff back as the lad leaned across, all fired up, ready to have a go. 'Don't be a hero, they're armed.'

A mite impatient, the raider smashed the gun's metal butt against the mesh-reinforced window.

'Hands on your fucking heads!'

The wagon shuddered and rocked – the dull boom of an explosion, a gush of white smoke as the rear doors were blown off. In the wing-mirror Harry could see the sacks being tossed from hand to hand. It was done a damn sight quicker than it had taken him and Cliff to load them. The man at the window never budged his eyes once, the large bore business end of the weapon pressed against the glass. Harry heard the distinctive *thwack-thwack-thwack* of a silenced automatic as the men pumped bullets into the tyres. The security wagon sank slowly onto its rims.

The raider in the ski mask jerked his head at his companions. 'Go – go – go! All clear!' They dived into the back of the van and pulled the big doors shut behind them.

Covering Harry and Cliff, the raider backed away a step. He glanced behind, judging the right moment to turn and jump aboard. The van came up alongside. The raider half-turned, getting ready. Harry threw the dead-lock bolt. He kicked the door open, catching the end of the sub-machine-gun, and leapt out. The raider staggered but kept on his feet. He turned and started to run for the van. Harry lunged, got a hand on his shoulder. The raider took a swipe with the weapon, missed, and Harry grabbed it off him. Still holding onto the raider's jacket shoulder, Harry tossed the gun to Cliff. The raider was half-in, half-out of the van door, Harry hanging on like grim death, both of them being dragged along as the van picked up speed. Cliff brought the gun up, sighted, but the two men were too close together to risk a shot. He saw Harry clawing at the raider's head, ripping the mask up so that Cliff snatched a glimpse of the man's left profile. Frantic now, the raider back-heeled, and lucky for him, unlucky for Harry, found a soft target in Harry's balls. Harry let go, dropped, rolled, curled over, hugging himself. Cliff let one off, aiming for the tyres. He missed with the first, bagged a rear tyre with the second. The van veered left, then right, straightened up and was off.

Harry was on the ground, bent over, clutching his property.

'You okay . . . Harry?'

Harry pulled his helmet off. His face was green. His lips were tight against his gritted teeth. 'Me voice sound higher? Ohhh . . . *Kerrrist!*' He started to heave, then held his breath to stop himself vomiting.

From the back of the wagon, Cliff yelled to him, 'they cleaned us out, Harry. Harry . . . ?'

Harry was on his knees on the grass verge, bringing up last night's Murphy's stout and vindaloo. He wiped his mouth and gingerly climbed to his feet, walking back towards Cliff doing an impersonation of John Wayne riding an invisible horse.

He gestured for Cliff to hand the gun over and checked it out. He thought it looked familiar. It was an L2A3 Sterling 9mm sub-machine-gun, a standard British Army weapon issued to tank crewmen and artillery support services. Harry tucked the triangular metal frame butt against his shoulder and blew out the wagon's windscreen. He fired again and shattered the driver's window. While Cliff stood gaping at him as if he'd lost his marbles, Harry walked up to the wagon and head-butted the armour-plated side panel. He staggered drunkenly backwards, a gash pouring blood.

'Go get the cops,' he told Cliff, sinking to the ground. 'Mess yourself up a bit!'

'For the law . . . ?'

Harry was in agony, clutching his head. 'No, you prat! The bloody laundry wages have gone! We got to look like we almost got ourselves killed for it!'

'What you mean, almost?' said Cliff indignantly.

'They were bloody pros, I tell you that much. Knew what they were doin', an' they could handle themselves.'

The same notion had occurred to Cliff. 'One of 'em,' frowning and shaking his head, 'I'm sure I've seen him before . . .'

Dillon picked up the Sterling from the desk and glanced at Harry, sitting looking sorry for himself with an ice-pack on his head.

'Cops knows about this?'

'Na, I stashed it under a hedge.'

'What about the laundry company, they know?'

Harry snorted. 'Guv'nor was grovellin' his thanks to us in front of the cops – you know, how we risked our lives, what's money!'

Cliff was drying his neck and hands on a towel. 'He's insured, won't hurt him.'

'Screw him!' Harry said. 'Our wagon's a write-off, Frank. They were good, an' you know somethin' – I think they were Army trained.' He indicated the gun. 'That's Army, similar to the one we used.'

Dillon said angrily, 'You should've handed it over!'

'We're insured, aren't we?' Cliff said with a shrug.

'Yeah, we're insured,' said Dillon grimly. 'Third party, fire and theft!"'

'Thank Christ for that.'

Dillon rolled his eyes to the ceiling. 'Theft of the vehicle, you prat! Oh Jesus, this is all we need . . .' He put the gun down and stared dismally at the dismal view of the basement steps. 'I don't believe it. Why is it every time we make two steps forward we take ten back? Why?'

'You think we'll lose the account?'

'We got no wagon, Cliff.'

'We got the Mercedes – an' I tell you,' Harry stabbed a finger, 'if we'd had that they'd never have got us trapped. I mean, our top speed in that bus was eight..' The phone rang and Dillon answered. 'An' then it shuddered, we were easy pickings.'

'Stag Security . . . hang on.' Dillon thrust the phone at Cliff. 'Shirley!'

Dillon paced up and down, rubbing his forehead. He said to Harry, 'This is a real downer, you an' me'll have to see if we can get another wagon.' He tapped the Sterling on the desk. 'Bloody get this out of the way an' all.'

Cliff was holding the phone away from his ear. Finally he managed to get a word in. 'Don't scream at me like it was our fault, I'm still shakin'. We were held up, yeah!'

Dillon gave Harry a look and walked out.

'I'll tell you everythin' when I see you . . .'

Harry tossed a bunch of keys onto the desk. 'Tell her now. You man the office, me and Frank'll see if we can sort a replacement wagon.' He lumbered to the door.

'Hey, Harry!' Cliff covered the receiver. 'What about tonight's job?'

'I'll be back. Get hold of Wally and Taylor, we need four blokes.'

Cliff gave the thumbs-up and went back to telling his fiancée about the morning's raid.

Shirley stared at herself in the full-length mirror, biting her lip. She smoothed her hands over the waist of the brocade and lace wedding gown and felt her stomach. Couldn't have grown *that much* in twenty-four hours, could it? What did she have in there, the next heavyweight boxing champion of the world?

'You'll have to let it out another inch, Norma,' she told her friend, kneeling at her feet with a mouthful of pins. Norma glared up at her, and Shirley spread her arms helplessly.

'*Shirley*!' Cliff pounded up the stairs. 'It's me!'

Shirley let out a small scream and dashed to the door.

As it opened she slammed it shut, nearly flattening Cliff's nose.

'Go away! You can't come in, I'm having a fitting!'

'I'm workin' tonight . . .' Cliff banged on the door. 'Shirley? Did you hear me?'

'Yes, I heard you,' Shirley snapped bad-temperedly. 'Go away!' She looked round. Norma was crouched double, clutching her throat, coughing, or trying to. 'Oh my God . . . are you all right? You haven't swallowed a pin, have you?'

'Don't bother to ask if I'm okay!' said Cliff furiously, thumping the door. 'Shot at! Held up in an armed bleedin' robbery! But don't bother – '

Shirley threw open the door. Cliff's furious expression sagged. He stood there with his mouth hanging open, and then he gave as low smile of rapturous wonder.

'Oh man . . . that's beautiful.'

37

Harry thought, Typical bloody cock-up. Down here in docklands somewhere, hired as bouncers for an acid house party gig, and they couldn't even find the place! Cliff was driving the Granada, he was supposed to know but of course he didn't have a clue. Berk!

They drove round the badly-lit, deserted streets, Wally and Taylor in the back, looking for signs of life. Trouble was, there wasn't a soul to ask – high gaunt buildings, not a chink of light to be seen, some of them derelict, boarded-up, everything sealed up tight. Not even a stray cat on the prowl. At last Harry spotted a phone booth and told Cliff to pull over. He was glad to get out of the car for five minutes, a brief respite from Cliff's latest wedding bleeding saga.

'Poor cow's clutchin' her throat, swallowed two pins, she was doin' the hem, so we had to get her rushed to the infirmary . . . can be dangerous, you knows, pins!'

Wally got out to stretch his legs. 'We all invited to this do, then?' he asked Cliff through the window. 'Who's your best man – Frank? Is he the best man?'

Taylor laid spindly arms along the back of the passenger seat. He was a thin, wiry bloke with close-set eyes and a pock-marked face, a compulsive nail-biter. Not a ladies' man. 'I wouldn't get married mate,' he said gloomily. 'Two mates just lost their houses, these mortgage rates.' He sniffed up a dewdrop. 'We gettin' cash tonight, Cliff? These acid house parties can get heavy, y'know . . .'

Harry came out of the phone booth and walked back to the car, his broad frame silhouetted in the lights of a vehicle coming down the road towards them. He leaned in. 'We're close, said it's a warehouse over by the docks,

299

they're expectin' about two hundred kids. It's off an alley – give us the *A to Z*, Cliff.'

Wally strolled round the car and started a quiet natter with Harry, who banged on the roof of the Granada. 'Cliff, you deaf? Look up Gables Yard.'

Cliff pinched his nose between finger and thumb, goggling as the vehicle rumbled past. It was a large removals van. The radiator grille was damaged, as if it had been bashed in. Or had maybe done the bashing. And the geezer he thought he'd recognised was behind the wheel. Cliff shot out of the driving seat for another butchers.

'Harry! . . . Hey, Harry! *Get in! Get in the car!*'

'*WHAT*?' Harry turned back to Wally, finger on his chest. He had wanted a private confab since they'd arrived at the office, but there had been no opportunity. He knew he had to warn Wally, just in case anyone should get wind that they had been given a tip-off about the safe house.

Wally looked Harry directly in the face. 'I dunno what you're talkin' about sunshine, I've not been up the base for months.'

Harry winked. 'Good, just remember that, you never told me nothin'.'

Cliff was hysterical as he yelled, 'Harry get in the friggin' car.'

Harry still took his time, easing his bulk into the passenger seat. 'What you gettin' your knickers in a twist about, we'll be on time.'

'Behind you, didn't you fuckin' see it?' Cliff jerked his thumb over his shoulder. 'It's that van from this morning . . . let's *move*.'

'What the bloody hell you doin'!' Halfway in the rear door, Wally hopped on one foot as Cliff did a tight U-turn, and scrambled in as the Granada screeched off down the road.

'It's Cliff! Yeah! Is Frank there?'

One ear covered by his hand, the other ear glued to the portable phone, Cliff did his best to make himself heard above The Happy Mondays. He was a big Diana Ross fan, and this lot sounded to him to be in the throes of terminal agony. Cliff shut his eyes to cut out the flashing strobe lights, face screwed up in a painful grimace. The narrow passage was only feet away from a vast, heaving, sweating mob of youth, the noise and heat wafting over him in waves.

'No, no, he's not with me, you know where he is? I've tried him on the portable an' I'm gettin' no answer. Listen, if he comes in, love, will you tell him it's urgent, I'll wait for him at the office . . . yeah! Yeah, I know what time it is. Okay, tell him it's urgent, an' I'm with Harry . . .'

'Come on, come on,' the young guy who was promoting the gig bellowed, beckoning to him. 'There's kids trying to get in by the back door.'

Cliff finished the call and scurried off.

'Oi! *Me phone.*'

Cliff handed it back. 'Thanks, mate.'

Dillon was doing his flunkey act, holding open the rear door of the Merc. He'd already taken the entire staff of the Chinese restaurant home, nine waiters and waitresses, dropping them off at their respective addresses, and now it was the turn of the manager and his wife. They settled themselves inside, and Dillon opened the front passenger door to get at the bleeping portable on the dashboard.

'Dillon . . . eh, can't hear, just take your time.' He glanced at his watch. 'I'll be back at base in about an hour . . . Okay, hang on.'

He leaned in and spoke to the Chinese man and his wife, reclining in luxury. 'You'll have to call another cab.' They both blinked up at him, totally bewildered. 'Out. Go on – out!'

Dillon slammed the door after them and said into the phone, 'Gimme ten minutes.' He climbed in and zoomed off, leaving the manager and his wife on the pavement staring at him, not quite inscrutably.

This had better be worth it. Three-thirty in the morning and they want a pow-wow. Plus losing the chink custom. And he needed his sleep, badly. If this was all over nothing . . .

Cliff opened the basement door and launched right in, gabbling ten to the dozen and waving his arms around. He followed Dillon into the office, where Harry was sitting with his feet on the desk, a mug of coffee in his fist.

'. . . so we're lost, right, Harry's tryin' to find the address, he's in a call box, over by Tower Bridge, the wharf, when I see the truck – '

'What truck?'

'The one from this morning' – the bleedin' furniture van, went straight past me.'

'What you do? Call the cops?'

'I called you! Where the hell you been?'

'With the bloody Chinese . . .'

'We tried to follow but we lost it, then we had to get to this gig!'

'Probably be stripped an' dumped by now,' Harry reckoned. 'There's a couple of crusher yards around that area, an' it – '

'Well, let the cops sort that out – it's nothin' to do with us.' Dillon rubbed his eyes. 'I better get home.'

Harry banged his mug down on the desk, slopping coffee.

'Tell him!'

Cliff jerked his head rapidly. 'Frank – the driver. I knew I'd seen him before. It was that Barry Newman's heavy . . .'

'Colin,' Harry said. 'One that picked your kids up,' he added softly, looking straight at Dillon with his shrewd baby-blues.

Cliff was nodding, more arm-waving. 'An' if you put two an' two together, I mean, he knows what business we're in – he even owns this place, right, he could have . . . he could . . .' He puffed out his cheeks. A thousand possibilities. Take your pick.

Dillon's head was down, staring at the floor. 'Here we

302

go again.' He swiped the air viciously. 'Why is it, every time I get a goddamned leg-up, something – somebody drags me down?' He stared at the desk for a second, nostrils flaring, breathing audible. He stared for a second more, then jerked his thumb at Cliff. 'Go out back, get some ropes an' that gear Jimmy left.' Dillon's eyes were suddenly hard, like shiny black pebbles. 'I'm gonna sort this bastard out once and for all.'

It was well after four, and Newman's warehouse was in darkness. Dillon and Harry got out of the Granada, looking up and down the dark empty street. Harry collected the gear from the boot and carefully pressed it shut. Dillon leaned down to Cliff in the driver's seat. 'We'll have a shufty around. Park it a good distance.'

The whites of Cliff's eyes gleamed. 'You mean walk back here?'

'Anythin' happens, our logo's on the side of the car, you pillock!'

Harry tapped on the roof, advising Cliff he'd got the rope and other stuff, and Cliff drove off. They approached the high gates, chain-link reinforced with iron bars, fringed along the top with razor wire. There was a snarling alsatian in a triangular metal sign with GUARD above and DOG beneath.

'Dog!'

'I can read, Harry! But I didn't see one when I was here, did you?' Harry shook his head. 'Just a front, cheap bastard,' Dillon said.

They moved further along, past the gates to a wall topped with broken bottle glass set in cement. 'Okay, my old son, how we gonna work it,' Harry said, unslinging the coil of rope from his shoulder. 'This wall's a piece of cake, an' I got a crowbar . . .'

'Let's just check out for alarms, no ruddy heroics. We've had enough for one day. We just sort the place out.'

Dillon's fear of alarms was unfounded, at least as far as the external windows were concerned. Harry jemmied the catch and the three of them slipped inside. They moved on rubber soles along the aisles, hands cupped around the torch glass so the light was focused into tight beams. The shelves were chock-a-block with Newman's Third World trade. One rack was completely filled with elephants, some without their decorative head-dresses, some in the process of being replaced with beads and coloured glass. At the far end they came to Newman's office, a partitioned structure of wooden panels up to waist height and panes of frosted glass right up to the ceiling.

Harry held up his hand. 'Hang about . . .' He did a slow sweep with the torch round the edge of the door. 'You see any wires?'

Dillon ran his fingers along the top and down both sides of the door frame. 'I'd say we're okay.'

Harry moved back a pace or two. He switched off his torch and craned upwards, peering through the frosted glass. 'Don't go in,' he warned Dillon. 'See that red dot? We got to find the main electricity circuit. We cross that beam an' all hell breaks loose. I'll go, just stay put.' He flicked on the torch and went off.

Dillon and Cliff hunkered down, backs to the wooden panels.

Down in the basement Harry followed the circuit cables along the wall, which led him eventually to the mains box. He opened the cast-iron cover and propped his torch at an angle to provide illumination. He leaned in, lifting two wires clear with his screwdriver, clippers poised. 'Our Father which art in heaven . . .'

He snipped. Nothing happened. He isolated two more and snipped again. Still nothing.

'Lovely,' Harry grinned, and carried on pruning.

Hunched against the wall of the office, Cliff shone the torchbeam on his wristwatch. Ten after five. 'It's gonna be daylight soon!' he hissed at Dillon. Drops of moisture filled the air. 'Christ!' Cliff stuck his hand out. 'It's raining. . . .'

Dillon squinted up, his face wet. The sprinklers had

come on. The wavering beam of a torch through the racks marked Harry's return. He came up grinning, dead chuffed with himself.

'I clipped every wire, turned off every main switch.'

'Yeah, an' put the sprinklers on.' Dillon got up, rubbing his knees. 'Can we go in now, or not?'

38

Dillon and Cliff knelt in front of the safe, a squat, old-fashioned green job with a brass handle, their heads close together as they studied the combination dial in the pale wash of light filtering through the windows. Harry was rummaging in the desk, still using the torch to peer into drawers, even though the office was brightening by the minute.

'Try it again . . . turn it left, left,' Dillon said. Cliff twiddled the dial. 'If we can't open it, we'll blow it. Harry, turn that off, or stop flashin' it around!'

'Hey, look at this – ' Harry reached into a drawer, a greedy kid who's discovered a cache of Mars bars. 'It's a 9mm Beretta. Oh very nice . . . it's got a custom-made silencer.' He checked it was unloaded, clicked the trigger on the empty chamber. 'I'm havin' this . . .'

'Leave it!' Dillon shot him a fierce look. 'We're not liftin' anythin', we're just lookin' for evidence.'

Cliff twiddled some more, then shook his head, mouth turned down. Dillon took out two small packs of plastic explosive, a wad of putty, and from a separate pocket a detonator with trailing wires. He nudged Cliff aside. 'Get back, lemme stick it.'

Harry rooted, searching for cartridges. Dillon set the charge, attached the detonator wires. 'Get under the desk,' he said to Harry. 'You too, Cliff.'

They took up positions. 'Okay. Here we go.' Dillon scuttled behind an armchair and put his head in the crook of his elbow.

It wasn't a huge bang, more like a heavy door slamming shut in the wind. Short and sweet. They waited till the puff of grey smoke had cleared and had a peek.

'Beautiful, Frank,' breathed Cliff. 'Neat as a whistle. That Jimmy's gear?'

Colin half-turned in the driver's seat, speaking out of the corner of his mouth. 'I sorted it personally, Mr Newman. The van's crushed, you could carry it in a holdall.'

At his ease, Newman sat in the back of the Jaguar Sovereign, gloved hands lightly clasped, resting in his lap. The car moved along the dingy street, passing a few parked vehicles; it stopped in the middle of the road and backed up. Newman operated the window and leaned his head out into the chill morning air. 'That's Dillon, isn't it?'

Colin went round to the Jag's boot, took out a short crowbar, walked across and broke the Granada's windscreen. He smashed the rear window and was about to start on the side windows when Newman said curtly, 'That's enough.'

Colin returned to the car. Newman leaned forward, rapped him on the shoulder. 'Let's go, they gotta be close . . . get some back-up round fast!' The car sped off.

'Take a look at what we got here!' Dillon slid open a deep metal tray, packed to the brim with small brown envelopes. He picked one up and tossed it to Cliff. 'The lazy so-an'-so's didn't even take it out of the wage packets.'

Cliff unzipped his windcheater and took out a foldaway bag. He batted it into shape and he and Dillon started scooping wage packets into it. Newman must have stashed the rest of the money elsewhere, Dillon thought, because this was only a fraction of the stolen payroll. But that didn't matter. The fact that Newman had some of the laundry wage packets in his possession was the real clincher. Let the slippery bastard try to wriggle out of this one!

Harry's eagle eye had lighted on a metal box, and his itchy fingers were in there quick as a shithouse rat. He rattled it and prised it open with his thumbnail. All shapes and sizes, several different hues, the heaped diamonds

307

sparkled in brilliant profusion. Harry hissed in a breath between his teeth.

'No, put them back! I mean it, Harry, put the box back,' Dillon ordered sternly. 'You're worse than a ruddy kid! Do as I say – just get the evidence.'

'Okay Sherlock!' Harry obeyed, though his heart was weeping.

The floor in the main warehouse was awash. Coat collars up around their ears against the sprinkler jets, the three of them legged it for the main entrance. Dillon slid back the bolts, eased the door open a fraction, then quickly slammed it shut.

'Newman's outside. He's out there!'

Cliff did a sliding turn, feet slithering on the wet floor. 'We go the back way across the roof!'

They set off down the central aisle, heading for the fire exit door. Newman and Colin burst in. As he ran, Dillon grabbed one of the racks and brought it crashing down behind them. Harry and Cliff got the general idea and did likewise, bringing shelves of elephants, brass trays, fertility totems, candlesticks, temple bells and earthenware pots tumbling down.

'Dillon – wait!' Newman ran forward, kicking an elephant out of the way. 'Dillon!' He stepped on a tray and went skidding into one of the racks, bringing the whole lot down.

Colin came panting back. 'The roof – they're goin' to try and cross by the roof, the crazy bastards. It won't hold their weight . . .'

Limping and cursing, Newman followed Colin into the yard. They stared up in the grey light to the three figures running as nimbly as cats along the apex of the old warehouse roof, crumbling yellow brick supporting a slanting metal-framed structure of skylights. They were balanced on a lead strip no more than six inches wide, sloping glass either side, so that a single slip could be fatal. Dillon, bringing up the rear, yelled down, 'I warned you to stay off my back, you bastard!' He hoisted the bag high. *'I got the wages, an' I'll have you, Newman!'*

As he turned to run on, Dillon's foot caught the lead flashing. He slithered down, a swinging foot smashing through one of the skylights. As the glass gave way he lost his hold, Harry snatching his wrist and hauling him back up. Cliff had the rope unfurled. He secured one end, tossed it down, and moments later all three of them vanished from sight over the rear of the building.

A truck piled high with the heavy mob pulled into the yard with a squeal of brakes. Colin ran up, waving his arms. 'We'll get 'em – back up, turn around! They'll be headin' for their car . . .'

'Leave them.' Newman walked back to the main door. *'I said leave it!'* He beckoned Colin. 'Get them inside.' As the men jumped down Newman said, 'One of you try and track Dillon, see where he is an' get back to me . . . *Move!"*

Three streets away, Dillon, Harry and Cliff were running like the clappers. As they rounded a corner Harry glanced behind, checking for signs of pursuit, but there wasn't a soul to be seen. 'We did it!' he exulted. 'Come on . . . *come on!'*

Even the sight of the Granada's shattered windscreen didn't wipe the smile from his face. He brushed the broken bits from the bonnet and unlocked the door. 'Get in – let's get out of here!'

The rooftop escape had infected the three of them with an adrenalin high. Dillon especially was abuzz, the joy of triumph so sweet he could almost taste it. 'We got enough evidence here to get that bastard ten years,' he chortled. 'Hey! That laundry offerin' a reward?'

Driving off, they were too busy laughing like drains and congratulating one another to notice the black Jaguar Sovereign creeping out from a side street and ghosting behind at a discreet distance.

Newman straightened up from the safe, the metal box in

his gloved hand. He could practically tell by the weight of it that the contents were untouched, but just to make absolutely certain he did a cool, professional appraisal of the stones in their padded velvet lining. Snapping the lid shut, he slid the box into his overcoat pocket. Colin was hovering by the door, cracking his knuckles.

'I want this place cleaned up – like now!' Newman said, his voice as lethal as cold steel. 'If it takes ten or twenty men, get 'em. This never happened, understand me?'

Colin glanced behind uneasily. The sprinklers had been turned off, but the warehouse was a total shambles, water inches deep in places. 'Barry, what about the lads, their cut? They won't go for this – '

'They'll go for anythin' I tell them,' Newman sneered, his thin, wide mouth twisting contemptuously. 'Fuckin' ex-soldiers are all alike, they're conditioned to take orders, why you think I use them?' He suddenly kicked out at the desk, livid with a furious spite and overwhelming rage. 'I made a point of helpin' the bastards, handin' out work to them. I did it for Billy, my Billy . . . well, not any more. An' that Dillon.' He spat the name. 'I tried! I'd have given that stupid bastard more money than he'd ever dreamed of, because he was good to my Billy – but no! Legit. He wanted to be legit. Well, we'll see how he gets himself out of this one!'

Breathing hard, Newman wiped spittle from his moustache. His voice sank to a murmur. 'He was never here, understand? And you get on the first plane . . .'

'I dunno.' Colin cracked his knuckles. 'What about my wife?'

'You don't know, son,' Newman sighed, managing to sound fatherly and patronising at one and the same time. 'I do. I survive, an' I got,' he patted his pocket, 'one-point-five million here. An' if you want your cut, you do as I tell you – you weren't here tonight. Nothin' went down here tonight.' He raised his eyebrows. 'Get over to Spain, call it a holiday!'

310

Colin nodded unhappily. It had the ring of a friendly invitation but he knew it was a command.

39

Dillon bounced into the office, dumped the bag on the desk.

'Cliff, get the motor over to Fernie, see if he can fix it up by tomorrow afternoon. Harry, check over the jobs we got lined up.' He unzipped the bag. 'We get cleaned up, then first thing I go to the cops.'

Eyes all aglow, Dilon scooped up wage packets and held them high, tightly bunched in his fist. 'We got that bastard!'

Newman paced along the aisles, head swivelling left, then right, left, right again, noting every tiny detail, every slight discrepancy. He adjusted the position of a set of brass candlesticks, nudged a china figurine back into line with its fellows. The boys had done good. Just over the hour it had taken them, and you'd never have guessed that at six-thirty that morning the place looked as though a bull had rampaged through it and pissed all over the floor. Three blokes were finishing off the mopping up at the far end; once the floor dried it would be as if nothing had happened. Newman pursed his lips and smiled. Nothing had.

He strolled back to the office. Derek, the guy he'd put on Dillon's tail, came in the main door and hurried over.

'Dillon went straight to his gaff,' he reported.

'You see him carry the gear in?' asked Newman quietly.

Derek nodded. 'You want us to pick him up?'

'No, but I'll get him picked up, all right,' Newman smirked. He held open the office door. 'Come on, you got a call to make!'

Derek stared at him, mystified, and in he went, scratching his head. Newman and his smirk followed.

'Morning!' Harry was using his electric shaver when Susie breezed in with a bag of shopping and a cheery smile. 'As Frank didn't make it home, I reckoned you had a busy night, so . . .' She held up three paper bags, their contents seeping through '. . . breakfast! Bacon butties!'

There was the sound of running water from the wash-room, where Dillon was engaged in his morning ablutions.

'How you feelin'?' Harry asked, unplugging the shaver. 'You okay now?'

'Yes, I'm fine.' Susie showed him her hand, now out of plaster, and waggled her fingers, almost as good as new. 'I'd have started back days ago but Frank wouldn't hear of it.' She opened a cupboard. 'No coffee? Any milk?'

Harry nipped out behind her back to forewarn Dillon. Susie switched on the overhead light and shook her head at the state of the place. Leave three fellas alone for a few days and they could turn a palace into a pig-sty.

Dilon appeared, drying his hands on a towel. 'Hello, love, you're early.' He gave her a peck. 'I was just havin' a wash. Kids get off to school okay, did they?'

'Yes.' Susie loaded a tray with dirty coffee mugs. 'Ket-tle's on. I'll get some milk. Looks as if I came just in time.'

'Cliff not back?' Dillon asked Harry as he came in.

Harry shook his head. His eyes flicked a sidelong look at Susie. 'How do you want to work it this morning?' he asked Dillon, making it casual.

Dillon gave a quick frown, gestured towards the pas-sage. He said, 'Can I borrow your shaver? An' get me a clothes brush . . .'

Susie was standing with an armful of empty beer cans, about to drop them in the waste basket. 'Frank!'

Dillon whipped round in the doorway.

'Is something going on?'

He blinked at her, wide-eyed innocence. 'No . . .' and went out.

When Harry came through into the washroom with the electric shaver Dillon had done a lightning change into a clean white shirt, black tie and neatly pressed grey trousers.

Dillon turned on the tap and started shaving. Under the sound of running water he whispered, 'I don't want Susie to know what went down last night.' He noticed his cuffs, slightly puckered, and fretted, 'Should have had it laundered!'

The phone rang and they heard Susie answer it. Harry rubbed his palms briskly. 'What we do? Go to the cops? If there's a reward, maybe we can do a deal – '

Dillon nixed that with a swift chop of the hand. He had other worries on his mind. 'We're bound to have repercussions from Newman . . .' He frowned towards the door. 'I don't want Susie left down here, that bastard could try to get my kids again. Soon as I'm cleaned up I go straight to the cops, no deals. Get that shooter they used, we'll need that.' He smoothed his hand over his chin. 'Gimme me jacket . . . tie okay, is it?'

Harry unhooked the chauffeur's grey jacket from behind the door and tore off the plastic cover. He helped Dillon into it, then climbed up on the lavatory seat, reaching inside the big old-fashioned wooden cistern. 'I stashed it up here.'

Dillon twitched as the phone went again. He fumbled with his jacket buttons, a bundle of nerves. 'We're doin' the right thing, Harry, trust me. I won't let you down. Cops'll want to question all of us.' Harry stepped down with the Sterling, wrapped in *The Sporting Life*. Dillon looked him in the face. Now it came, what was really troubling him. 'You and me made a terrible mistake.' he said in a hoarse whisper. 'One we have to live with, but, we're for it if so much as a word gets out about what we done, right?'

'Yeah.'

'So, that's finished, that never happened, we never discuss it, agreed?'

'Yeah.' Harry nodded. 'I hear you, gov'nor. I'll put this with the dough.' He grinned. 'You're lookin' good . . .'

Dillon turned to the door, whitewash all down the back of his jacket.

'Hang on!' Harry batted it off. 'Whitewash on the back . . . s'okay now!' He brushed Dillon's shoulders. 'You sure about this, Frank, maybe we can do a deal – not with Newman, the geezer from the laundry, he hadda be insured.'

'I said no deals.' Dillon ground it out so that it stuck. 'We play it straight. So far we been lucky! Don't push it, Harry. I'm going in, that's final.'

He took down his chauffeur's cap, flicked off an imaginary speck of dust. He opened the door and Cliff came barging in, face shiny, out of breath. He'd changed too into his chauffeur's gear. 'I've left the motor at Fernie's. Where's the dough?'

'Where's Susie?' asked Dillon, fractious and fussing. 'I look okay?'

'Gone for some milk.' Cliff squinted sideways at his shoulder, brushing it. 'Mind the walls . . . whitewash comes off!'

'Come on then,' Dillon said decisively, 'before she gets back, let's get this sorted between us – ' Cliff started to move as the telephone rang, and Dillon hauled him back. 'Just leave it, we got to talk.' Dillon emphasised his words with his bunched fist. 'When we go to the Old Bill, we got to all have the same story. Why we went to Newman's, why we got that gun . . .'

Cliff's eyes shifted uneasily to Harry, who was sucking his moustache. Two very unwilling volunteers, the pair of them couldn't have looked less enthusiastic if they'd rehearsed. Dillon faced them, attempting to chide and jolly them along. 'Come on, this is the only way . . . we sort this out, well, like Harry says, might even get some kind of reward, right? But what is important, and it's gonna stay that way – we're legit, an' we stay legit, an' I reckon we got a future, one we can all be proud of . . .'

Dillon's fist shot up.

'We made it! an' we're gonna go on makin' it! What's past is past, agreed?'

He spread his raised hand. 'Harry?'

Harry whacked it.

'Cliff?'

Cliff whacked it.

'*Yes . . . !*'

Dillon was convinced himself. Edginess, uncertainty, doubt were banished, he was psyched up and raring to go. A new confident Dillon now, on his way to the top, and nothing on the planet short of a thermonuclear warhead could stop him. At last he was in control. He had a grip. He felt great!

'I'll level with them, tell exactly what went down, an' then we're in the clear. We learn from our mistakes. Only one way to go now, an' that's *up!*'

'Frank . . . ?' Susie's voice started low and ascended the scale like the shrill whine of a thermonuclear warhead homing in on its target.

'*Frank – will you get in here!*'

Harry appeared in the doorway, sent to forestall nuclear armageddon.

'Where's Frank? You get in here, now!' Susie was blazing.

Cliff came in behind Harry and she let them both have it.

'Fernie left a message for you. He said – and I won't repeat it word for word – but he said unless you pay what you owe him he's keeping the car, smashed up as it is, but it's nothing to what he intends doing unless he gets paid – '

'Oh . . .' Harry feebly waved a pacifying hand. 'We had a bit of a prang last night . . .'

'I haven't finished. He also said he's keeping the portable phone! And – '

'Oh man,' Cliff moaned. 'We need that!'

'*I haven't finished Cliff!* The bank called, wanted to know if there was a problem. There's not been *one* repayment on their loan, and the Stag Security account is overdrawn up to . . .' Susie snatched up her notepad. 'Three and a half thousand pounds. And *don't either of you tell me that's Frank's business* – '

'I dunno anythin' about the loan, Susie,' said Cliff lamely.

Susie yanked a drawer open. 'Do either of you know about these betting slips?' He glare would have blistered paint. 'Or is that Frank's business as well, like the account at the betting shop. Eight hundred quid outstanding! My friend went out on a limb for you lot, is this how you repay him?! Don't you understand what'll happen to him?'

Harry stepped up to the desk, hands raised. 'Just calm down, love . . .'

'*Calm down!*' The nuclear warhead was about to explode. 'They'll take his taxi firm – he's guaranteed your loan!'

Dillon came in, smart in his chauffeur's grey uniform, bag of money in one hand, the Sterling sub-machine-gun wrapped in newsprint under his arm. 'Okay, we all set . . . ?'

All four heads jerked towards the window. The sudden loud wail of police sirens, the screech of brakes in the street outside.

A look of bewilderment on Dillon's face. 'You didn't call 'em, did you?' he asked Harry.

Car doors slammed and the basement steps were immediately filled with dark blue trousers, the thump of heavy boots, a fist hammering on the door. 'This is the police! Come on, open up, we have a warrant to search the premises. This is the police!'

Dillon was rooted to the spot, staring blank-eyed at Harry and Cliff. Harry and Cliff, blank-eyed, stared back at Dillon. Standing behind the desk, Susie's face had drained to a whiter shade of pale.

'This can't be about the Newman business,' Harry muttered, blue eyes vague and confused. 'Can it . . . ?'

More hammering, the shouts getting louder and angrier. These weren't bumbling PC Plods, they were the hard squad, as tough and ruthless in their methods as the villains they picked up.

Dillon felt a sick fearful panic knawing at the pit of his

stomach. He had a terrible vision, seeing once again the door open, the pale blue light splashing into the hallway, the man framed in the doorway with the TV flickering behind him, frantically pushing the door shut, and then the blast of the rifle, the body hitting the floor, the electric fire turned on its side. He gripped Harry's arm, fingers digging in. 'How much you tell Wally? He wouldn't have opened his mouth, would he?'

'He knows nothin', I swear, Frank. I told him nothin'.' Harry was shaking his head, all at sea. 'It's got to be about last night, nothin' else . . .'

Dillon recovered himself, his face hardening. He looked at the two men, holding their eyes with a deadly fixed intensity. 'Say nothin' – hear me!'

Susie came slowly around the desk, not a shred of colour in her face, arms lifting up beseechingly.

'Oh God, Frank, what have you done?'

Harry was taken out, handcuffed to a uniformed officer. Cliff was next, handcuffed to another. Dillon followed, hands cuffed behind his back. Going up the steps he yelled out, 'You don't say a bloody word! Let me explain it . . . you don't say nothin'. *You don't know anythin'* – '

For that he got his face rammed into the iron railings. The officer jerked Dillon's arms up his back, nearly pulling them out of their sockets. Then he was shoved, staggering, into the street towards the open door of the police car.

Finally, an officer came out carrying the zippered bag and the Sterling, its muzzle peeping through *The Sporting Life*.

Susie trailed after him. Her arms hung limply at her sides, head thrown back as she sobbed her heart out. Coming up the steps, she was met by the lowering bulk of Detective Chief Inspector Reg Jenkins. He looked like the kind of copper who enjoyed pulling the legs off tarantulas. Waving the search warrant in her face, he gestured her back down. Standard procedure that someone had to be present when premises were searched, and in this respect, at least, Detective Chief Inspector Jenkins always went by the book.

40

A cigarette dangling from the corner of his mouth, DCI Jenkins leaned against the window sill, arms folded, squinting through the smoke at the tagged evidence arranged on the table, some of it still bearing traces of fingerprint powder.

Item: Black ski hood, slits cut through for eyes.

Item: Black ski hood, identical, also with slits.

Item: Blue plastic bag with zip. No markings.

Item: Wage packets marked 'Roche Laundry Services', sealed.

Item: Sub-machine-gun with magazine, classified by ballistics as a 9mm L2A2 Sterling, as used by the British Army in Northern Ireland and elsewhere. Recently fired. Four cartridges missing from the 34-round magazine capacity.

Jenkins pushed himself up. Unhurriedly he removed the cigarette from his lips, blew out a plume of smoke, and made the slightest of shaking movements of the head. This was almost going to be too easy.

There were footsteps in the corridor and Detective Inspector Briggs came briskly in carrying a document file. Jenkins took a deep drag, holding out his hand. 'That from their statements?' He opened the file on the corner of the table and fanned out the reports so he could refer back and forth.

Riggs stood by Jenkins' shoulder, trying to avoid the cloud of smoke. He might at least open a window. The place stank. Jenkins skimmed through. 'Dillon's been held before, you read this?' He sucked in another satisfying lungful. 'Let off with a warning! Wrecked a patrol car . . . he still refusing to talk? Well, we got 'em bang to rights on this caper.'

'You see who owned the car he and . . .' Riggs craned

forward. 'Driven by Steve Harris, but the motor they were driving was owned by . . .' He tapped the report.

'One Barry Newman.' Jenkins read on, nodding, flakes of grey ash drifting down. 'No charges. What about bringing in this Steve Harris, see what he has to say?'

'Be pushed, he's dead. I've already checked.'

Jenkins leaned across to stub out his cigarette. He braced both arms on the table, head sunk between his shoulders, gazing down at the documents. 'Dillon and Travers won't budge, let's go for the black bastard . . . somethin' stinks.' His eyes roved up to the ski hoods, money, gun. 'None of 'em'll get bail this time! Not with that lot . . .'

Not gloating exactly, but with the deepest satisfaction.

Dillon was wiping up bacon fat with a piece of bread when a small, round-shouldered man with thinning sandy hair pushed open the door of the holding cell. Clutching a rather tatty briefcase in pale, freckled hands, he blinked at Dillon through a pair of horn-rimmed spectacles with thick, distorting lenses. In other circumstances he might have been taken for someone trying to flog an endowment policy or double glazing on the never-never.

'Mr Dillon? I'm Arthur Crook. I've already spoken to Mr Travers and Mr Morgan.'

Dillon pushed the tin tray further along the bed and made space for him to sit on the grey blanket.

'I've been appointed to represent you.' The voice was bland and diffident, as colourless as he was. 'Is this acceptable to you?'

'I have an alternative?' said Dillon, testily.

'If you don't wish me to represent you, that is your prerogative, I can ask for someone else. But I am experienced in criminal – '

'*They got no right to hold me here!*'

Dillon's outburst set the little man to blinking once again. Almost in a tone of apology, he said, 'Mr Dillon, they have some very tough evidence against you.'

'An' I explained how we came to have it. I told them . . .'

320

Dillon stared at Crook, his mouth suddenly dry. 'There's nothin' else, is there?'

'I've read your statement, Mr Dillon.' Either Crook didn't understand the question or had chosen to ignore it; Dillon couldn't decide which, and he was frantic to know. 'Unless you are prepared to name the man who you say instigated the robbery, well – ' A small shrug of the rounded shoulders. 'If you name him, then we can check out your story.'

Dillon rested his elbows on his knees, hands working restlessly, gazing at the wall opposite. 'I got two kids,' he said in a low, harsh voice. 'I start naming names while I'm in here, who's gonna protect them? You get me bail, then I'll talk.' He swung his head at Crook. 'But I need to take care of my family first!'

Crook opened his briefcase and took out several typed sheets. Dillon watched with hooded eyes as the solicitor looked through them, and then he tried again. 'They're not chargin' me with anythin' else, are they? Just the robbery . . . ?'

'I'd think seriously about giving the name of this man,' Crook advised in his bland legal tone. 'If he's a suspect, the police will protect you . . .' He had the typewritten sheets in order, placed neatly on the briefcase resting flat on his knees. He cleared his throat. 'Now, I have been asked to tell you that there have been three robberies, all carried out in a similar way, and – the police believe – with military precision.' The pale blue eyes, magnified by the thick lenses, bulged up at him. 'Mr Dillon, they are all very aware that you and those arrested with you are ex-Parachute Regiment soldiers.'

It was Dillon's turn to blink. He'd been worrying himself sick about the Irishman in the derelict house and suddenly he was being dumped on from a different direction entirely. What the hell was happening?

'Now, these robberies took place in Surrey, Brighton, and Whitechapel.' Crook held out the top sheet. 'I will need to know where you were on these dates.'

321

Dillon looked at them blankly. He shook his head, thoughts in a whirl, unable to take this in.

'Look, check my diary. We've been runnin' a business. I dunno where I was right off, but the diary gives all the jobs we done.'

Crook took the sheet back. 'They have also found a weapon at your office.' He looked gravely at Dillon. 'You have anything to say about that?'

'You mean the gun used in the hold-up?'

Crook gave a slight nod.

'I can explain that,' Dillon said, starting to feel very sick again.

'Mr Travers, they have the sub-machine gun used in the robbery,' Crook said. 'The same gun had been determined as the one used to damage your security wagon. They have black hoods, they have the wage packets you insist were stolen – '

'I'm not sayin another word. Frank will tell you what went down. Ask Frank Dillon.'

The line-up was already in position, Harry the second man along, as Dillon was led in. His handcuffs were removed and the officer indicated he could could stand where he wished. Dillon chose roughly midway and faced the darkened viewing window which reflected the twelve men under the spotlights. Some wore jackets, some were in shirtsleeves like him, but only Harry and himself were unshaven, he noticed. Perm any two from twelve, so long as they got five o'clock shadows, Dillon thought sourly.

'We're in the clear, they don't know nothin',' Harry called to him, and then louder, 'How ya doin', Frank!'

'No talking! Look straight in front, eyes to the front!'

Behind the window, a uniformed inspector ushered in a portly middle-aged man in a smart pinstripe suit.

'Just take your time, sir. You say you got a good look at the man as he approached the bank tellers. If you seen him, want him to turn right or left, just say so.'

The portly man nodded and took his time, studying each face for several seconds. Twice he leaned forward, his gaze lingering, before passing on. He came to the end of the line, and after a brief pause, shook his head.

The inspector spoke into the microphone. 'Thank you, gentlemen. You can go!'

That was the only time he'd seen Harry since their arrest, and he hadn't seen Cliff at all. Obviously, Dillon thought, they were grilling each of them separately, cross-checking their stories, trying to break each of them down. But if the other two said nothing, left it to him, what was there to fear? He could explain everything, given the chance. As for the other robberies, the evidence was purely circumstantial. Wasn't it?

He was taken out to the Black Maria and handcuffed to the iron guard rail which ran along the side of the van above the slatted wooden seat. Two teenage boys, who looked comatosed on drugs or glue or something, sat huddled together in the corner next to the cab. A uniformed officer, a bear of a man with no neck, climbed in and sat opposite Dillon. He pulled the door shut, so the only light came from the two narrow slits in the rear doors.

'How many more line-ups you bastards want me in?' Dillon asked, not expecting a reply, and not receiving one. The officer sat back, folded his arms, and contemplated eternity, or maybe his pension.

By raising himself slightly off the seat, Dillon could see through the slit. Another Black Maria had pulled up in the yard, and Cliff was stepping down, handcuffed to an officer. He seemed more bewildered than frightened, and Dillon wanted to yell out, tell him to keep stum. If the kid lost his nerve, did something stupid, he could land them all in it.

'Sit down,' the bear with no neck said. '*Sit – down!*'

Dillon slowly sank back, but then leaned forward sharply. At the wheel of his black Jaguar Sovereign,

323

Newman was rolling to a halt. He slid the window down and reached out his hand, a faint smile on his thin lips. Detective Chief Inspector Jenkins strolled forward. Dillon stared as the two men shook hands. He pressed himself closer to the slit, feeling the flesh of his face tight to bursting, and a large hand shoved him roughly back onto the bench.

'Sit! You deaf?'

Dillon slumped down, his heart trip-hammering in his chest. The door opened and a sheaf of folded release papers was thrust in. The door was closed, the handle locked, and the officer banged on the side to indicate all present and correct. The van jerked forward, dragging Dillon by his handcuffed wrist against the guard rail, and moved off. Dillon hardly felt it. What he did feel was a crawling panic in his bowels. Barry Newman and the cops, all mates together. Was he being fitted up? What was Newman telling them? What the fuck was going on?

41

'Believe me,' Newman said, 'if somebody had broken in here I'd know it. Besides, who'd want to nick this stuff, weighs a ton.'

Jenkins looked along the aisles, at the racks and racks of artifacts which to his eye were the kind of cheap trash you might see in a fairground, prizes for getting three double-tops in a row or potting clay pipes with a .22 that had had its sights doctored. Three of his uniforms were poking about, but probably they had less idea what they were looking for that he had.

'What about the office?' he asked, nodding towards the partitioned glass-panelled enclosure.

'Follow me!' Newman beckoned, the good citizen only too happy to co-operate with the law. 'Watch your footing, I've had problems with the sprinklers.' As they walked along he pointed up to the cables running along the walls. 'Alarm system. Anyone trying to get in here and this baby would go off like a time-bomb.' With an indulgent wave of the hand, Newman called across, 'Any of you lads got kids, take what you want. Business is bad, I can't give this gear away.'

A few paces behind, Jenkins said casually, 'Your boy was a Para, wasn't he? A soldier . . .'

And noted the stiffening of Newman's spine. Newman stopped to face him, but he wasn't angry or defensive, the inspector saw, he was proud, even a little defiant.

'Yes. I got a medal to prove it! He was killed in a club, he wasn't even on duty. Nineteen years old.' Newman looked away, and in profile the hollow cheeks and scrawny neck made him look old and haggard, a distinguished roué long past his sell-by date. 'His mother never got over it . . . his name was Billy.'

'So you know Dillon then?'

Newman walked on. 'He was his sergeant! I met up with him when he first came to civvies, while back now.'

'Meet some of his pals too, did you?'

Newman paused at the office door. He turned slowly, gave Jenkins his full dead-eyed stare. Touched a spot there, Jenkins thought, half-expecting a flat denial, but didn't expect what he got, an acid, withering bitterness, a raw open wound that had never healed and never would.

'Look, this Dillon. I tried to give him a leg-up, know what I mean? The thanks was, he borrowed my motor and totalled it, an' that's been my only interaction with him. Maybe I should've tried to do somethin' for him, but that was thirty grand's worth! I reckoned whatever he'd done for my boy, we were quits – an' I'm not a charity.' Newman held up his thin hand, pointed a long skeletal finger. 'I'll tell you who should watch out for these lunatics, the ruddy government. Most of them need rehabilitation, they're all screwed up.'

Whatever lies he might tell, whatever descriptions he might perpetrate, Newman was on the level with this, Jenkins thought. It came straight from the heart, no question. Newman gestured brusquely. 'Here's my office, come on through.' Jenkins followed him inside.

She wouldn't cry. Susie had made this promise to herself. She had to keep Frank's spirits up. The last thing he wanted to see was a red-eyed bawling wife. But it took every ounce of self-control as the woman police officer led her into the interview room not to let the calm outer surface crack wide open. It was the sight of him sitting hunched in the chair, hands clasped on the bare table, shackled by handcuffs. He looked so lost and helpless. From somewhere Susie summoned up a pallid smile. She sat down opposite him, while the WPC took up a position behind her and a male officer stood with arms folded at the door, like a bouncer itching to sort out the troublemakers.

326

'I've been here every day but they wouldn't let me see you. Mr Crook arranged it in the end.' Susie wore a plain dark skirt and a pale yellow blouse under her coat that she knew Frank liked, but he hadn't even looked at her. She reached out, not quite touching the bunched hands, fingers squeezed tight. 'Are you all right?'

'This is all a mistake.' Dillon stared sullenly at the table. His cheeks were smooth and pale, freshly shaved, dark rings under his eyes. 'I haven't done anythin' wrong. They can't keep me here without chargin' me.' His lips thinned. 'I haven't done anythin'.'

'Mr Crook's tried for bail, Frank, but it was turned down at the Magistrates Court. He said he'll have to wait a few more weeks before he can apply again – '

'You think I don't know?' He raised his head sharply. His mouth twisted as the anger spilled out. 'He's a useless twat!'

Susie hesitated. 'He says you're not helping.'

'I didn't do anything wrong!' said Dillon hoarsely.

'You know Cliff told them about Newman?' Dillon glared at her. 'What are you protecting him for?' Susie asked, genuinely puzzled.

'You don't understand.' Dillon was nodding to himself, an ugly smile smearing his features. 'I'm gonna give you some names, friends, if that bastard shows his face – '

'Frank!' Susie leaned towards him. 'He said you never worked for him, he says his place was never broken into . . . that it was lies, all lies.'

'Marvellous innit – they believe that villain, but not me? I told Cliff to keep his bloody mouth shut. Typical. But what can you expect, he was only on transport, he's never seen any action. They won't get Harry to – '

Susie's fist drummed impotently on the table. 'I can't believe I'm hearing you right! Cliff was going to be married, don't you care? He's in a terrible state . . . Shirley's pregnant.'

'You think I'm allowed to see him? See Harry?' Dillon didn't hear, didn't care. His eyes were a bit wild, his brain

327

locked on the single track it had been on, ceaselessly, every waking moment. 'Bastards have segregated us. Four line-ups they had me in – I been in four line-ups, for what? They're tryin' to pin every robbery pulled in England on us. It's crazy, it's all crazy . . .'

He calmed his breathing and looked at her from under his brows. 'They not said anythin' about anythin' else?' he asked uneasily. 'Have they . . . Susie?'

A fist rapped on the door. The officer unfolded his arms. He waved to Dillon to stand. Susie pleaded, 'Ah, not yet! Please, not yet . . . !'

The officer got Dillon on his feet. He opened the door. Dillon said desperately, 'Are the kids all right?'

'Yes . . .' And the promise she had made herself was broken as a sob came up, nearly choking her. Still she struggled to hold on. Dillon tried to turn back. The officer would have none of it. He had Dillon under the armpit, and the officer outside grabbed the other arm and he was bodily hauled away.

Susie laid her head on her arms and had to let it all come out, promise or no promise.

Twenty-seven. Twenty-eight. Twenty-nine. Thirty. Thirty-one. Thirty-two. Thirty-three . . .

Sweat dripping off his nose, Dillon pushed himself up from the cell floor. Susie had brought in some of his gear, and he wore a singlet, track-suit bottoms, and his faithful old Pumas. If he shut his mind to everything, it was like doing Basic again. He was back at The Depot.

Forty-three. Forty-four. Forty-five. Forty-six . . .

Do eighty of the bastards and he'd be ready for a pint with the lads in the NAAFI. Have a sing-song, good old Taff booming out in his big Welsh voice, the prat. Get Steve up on a table, doing his Tom Jones with a baton down his inside leg. Jimmy fiddling the one-armed bandit. Harry remembering that long day's tab up to Wireless Ridge, when Wally's frostbitten toes dropped off.

A bell rang out and the caged wall light went out, plunging the cell into darkness.

Fifty-eight. Fifty-nine. Sixty. Sixty-one. Sixty-two . . .

Susie moved silently into the boys' room, careful not to disturb them. She left the door slightly ajar so that she could see by the landing light. There were one or two gaps on the walls where Dillon had taken down the photographs. And what Dillon had started, Susie now finished, dropping them one by one in the cardboard box. His face looked out from nearly all of them. Sometimes clean and shiny, sometimes streaked with brown camouflage cream and dirt. Mostly unsmiling, but in a couple there was that rare Frank Dillon grin. It was there, broader than usual, in a photograph of him and his lads, grouped round a table in a bar, brimming pints of Guinness and Murphy's in front of them. Six young Toms, just kids, sitting at the table, with Dillon standing behind, flanked by Jimmy Hammond, Taffy Davies, Steve Harris, Harry Travers. They looked to be having a great time, and probably were. The very best of times.

Susie took it down and looked at it. Then she dropped it in the box with all the rest and shut the lid. She went to the door and paused, gazing round. The little room seemed empty and desolate, the walls naked. Just pale rectangles and pin-holes to indicate where the gallery of memories had once been. The boys would miss them, no doubt, but it was time to move on, to grow up. You couldn't live in the past for ever. Susie went out, closed the door on it.

42

It was called the Visitors' Room but it was more like a public meeting hall or a large works canteen. Not dissimilar to a canteen, with tables spaced equidistant on the squeaky composition floor, except the tables were quite small, with plain grey plastic tops, room enough for just one remand prisoner, one visitor. The kids had to stand or play on the floor. Four uniformed wardens patrolled the perimeter, constantly on the move, eyes alert for any communication between prisoners – strictly forbidden. Two senior wardens sat like tennis umpires on high chairs, keeping a general watch on the proceedings. The prisoners were rotated in batches of twenty, over a hundred in the hall at any one time. Once seated, their visitors were allowed in, while the previous batch of visitors streamed out, so there was continuous noise and bustle and movement, the scampering and crying of children, the muffled weeping of women, the rumbling hum of a hundred conversations.

Shirley was in the first batch. She came in with other wives, girlfriends and mothers, heads craning for their loved ones. There were a number of black prisoners, but she spotted Cliff at once, his hand slightly raised, a shy, almost painful smile on his face. Like all the others he was dressed in a blue shirt, dark trousers without a belt, black slip-on shoes with soft soles.

'How you keeping?' asked Cliff, eyes very large and suspiciously bright, fixed on her as she sat down.

Shirley placed a paper bag on the table. She slipped off her shoulder bag and put down the styrofoam cup of coffee she'd only taken a couple of sips of before the name Morgan came up over the PA.

'There's chocolate, crisps and cigarettes.' She pushed the bag towards him.

'I don't smoke,' Cliff said.

'Susie said to bring them in, you can trade with them. She takes in some for . . .' Shirley glanced around the crowded room. 'Have you seen him yet?'

Cliff shook his head. 'They keep us segregated. I got a message to Harry, but he . . .' Cliff gulped, and the tears that were there, waiting to be shed, suddenly filled his eyes. '. . . he sent it back. I just had to tell them what went down, Shirley, this is all a mistake, we didn't do it.' Out it poured in a frantic gabble: 'You see I saw the van, the furniture van that was used in the robbery, and I saw the guy drivin' it, it was me that told Frank, that Newman's put us all in the frame. I had to tell them, but they twist it, they twist it around. I know they found the gear at our place, but we'd come from Newman's, we were gonna hand it in. I think Frank's scared that Newman'll do somethin', he reckoned we'd get bail you see, an' — '

'Cliff — Cliff, you've told me all this, you tell it to me every time, but why won't they give you bail?' Shirley searched his face. 'None of this makes sense to me. Why are they askin' about other robberies unless . . .' She leaned over until their faces were nearly touching. 'Cliff, don't protect them, will you?'

Cliff's mouth was quivering. Tears had made wet pathways down either side of his nose. He was looking at Shirley but he wasn't seeing her. The inside of his head was spinning like a merry-go-round, the same endless, obsessional whirl of facts, events, places, names blurring in front of his eyes. She tried to stop him, to stem the flow, but he was unstoppable.

'. . . I said to Frank we should go straight to the cops, but we had to clean ourselves up an' then there was the car, windscreen was wrecked . . . now the gun, Harry took it off the blokes, I mean I nearly got myself killed. I explained all this. I told them all this. I recognised one of the guys, I said to Harry, I said . . .' He blinked, tears

331

splashing down. 'I dunno why he kept it, we should have handed that gun back. It'll be sorted. It'll all be sorted, we'll be out of here . . .' Cliff wept openly. 'Shit, why didn't we hand over that bloody shooter . . .'

Shirley could hardly hear him for all the racket going on around them. Not that it mattered. She'd heard it ten times before. She simply sat and gazed at him, at the merry-go-round spinning madly out of control.

A bell rang, signalling a changeover of batches. Twenty in, twenty out. There was a clicking and crackling from the PA, and a voice announced in a monotonous drone: 'Allen, Alcott, Allerton, Anthony, Daneman, Dillon, Dupres, Hoyle, Knight, Morris, Mayfield, Mayell, Netherton, Normans, Orchard, O'Rourke, O'Neill . . .'

Dillon was brought in and directed to a table on the far side of the room from Cliff. He sat down and looked expectantly towards the door as the visitors filed in, eager for his first glimpse of Susie. The clamour was tremendous, women moving along the aisles, many with toddlers in tow, some carrying babies. Around the human arena the wardens kept up their steady pacing and relentless steely-eyed scrutiny. At last he saw her, moving through the tables, and something strange happened. He thought he was strong, that he could face anything, had built up his resolve to get him through each minute of every day as a prisoner on remand. But the moment he saw her his strength and resolve just crumbled away. His insides seemed to shrink, and he had to turn away because his face was too naked and vulnerable. Tough guy Dillon who could throw himself out of a Herc at 800 feet, and yet this particular ordeal nearly did for him. He understood now how a man's reason could snap, as easily and suddenly and fatally as a brittle pencil point.

'They made me wait almost two hours.' Susie gave him a quick smile, sounding out of breath. She had a paper bag with her, and from her handbag produced a manila

332

envelope. 'I brought all your letters from the C.O. You'll give them to the lawyer?'

Dillon nodded. He couldn't trust himself to speak. He took the envelope to give his hands something to do. His mouth was dry as dust and his palms were cold and damp.

'Is there anything else you need?'

'No,' Dillon croaked. He cleared his throat. 'I got everything.'

'He said the trial will be in ten – ten to twelve weeks.'

'Yeah. That's right.'

'He said you'd moved cells. You're sharing now. All right, is it?' Susie raised her eyebrows. It was stupid small talk, but what else was there? You couldn't talk about the weather to a man inside.

'Guy's a nutter, but I'll make out,' Dillon said, making an effort. He found the strength to look into her eyes, and that gave him hope. He said, 'We been set up, it'll just be a question of gettin' the facts right, that Newman's got to be palmin' somebody. He denies we were in the warehouse, he's a liar, he's got them in his pay. I sussed that out.' His voice hardened as his confidence grew. 'Cliff saw the furniture van, he saw it, that's why we knew he was involved, right? That's why we went to his place, that's where we got the wages, they were still in the packets.' Faster now, gathering pace, urgent. 'I mean, if we'd been gonna rob somebody, we had every opportunity. He had the stolen gems, diamonds. If we'd been gonna pull a robbery we'd have, we'd have . . .'

His voice faltered, tailed away. Susie waited a moment. Then she said, as gently as she could with all the racket going on, 'Frank, you said this last time I was here . . . it's me, and I believe you. You don't have to prove anything to me, you know that. I believe you.'

Dillon nodded. He glanced away, as if embarrassed. 'Sorry, it's just that's all I keep thinking about. I'm sorry.' He looked at the envelope, rolled into a tight tube in his hands, and then up at her. 'They not mentioned anythin' else to you, have they? The cops?'

Dillon looked relieved when she shook her head, though Susie had no idea why. It was something he kept harping on, every time she visited, and she was too scared to ask the reason. What else could there be?

'We'll be out,' Dillon said, and this time his confidence seemed real, as if he actually believed it himself. 'They can't keep us in here. Me and Harry'll get the firm back on its feet in no time.' He even found the old Dillon grin. 'I can keep Harry in line – I told him he should've handed over that ruddy gun, but . . . but . . .' His head dropped, eyes shut tight. 'Sorry, I'm sorry.'

Susie looked away. Her face had gone bright red. She bit her lip and stared at a toddler on his mother's lap. She opened her hand and discovered a wadded-up tissue, but didn't dare use it.

'Do you want to see the boys?' Susie glanced again at the toddler and back at him. 'Frank?'

'No. Not here. I don't want them to see me in here. Besides, I'll be out soon, lawyer's very confident, well as confident as a twat can be. Did you bring all my papers, letters from the C.O.?' He then remembered he was holding them. 'Oh yes, yes, thanks . . . cigarettes?'

Susie pushed the bag towards him. Dillon stared at it, eyes glazed, nodding like a mechanical doll. There was a silence between them, a dreadful chasm of silence too wide to shout across. Susie's fingers crept forward, nearly touching his, then curled up, like a plant withering in the frost. Dillon was dumb, no words left in him, no sounds at all, except screams.

Susie burst out brightly, 'I've got a job – restaurant. Pay's not bad, and Mum's been . . . I'll look round for something better. Mr. Marway's sorting things out with the bank, his family have rallied round. I don't think he'll lose his business. I passed on any accounts we still had left. Not much, but . . .' Huge glistening tears rolled down her cheeks, dripped off her chin. '. . . the Chinese an' . . .'

Susie gulped but kept right on.

'Shirley and me came here together, she's really showing

now. I see her when I can, an' – oh Harry, he gave her his microwave an' I gave her the Hoover from the office. Mum was uptight, said she could've done with it.' Susie used the tissue to wipe her face, blotchy red and swollen. 'I'm sorry. I'm sorry.'

The bell rang. Two minutes to changeover. Twenty in, twenty out.

Dillon came back to life. He took a deep breath and said breezily, 'Well, that's it. Thanks for coming all this way. Give the boys my love. You tell them I joined up, gone abroad. Maybe tell 'em I'm with Jimmy in Colombia. I can get the lads to send cards, put my name on for me . . .'

'I won't lie to them, Frank.' Susie's eyes were moist but she wasn't crying any more. 'There's been enough of that. I'll see you in two weeks' time. You sure there's nothing you want . . . ?'

The bell rang again. Final warning.

'. . . they said I can send in paperbacks.'

'No.' Dillon was deathly pale. 'I'm fine.'

Susie pushed herself up, the wet tissue tight in her fist. She came round the table and bent to kiss him. Dillon averted his face, and she kissed his cheek. A warden passed by, making sure nothing was exchanged except this brief, formal token of affection, and carried on pacing, eyes on the next couple.

Women were moving along the aisles towards the main door. Some of the children were crying. Susie followed the woman and the toddler from the next table. She turned back, raising her voice above the shuffle and squeak of feet on the composition floor.

'I forgot to tell you – I passed my driving test!'

Sitting with his hands clasped on the table in front of him, Dillon slowly turned his head. He nodded, and with a supreme effort, forced a frozen smile. Susie looked at him across the unbridgeable chasm of perhaps ten feet that separated them. She took a pace towards him. Her hand came up, pressed flat against her chest, fingers splayed. She turned and followed the woman and toddler out.

Dillon looked straight ahead, no expression on his face, no movement in his body, arms and shoulders locked solid, his spine an iron bar, holding onto himself with a rigid, unbearable tension, so that the single thin strangulated sound that escaped from him seemed to come from nowhere, from the ether, or a part of him that has no name in human anatomy. A silent cry from his heart, as if it were slowly being torn apart, his sense of loss consumed him, remaining locked tightly inside as he was led back to his cell. There the loss remained, as if held in by steel straps. He was sitting on his bunk, dead-eyed, unaware of where he was or of the man lying prone on the next bunk. Held inside him, as if bound by mental steel straps, was the mounting fury, like a fever. He had no one and no place to let it free. He knew he had brought this on himself, it was his fault, no one else's.

Dillon refused his evening meal. He remained in his cell and it took all his will power to uncoil his stiffened body and lie flat, rigid, eyes staring at the ceiling.

Harry Travers also lay on his back, his head resting on his hands, staring at the ceiling. He had no visitors, he only had his sister in Manchester, and she hadn't the money to come down, not that he had even told her where he was. Apart from her he had nobody. He'd written to Susie, told her to give his microwave to Shirley, for safe keeping, as he didn't want the Pakki landlord nicking it whilst he was inside. There were only a few other things he'd mentioned to Susie to keep safe for him, he had nothing else. He was going to write to Trudie, but didn't bother. He wasn't foolish enough to think she cared what happened to him – he was a fifty-five-quid full job, nothing more. Well, he had been given a few freebies, but mostly he paid up, paid for his loving, always had. In the darkness of his cell he began to remember all the tarts, in all the countries, he'd had some beautiful women, and some dogs, but he'd never had any long-term relationship, never had felt the need. He'd almost been snared once, a long, long time ago. The girl had lived next door to his auntie, a skinny little thing with a funny lop-sided smile. He had been her first and she had believed he would marry her, maybe he had even promised, he could no longer remember that far back, but he'd seen a lot of her just before he joined up. On his first leave he had called round, but she was going steady with a bloke from the local factory, he shoved over a few trinkets he'd bought for her, told her he hoped she'd be happy and got legless with a mate who'd arrived home to find his wife in bed with his best friend. Women were like that, couldn't trust them, and Harry reckoned he'd lost nothing, not missed out. He gave a few moments over to Jummy, wondered how he was getting on, and decided that when he got out, he'd sign up, do a mercenary stint. He wasn't cut out for civvies, not enough action, the action made up for the loneliness. He seemed to see the word printed in front of his eyes, and for the first time in his life he knew he was a lonely man. He turned over and buried his face in the pillow, suddenly wanting to have someone, even that funny, skinny little girl who had lived next door to his auntie's.

Cliff had been knocked around in the exercise yard, his lip was swollen, and he felt exhausted. Seeing Shirley had really upset him. The baby was showing now, and he knew her Dad had gone apeshit, and all the wedding plans had been cancelled. Well, there would be one person who was pleased, Shirley's Dad, he'd never liked Cliff, now he must be rubbing his hands together, saying to poor Shirley, 'I told you so, what did I tell you . . .'

Cliff wrote copious letters, every spare moment he had, he wrote to Shirley, explaining over and over that it was all a terrible mistake, that he would be out and they could still get married, she would have the baby and they would be okay. He would get a decent job, he would provide, he would make it, and Shirley had promised to stay with him, no matter what her father said. She knew he would be out in time for the baby, and even joked in her letters that poor Norma would then have to take her wedding dress in, as she would be back in shape.

Cliff wrote to his mother and father, his brothers and sisters, he wrote to everyone he could think of, desperate for everyone to know that it was all a terrible mistake. Hunched on his bunk, hardly able to see the page in the darkness, he started another letter, one he had begun over and over. It was to Frank Dillon, an attempt to make him understand why he had to tell the law about Newman, that he knew he should have kept his mouth shut, knew that Dillon was sorting everything out, but he had just been unable to keep quiet. The letter was written, re-written and torn up time after time. He had sent round a note to Harry, and it had really hurt him when it had been returned. Dillon had not looked at him, or spoken to him, and that had hurt, he had always believed Frank Dillon was his friend, his best friend, and he tried one more time to put into words what he felt.

'Dear Frank, Please don't think any the worse of me, I only did what I felt was the best for all of us. I know we'll get out, and I reckon we can still make the business work. We are innocent, the case against us will be thrown out. Good luck, I guess I'll see you in court. Your Friend Cliff.'

The truth was, Cliff was the only true innocent, and because of Dillon he had lost his job, because of Dillon he had pooled his money from Scotland into the security firm, and because of Dillon he was banged up in a prison cell, but the latter Cliff would never admit was in anyway Dillon's fault. He loved Dillon and admired him, and he was ashamed he had not kept quiet, ashamed he had bleated out about Barry Newman. It seemed to obsess him even more than the cancellation of his wedding, and Shirley's pregnancy. Mr. Crook had said to him that he had better look out for himself, not worry about Frank Dillon, but Cliff did worry, he cried himself to sleep, because he knew he had let Dillon down.

43

'Stand up the three of you.'

The judge pushed his gold-rimmed bi-focals more firmly onto his nose, eyes downcast on the papers before him. He looked up at the men in the dock. The court waited. The stenographer settled herself, hands poised over the keys. From outside, the faint hum of traffic from Camberwell New Road. Somebody coughed, and the judge waited a moment longer. Then he began.

'You have all been convicted after a long and difficult trial of a serious conspiracy to steal. You are also convicted of possession of a firearm for use in connection with the commission of that offence, and in your case, Dillon, that charge is made out because you supplied the firearm to Travers and Morgan. We have listened to the evidence in this case and I am appalled at the deliberate premeditated planning and execution of these offences, offences committed with military precision. You three men planned to steal money entrusted to you in breach of the substantial confidence placed in you, and to dress up your offences so as to incriminate others.'

The judge glanced at the papers and leaned forward on his elbows, fingers laced together.

'You, Dillon, until recently a sergeant in Her Majesty's Army, brought all your military training to bear in the preparation and planning of these offences. You procured equipment and drilled your men, Travers and Morgan, going so far as to require them to inflict violence upon each other and to discharge a firearm in a public place so as to mislead the police.'

From the tiered bank of seats to the judge's left, behind the two rows reserved for the press, Susie's eyes were fixed, dry and unblinking, on her husband's face. Beside her sat

Helen, recently blue-rinsed and wearing a new chiffon scarf. Shirley sat two seats along, her head bowed, rocking slightly, a handkerchief pressed to her mouth. Marway and his wife were in the row behind, he in his turban, she with a silk shawl draped over her head. In the back row, an empty seat either side of him, Barry Newman sat with one gloved fingertip stroking the tip of his chin.

'Despite your absence from the scene at the time of the commission of these offences,' the judge continued, addressing Dillon directly, 'I take the view that you are the ringleader in this case, and that the most severe penalty must be reserved for you.' His gaze shifted to include the others. 'I have taken into account your exemplary military records, having heard from the many character witnesses that you have called. I'm sadly aware that all three of you have fought bravely for your country and have been decorated. I am also aware that none of you has appeared either before a court martial, or since your discharge from the Forces before a civilian court.'

The judge leaned back and straightened up in his chair. His voice straightened up too, stood to attention.

'For offences of this sort the court has no alternative but to pass an immediate prison sentence. That sentence must reflect the gravity of the offences, and it is all the more sad in this case that none of you has had the courage to plead guilty, despite overwhelming evidence against you.'

Dillon stood hands by his sides, Harry and Cliff either side of him. Since rising none of them had moved a muscle. Three uniformed officers stood directly behind the three men. In the well of the court, Detective Chief Inspector Jenkins watched the faces of the three leading actors in the drama. It had unfolded beautifully, he couldn't have written it better himself. Now he was anticipating with great relish the climax to the third act.

'Morgan, I take the view that your part in these offences was as culpable as Travers, but nonetheless I take into account your youth, and for the offence of conspiracy to steal I sentence you to six years' imprisonment and three years' concurrent in respect of the possession of the firearm. Take him down.'

Cliff's knees buckled. He might have fallen but for the officer, who gripped his arm and supported him. In a state of total shock, Cliff was too stunned even to look at Shirley, or to hear her sobs as he was led down the stairs.

'Travers, you will serve a sentence of eight years' imprisonment for conspiracy with three years' concurrent for possession of a firearm with intent to commit an indictable offence. Take him down.'

Harry glared. At everyone – judge, court, Jenkins, reporters, the whole swinish, double-talking, fixing, finagling, fucking lot of them. His final verdict as his head disappeared below the level of the dock was one enraged bellow of defiance.

'*Bastards!!!*'

Alone in the dock, Dillon awaited his fate. Susie's wedding ring cut into her flesh as she gripped her mother's hand. Two rows behind, gaunt face completely impassive, Newman stroked his chin.

'Dillon, the sentence of this court for conspiracy to steal is that you shall serve nine years' imprisonment; for possession of a firearm with intent to commit an indictable offence, three years to run concurrent. Take him down.'

Dillon stood his ground. He wouldn't be budged, this was madness. Handcuffed, his hands, with his fingers tattooed with the words 'love' and 'hate', clasped tightly. An officer came up the stairs to assist his colleague. Between them they wrestled Dillon round. He looked up to Susie but she bowed her head. Her mother clung onto her hand, crying; no matter how she had gone on and on about her son-in-law, she loved him, and she felt the betrayal of her trust in him as devastating as Susie did. It was Susie who patted and comforted her mother, watching her husband's straight back as they frog-marched him down to the cells below the court.

Not until he was in the holding cell did Dillon's

341

shoulders slump, his head go down. He felt all his will-power and all his strength seep from him. There was no more fight left in him, the fight was gone. They led each man out, Cliff first, Harry second and then Dillon. Harry had to be pushed hard up the steps of the van, he stumbled forward cursing, Cliff, already inside, sitting dull-eyed, still in shock. Lastly Dillon stepped in, and they sat side by side, as the handcuffs were attached onto the steel bar.

The clang of the heavy doors left them in almost total darkness and the small slit windows high above their heads sent shafts of sunlight across the interior of the van. In the darkness, as the engine ticked over, their eyes searched for each other, locked, and then looked away again. There were no words, not at this stage, nothing to be said, they were all in shock at the harshness of their sentences, the loss of their freedom still not fully comprehended. They were mute, as if the stuffing had been punched out of them.

Dillon closed his eyes and the van became the old Hercules. He was standing at the open door, the wind rippling his cheeks, the lads lining up ready to move to the open door. 'Tell off for equipment check . . . shuffle forwards!'

He stepped out, and felt the rush of the howling wind, the explosion inside his chest, the exhilaration of the air itself, the tug to his guts as the parachute opened up, like a glorious white cloud, and suspended, with sky below and above, you were the hawk, you were the eagle, the swallow. You never mentioned this because they'd call you a wanker, but there was that moment when the feeling of freedom was the sweetest most precious thing in the world. Afterwards came the fighting, the killing, the anger, the feverish rage when your mates died, the blanking off of feelings, the sick jokes about the injured, because you were relieved it was somebody else's legs blown to smithereens. It was as if all those early days, those first jumps, merged into one mass. Why now, just 'as his freedom had been taken from him, did Frank Dillon remember, with crystal clarity, the way he had felt all those years ago, when he was young, he was healthy, he was a bit wild, he had his whole life ahead of him? And that life for eighteen years became the Army's, was the Army. He had placed it before his wife and sons, had given the Army himself one hundred per cent, and left little for Susie and his family. He knew he had been given chances, like the bank loan, but he was just ill-equipped to deal with it, he was almost as inept now as he was when he first enlisted, he'd never even had a job before he signed on the dotted line. How could he have cared and trained blokes and yet remained such a fucking walking liability in civvies? He shook his head in confusion, and turned to Cliff.

Cliff bowed his head, as if unable to meet Dillon's eyes.

'S'okay Cliff, you did right son, it was me that fouled up, and I'll . . .' he was going to say he would sort it, like he tried to sort everything, everybody. 'I'm sorry, sorry about Shirley and the weddin'.' Dillon leaned over and patted Cliff, who gripped his hand tightly.

'We'll get a re-trial, we will won't we?' Cliff asked.

Harry elbowed Cliff away. 'Not with that bloody Arnold Crook! We need a better friggin' lawyer, he couldn't get a hard on, never mind fight a bleedin' complicated case like ours, we was framed. Did I ever tell you about that time in Argie? Well, Dick the Armpit, you remember him don't you Frank? Well he's got a bag full of smoke right and . . .'

Harry nattered on, Cliff only half-listening, his eyes straying to look at Dillon, who sat staring ahead, deep in thought. As if he knew Cliff was watching he turned his head a fraction.

Harry continued . . . 'I said what you got in the bag Armpit? It smells like camel's shit! It is, he said, that bastard Blackie Hardcastle sold it me, said it was Colombian Gold, so I said to him . . .'

Dillon smiled, the smile Susie fell in love with, the smile that came across his dark features so rarely. It stunned Cliff, because he saw the vunerability, almost the youth of the man he had believed was so invincible, the man he

had trusted. The smile disarmed him, he was no lo...
sergeant, just an ordinary bloke.

Harry continued, 'In shit up to his armpits, so I said . . .'

Cliff leaned back and Dillon returned to leaning against
the wall of the van as it continued its journey to the prison.
They were in it all right, up to their armpits, and Harry
realising no one was listening to his camel dung story went
quiet. They remained silent for the rest of the journey,
each wrapped in his own thoughts until the van stopped
as Brixton Prison gates were opened. Their papers were
checked, the door opened and the wardens peered in to
view the three new prisoners. The door clanged shut again,
and a disembodied voice was heard discussing the new
arrivals. The driver leaned out, jerked his thumb to indicate the back of the transport van.

'Got the Army back here, mate!'